Praise for Fiona Riley

Bet the Farm

"Riley winningly showcases women's friendships as integral to romantic success. This is a fluffy delight."—*Publishers Weekly*

Bet Against Me

"Ms. Riley's readers know that her books feature likable characters with great chemistry between them. This book has it in spades and, as usual, the author delivers pent-up sexual tension and hot intimate scenes...Overall, another entertaining, fun, and hot romance by Ms. Riley. I can't wait to see what's next in the series. 5 stars."—*Lez Review Books*

"This book is almost too sexy...almost!...This book is quintessentially Fiona Riley with the characters having off the chart chemistry, sizzling tension, and sexy sassy dialogue. I knew it would be a winner when I listened to Fiona read a scene from it recently in an author reading video. It screamed all the things I love about this author. It is 100% my new favourite Fiona Riley book. 5 Stars."—*Les Rêveur*

A Christmas Miracle (in *All I Want for Christmas*)

"A girl walks into a bar and, wham, chemistry flares. Mira and Courtney are great together. Courtney brings out the best in Mira. Their connection and conversation is fabulous. Courtney's sense of adventure and fun is the perfect way to end this anthology. Riley gives us a good old-fashioned holiday romance to celebrate Christmas with."—*Phoebe's Randoms*

"[T]hese three short Christmas stories were worth the read and put me in the holiday spirit. *A Christmas Miracle* by Fiona Riley gives us a trillion tons of chemistry for the finale. A scrooge bar owner has to host a holiday party that Courtney is throwing for her workplace so that they will recognize her efforts to get that overdue promotion. The flirting in this story was top notch. D...ll...r...d...l...*rk*

No

"Riley strikes an impressive b⋯⋯⋯⋯⋯s and sweeping romance in this tend⋯⋯⋯⋯Riley endearingly captures the growth of Charlotte and Lexi's relationship from when they were in high school to when they are reunited as adults. Readers will root for this well-matched couple."—*Publishers Weekly*

Not Since You "is well written and hot. So hot."—*Jude in the Stars*

"This book has all the elements of a perfect romance—beautiful characters seeking to rekindle a lost love with heat and passion under sunny skies and starry nights on a cruise ship traveling to a tropical paradise."—*The Lesbian Book Blog*

Media Darling

"A great mix of characters, some great laughs, and a good romance. A great well written read that was emotional and fun."—*Kat Adams, Bookseller (QBD Books, Australia)*

"{A] sweet romance with the addition of a critique of the media role in their portrayal of celebrities. Both main characters are multi-layered with their personalities well defined. Their chemistry is absolutely off the charts…an entertaining, poignant and romantic story with a side of social critique to celebrity culture and the media. Five stars." —*Lez Review Books*

"I really dig the way Fiona Riley writes contemporary romances because they're sexy and flirty with a whole lot of feelings, and *Media Darling* is no exception."—*The Lesbian Review*

Media Darling "was well-executed and the sex was well-written. I liked both of the characters and the plot held my interest."—*Katie Pierce, Librarian, Hennepin County Library (Minnesota)*

Room Service

"The sexual tension between Olivia and Savannah is combustible and I was hoping with every flirtatious moment they would jump each other…[A] sexy summer read."—*Les Rêveur*

"*Room Service* by Fiona Riley is a steamy workplace romance that is all kinds of fabulous…Fiona Riley is so good at writing characters who are extremely likeable, even as they have issues to work through. I was happy to see that the leading ladies in *Room Service* are no exception! They're both fun, sweet, funny, and smart, which is a brilliant combo. They also have chemistry that sizzles almost from the get-go, making it especially fun to watch them grow in ways that are good for them as individuals and as a couple."—*The Lesbian Review*

"*Room Service* is a slow-burn romance written from the point of view of both main characters. Ms. Riley excels at building their chemistry that slowly grows to sizzling hot."—*Lez Review Books*

"Riley is a natural when it comes to delivering the heat between characters and undeniable chemistry."—*Book-A-Mania*

Strike a Match

"Riley balances romance, wit, and story complexity in this contemporary charmer...Readers of all stripes will enjoy this lyrically phrased, deftly plotted work about opposites attracting."—*Publishers Weekly*

"[A] quick-burning romance, with plenty of sex scenes hot enough to set off the alarms."—*RT Book Reviews*

"*Strike a Match* is probably one of the hottest and sexiest books I've read this year...Fiona Riley is one to watch and I will continue to get extremely excited every time I get one of her books to read."
—*Les Rêveur*

"While I recommend all of the books in the Perfect Match series, I especially recommend *Strike a Match*, and definitely in audio if you're at all inclined towards listening to books. Fans of the other two installments will be happy to see their leads again, but you don't have to have read them to pick this one up. It's sweet, hot, and funny, making it a great way to spend a day when you just want to hide away from the world and immerse yourself in a lovely story."—*Smart Bitches, Trashy Books*

"*Strike a Match* is Fiona Riley's best book yet. Whether you're a fan of the other books in the series or you've never read anything by her before, I recommend checking this one out. It's the perfect remedy to a bad day and a great way to relax on a weekend!"—*The Lesbian Review*

"I love this series and Sasha is by far my favourite character yet. I absolutely loved the gritty firefighter details. The romance between Abby and Sasha is perfectly paced and full of wonderful grand gestures, magical dates, and tender, intimate moments."—*Wicked Reads*

"Fiona Riley does a nice job of creating thorny internal and external conflicts for each heroine…I was rooting for Abby and Sasha, not only to be together, but also that both of them would grow and change enough to find a true HEA. The supporting cast of family members, friends, and colleagues is charming and well-portrayed. I'm looking forward to more from Fiona Riley."—*TBQ's Book Palace*

Unlikely Match

"The leads have great chemistry and the author's writing style is very engaging."—*Melina Bickard, Librarian, Waterloo Library (UK)*

"Two strong women that make their way towards each other with a tiny little nudge from some friends, what's not to like?"—*The Reading Penguin's Reviews*

"*Unlikely Match* is super easy to read with its great pacing, character work, and dialogue that's fun and engaging…Whether you've read *Miss Match* or not, *Unlikely Match* is worth picking up. It was the perfect romance to balance out a tough week at work and I'm looking forward to seeing what Fiona Riley has in store for us next."
—*The Lesbian Review*

Miss Match

"In this sweet, sensual debut, Riley brings together likable characters, setting them against a colorful supporting cast and exploring their relationship through charming interactions and red-hot erotic scenes… Rich in characterization and emotional appeal, this one is sure to please."—*Publishers Weekly*

"*Miss Match* by Fiona Riley is an adorable romance with a lot of amazing chemistry, steamy sex scenes, and fun dialogue. I can't believe it's the author's first book, even though she assured me on Twitter that it is."—*The Lesbian Review*

"This was a beautiful love story, chock full of love and emotion, and I felt I had a big grin on my face the whole time I was reading it. I adored both main characters as they were strong, independent women with good hearts and were just waiting for the right person to come along and make them whole. I felt I smiled for days after reading this wonderful book."—*Inked Rainbow Reads*

By the Author

Miss Match

Unlikely Match

Strike a Match

Room Service

Media Darling

Not Since You

A Christmas Miracle (In *All I Want for Christmas*)

High Stakes Romances

Bet Against Me

Bet the Farm

Beginner's Bet

BEGINNER'S BET

by
Fiona Riley

2021

CREDITS
EDITOR: RUTH STERNGLANTZ
PRODUCTION DESIGN: STACIA SEAMAN
COVER DESIGN BY TAMMY SEIDICK

Acknowledgments

There are so many ways to have a family in this world, and each one is so, so important. I've been wanting to write Ellison's story since the very beginning of storyboarding for *Bet Against Me* (Book 1 in the High Stakes Romance Series). I knew from the start that writing Ellison's path was going to be challenging for many reasons, but perhaps the most challenging part was how closely her story of wanting to be a mother overlapped with my own.

As many of you may or may not know, my journey with cancer is what got me into writing. And eventually, that same journey is what helped me realize my dream of becoming a mother. But it was a long and hard road with losses, disappointments, new cancer diagnoses, and a seemingly infinite number of setbacks along the way. I have spent many long hours in waiting rooms and doctor's offices, weighing what seemed like unachievable options against impossible odds. But then I got lucky, because all those shots and procedures and tears and losses resulted in the birth of my first child. And then another. And while writing this book, we had another. Three perfect miracles in an imperfect world. And I know how very fortunate I am.

There are so many ways to have a family. I'm glad I was able to tell a part of my story in Ellison's and Katie's. Because loss and love go together sometimes. And that's an important story to tell, too.

Thank you to everyone at Bold Strokes Books for encouraging me to tell the kind of stories that I want to see in the world. Your support is invaluable.

To Jenn Rieken: There is no one in this world who understands what it's like to be in my shoes more than you. Even though you have way more fashionable shoes. ;) I love you. Forever and always. You will forever be my sister, my confidant, and my heart. I don't think you could ever understand how much just texting back and forth with you changes my whole day. I miss your face. Let's get together again soon.

To Ruth Sternglantz: Thank you for keeping me on schedule and for bending over backwards when our newest little love graced us a bit early and halted my book progress. Your patience is endless. And your heart is infinite. Much love to you, always.

To Kris Bryant: Can you believe we had another baby while we wrote this book? Thanks for always making time to help me work out story issues and for sending diapers. Best. Auntie. Ever.

To Melissa Brayden: I'm so glad we got to go through our pregnancy and motherhood journeys together during the writing of this book. And I'm so glad our littles nearly share a birthday—that's something very special. You have been a gift in my life. Thank you.

To my now *three* little gingers: Momma loves you!

For Jenn.

My journey to motherhood would simply not have been possible without you. You are my whole world and you have given me the whole world—over and over again. Thank you for my beautiful family. And thank you for making this wild and wonderful parenting adventure so much fun. Because even on our most tired, sleep-deprived, and nerve-frayed days, you always make me laugh and remind me not to miss the littlest things.

There is no one else I'd want to share my life with or build a family with. You're simply the best.

CHAPTER ONE

Ellison Gamble's every accomplishment had come through hard work, dedication, and tenacity. She'd made a career on taking chances and doubling down on success. And it had served her well in her forty-two years—she was more successful than she could have ever imagined. But all those successes amounted to nothing in this moment. Because this time she had gambled and lost. And there was nothing she could do about it.

"Ellison?" Her fertility doctor, Dr. David Brinkley, looked concerned.

"Hmm?" She knew he'd said something, but whatever he'd said after *I'm sorry, you'll never be able to successfully carry a baby to full-term* had sounded like a rush of water in her ears. And the loud, thunderous roar that followed that statement made her feel like she was drowning.

"Here," he said as he handed her a box of tissues.

She accepted one to be polite, but she wasn't crying. She couldn't cry. She was too shocked. She knew after her most recent miscarriage that they'd have to reevaluate things, but she wasn't prepared to hear that just yet.

"I know this is disappointing, but we have options," he said as he came to her side of the desk. The pitifulness of the situation wasn't lost on her when he sat next to her in the seat usually reserved for a patient's significant other. She had none. Like everything else she'd done in her life, she was alone in this endeavor.

She looked at him. He had a kind and ageless face. He was nearly twenty-five years her senior, but you'd never be able to tell by looking at him. She only knew how old he was because one of his nurses had let it slip when she'd started on this path nearly a decade ago. Her physician had encouraged her to harvest her eggs after her endometriosis diagnosis and had practically insisted on it once her mother died of cervical cancer shortly thereafter. That was about the same time her marriage to Peyton Stroker had started to dissolve, when after years of promising to start a family and telling Ellison she wasn't ready yet, Peyton dropped the bomb that she'd never wanted kids to begin with. And try as she might not to hold contempt for Peyton, Ellison still failed miserably. Because Peyton was every bit the charming, silver-tongued art dealer in her personal life as she was in her professional one. After all, she'd sold Ellison on a picture of their future that was a fake. And a childless one, at that.

Ten years. A lot had happened in those ten years, including the formation of her incredibly successful luxury real estate firm, Gamble and Associates, of which she was beyond proud. And though professionally she had prospered beyond her wildest dreams, her marriage to Peyton had combusted. Her attempts at subsequent romantic relationships had sputtered and flopped following her divorce, and her efforts at becoming a mother had stalled to the point of failure, it seemed. But not without complications, miscarriages, and devastation first. Because though she'd never wanted this day to come, deep down she knew it was inevitable.

Dr. Brinkley placed a tentative hand on hers, drawing her back to reality. A reality that reminded her that now, though they were both a decade older since their first meeting, his unwaveringly youthful face was in better shape than her apparently hostile and aging uterus.

He looked uncomfortable by her silence. She felt bad for him. No one wanted to deliver the news he just had. Too bad hearing it was worse than giving it.

"Ellison," he tried again.

She sighed. "I'm fine."

She wasn't. But she could wade through those feelings in the privacy of her Maserati on the way back to the office, where she was expected to be a totem of support for everyone else. She'd use those twenty or so minutes to fall apart if she needed to.

He didn't look like he believed her. "Look, we were friends long before you became my patient. And as your friend, I call bullshit on that."

Ellison laughed. She'd been instrumental in securing a sale on his city home as well as negotiating a sweet deal on his weekend home in the country long before she'd become his patient. David was a good man. And his husband Cole was absolutely darling. That was why she'd taken the steps to come to his practice to achieve the one thing she wanted more than anything in this world—to be a mother. She trusted him. She always had. And through her lowest fertility lows, he had been there with a strong hug and a level head. David never seemed to lack optimism or solutions. And she needed both right now.

"I'll be fine, eventually." She humored him.

He gave her another look before continuing. "We have some choices."

She waved him off. "I'm not—"

"Listen," he tried again, his voice calm and full of empathy. "We have two eggs left. We're all out of donor sperm, but that's an easy fix. Pick some more, and let's fertilize those last eggs."

She was okay with this option. That part felt like a fresh start since she'd picked the last donor during her divorce from Peyton. Though she was sad that donor was no longer available, she knew there were thousands of more choices now since then. She'd figure that part out. "And then?"

"And then we try the surrogate route. Past testing has shown that the eggs are good, but just to be sure, we'll test them once they fertilize, and we'll try again."

"With someone else's significantly less hostile uterus," Ellison replied sarcastically.

"Exactly."

"And if that doesn't work?" Ellison didn't want to know that answer, even if she felt like she might already know.

He shook his head. "We're not there yet. Think about surrogacy. You already have the eggs. And we know how hard you had to work for those."

That was an understatement. She'd gone through dozens and dozens of injections, hormone treatments, painful egg extractions, tests, and scans to get those eggs. And at forty-two, she knew those were likely her last. If there was any chance of her having a biological child, those eggs were it. But they'd have to grow in someone else, it seemed.

"That's a lot of control you're asking me to relinquish, David," she joked. "You think I'm just going to be able to put my precious little DNA sacs in someone else and sleep soundly at night? We both know I'm too Type A for that."

"*DNA sac* isn't exactly a medical term, and a trained professional would be doing the implantation, not you. So I think we're good." He smiled. "We might have to medicate you to sleep, but I know a guy for that."

"You're too good to me," she replied.

"I do what I can," he said with a shrug. She appreciated his fake nonchalance. She needed the levity of sarcasm and teasing right now. She could get through the rest of this meeting if they could keep it light.

"Okay, so what do we do now?"

He stood and returned to his side of the desk. She watched as he opened a folder and procured a brochure for her.

"Full Circle Surrogacy?" Ellison read the name aloud as she thumbed through the trifold.

"There are a few options in the area, but I'm friendly with one of the partners that runs this group," David replied.

Ellison looked at all the happy couples in the pictures as she skimmed over the words on the page—she'd read this more carefully later. She smiled at the multiple gay couples pictured. It was important to her to work with companies that represented her community.

David pointed to a particularly handsome couple as he said, "That's Kevin and Philip. They're friends of mine and Cole's. They have the most beautiful twin boys. Full Circle helped them build a family they otherwise wouldn't be able to have."

The one David identified as Kevin was older with a dash of gray at his temples and in his goatee. Philip was equally handsome with a clean-shaven face and square jaw. He looked like a younger version of Alex Landi.

"God, they're obnoxiously attractive. Aren't they?"

"They're the worst. Kevin is constantly being mistaken for Idris Elba. And I'm personally offended by Philip's jawline." David rolled his eyes. "No one should be gifted with such beauty. It's unfair to the rest of us."

"Agreed," Ellison said as she closed the brochure and slipped it into her purse. "I'll give this some real thought."

"Good. I'm glad." David met her at the door to give her a hug. "Call me in a few days, and let's see where you're at."

"I will," she promised.

"Oh, and Cole wants to get drinks again soon," David added as he opened the door for her. "Give us a few dates that work for you, and I'll make it happen."

"Sounds good," Ellison replied. "I'll be in touch."

She made her way to her Maserati, slipping into the driver's seat and shutting the door as she let out a long, slow exhale. She started the car and focused on the purr of the engine that she loved so much. This car had been a gift to herself, one that was completely over the top and entirely necessary. Though she had beautiful clothes and expensive taste, this was the third version of the first real extravagance that she'd ever bought herself. Well, besides the multi-million-dollar beach house she almost never stayed in.

She ran her hand along the smooth leather of the steering wheel as she thought of the house that sat uninhabited most months of the year. She'd bought that on a whim after Gamble and Associates had begun to flourish. It was both a distraction and a reward for surviving her divorce. The property was gorgeous—walking distance from a private white-sand beach—and only an hour from her office. But the house that had previously occupied that land had been in shambles. So she'd spent more than a year and a half on construction to start new—building it and healing herself—from the ground up. That had been her first taste for new construction. A taste that was further piqued when her star Realtor Trina Lee and her now-girlfriend Kendall Yates got into a sales war over the luxury condominiums of the Harborside in the Seaport. Soon after Trina bested Kendall—and bedded her somewhere along the way—Ellison had started her own commercial building project with the Newbridge on the Gardens. She entrusted the success of that to numbers phenom Lauren Calloway and up-and-comer Jax Pearson. None of her team had let her down, and due to their incredible and continued successes, Ellison had been able to build her own dream home. One that sat empty except for a few weekend stays here or there. But those were few and far between.

"Because you made the beginner's mistake of putting in more

bedrooms than you could fill," she said to herself as she pulled out of the parking lot and headed in the direction of her office. "A typical beginner's bet—foolish, rash, and overenthusiastic."

That was the truth of the matter. The house was everything she'd ever dreamed of—designed with the highest luxury and function and perfect in every way. She'd agonized over every detail, every fixture, and every drawer pull. It was the most magnificent beachfront home she had ever seen. And it was the product of her vivid imagination and deep pockets. And she had no one to share it with. A five-bedroom, five-and-a-half-bath McMansion with a separate guest residence over a three-car garage, all for exactly one person—Ellison.

The tears she'd held at bay until this moment started to fall, and the gravity of David's statement settled on her chest like a hundred-pound weight. She'd never carry her own child. She'd done everything in this life by herself. All of her greatest accomplishments had come by her own hard work and determination. But no amount of trying would fix this. Nothing could fix *her*. She was the broken piece this time. And like the too big dream house that sat empty, waiting in vain for life to fill its halls, her heart felt just as hollow. Just as empty. She'd never give birth to her own child, and the sooner she came to terms with that, the sooner she could bury that dream. The sooner she could try to accept David's suggestion. If only she had any fight left in her heart to try.

Chapter Two

Katie Crawford's head was pounding. She wasn't sure if it was because she'd collectively slept five hours the last two nights or because the spa was busier than it had ever been, and she was completely ill-prepared for the type of face-to-face client interaction that filling in for Marcio would require today. But she was sure it was a combination of the two. She was short on sleep and patience. And stressed. Stressed about her mother. And about how expensive everything seemed to be. Every little thing seemed like more than she could handle, and she couldn't remember another time in her life when she had felt this utterly helpless.

"Katie," Shaina Farrington said. Her best friend and work colleague looked concerned. "You want me to get that?"

"Get what?" Katie asked as she rubbed along her temple.

"The phone." Shaina gestured to the blinking line before her. "It's ringing."

"Oh, that's not just in my ears?" Katie asked as she clumsily reached for the phone.

"I'll get it. Maybe get some water or something," Shaina said as she caught the receiver that flew out of Katie's hands, giving her a sympathetic smile.

"Thanks," Katie said as she slipped out from behind the desk in the direction of the small but posh break room between the reception area and the treatment rooms.

She opened the door and let out a sigh of relief to find the quaint space uninhabited. She grabbed a bottle of water from the staff fridge and dropped onto the plush faux-leather couch in the corner. She sipped the cold beverage, closing her eyes as she silently counted down from ten, trying to calm her nerves and steady her breathing.

She had really, really needed today off. But she'd also needed a distraction. So when Marcio had called out of his reception position last minute, she jumped at the chance to pick up more hours and make more money. Even if working the desk was her least favorite job. She'd do just about anything, and her boss, renowned spa owner Pietro Ferrazi, knew that. He didn't hesitate to ask her to fill in last minute, and they both knew it was because she'd never say no.

She leaned back against the couch as she took in the pleasant and soothing smell that was in this room—like every room—in the Indulgent Tranquility Spa. She had to give it to him—Pietro had found the perfect fragrance to calm and relax. Katie wondered if she could bathe in this scent. She would bet he had samples of this in bath bombs in his office. Maybe she'd ask later.

Not that she had a working bathtub to indulge in an essential oil soak. She'd given up her apartment when it became evident that her mother was unable to live alone, but she had sorely underestimated the disrepair her childhood home was in. Nothing worked, everything leaked, there were boxes piled high in most of the rooms—it was a condemnable mess. But she had nowhere else to go. She'd sold everything she had of value to help her mother out. As it was, she barely had anything left to her name besides her clothes and her car, Bertha. She sighed. Bertha needed an oil change and probably an exorcism. She was held together by duct tape and a prayer, and the rattling on the highway had gotten worse of late. So she either had a poltergeist in the back seat, or that car—like her patience—was on its last leg.

"How did I get here?" Katie asked no one.

"You applied for a massage therapist job three years ago and became obsessed with the on-site esthetician, unable to leave without being her friend and learning her craft, further deepening your soul-sister connection, and nurturing your sister-from-another-mister bond with your Nubian queen bestie." Shaina's voice was a welcome surprise.

Katie opened her eyes to find Shaina perched on the table in front of her. Her brown eyes sparkled, and her flawless complexion taunted her. Thank God Shaina had helped her learn to manage her naturally oily skin. Because besides being the best friend she'd ever had, Shaina's professional insight was invaluable. "This is true. But be honest—before me your life was very boring."

"So boring," Shaina said with a solemn nod. "I was barely keeping myself awake at work. You know, like you, just now."

Katie frowned. "I wasn't sleeping. I was meditating."

"You were snoring," Shaina said. "But it was cute snoring."

Katie wanted to argue, but her headache felt like it was finally receding, so she decided not to push it. "Are all the clients checked in?"

"Yup and there's a gap in the schedule for the next few minutes, so we're good. I put up the *Be Right Back* sign so I could make sure you hadn't crawled out the window and fled in Bertha."

"We both know I'm not flexible enough to fit through that window," Katie said as she motioned to the small window on the far side of the room. "Not to mention, I'm sure you would have heard Bertha making her getaway if I had." Bertha just about always backfired as she pulled away these days. It wasn't uncommon to see people nearby jump when she accelerated from a stop.

"That car needs to see a professional," Shaina said as she pulled Katie up to a standing position. "And maybe you do, too."

Katie frowned as she stepped into Shaina's embrace. She was right. Her life was a mess right now.

"You want to talk about it?" Shaina asked as she swayed them in place.

"What's to talk about? I put my mother in a long-term care facility this morning and just fell asleep on the staff couch. Basically, I'm winning at life." Katie had to bite the inside of her cheek to keep from crying. Her mother's stroke three months ago had felt like a surreal nightmare. And yet, here she was, barely keeping it together and very much awake. Well, mostly awake. Sleep gave her no peace when her waking hours reminded her of her mother's decline.

"Hey," Shaina said as she pulled back. "That was the best decision for you and her. You know that."

"I know," Katie said as she looked down, unable to bear the pity in Shaina's face. "But it doesn't make it any easier. If I had known all of this was going to happen, if I had moved back sooner…"

Shaina guided her face up by her chin, brushing a tear off Katie's cheek as she shook her head in disagreement. "You were living your life. And that's what your mother wanted. And you've been here ever since the accident, making sure she got the best care possible. You've done the best you could. That's all you can do."

Katie didn't feel like she'd done her best. Desperate for a fresh start after high school, she'd gone to college across the country and stayed there, only coming home for holidays and occasional long weekends. But all that changed a few years ago over Christmas when her mother fell asleep at the wheel while driving home from her overnight hospital shift as a nurse. The single car accident put her mother in a coma for months, and when she awoke, it was clear she had a traumatic brain injury. Katie left her life in California and became her mother's full-time caregiver, adjusting her work schedule the best she could around the aides and nurses she employed privately. But her mother's recent stroke took away what little independence she had retained after the accident—she was no longer able to participate at all in her own self-care, even the little she had been doing before. And what was worse, now her mother was barely there at all. They had managed to maintain some of their mother-daughter familiarity before, but now...Katie hated to think about the stranger she was to her mother.

Her mother barely spoke, and when she did, it was mostly nonsensical word salad. Katie's heart broke for so many reasons—the least of which was that she knew New Beginnings' long-term care facility wasn't an option she could financially sustain for very long. Even if it was the only option she could come up with. Because Katie was still in debt from her mother's first hospitalization after the accident and the newest rehospitalization, and her mother's increased care needs had proven to be too much for home care. To make matters worse, the house wasn't suitable for her mother's needs, and its neglected state had made it unsafe for her.

Katie had yet to forgive herself for abandoning her mother to chase her California dreams. It was a decision that she regretted endlessly the more her mother slipped away. They could have had so many more moments together—so many memories—had she stayed. And try as she might to make up for lost time between her shifts as a massage therapist, it was clear that Mae Crawford needed more help than Katie could provide, and New Beginnings offered her the best care money could buy. Too bad Katie didn't have any.

"What am I going to do?" she asked Shaina, like she asked her reflection every night. There was no way even picking up extra shifts would cover the cost of that facility. She could manage three, maybe four months before her and her mother's savings were depleted. And that was if she kept working herself ragged seven days a week. It all seemed so hopeless.

"Cry it out for a few more minutes before you come back out there and finish up the front desk duties," Shaina said, hugging her one last time. "Then you're going to let me take you out for dinner and drinks and get a good night's sleep."

That sounded like heaven. Well, except for the go back to work part. "Okay."

"One day at a time," Shaina said with such confidence that Katie momentarily believed her. "Now let's get out there before Mrs. Grossman files a complaint with Ferrazi and we both end up jobless."

"Don't joke about that," Katie said, picking up her pace. "New Beginnings isn't cheap, and I'm already working double overtime."

"I know you are," Shaina said, her voice full of compassion. "You're a good daughter, Katie Cat."

"I hope so." But Katie felt that was as far from the truth as possible. What kind of daughter put her fifty-eight-year-old mother in a home? Evidently, she did.

CHAPTER THREE

Ellison was scanning her email as she walked, trying to distract herself from the car ride and the emotions she'd stifled once she'd pulled into the parking lot at work. An email from the management office of her luxury apartment building had just arrived, informing her that Mr. Stetler and his new wife would be renovating the unit next to hers in the upcoming weeks, which Ellison didn't care much about. What she *did* care about was that the timeline for the work was projected to last until the end of the summer. Fucking great.

"Ellison," Pietro Ferrazi lunged out of her peripheral, startling her. "I'm glad to have caught you."

Ambushed was more like it. She composed herself, glad that her oversized sunglasses hid her red-rimmed eyes. "Oh? What can I do for you?"

"Ah, it's what I can do for you," he said as he stepped beside her, matching her cadence.

She cast him a brief glance. Pietro had recently opened a new location to his extremely popular Indulgence Tranquility Spa in the building adjacent to Ellison's office. From what she understood, his Newbury Street location was bustling, and this location was both to accommodate demand as well as an experiment to attract a younger clientele. If the seemingly always full parking lot in front of his building was any indication, he was doing just fine. And since her office managed the rental agreement for the building owner, GM Enterprises, she could also attest to the fact that his rent was early every month.

"I'm listening," she said without breaking her stride. She *was* listening, but only to be polite. Small talk was the last thing she wanted right now. She didn't mind Pietro—he seemed nice enough, though they'd only had a few interactions—but she just didn't have time for him.

"Listen, I know you're busy."

Uh-oh. That was something someone said right before they were about to inconvenience you. Her waning patience started to plummet.

"I am," she said, careful to keep a small smile on her lips. She'd perfected that trick throughout her years of luxury realty work—it was important to maintain an air of congeniality even if the client, or spa owner in this case, tested her patience. She'd never fully embraced that *you catch more flies with honey than with vinegar* proverb, but she did know that appearing to be open-minded had secured her numerous sales and professional victories. She'd built her entire career on seeming unflappable and rarely losing her patience even in the most stressful or high stakes of situations. That was a trait she'd inherited from her mother, but not one that she hadn't had to work very hard at over the years. She knew remaining calm and in control was the best option. Always. Even if she felt anything but that right now.

"Right. Which is why I wanted to circle back to our discussion a few weeks back. I'd like for you to take me up on that offer of a massage and spa treatment." Pietro stepped into her path, slowing her progress. "It would mean a lot to me to have your input. It'd be on the house, of course."

Ellison raised an eyebrow in his direction. He'd come into her office a while back and offered all the Gamble and Associates team members a series of free treatments—she assumed to drum up business. She knew that Trina and Lauren had taken him up on his offer and raved about the spa afterward. But what did he want with her? Trina and Lauren would certainly have more peers to advertise his services to than she would. It wasn't exactly as if her friend pool was spilling over these days.

"I'm happy to pay for any services I use," she said as she stepped to the side. "I'll review your spa options and let you know if I'm interested."

Pietro sped up to catch her again. "Whatever you choose will be my treat. Please."

Ellison stopped short, and he nearly stumbled into her. She was no longer interested in this volley of pleasantries. She'd been counting on the last few moments of quiet from her car to her office to stifle her lingering emotions from her appointment with Dr. Brinkley, and Pietro was wasting her few precious steps. "Is there something you need?"

Pietro looked like a deer caught in headlights. He ran his hand over his thin mustache as he stalled. Finally, he said, "Business is going well. And I know you're friendly with the building owner. I'd like to pursue expansion here—"

"And you want my input on the quality of your spa to help sway that request?" Ellison took a moment to appreciate how anxious Pietro must be to even ask this of her.

"Well, the quality is superb. I have no doubt that you will find that to be true." Pietro straightened up, standing a bit taller. "I, of course, want you to be satisfied. But I also want you to see the sustainability of a business like this. With more space, we could offer so much more in the way of treatments." He paused. "I want you to try the spa because I'm confident in our ability to bring relaxation to your existence. But I also want you to see the space for yourself and perhaps relay those observations to the building owner to help my pitch for expansion be more successful."

Ellison reached into her purse and pulled out her business card. "My cell is there. Have them put me in the system, and I'll call later to set something up."

"Thank you," Pietro said as he slipped the card into the breast pocket of his designer suit.

"I think you're placing far too much weight on my opinion, though, Pietro," she said as she continued toward her office door. "I just collect the rent checks."

Pietro shrugged. "Anyone can collect rent checks. If the incredibly successful GM Enterprises chose your office to represent them—and your office, which has its own indelible legacy, agreed to take on such a menial task—then your opinion must matter. I'm willing to bet the expansion of my business on it."

Ellison liked his tenacity. She favored those willing to take risks because with great risk came great reward. And that was something she'd built her career on. "I'll be in touch."

He smiled and bowed his head, holding the door for her as she entered her office.

She took a deep breath as she stepped over the threshold, shouldering the responsibility of being a boss with each step of her Manolo Blahniks. The time to mourn was over for now. It was time to get to work.

❖

Ellison rubbed her forehead as she looked at the seemingly endless stack of papers before her. Today had been long enough already.

A knock at the door got her attention. "Ellison?"

She looked up to find Jax Pearson, one of her younger, rising star agents, standing by the door with another stack of papers. Jax's journey in life and in work had been long and complicated, but Ellison was glad to have been a part of it. Jax had come to her as a dedicated but anxious trainee with the best intentions but had needed to be groomed and sculpted into the capable and talented salesperson they were today. With Ellison's guidance and Lauren and Trina's assistance, Jax had surpassed their own expectations. Ellison had known they would, but Jax had to see it for themselves. And since their top surgery last year, Ellison had noticed a steady change in their confidence and success as well. Jax had earned every triumph, and she couldn't be happier about it.

"Tell me those aren't for me," Ellison said, wearily eyeing Jax's paper stack.

Jax winced. "I can put them on Lauren's desk and pretend they aren't."

"Put what on Lauren's desk?" Lauren showed up over their shoulder with that carefree, breezy smile that she wore so well. Where Jax was a rule follower and meticulous about lists and notes, Lauren was everything but. Ellison assumed that their friendship worked because they were so different. Lauren made everyone feel welcome—she was an open book. And a numbers phenom, though you'd never know that by her model-good looks and easygoing nature. She was brilliant, and she brought a different perspective to realty and life. She'd helped Jax come into their own. Lauren was an asset here.

"These papers that Ellison doesn't want," Jax replied.

"It's true. I don't want them," Ellison said as she leaned back.

"Then put them on Trina's desk. That way you'll never see them ever again. It'll be like they never existed in the first place," Lauren supplied with a wink.

"I heard my name." Trina's voice sounded from behind Lauren. Ellison's doorway seemed to be the new gathering place.

"Did you hear something?" Lauren teased as she looked at Jax. The mischievous reference to Trina's diminutive stature caused Jax to snort.

"You mean besides all the moans coming out of Thea's back seat this morning before the staff meeting?" The playful edge to Trina's voice wiped the smile right off Lauren's face. Trina pushed Lauren aside and stepped into Ellison's office with a teasing grin of her own.

Trina completed the best friend trifecta before her. Trina was sure of herself like no one Ellison had ever met. She was a masterful Realtor and charming beyond measure, with a wardrobe and fashion sense to envy. And though she always looked like she stepped off the page of a fashion magazine, she wasn't cold or aloof. She just didn't put up with anyone's bullshit. She could be sharp—prickly, even—to those that crossed her or her friends. But Ellison knew she loved deeply and was loyal to the core. If Trina had your back, you'd be fine. Because what she lacked in height, Trina made up for tenfold in everything else that she did. Confidence being number one.

Lauren's cheeks pinked as she cursed under her breath. "I told her that was a bad idea."

"So, things are going well with Thea, I assume?" Ellison asked, amused. Lauren had fallen in love with Thea Boudreaux, the daughter of an old family friend that Ellison had asked Lauren to help with the sale of their Maine dairy farm. From what she could understand, the relationship had come as a surprise to both Lauren and Thea, but she could see their match was strong. They were cute together—Lauren's city slicker humor and wit paired well with Thea's country grown charm and strength. They were the perfect rom-com mix for success.

"Uh, yeah." Lauren's blush deepened. "It is."

"I'm glad," Ellison said, and she was.

"They're ridiculously cute," Trina said as she examined her manicure. "It's annoying, actually."

"Oh, please. Do you and Kendall have matching pajamas yet? Or did you just stop at matching diamond rings?" Lauren joked.

Trina held up her right hand and fluttered her fingers, the large diamond band twinkling as the light caught it. "She's a smart woman. She put a ring on it and everything."

"On the right hand," Jax teased before cowering slightly in response to Trina's death glare.

"Better than the *wrong* hand," she said, admiring the no doubt flawless stones. "This is just totally our speed right now. I'm soaking in every delicious moment of it."

Ellison smiled at the genuineness of Trina's statement. Trina and Kendall had moved in together at the end of last summer, and Ellison assumed it was only a matter of time before there were wedding bells in their future. Kendall was every bit Trina's match, a feat not for the faint of heart. But Kendall had loads of heart. And patience. And money, thanks to her family's successes in addition to her own. Trina was a happier and gentler person with Kendall in her life. Ellison was happy for her as well.

"Anyway," Lauren said, bumping Trina's hip and distracting her from staring affectionately at her right ring finger. "We're getting ready to head to The Mirage for drinks. Would you like to join us?"

Ellison wanted nothing more than to avoid the stack of paperwork Jax was still holding hostage, or the empty house and creeping depression that awaited her when she got there. She still had a lot to unpack about her appointment with Dr. Brinkley earlier. She could only avoid it for so long. "I'd love to, but"—she beckoned for Jax to bring her the papers—"I have to sort through this. And by the looks of it, I'll be here until morning."

"Some of it's mail," Jax offered. "Maybe that'll go quick?"

"Maybe," Ellison said as she looked up at the full brown eyes before her. Jax's kindness flowed off them like an ocean. She let herself bask in it for a moment. "If I finish early, I'll text you."

"Score," Lauren said with a fist pump. "Trina's buying."

Trina laughed, rolling her eyes. "It's the least I can do to repay that parking lot performance you gifted us all with this morning." She fanned herself. "But maybe Thea should buy me a drink after that eyeful."

"I hate you," Lauren deadpanned.

"You love me," Trina challenged.

Lauren sighed. "I do. Dammit."

"C'mon." Trina ushered her and Jax out the door. "The sooner we stop bothering Ellison, the sooner she can join us at the bar."

"Maybe," Ellison added, though she doubted she'd make it. She thoroughly enjoyed her team. And perhaps if things were different—and she weren't their boss—she'd be as close with them as they were with each other. But she was grateful for the relationship she had with them anyway. They welcomed her with open arms, and she made sure to show up as often as she could to show her appreciation for that. But she knew that tonight was not that night. Tonight, she needed to be alone.

"Maybe," Trina said with a nod. "But the likelihood improves with fewer distractions." She motioned to Lauren and Jax, who seemed to be engaged in a tickle fight. "And by distractions, I mean these two goofs."

"Have fun," Ellison said with a wave as she watched them head out toward the parking lot.

As the last of the remaining staff trickled out, she sorted the stack of papers into important documents, advertisements, and mail. The quiet of the office was a welcome accompaniment to the tedious task in front of her. But the quiet didn't last long. Because her cell phone started ringing and didn't stop.

"Ellison Gamble," she said. She didn't recognize the number, but that wasn't unusual in this business.

"Hello, gorgeous! This is a reminder call from Indulgence Tranquility Spa for Sarah about your upcoming massage on Thursday at ten a.m. We can't wait to see you—have a relaxing day!" The friendly automated female voice disconnected before Ellison could sort out what had happened.

Ellison felt badly that Sarah—whoever she was—wasn't going to get her reminder call, but before she could dwell on it any longer, her phone rang again.

"Ellison Gamble," she said. This number was also one she didn't recognize, but it seemed to be only a digit or two off from the last number that called her.

"Hello, gorgeous! This is a reminder call from Indulgence Tranquility Spa for Beatrice about your upcoming pedicure on Thursday at three p.m. We can't wait to see you—have a relaxing day!"

Ellison disconnected the line only to have the phone ring in her hand again. She answered the line without speaking, and sure enough, that same overly cheerful voice was there, this time notifying her of a facial rejuvenation session for Christopher.

"What the fuck is going on?" The phone rang again and again, and before she knew it, her voice mail was full. Why was the spa next door calling her with every appointment notification under the sun? She'd never been there, nor had she ever booked a—Pietro. Dammit. He must have added her name to their call system, and something got fouled up.

She put her cell on silent and reached for her office line as she looked up their number. Hopefully this was something she could quickly rectify over the phone. She couldn't run her business with her voice mail at capacity full of wellness and bikini-wax reminders.

"Indulgence Tranquility Spa, this is Katie," a pleasant-sounding voice answered. Ellison breathed a sigh of relief. She'd noticed the spa hours when she'd tracked down the phone number online, and it seemed they would be closing shortly. With the luck she'd had today, she was sure she'd have missed them.

"Hi, Katie, my name is Ellison Gamble. I seem to be receiving *all* the appointment notifications for the entire spa to my personal cell phone. And now my mailbox is full. Is there a way you can remove me from the system to stop the call inundation?" Ellison thumbed through the mail pile as she spoke, separating bills from junk mail.

"Oh my. Of course. Let me just take down your information, and I'll see what I can do."

"Thank you," Ellison said before relaying her contact information and disconnecting the line.

She paused her sorting to clear her voice mail between calls, but when they continued, she tossed her cell to the side. She figured they would need a few minutes to rectify the issue, and there was no point frustrating herself while they fixed it.

She dropped a pile of junk mail in the trash, but a small card missed the bucket and floated down to the floor by her feet. She must have missed that when she was sorting—that's what she got for multitasking. She scooped it up and groaned when she read the front. The handwriting was unmistakable—loopy and carefree, almost juvenile. It was exactly the type of handwriting an annoying twentysomething bubbly blond ex-cheerleader type would have. This was the handwriting of Ilaria Forrest-Stroker, Peyton's new young wife.

"What could you possibly want from me?" Ellison asked with a sigh as she opened the envelope. Ilaria, for some reason completely unfathomable to Ellison, had repeatedly reached out to her once she and Peyton got together. She'd even invited Ellison to their wedding. Ellison had politely declined, but she'd sent a small gift. She wasn't an animal, after all. Plus, Ilaria seemed nice enough, if not a little naive. Personally, Ellison felt a little sorry for her. She knew how manipulative and emotionally devoid Peyton could be.

She got the card about a quarter of the way out before the image at the top made her freeze. Her breath caught in her throat, and her heart rate increased as a wave of nausea swept over her. No. This had to be some sick fucking joke, right?

Her hand shook as she discarded the envelope. The embossed image of an ornate antique stroller at the top of the expensive card stock mocked her as she reread the card over and over. Peyton and Ilaria were having a baby. Peyton. The same woman who had convinced her for years while they were still married to push off her dream of having children only to end that marriage when she admitted that she'd never wanted kids to begin with. That Peyton.

The card slipped from her hands when her cell phone rang, startling her. She fumbled to reach it, her hands still shaking from the shock of the announcement and the accompanying invitation to the baby shower she would never attend. It didn't occur to her that the phone shouldn't ring while it was on silent until she recoiled at the name on the screen. Peyton was calling. She must have called enough times in a row to engage the emergency break-through setting on the phone.

The nausea quickly turned to rage as the ringing continued. All of this morning's suppressed feelings rushed back to the surface, and before she could stop herself and calm down, she'd slid her thumb across the screen and answered the call.

"Are you fucking kidding me?" she hissed into the receiver.

"Shit, I was trying to reach you to warn you. But your line has been busy for like an hour, and your voice mail is full. I had no idea she'd sent you the—" Peyton evidently still rambled when she was nervous.

"Pregnancy announcement?" Ellison could barely get the words out. The irony of the situation wasn't lost on her—here she was, childless and desperate to be a mother, while the woman who left her because she didn't want children was about to become one. With someone else. "And here I thought you never wanted kids. Wow, Peyton. Just, wow."

"I never would have—It's not—" Peyton stumbled, and that enraged Ellison even more.

"The card stock is nice. Expensive. And the calligraphy is a wonderful touch. Clearly this was given a lot of thought. Lots of love went into this. And planning, I bet. Like the way one plans to have a child and be a parent for the rest of their lives. Big leap, that decision. Right, Peyton?" Ellison made sure her voice dripped with sarcasm. "Seems like that wasn't such a hard choice to make with someone else, huh?"

"Ellison," Peyton tried. "It was never about you. I didn't want kids. Things have changed."

Oh? This should be good. "And what changed, Peyton? Are you suddenly less selfish?"

The line was silent.

"I didn't think so."

Peyton sighed. "We agreed it was time."

"You agreed? Or she decided it was time, and you weren't looking for another costly divorce?"

"Our divorce cost almost nothing," Peyton bit back.

"That's because I paid for everything. Including the irreplaceable cost of wasting my youth on you." Ellison was surprised by the edge in her voice. She and Peyton had split amicably, even if Ellison had footed the bill. It had been a mostly clean break. But as Ellison's rage continued to increase, she started to wonder if maybe it wasn't as clean a break as she thought.

"Fuck you."

Ellison smiled. She'd struck a nerve. Good. "I think we're done. I won't be attending the baby shower. But I think we both knew that. Best of luck on all your endeavors, Peyton. Feel free to stop including me in the updates of your woeful existence. You said yourself the divorce cost almost nothing—let me be finally free of you."

She disconnected the line and cursed modern technology. The dramatic yet satisfying finality of physically hanging up on someone was lost in the days of cell phones and touch screens.

The phone instantly rang in her hands, but it wasn't Peyton. She knew Peyton was too prideful to call back—maybe Ellison *was* finally done with her. No, it appeared that someone had not removed her from the Indulgence Tranquility Spa calling list as promised. A brief call to their main line again resulted in hearing their voice mail. Shit. Maybe if she hurried over there, she could catch them before they left for the night.

Ellison pushed back from her desk. As she shrugged on her coat and grabbed her purse, she cast one last look at the work that would await her tomorrow. She had one more fight to pursue tonight, and that was freeing her mobile number from the clutches of Pietro's robo-dialer. Work could wait. She had to fix this problem now, and she wasn't in the mood to be polite about it anymore.

CHAPTER FOUR

Katie stared at the computer screen, baffled. She was good with technology. She was on all the apps, had handles for all major—and some minor—social media avenues and dating sites, and yet this issue with the phone system was stumping her.

"Where the hell is the cancel option?" she said aloud to no one. The office was closed now and empty. Well, except for her, Shaina, and Pietro—who had not emerged from his office after walking in a few hours ago. She had just finished running through the end of day checklist for the front desk while Shaina cleaned the treatment rooms when she returned her attention to the reminder call problem. She'd hoped to resolve this phone issue before Pietro finished his scheduled conference call, so she could leave soon. But she wasn't having any luck. If she couldn't get this fixed, she'd have to wait on him before leaving, and she had no idea when he'd be done.

Katie was reviewing the PDF on how the computer and phone system worked when she heard the door open in front of her.

"I'm sorry, but we're closed for the evening," she said without looking up. Dammit. She thought Shaina had locked the door after that last client left.

"I figured as much since the nightly reminder calls have continued to flood my phone, and yet your office line has rolled over to voice mail. Too bad for me, it seems," a woman's voice replied.

Katie looked up to find an attractive woman before her. Her blond hair was swept into an intricate updo, and her outfit screamed money and power. Her heels accentuated what Katie could tell from her seated position was an already considerable height, and the matte pink color on her lips perfectly complemented her skin tone and coloring. The pursed smile on her lips told Katie that though her tone was bordering on annoyed, she was trying hard to remain polite.

"Oh, uh"—she glanced down at her notes—"you must be Ellison."

"In the flesh," she said as she stepped closer. Katie noticed her blue eyes and how intense her gaze was. This woman looked like she owned things. Which wasn't unlike most of the clientele Katie saw at this location. She was used to being around women and men of means, but something about this woman was different. She was oddly powerful. Katie could feel it in the air.

"I'm sorry"—she checked her notes again—"Mrs. Gamble. I'm working on it. I'll get this fixed tonight, I promise."

"Ms.," she corrected, and Katie's gaze unintentionally dropped to her ringless finger. Why had she assumed she was married? "And I'll wait until it's done."

Katie looked up to find an eyebrow raised in her direction. Suddenly she felt a little nervous. She'd wait? Who did this woman think she was?

"Well, that could take some time," Katie reasoned. "I'm doing everything I can to correct the issue, but—"

Ellison stepped up to the desk and looked down at her name tag. "Katie. You're the person I spoke with before."

"I am." Katie felt like she was examining her.

"It's nice to put a face with the name," she said, her tone light. "And I'm sure you'll have no trouble rectifying whatever phone snafu occurred. I bet you'll get it done in record time, too. I have the fullest confidence in you."

"I'll certainly do my best," Katie said, not sure why she was having a hard time breaking eye contact with this woman. She wasn't threatening her, but Katie felt compelled to retain her full attention, for whatever reason.

"Then I'm sure we'll both be out of here in no time." Again, not a threat, but not exactly a passive response either.

Katie watched her for a moment. Ellison was older than her, but she couldn't tell by just how much. She'd clearly taken great care of her skin and body—she was like some Grecian goddess standing before her, slightly tanned and incredibly toned in those skintight dress slacks. She had the kind of high cheekbones runway models seem to all be blessed with. And there was something else. Something about her was familiar, but Katie couldn't place it.

Ellison's pursed smile broadened, and Katie knew she'd been caught staring.

"I can assure you that the answer to the phone thing isn't here," Ellison said as she gestured to her face.

Katie felt her face heat. "Sorry. You look familiar. Do I know you?"

This seemed to amuse her. "I don't believe so. But you are holding my phone line hostage, so at this point I think it's safe to say we are quickly becoming more than acquaintances.

Katie winced. "Sorry. Really. I'm doing my—"

"I'm sure you are," Ellison replied, and Katie had to pinch her thigh from under the desk to stop from staring at the full pink lips before her. What was her problem tonight? She wasn't even into women, and yet something about this woman had her entirely captivated.

"Katie," Ellison said, and Katie didn't hate the way her name sounded on her lips.

"Yes?"

"The phone issue," Ellison said as she pointed toward the desk between them.

"Right." Katie shook her head, trying to clear the fog in her brain. She needed sleep. Her stomach growled obnoxiously, reminding her that she also needed to eat.

"Hey, Katie Cat. Ready to grab that dinner and those much-needed drinks—" Shaina's voice halted as she turned the corner. "Oh, you're with a client. Sorry."

"Not a client. Just someone trying to access her voice mail without being called *gorgeous* by a pleasant but persistent female stranger confirming Darnell's bikini wax with mineral soak afterward." Ellison made a face. "That one sounded painful."

Katie laughed. Darnell was local drag queen Roxxy Corazon's real name, and he was a regular wax client of Shaina's. He'd been waxed there so many times he hardly flinched anymore. Katie was—frankly—amazed by it.

"Oh, my, that's not good." Shaina rushed over to the computer to help, and Katie was beyond grateful.

Her stomach growled again, and Shaina gave her a look.

"What? We're all trapped here until we fix this. My stomach will have to wait."

Shaina looked at Ellison and gave her a sympathetic smile. "You don't have to wait, ma'am. We'll get it sorted."

"She's not leaving," Katie replied, surveying Ellison again. She was scanning her phone screen, with her brow slightly furrowed. That was the only wrinkle she had on her entire face from what Katie could tell, and it was clearly a thought wrinkle and not an age one.

"She's right. We're all in this together now." Ellison glanced up with a smile. Katie appreciated her sarcasm. Though she was sure this was beyond annoying, Ellison was being a surprisingly good sport about the whole thing.

"Ellison." Pietro's voice sounded from over their shoulders, and Katie's fingers froze on the keys. "Are you here to schedule a session?"

Ellison laughed. "No. Not exactly."

"Oh? What can we help you with? They have been helping you, right?" Pietro sounded somewhere between flustered and confused. That was a new one for Katie. Pietro rarely seemed unsure of himself.

"They're trying," Ellison said, and Katie started to sweat a little.

"Somehow Ellison's phone number got into the call system, and she's receiving everyone's appointment updates, directly to her personal cell. Incessantly. And I can't figure out how to fix it," Katie said.

"Well, that's unacceptable." That was the tone of Pietro's she was more familiar with. "Let me see what I can do."

Pietro ushered Shaina back and Katie out of the chair as he began pecking at the keyboard in an almost comical way. She rolled her eyes as he repeated the steps she'd tried a dozen times before like she was someone incapable of problem solving. It was decided. They were doomed to stay here forever.

Shaina gave her a shrug as she wandered out back, shutting off the lights beyond the front desk.

Katie shuffled some papers around the desk just to have something to do when she felt Ellison's gaze on her. She turned to catch her giving her a once-over. Ellison held her eye contact briefly before returning her attention to her phone with a small smile on her lips, and Katie wondered what she was thinking.

After a few mumbled curses from Pietro, Ellison said, "Pietro. Katie and her friend have dinner plans, and the workday is over."

She motioned to the clock over his head. "If we aren't any closer to resolving the problem, might I suggest shutting off the automated call service until someone *can* fix it?"

"Duh," Katie said, palming her forehead. Why hadn't she thought of that? "I'll leave a note for Marcio to make the calls manually tomorrow. I'm sure you can shoot off an email to IT tonight, and they'll have it corrected by the morning."

Pietro shot her a look.

"Or I can email them," she backtracked.

Shaina reemerged, holding Katie's purse and their jackets, as Ellison said, "That sounds like a solid plan. And I'm sure you're fine with the email task, right, Pietro? That's certainly easier than paying overtime to these ladies, right?"

Katie knew she was mirroring Shaina's look of surprise. Ellison Gamble did not fuck around.

"Absolutely. I'll take it from here. Thank you, ladies." Pietro dismissed them with a wave before seeming to reconsider that. "Thank you for your help. And Ellison, my apologies for the inconvenience."

"Just ensure that it doesn't happen again, and we're good." She strode toward the door, holding it open as she asked, "Ladies?"

Katie tossed down the half-legible note to Marcio before hustling with Shaina toward the door. She wasn't about to miss her exit window, especially if Pietro was sore about what had just happened. The sooner she was out, the better.

"Enjoy your dinner," Ellison said with a nod as she let the door close behind them.

"Thanks," Katie replied as she watched her head across the parking lot toward the adjacent building. The lights to the Maserati parked out front flashed, and Katie laughed. That's how she knew her. The Maserati. Though she'd seen her enter and exit her vehicle dozens of times, she'd never seen her without large sunglasses obstructing her flawless face. And after spending only a few minutes in her presence, it made perfect sense to her that Ellison was the owner of the most expensive car in the lot.

"What was all that about? Did you see how fast she put Pietro in his place? And why was he so nervous around her?" Shaina asked.

Katie watched Ellison pull out of the parking lot before them into the dark night, and she shrugged. "I have no idea."

CHAPTER FIVE

"Drinks! Refills for everyone," Lauren cheered, and Trina laughed. "Ellison is here, and we're celebrating."

"Celebrating what?" Ellison asked as she drained her martini.

"You being here, of course." Jax gave her a nudge before seeming to think they'd crossed a line.

She placed a hand on Jax's forearm and gave it a squeeze. "Thank you."

Jax blushed and Trina laughed again.

"Don't mind them—they aren't used to seeing unicorns out around town," Trina said with a wink.

"I come out with you guys a lot," Ellison argued.

"Define *a lot*," Trina replied with a smile. "Don't get me wrong, I'm thrilled you're here, but we invite you out at least once a week, and it's been months since you took us up on it."

"Which is why we're moving on to shots," Lauren said as she returned with a tray of shot glasses full of clear liquid.

"Oh, I don't know about that," Ellison said, raising her hands in surrender.

"Please?" Jax's big brown puppy-dog eyes were too adorable to ignore. "We always do a shot when we celebrate."

"Again, no need to celebrate," Ellison said as she took the glass Lauren offered her. "And I'm not a unicorn. Just busy."

"One could argue too busy," Trina said as she raised her glass. "To Ellison working less and socializing with her favorite employees more."

"Hear, hear," Lauren said, and they all laughed as Jax nearly choked into their glass.

Ellison closed her eyes as the liquid warmed her throat. She couldn't remember the last time she'd had a shot of tequila.

She stayed a while longer, laughing with them and enjoying the moment until a text from David Brinkley checking in on her thrust her back to the reality of her life.

"Uh-oh. That's a serious face." Lauren shook her head. "We have a strict no cell phone rule during colleague cocktail hour."

"Hours. Cocktail hours," Trina corrected. "But she's right. Only girlfriends and potential girlfriends"—she nudged Jax, who immediately turned bright red—"are allowed to interfere with best-friend time."

Ellison warmed at being included in that very valuable time. That feeling doubled when Jax shyly checked their phone only to be teased by Lauren and Trina. Ellison knew that Jax had a significant crush on her personal stylist, Talia French. She'd gone out of her way to put the two of them together, and after Talia helped Jax redesign their wardrobe after their gender-affirming top surgery, they *had* become closer. But maybe not as close as Jax had hoped. Just yet.

"Unless that's a text from a special lady friend that you want to tell us about?" Lauren asked boldly as she tried to catch a glimpse of Ellison's phone screen.

Ellison moved her phone back to her purse with a coy smile. "Maybe it is."

Lauren's face lit up. "I knew it."

"She's teasing you, Lau," Trina said as she wrapped her arm around Lauren's shoulders. "Ellison is way too classy to kiss and tell."

"Thank you," Ellison said as she stood, pulling on her coat.

"Dammit." Lauren frowned adorably, and Ellison felt a little bad.

Trina kissed the side of her head as Jax scrolled through their phone, looking sad.

Ellison leaned in toward them and said, "Talia's aunt is in town this weekend. We're meeting for dinner. I can put in an encouraging word or two if you think that would help."

Jax was out of their chair so fast it almost tipped over. "Really? Faith is in town? Would you?"

Faith Leader, Ellison's first love and occasional friend with benefits, had called Ellison last night to see if she was available this weekend. That meant two things: Ellison was getting laid, and she was going to get all the behind-the-scenes gossip on Talia and her dating life from her beloved auntie. She loved when Faith visited. Maybe she could angle this visit to help Jax out, too.

"If you want me to. I'll be subtle about it. I promise," Ellison reassured them.

Jax ran their hand through their hair, messing it up a bit. "Yes? I think so. Totally. Yes. But..."

"But what?"

"But maybe don't tell me if it's bad news. Maybe I'd rather not know that," Jax replied, eyes cast downward.

"It won't be bad news. You're a fucking catch," Trina said as Lauren helped her into her designer coat. The tan fabric with chunky leather buckles was incredible. Ellison made a note to inquire about it later.

"She's right," Lauren replied.

"Always am," Trina said as she patted Jax on the shoulder. "You're amazing. And Talia sees that. How could she not?"

Jax gave them all a shy smile, and Ellison wished more of Trina's confidence had rubbed off on Jax.

"I'll let you know what I find out," Ellison said as she pulled them into a hug. She whispered, "And I'm sure it won't be bad news. You *are* a catch. She'd be lucky to have you."

"Thanks," Jax mumbled into her shoulder, and Ellison gave them an extra squeeze before turning her attention to the ladies.

"I'm off. I trust that you're all safe enough to get home?" she asked.

"Lauren's coming to my place, and Thea's going to pick her up on the way home from softball practice with Kendall and the team. But I see pizza in our future, so we're good," Trina replied.

"Pizza? Hell yes," Lauren said as she gave Trina a high five. "Jax, you in for pizza?"

"Can't." Jax frowned. "I have a Twitch game in a bit. I gotta be home."

"Kick some ass, Jaxy," Trina said. She looked at Ellison and added, "Pizza will be at the next best friends' night. Make sure you're there."

"I'm in," Ellison replied. "But only if you let me buy tonight's drinks. Deal?"

"You drive a hard bargain, Gamble," Trina teased. "Deal."

Ellison bid good-bye to her colleagues and headed to the bar to close the tab. She was waiting for her receipt when she heard a frustrated sigh to her left.

Katie from the spa had just stepped up to the bar and was rummaging through her purse with a deep frown. Her curly dark red hair fell around her face, mostly shielding it from view, but Ellison could easily recall her deep green eyes from before. She never forgot a face. Especially one as attractive as Katie's. What she hadn't noticed before at the spa was how soft looking those loose curls were—but now, standing next to her, she had the desire to gently tug on the mid-shoulder-length locks to watch them spring back up.

After what seemed like a fruitless search, she gave up. "Fuck this day."

"You okay?" Ellison asked as she signed the receipt the bartender had dropped off.

Katie startled, placing her hand over her chest as she replied, "Ellison. Hi."

"Hi," she said. "Is something wrong?"

"Everything is mostly wrong. But..." She paused. "Did the reminder calls stop?"

Ellison nodded. "They did."

"Well, at least something went right, then." Katie sighed again. It was the kind of sigh that was so heavy it brought the room down with it. Ellison knew the emptiness that accompanied that sigh.

Mira Donahue, The Mirage bar's owner, emerged from behind the bar with a sympathetic smile. "Rick's here. I told him you'd be right out."

"Thanks for calling him, Mira."

"Anytime. Oh, hey, Ellison. Good to see you." Mira gave Ellison a brief nod before disappearing behind the bar again.

"Boyfriend waiting for you?" Ellison asked, because Katie looked distraught, and sure, she didn't know the woman, but no one should look that sad. Or overwhelmed. And something about that sigh told Ellison she was both of those things right now.

Katie laughed. "I haven't had one of those in months." She slung her purse over her shoulder and adjusted her coat, pulling it tightly around her body as she said, "Bertha's backfire finally, well, backfired."

"Bertha?" Ellison wasn't quite following.

"My car," Katie said with a sad smile. "Rick is the tow-truck guy Mira knows. He's here to take Bertha to his shop. Or her final resting place. Which is probably the same location, if I'm being honest."

"Oh, I'm sorry." In her previous life, Ellison had had many a car that she'd sent to the junkyard. She had always found it a rather sad experience, like breaking up with an old friend. The look on Katie's face told her she felt the same way.

Katie shrugged. "It's sort of the way my life has been going these past few months." She swept an errant hair behind her ear. "Mostly I'm sorry I left my charger at work and that my phone is dead. Because now I have to charm Rick into taking me to a bus stop that hopefully is on my route home."

Ellison frowned. A quick glance at the clock above the bar confirmed what she already knew—it was late. And if Katie had to take multiple bus routes to get home, then she'd never get there.

"Where is home, exactly?" Ellison asked, buttoning her jacket.

"Brookline. So not far."

"But far enough," Ellison said, giving her a look. "I'll call you a cab."

Katie winced. "That'll be a fortune, and I was already panicking about calling an Uber when the dead phone sort of resolved that issue for me. Honestly, I'm sure Rick will drop me at the T or something."

Ellison had fully intended to pay for the cab in question, but Katie's resistance gave her pause. She wouldn't push anything on anyone if they didn't want it. Even generosity.

"Well, I'm parked out back. So I'll walk out with you," she said. "You know, just in case Rick is creepy or something."

Katie gave her the first genuine smile she'd seen from her tonight. "Oh? And if he is, are you going to defend me in those heels and that designer coat of yours?"

Ellison feigned offense. "Are you trying to insinuate that I'm any less lethal in this outfit than some other one? Because I've got moves like you wouldn't believe."

"Oh no. Far from it. I saw how you told Pietro to send his own damn email," Katie said with a laugh. "I'm sure you've kicked many a man's ass in those shoes. And that coat. Which is gorgeous, by the way."

"I have. And thank you." Ellison held the door for her as they left the bar.

They walked in silence for the few dozen feet until they found Rick and Bertha in the back lot. And contrary to Ellison's jest earlier, Rick seemed like a genuinely nice guy.

"Okay, she's all loaded up and ready," Rick said, motioning toward the old beaten-up car on the elevated flatbed behind his truck. "I'll take her to the shop and look at her first thing in the morning."

"Thanks, Rick. I really appreciate it." Katie shook his hand and took his card. Ellison watched her hand off her keys and chat for a bit. Before long, Rick and Bertha were out of sight.

"So, about that bus stop," Ellison said.

"Shit!" Katie groaned. "I was so flustered about Bertha I completely forgot."

"I'll take you. Brookline is on my way home. C'mon." Ellison unlocked her car and waited for Katie to join her.

Katie looked unsure.

"If you'd feel more comfortable, my offer to call you a cab still stands. And I'll pay for it, if you're worried about that."

"I'm not worried about anything. Except for sitting in your car," Katie said as she pointed to the Maserati.

"You're worried about *my* car? When yours was just towed away?" Ellison asked.

"No, I'm worried because I've never sat in such an expensive vehicle, and I just don't trust myself."

Ellison laughed. "Why? Do you have an incontinence issue I should be concerned about?"

"Pee? Do I spontaneously pee? No." Katie shook her head, looking mortified.

"Then what's the problem?" Ellison opened the passenger side door and motioned for her to get in. "The seats are leather anyway. They clean up nicely."

"I can't believe you just suggested that I have bladder control issues," Katie grumbled as she sat in the car.

"You're the one that was worried about getting in, not me," Ellison said as she closed the door and headed to the driver's side. Once seated, she continued, "If you told me you were worried about me murdering you, then I'd think that was a legitimate reason not to get in. But if you're worried about somehow messing up the interior of my car—if you are, in fact, in control of all your faculties—then that seems silly."

Katie settled into her seat and rested her head on the headrest. "I'm not worried about you killing me."

"Good, you shouldn't be." Ellison pulled up the GPS and waited for Katie to give her an address to punch in. "I've met my murder quota for the month."

"It's the first week of May," Katie said, giving her a look.

Ellison shrugged. "I like to check things off my to-do list quickly."

Katie laughed, and Ellison was glad to see her mood was improving a bit.

"So, tell me about Bertha," she said. She figured since she was driving Katie home, she might as well get to know her a bit.

"Bertha and I go way back." Katie leaned her elbow on the passenger window as she spoke—Ellison could feel her watching her as she drove. "I got Bertha my senior year in high school, and I drove her cross-country to California for college. We've been together ever since. I've gone through many a breakup and learned countless life lessons with Bertha by my side."

"You got Bertha in high school?" Ellison didn't know much about cars, but she could tell Bertha wasn't an antique. So how old was Katie?

"Secondhand, at that." Katie stretched. "I logged long hours at Subway and babysitting to afford her. I bought her off the used car lot on my seventeenth birthday—she was the first real gift I ever got myself."

Ellison glanced in her direction, and she found that Katie was in fact watching her. "So you've had the car, what, about a decade? I'd say that's a good long run."

"Eleven years next week," Katie corrected her. "And yeah. I suppose it's time to accept the inevitable."

"Well, maybe Rick can pull out a miracle for your birthday," Ellison said, trying to be positive.

"Maybe. But I'm in no rush to turn twenty-eight and be carless if he can't. That's more pathetic than my current predicament. At least now I can feign nostalgia about still driving Bertha." Katie shifted and looked out the front windshield. "Birthdays can go screw."

Twenty-eight was so far in Ellison's rearview she had to really focus to remember what that was like. At twenty-eight she was newly married and ignorant to the cancer brewing in her mother. She'd lose her shortly, in her early thirties. A lifetime ago.

"Well, if it makes you feel any better, my birthday is also next week, and I completely agree with you. Birthdays can go screw." Ellison was not looking forward to next week. Though now that Dr. Brinkley had encouraged her to unshoulder the burden of carrying a pregnancy, she supposed the numbers on the cake didn't matter anymore. It's not like anyone would remember or acknowledge her birthday anyway. She could let the day slip away like it was any other. That was just fine by her.

"We can be un-birthday buddies, then," Katie said, sounding amused.

"I like the sound of that," Ellison said as she steered them onto Route 9. "So, California, huh?"

"I wanted to be by the water and away from my past," Katie said. "Although UC Santa Barbara was my first choice, I think I would have gone to any school on the West Coast that would have me. I needed a change of scenery."

"Oh? And why's that?"

"My dad left when I was in middle school, and my mother had a hard time adjusting to being a single parent. And I had a hard time being abandoned. But in the end, I guess I left just like he did, as soon as I was able to." Her voice was soft. "I regret that now."

Ellison spared her a glance. Katie was looking out the passenger window, tracing her finger along the window frame where the glass met the car's interior.

"Sometimes you have to leave to find what you're looking for. Home can be a hard place to find yourself," Ellison said.

"You sound like someone speaking from experience," Katie said, looking at her again.

Ellison smiled at her before redirecting her attention to the road. "I've done my fair share of running."

"So, you know all about me and my short stint in Cali, and my abandonment issues. Which was probably an overshare, but here we are." She laughed, and Ellison loved the melodious nature of it. "What about you? Where did you run away from?"

"Rural Maine," Ellison said. "The real sticks."

Katie let out a low whistle. "And look at you now, Mrs. Maserati."

"Ms.," Ellison corrected. "I did this all on my own."

"I bet you did," Katie said. "You strike me as very independent."

"I am," Ellison replied as she turned them onto a side road. She was familiar with this area—she'd sold more than a few properties in this zip code over the years. The homes were large, and the lots were spacious, considering its proximity to the city. This was an expensive area to live in—the schools nearby were rated some of the best in the state, and the neighboring shopping and grocery stores were high-end and easily accessible. Houses around here sold fast and for a fortune.

"Did you enjoy California life?"

"I loved it," Katie replied without hesitation.

Though Ellison had only visited the left coast for work, she could see why people loved it. The vibe was different, more relaxed. And the sun was almost always shining, especially in Southern California. "What brought you back here, then?"

Katie didn't answer right away, and Ellison worried she'd overstepped.

"My mother was in a bad accident. And life changed. I moved back to help her out." Katie sounded distant.

Ellison examined her. Katie seemed much older than her years in this moment. "I'm sorry to hear that. Is she okay now?"

Katie shook her head. "No. Not really."

"Oh." Ellison wasn't sure what to say. "I'm sorry."

"Me, too," Katie replied, and that heavy sigh from the bar was back. The one that felt like the weight of the world, and Ellison was only an observer to it.

After a long pause, Katie said, "I owe you an apology."

"Why?" Ellison slowed as she turned onto Katie's street.

"Because it's totally my fault that your phone line got hijacked, and I realized it as soon as Shaina and I got to dinner, but I wasn't sure I'd ever see you again and have to cop to it. But you're driving me home on what is probably the worst day of my life, and you're being so nice about it. And I'm really, really sorry about the phone thing."

Ellison pulled over when the GPS pinged and put the car in park. "Why was it your fault?"

Katie massaged her temple. "Pietro came in buzzing with excitement earlier in the day and told me to add your number to the call list. He was rambling about VIP something or other, and I was on the phone with a client while checking someone in at the front desk at the same time, and I probably definitely input your number into the wrong place as he was breathing down my neck. And I'm sorry."

"Mistakes happen. Plus, it sounds like Pietro should have been more patient. Or done it himself," she offered. Ellison had little patience for people too lazy to help themselves. Especially people who thought a task was below them. "But what about the other part?"

Katie looked at her, and Ellison loved the green of her eyes even if they seemed a bit sad and tired. "What other part?"

"The part where you sort of casually mentioned that today was the worst day of your life. That part."

"Oh, right." Katie looked out at the house they were stopped in front of, and Ellison leaned forward to see it.

A large, stately Victorian occupied the spacious lot before them. All the lights were off, and the path to the front door was overgrown, but even in the shadows Ellison could see its exquisite beauty and charm. This home was an original to the area, a towering giant bathed in history and rich in architectural style. But she could see some of its regal character had faded. The portions illuminated by the streetlight showed chipping paint and neglected, rotten woodwork. What once must have been a grand front porch now sagged from years of being overlooked and under cared for. This diamond was certainly rough.

"Mom took a turn for the worse a few months ago. And it became apparent that I couldn't care for her like she needed. So today she moved into a long-term rehabilitation facility." She shook her head. "No. That's not right. I have to start saying it out loud because it's real. She didn't move anywhere. I *put* her into a long-term rehabilitation facility. Because I can't take care of her."

The pain on Katie's face was unmistakable, and Ellison's instinct was to reach out and touch her hand. The hand of a stranger in anguish. Someone she knew next to nothing about.

Ellison couldn't imagine what Katie was feeling or even thinking in that moment, but she could listen. And offer some levity. And right now felt like a good time for that.

"I thought I was having a bad day, but you win," she said, turning her palm over in Katie's direction. "Low five for your lowest day?"

Katie laughed and briefly touched her palm before quietly cheering, "Worst day ever winner. Woo."

"A win is a win," Ellison said. "You're the winningest loser I've met today."

Katie chuckled, and a small smile returned to her lips. "Share some misery with me. What happened today to make it shitty for you? Besides getting endless calls about random people's body waxing appointments, I mean."

That felt like a different day entirely. "Well, first my fertility doctor told me I'll never be able to successfully get pregnant and carry to term. And then when I got back to my office, I found a birth announcement from my ex-wife and her current wife. This is the same woman who left me because I wanted a baby, and she didn't. So she'll have one, and I still won't. Which seems cruel in so many ways, but not as heavy as what you're going through at the moment. So you still win."

Katie's hand rested on her forearm. "Ellison, I'm so sorry."

"I'm not really sure why I told you that," Ellison said, feeling guilty and exposed at the same time.

"I asked you to share your misery," Katie replied. "Thank you."

Ellison looked back at the darkened house and frowned at the thought that Katie would be walking into it alone. "Have you lived here long?"

"I grew up here. My grandparents left it to my mother, but they'd let it start to fall apart long before Mom got it. She hung on to it as best she could, but the house needed more work than she could complete. She did her best, but in a lot of ways I think she felt burdened by the house."

"And you?" Ellison asked, knowing that restoring and upkeeping this kind of house was a labor of love.

"Everything feels burden-y and overwhelm-y at the moment," she said with a sad smile.

"I bet," Ellison replied. She glanced into the space behind Katie's seat, glad her Realtor bag was there. She reached into it and pulled out the flashlight she kept there. "Here. I'll walk you to the front door."

"It's okay, I'll use my—" Katie palmed her forehead. "I was going to say my flashlight app, but my phone is dead, so…"

Ellison winced. "I'm sorry my car charger didn't work for you."

Katie shrugged. "That's what happens when you have a model that's one step away from a flip phone. Antique charging port and all." She shook her head. "Of all the days to forget to leave the porch light on."

"C'mon. Let's get you inside, so you can try this day again tomorrow," Ellison said with a smile. "It has to be better than today."

"I hope you're right," Katie said, but she didn't sound enthused by the suggestion. "Why do you have a flashlight in your car, anyway?" Katie asked as she stepped out of the car door Ellison held open for her.

"It's part of my Realtor emergency kit. Although I don't use it much these days, there have been plenty of times in the past when a light blew or there was a darkened basement area I needed to show some clients. I have a bunch of little odds and ends in there. You'd be surprised how much they come in handy," she replied.

Ellison used her flashlight to safely navigate the uneven masonry of the front walk and avoid the stones disrupted by roots and sunken over time. Katie walked to the far right of the stairs, and Ellison followed.

"Careful," Katie said, pointing to the center of the top step, and Ellison could see why they'd taken the longer route—a boot-sized hole in the floorboards indicated that someone once hadn't been so lucky.

"I nearly lost a Timberland into that black hole," Katie said with an ironic laugh. "This house is trying to kill me."

Ellison glanced around the porch, briefly casting light along the surface for fear of any other dangers, when Katie cursed next to her.

"What? Are you okay?" she asked, whipping the stream of light back in Katie's direction.

"Well, that depends. Do you have a lock-picking set in that emergency bag? Because in my frazzled state, I left my house key on the key ring I gave Rick." Katie looked even more defeated than before.

Ellison frowned. "Do you have an alarm system on this place?"

Katie gave her a look. "You're kidding, right?"

"Okay, then, how about a credit card?" She motioned toward Katie's purse. "Got one of those in there?"

Katie rummaged through it, pausing to ask, "Does it matter if it's maxed out?"

"That might be better if I snap it in half trying to break in to your house. At least that way it'll keep you from overextending yourself."

"Too late." Katie laughed as she handed over a debit card. "This is easier to replace if it gets broken. Plus, there's nothing in there to use in the next few days anyway."

Ellison took the card, handing Katie the flashlight as she reached for the door handle. "Can you shine that here for me?"

"I mean, if you get me into this house, I'll do anything you ask." Katie held the light steady. "At this point I think I owe you my life."

"Why's that?" Ellison asked as she leaned against the door and jiggled the handle. She slipped the card into the tiny gap next to the lock and carefully maneuvered it up and down.

"Because you saved me at the bar and drove me home. And now you're breaking me in to my own house because I'm a helpless fool who doesn't have a spare key hidden under that decorative porch planter like my mother always told me to."

"Did you ever?" Ellison asked as she worked.

Katie replied, "Oh yeah. The really embarrassing part of this whole thing is that the key on my key ring *is* the spare. I lost my original key months ago."

After a moment or two of struggling, the lock popped and the knob turned, opening into the pitch-black foyer of Katie's home.

Katie cheered. "My shero."

Ellison handed her back the card. "I hope I didn't ruin it. Or the lock."

Katie fiddled with the knob, locking it and unlocking it. "Nope, looks good. And I have the dead bolt in case you did. But I wouldn't have cared either way, because you literally saved my day."

"Glad to have helped," Ellison said, stepping back onto the porch as Katie stepped inside.

"How did you learn to pick locks, anyway?" Katie asked as she flicked on the porch light. "Is that a Realtor skill as well?"

Ellison shook her head. "I grew up in an old, dilapidated farmhouse. The front door got stuck all the time. Even with a key, I had to break in often. I doubt I could get into a newer lock system, but with an old door and mechanism like this, I figured it was worth the gamble."

Katie smiled. "I'm glad you tried."

"I'm glad I succeeded," Ellison said. "Have a good night. And I hope your tomorrow is better."

"Thanks. For everything," Katie said. As Ellison turned to go, Katie called out, "Watch that top step."

"I will."

"Good night, Ellison."

"Night, Katie."

Ellison glanced back at the house before climbing into her car. Katie was still in the doorway, waiting. She waved and waited until Katie disappeared before dropping into the driver's seat, tired from the long day filled with so many unexpected twists and turns. And as she drove away—headed to her empty luxury apartment—her mind wandered back to the charming and funny woman she'd left at the enormous empty home. They were both alone tonight, but their circumstances could not be any more different. And for some reason, that sat in Ellison's stomach like a pit.

"You need to get a girlfriend, Gamble," she said to herself. "Not a project."

CHAPTER SIX

E llison rolled onto her back, sated and out of breath.

"That is never not good," Faith said next to her with a laugh. The velvety timbre to her voice had always brought Ellison joy. Especially after they'd shared a few orgasms.

"Agreed," Ellison replied once she caught her breath. She could hear the waves crashing in the distance. She was glad they'd come to the beach house for the weekend. Ellison hated being here alone, even though it was paradise. So Faith's visit and company were the perfect motivation to open the house for the summer season. And she was glad she had because she absolutely loved it here. "We certainly are magical together, aren't we?"

Faith rolled to her side to face her, and Ellison intertwined their fingers, loving the contrast between their skin tones. Though Ellison tanned a bit in the sun, her blond hair and blue eyes were a complete opposite to Faith's endlessly deep brown eyes and gorgeous dark brown skin. Ellison had always found such beauty in their differences, especially when they were naked together. She loved Faith. She knew she always would. Because Faith had a part of her that she never wanted back, and she knew the same was true for Faith as well.

"At least in bed we are," Faith said as she kissed her lips slowly.

"Oh, come on," Ellison teased. "We get along out of bed, too."

Faith laughed as she counted out on her fingers, "And on the sofa, the kitchen counter, the back of the barn during senior prom when we dumped our dates for a literal roll in the hay…"

That was a fond memory of Ellison's. "We very nearly got caught."

"That was half the fun." Faith yawned.

Ellison poked her in the side. "You getting old on me, Leader?"

"Oh, I can keep up with you just fine," she said with a wink. The truth was that Ellison had to work hard to keep up with Faith. Faith had been an elite runner, diehard weight trainer, cyclist, and yogi for as long as she'd known her. Faith was in better shape now than she was in high school, which didn't seem possible since she was a goddess back then, too. "Plus, you're a month older than me."

Ellison groaned. "Don't remind me."

"Happy early birthday, by the way."

"Thanks," Ellison said. "Is that why you're in town this weekend?"

"I wouldn't miss your birthday," Faith said, nuzzling her nose briefly.

"Thank you." Ellison meant that all the way down to her soul.

"And"—Faith pulled back, watching her as she said softly—"I got Peyton's baby announcement."

"She lost you in the divorce. You're my friend, not hers," Ellison said with a hiss as she closed her eyes. The last thing she wanted was to talk about Peyton.

"I know." Faith's tone was soothing. "But you know that child bride of hers likes to try to keep everyone connected for whatever reason. I was surprised by the news."

Ellison grunted and rolled to her side, turning her back to Faith.

"And I was worried about you," Faith said as she turned Ellison back to face her.

Ellison opened her eyes to Faith's concerned expression, and the walls she'd put up slowly crumbled.

"It's okay." Faith wiped her cheek as she silently cried, and Ellison hated that the short amount of time they had together would be marred by sadness. Faith was her escape from the world. She always had been. She'd desperately missed their closeness during her marriage to Peyton, but she'd stayed loyal to her wife. She'd never cheated with Faith—not once, since they'd parted ways during college. Still, they'd always seemed to find each other when they were single, and she'd been enjoying more of her in the last few months. But like all things with Faith, she knew that would come to an end soon. That was why every moment mattered so much. Because they felt fleeting.

"David told me the jig is up," Ellison said, wiping her eyes. "It's time to seek out a surrogate or give up on having a genetic child altogether."

Faith hugged her. "How many eggs are left?"

"Two." Faith knew all about her fertility woes. She'd been her best friend all along, after all—sex or no sex.

"What does he think you should do?" She caressed Ellison's hair.

"Get some more donor sperm and hire someone with a far less hostile uterus to carry the embryo to term." Ellison had spent the last few days agonizing over the decision, but she'd settled on moving forward with surrogacy this morning.

"Did he say that? That you have a *hostile* uterus?" Faith sounded annoyed.

"He did," Ellison said, looking up at her. The look on Faith's face was adorable—she loved that she was so protective of her. "It's fine. Facts are facts."

Faith pouted. "Are you sure? Because I'm not above throwing hands."

Ellison laughed. "I'm sure. But…"

"But what?"

"You sure you don't want to reconsider this best friend with occasional casual sex thing and raise a baby with me? I promise you great orgasms all the time. Whenever you want." Ellison was half joking. Half.

Faith stroked her cheek. "You know I love you."

"I love you, too." Ellison knew there was a *but* coming, so she wasn't unprepared for what Faith would say next.

"But you know how I feel about kids. I love being an auntie. I'm the best damn auntie on this planet, and you know I'll spoil those babies of yours something serious. But being a mom isn't in the cards for me, Ellie. That's not the life I want for myself." Faith had never wavered on that. Not even when they were teenagers. And Ellison knew that. She knew to trust Faith's conviction on the matter. And she also knew Faith would help her with whatever path she chose, even if it wasn't one she'd take with her.

"I know. I just figured I'd double-check," Ellison teased, taking Faith's hand in hers. "In case you could be swayed by sex."

Faith chuckled. "You know I can't say no to you. But no."

"*Fiiine.*"

Faith smiled at her. "You're gonna be a great mom, Ellie. However and whenever that happens—and it will—you're going to be the best there is. I have no doubt about that."

Ellison warmed at that statement. "You're not going to Peyton's baby shower though, right?"

"Hell no," Faith clucked as she slipped out from under the sheets. Ellison watched her walk to the panoramic glass doors at the foot of the bed, sliding them fully open and welcoming in the warm breeze and the sounds of the ocean that was only a few hundred yards away. "You said it yourself. I'm yours, not hers. I never really liked her anyway."

Now it was Ellison's turn to laugh. "Liar."

Faith shrugged as she hovered, naked, in the doorway facing the ocean. "I mean, she was fine. But she wasn't right for you."

"And you are?" Ellison was surprised Faith didn't just walk her gloriously naked self out onto the expansive porch she had off the main bedroom. She had neighbors, but none close enough to notice if anyone was sunbathing on this second-story balcony.

"You know how I feel about being tied down." Faith gave her a small smile over her shoulder.

"You like it *a lot,*" Ellison said, knowing what she meant.

"Only when you do it." Faith took in a deep breath, spreading her arms out to the sides with a stretch. "You were the only one who could tame me."

"But you aren't someone who should be tamed." Ellison ran her hand through Faith's short hair when she crawled back in bed. "I love how things are between us. I'm good with that. I don't need more from you than you are willing to give to me."

Faith gave her a genuine smile, and she knew the message was received. She *didn't* need anything from Faith other than her friendship, and their history together was proof of that. She knew that she'd have Faith in her life forever—that was a constant she could trust.

"You need to spend more time here. This view is fucking outrageous," Faith said, propping her hand under her head and looking beyond the foot of Ellison's California king bed to the porch and ocean before them. "You really designed the hell out of this house, Ellie. If I were you, I'd never leave."

Ellison rested her head on Faith's chest, looking out at the waves.

She'd always found such peace by the water. Maybe she needed to slow things down and spend more time here. She loved it once she was here, and she hated leaving. So why not stay? It's not like she had a girlfriend or a family to worry about. Only work waited for her back in Boston.

"Maybe I'll make this a long-weekend place this summer and work remotely for a bit. Old man Stetler is renovating the condo to the tastes of his new bride, so the city will be very noisy from eight to four all summer long, starting in about a week or so."

"He got married *again*?" Faith's chest vibrated with laughter.

"I know," Ellison said, rolling her eyes. This was his second marriage since she'd become his neighbor six years ago, and rumor was he'd been married three times before that. And with each new marriage, it seemed, the apartment got a face-lift. "I don't know where he keeps finding these women."

"A catalog," Faith mused. "Because he has the personality of a slug. So it's gotta be about the money, not the dinner conversation."

"Oh, that's for sure."

After a few moments of cuddling with her, Faith asked, "So, when are we making that call, then?"

"What call?" Ellison asked with a yawn.

"The one to the surrogacy agency."

Ellison sat up and looked at her. "Are you serious?"

"Did I stutter?" Faith nudged her. "I'm not looking to be someone's momma, but I'll be your best friend and hold your hand while you make the call I know you've probably been avoiding."

"Rude," Ellison said, even if it was true.

"Get your phone, and let's do this," Faith said with a wave of her hand. "Then we can celebrate a new chapter in your life once you take that first step."

Ellison reached for her phone before pausing. "Can we celebrate any way I want?"

"As long as it involves me and you in this bed. Then yes. Anything you want, Birthday Girl."

"Happy birthday to me," Ellison said as she grabbed her phone off the bedside table. She unlocked the screen and took a breath. She could do this. Especially if Faith was with her when she did.

❖

"Hey, Mom," Katie said as she entered her mother's room at New Beginnings. She said that every time she entered any room her mother occupied, but her mother rarely looked in her direction. So when she did today, Katie nearly dropped her travel mug of coffee. "Oh."

Mae Crawford blinked her familiar but mostly vacant pale blue eyes twice in her direction before offering her a small smile.

A smile. Katie's heart swelled. "Are you having a good day today, Mom?"

Her smile broadened briefly before vanishing, though she maintained Katie's eye contact. That was something else that was new since she'd moved into New Beginnings a week ago—she seemed more alert. Even if only momentarily. That gave Katie hope that she'd made the right decision moving her here.

"Your nurse Karen told me that you had a great breakfast and even played some cards today," she said as she sat on the edge of her mother's hospital bed, facing the recliner her mother sat in nearby. "She said you grouped all the reds and blacks together but kept them in separate piles, as if you were organizing them. That's great, Mom."

Her mother's gaze dropped to the small table before her, and Katie watched her move the playing cards around randomly with her left hand. Though the brain injury from the car accident had significantly weakened her right side, she still had some use of her arm and hand. Since the stroke, though, she'd stopped using her right side altogether.

Katie reached into her mother's lap and pulled her right arm up on to the table, stroking her palm and teasing her clawed hand open with gentle pressure. It was times like these she was glad she had knowledge of muscles and movement. Never did she expect her exercise physiology and massage therapy background to become so important to her non-work life as it did after her mother's accident. During the past few years, she'd even started taking night classes to cover the prerequisites to pursuing a doctorate in physical therapy, in hopes of offering her mother more help. But the stroke halted all the progress they had been making—and in a lot of ways, this felt like square one again.

After a few minutes of passive stretching and caressing, the spasm in her mother's hand dissipated, and Katie was able to place it flat on the table before her. She rubbed her thumb along the back of her mother's hand as she sipped her coffee, enjoying the quiet of the moment.

Her mother's room was on the first floor in the rear of the building, and the window next to her bed faced a beautiful courtyard. It was warm today, and Katie could see families visiting with other residents, sitting on the evenly spaced benches along the path. One family had two little kids—Katie assumed they were the resident's grandkids—playing tag around the adults.

Kids. She shook her head with a heavy sigh. Prior to her mother's accident, she had teased Katie about settling down and having kids someday. Which was something Katie had always thought she would want, but the last three years had been hard. And with no romantic relationship anywhere in the near or distant future, the prospect of having kids seemed like a pipe dream. The one thing she'd learned about being the sole caregiver for her mother these few last years was that she didn't want to be a single parent. Her mother had struggled so much raising Katie alone, and that wasn't a world she wanted to bring children into. And honestly, she was a mess. She couldn't even afford to keep her mother in the place that seemed to provide her the best care possible. Children were out of the question. She wondered if that would disappoint her mother—or if her view of the future had changed as well.

She watched them play for a bit, smiling despite her own feelings of loss around the life that had taken such an unexpected turn. She made a note to take her mother out there next time she visited, when she didn't have an afternoon of clients booked at the spa. Her mother loved being in nature—and sure, it wasn't the intricate and lush garden oasis her mother had cultivated over the years at their Brookline home, but it was something other than these four walls.

"How's Super Mae today?" her cheery health aide Dennis asked as he bounded into the room. Dennis was probably in his mid to late fifties, but you'd never know it by the way he bounced around like a teenager. And he had seemingly endless amounts of enthusiasm and positivity, which Katie appreciated when she saw how much her mother brightened at his arrival. "There's my favorite smile."

"Hi, Dennis," Katie greeted him.

"How's it going?" Dennis adjusted his navy-blue scrubs before kneeling in front of them to tighten his shoelaces. "Staying for lunch today?"

Katie frowned. "I can't. I have to head to the spa for work. I just wanted to stop in and see Mom for a bit."

Dennis gave her a knowing smile. "You miss her, huh?"

"I do." The house felt so empty without her in it. And though Katie was glad to see her mother was acclimating nicely to New Beginnings, she still missed having her around. It had just been the two of them these last few years. It was like it had been when Katie was little. She missed that. "But she's in good hands, so I'm happy if she's happy."

Dennis seemed touched. "Thanks. We love Mae. She's family now."

Katie glanced at her watch—she'd have to leave soon.

"Tell you what," Dennis said as he stood. "Why don't you two catch up a bit without me causing any distractions, and I'll pop in after you leave and take her down to the common area for some pre-lunch socializing."

"That's okay, Dennis," Katie replied. "I really should get going." She placed a kiss on her mother's cheek and squeezed her hand before standing to go. "I'll be back again soon, Mom. Next time I'll bring you some cake."

"Cake?" Dennis cheered. "That sounds awesome. Is it your birthday this week, Mae?"

Katie gave him a sad smile. "No, it's mine."

"Oh. Well, we'll make sure she's all fancy for you. What day is it?"

"Today."

A look of acknowledgment and pity crossed his face. "Well, in that case, happy birthday, Katie."

"Thanks." But as she watched Dennis wheel her mother toward the community room, she felt anything but happy.

CHAPTER SEVEN

Katie was late, again. Ever since Bertha's final backfire last week, she had been carless. And trying to get over to see her mother this morning *and* get to work on time using mostly public transportation proved to be an impossible feat. The only reason she was even going to sneak into the office before her first client today was because she'd called an Uber she really couldn't afford out of frustration over bus delays.

She was jogging through the parking lot toward the spa when something a row over caught her eye. Ellison was at her car, embracing a woman. Katie wasn't close enough to hear what they were saying, but she could hear the carefree laughter. She was, however, close enough to see the kiss that followed. And it wasn't a brief one, either. The shorter woman stood on tiptoe to kiss Ellison, and Katie watched as Ellison's arms looped around her waist in a comfortable embrace.

"Are you coming or going?" someone yelled, and Katie jumped at the sound of a horn next to her.

She hadn't realized she'd stopped walking in the middle of the parking lot, but the line of cars behind the rude guy slamming on the horn indicated she had.

"Sorry," she said as she ducked her head and slipped between the parked cars toward the spa entrance.

"What are you sorry for?" Ellison asked, appearing by her side.

She looked back toward Ellison's parked car, but the other woman was gone. "I, uh…" For staring, she thought. "I wasn't paying attention and was holding up traffic, I guess."

"Or that guy was a jerk," Ellison supplied.

Katie winced. "You saw that?"

"It was hard to miss with all the honking."

"Sorry if I, uh, interrupted you," Katie said, feeling bad.

Ellison raised an eyebrow in her direction. "Interrupted me from what?"

"Kiss—" She paused, deciding to rephrase that. "Doing whatever you were doing."

Ellison laughed. "I was saying good-bye to a friend."

"Do you kiss all your friends like that?" Katie hadn't meant to blurt that out, even if she was thinking it. She also hadn't meant to stare—it's just that the two of them were so freaking gorgeous, it was unreal.

"No," Ellison said coyly. "Not usually."

"So she's a special friend then?" Katie asked.

"It's complicated," Ellison replied, though she didn't seem bothered by the question. "We used to be more than friends. Now we're just friends—"

"With benefits," Katie said.

"Occasional benefits," Ellison corrected. "She was in town visiting family and is heading back home now."

"Sounds nice," Katie said, feeling envious. She couldn't remember the last time she'd gotten laid. Or been kissed like that.

"It was."

"Katie." The sound of Pietro's voice made her cringe.

"Shit," she mumbled before plastering on her best smile and turning toward him. "Good morning."

"Cutting it close again, I see." The judgment in his tone was thunderous.

"But not late," she replied, pointing to her watch. She still had five minutes until her first appointment.

"It's my fault," Ellison chimed in. "I slowed her down."

"Oh. Is that so?" Pietro seemed to soften at this. "Well, Katie is our best staff massage therapist. I hope she was encouraging you to set up that free appointment we had been discussing."

"I, uh, totally was," Katie lied.

"Great. Then it's settled. She'll fit you in immediately. Won't you, Katie?" She could tell this wasn't a request so much as a command.

"You bet." She gave him an unenthusiastic thumbs-up and managed to hold in the laughter until after he'd said his good-byes.

"He's charming," Ellison said sarcastically.

"He's not so bad. Except when he is," Katie replied. "Thank you for intervening at the beginning. I think he's afraid of you."

"I think you're right. And I do feel partially responsible for you almost getting run over in the parking lot."

"I mean, I shouldn't have been staring." Katie hadn't meant to admit that she was.

"Were you?" Ellison's lips turned up at the corner into a small smile.

"Maybe? It's all a blur. Today's been kind of a circus already."

Ellison looked beyond her, back at the parking lot. "Where's Bertha?"

Katie frowned. "In her final resting place. That's why I'm latish. I've been patching some things together while I figure out my next step."

"I'm so sorry." Ellison placed a hand on her arm. "I know she was special to you."

"Thanks," Katie replied, touched by how sincere Ellison was. She barely knew this woman, yet she felt a connection and warmth from her like they'd known each other forever. "I should probably get inside before I *am* late."

"Of course." Ellison withdrew her touch, and Katie missed it immediately. She missed physical affection. Things had been so complicated with her mother lately that she'd let her personal life fall by the wayside. She didn't realize how much she missed touch until Ellison gave it so freely. "I'll call to set up an appointment, so you don't get in trouble. If that's all right with you?"

"It's more than fine with me. Honestly, it'll be a relief working with someone I like for a change," Katie replied. She'd had a run of frustratingly entitled clients lately who never seemed to be satisfied no matter how much or how little pressure Katie applied during her massages. She was either losing her touch, or her patience was too thin for the usual mindless chatter and complaints her clients filled the air with. What she liked about massage was the healing impact it could have and the therapeutic aspect of it. But lately she'd found herself annoyed with her clientele, which was probably on her. But she'd worry about that another day.

Ellison's smile broadened. "So, you like me then, huh?"

Katie laughed. She hadn't meant it like *that*. But she did enjoy the few exchanges they'd had up to this point. "I do."

"Well, I like you, too," Ellison said. "I'll pop by later. Will you be working all day?"

"Right up till close," Katie said with a heavy sigh. She hated having to work on her birthday. But at least she had dinner plans with Shaina later. That helped.

"All right, I'll see you before then," Ellison said with a wave. "Have a good day."

"Thanks." Katie watched her walk away a bit before turning and jogging toward the spa. Her grace period had ended. She was officially late.

❖

"You ready, Katie Cat?" Shaina placed her hands on Katie's shoulders as she finished entering her hours for the day.

"I'll give you a hundred dollars to keep doing that," Katie said as she closed her eyes. Her body was sore from the day, and she could really use a massage herself.

Shaina humored her for a few more moments before patting the top of her head. "This manicure is brand new. I'm not busting a nail on you when you get discounted massages anytime you want here."

Katie laughed. "First of all, you don't massage people with your nails—that sounds painful."

"There are plenty of kinky dudes on your schedule who would probably love that," Shaina said.

Katie scrunched up her nose at that. "Ew. You're probably right."

"I definitely am." Shaina examined her manicure before asking, "Was there a second part after the first?"

"And secondly, no one here is—" She wasn't sure how to say the next part delicately.

"Any good? You don't need to play coy, girl. We all know you're the busiest because you're the best. But still, get two subpar massages, then. That should equal a good one, right?"

"You'd be surprised." She liked her colleagues, but she *was* the best massage therapist on staff.

The front door opened, and she looked up. "Ellison, hey."

"I hope you weren't sticking around waiting on me," she said as she walked up to the desk.

"I totally was," she said with a wink.

"Liar."

Katie laughed. "Are we finally booking you a spa treatment?"

"I think so," Ellison said with a shrug. "It's my birthday week and all."

Katie's eyes fell to the sunglasses that were resting in the low-cut V of Ellison's blouse. They looked as expensive as the rest of her and were no doubt a designer Katie had probably never heard of and could never even dream of affording. Katie surveyed the rest of her outfit—she hadn't noticed the faint pinstripes on the tailored suit she'd been wearing before, but that was probably because she'd nearly gotten mowed down when she first saw Ellison. And because she was locking lips with that gorgeous Black woman who was equally well-dressed.

"It's your birthday this week, too?" Shaina's voice chimed in behind her. Katie had sort of forgotten she was there.

"It is," Ellison replied. "I figured I should treat myself. Know any good massage therapists?"

"Katie's the best in the biz," Shaina replied. "Too bad for her because she really could use a massage herself."

"Ow," Katie complained as Shaina poked the giant knot in her upper trap.

"You should have taken Ellison's lead and booked yourself a massage today, Birthday Girl. Now you'll just have to settle for wings and fries with me," Shaina teased.

"Today's your birthday?" Ellison asked, looking surprised.

"All day," Katie said. "Well, since six nineteen a.m."

"Oh, wow. You really know your birth time, too?" Ellison asked.

"My mother never let me forget it. She was a nurse at the time, and I popped out before her shift ended at seven. She regularly reminded me that I cost her an hour of pay," Katie said, remembering the playful ribbing from her mother. "I argued that no one that pregnant should still be working, but she assured me that the hospital was the safest place for her to be. Turns out she was right. I guess I came out pretty quick."

"You were in a rush to see the world," Ellison said with an easy smile. "I get it."

"Yeah, maybe I was." Katie hadn't thought of it that way.

"Well, happy birthday," Ellison added.

"Thank you." Katie watched her for a moment before remembering that Ellison was there for a reason. "Sorry. I just totally monologued at you for no reason. You were here to book a massage, right?"

"Right," Ellison replied, though she didn't look put out at all. "Do you have anything Thursday?"

Katie scanned her schedule. She had two openings at the end of the day. "I have a four and a five that day."

"I'll take the five o'clock," Ellison said as she pulled out her phone.

"Would you like sixty or ninety minutes?" Katie typed Ellison's name into the system and waited for her reply.

"Sixty, please."

"Great, you're all set."

Katie held up a reminder card, but Ellison waved her off. She motioned to her phone as she said, "I lose papers. The only reliable way to reach me or keep me on schedule is with this."

"Fair enough." Katie nodded. Most of her clientele navigated their appointments the same way.

"Well, enjoy your dinner," Ellison said with a wave. "I'll see you Thursday."

"Wait," Katie called out. "What day *is* your birthday this week?"

"Thursday," Ellison replied with a smile.

"I'll see you on your birthday, then," Katie said as she stood, pulling on her jacket.

"Sounds great." Ellison opened the door to leave before pausing to add, "Do me a favor, though?"

"Sure, anything," Katie replied.

"Don't put me on the reminder call list."

Katie palmed her face. "I'm so sorry about that."

"Bye, ladies." And with that, Ellison was gone.

❖

"So, are we going to talk about earlier? Or what?" Shaina asked between bites of her honey hot wing plate.

"What about earlier? God, this is hot," Katie said, fanning her mouth in between sips of water. They'd ordered a small of just about every wing plate on the menu, and the Jamaican jerk ones were way hotter than advertised. "I can't even feel my tongue."

"Use some blue cheese," Shaina said as she pushed a dish toward her. "Or grow some ovaries, because it's not that hot."

Katie dabbed her napkin under her eyes. "I can't argue with you— I'm dying."

Shaina sighed and handed her the remainder of her frozen margarita. "Try this."

Katie guzzled it so fast she nearly choked.

"Better?"

"Much," she said as the feeling slowly returned to her tongue.

Shaina motioned to the server for two more drinks. "I know that was just a sneaky way of you finishing off the rest of my drink."

"I assure you it was a matter of life or death," Katie replied. "You saved my life. You're a lifesaver."

Shaina laughed. "Well consider that your birthday gift, then."

"Isn't dinner my birthday gift?"

"Good point," Shaina said as she took another bite of her wings. "I'm far too generous with you."

"Can't argue with that," Katie replied. She was so grateful for Shaina for so many reasons. But spending tonight with her when she would have otherwise been alone meant a lot to her.

"So—now that you're not on death's door—can we talk about how you and Ellison were flirting up a storm today? Because I didn't realize you were into women. Or that she was. Or that you both were into each other."

"What?" The celery stick Katie was about to eat hovered in midair by her mouth, and a glob of blue cheese hit the table with a thud. "Shit."

Shaina handed her a clean napkin. "Yeah. You two were totally in the zone or something."

"I don't know what you're talking about." She cleared up the blue cheese mess and finished her celery to further cool the fire in her mouth. "We're just friends. I think."

"What do you mean you *think*?" Shaina said, looking dubious.

"I mean, I don't know her very well, but she's nice. And, I don't know, really thoughtful and sweet."

"And how would you know that?" Shaina had abandoned eating for this interrogation.

Katie shrugged. "It's just a vibe I get from her. Like, she went way out of her way to drive me home last week after our last dinner. Which means you are super generous because you've now taken me out two weeks in a row—anyway, that's not the point. She drove me home, and she totally didn't have to—"

"She drove you home last week? Whoa. You need to back up a bit." Shaina held up her hands in protest. "What happened?"

"I thought I told you about it," Katie replied.

"Um, no."

"Oh. Well, after dinner last week, I walked back to the bar where I'd parked Bertha, and she wouldn't start. So I went into the bar, and Ellison was there. And she drove me home." Katie could have sworn she'd mentioned that to Shaina.

"At no point when you told me about Bertha did you mention that Ellison Gamble drove you home."

"Really?" That didn't seem possible.

"Really. Now, spill."

"There's not much to tell. She was there when Rick took Bertha—"

"Who's Rick?"

"The tow-truck guy," Katie replied. "Ellison went with me into the parking lot to protect me in case Rick was some cretin. But he wasn't. He was super nice. And I meant to ask him for a ride to the bus, but then I forgot. So Ellison drove me home."

"You were going to take a bus home?" Shaina looked confused. "Why didn't you just call me? I would have circled back for you."

"I know, but my phone died. And you were meeting Raul. And I didn't want to bother you." Shaina and her boyfriend had been on the rocks lately, and the last thing Katie wanted to do was be a burden. Well, be more of a burden than she already was since her life was mostly in shambles.

"So that's it? She just saw you in need and drove you home?"

"I mean, yeah." Katie thought for a moment. "That's not entirely true. She also broke me into my house because I forgot to take my key off the ring before I gave it to Rick."

"She broke into your house?" The look on Shaina's face was almost comical.

"Well, that was after she helped me up the front walk with a flashlight because of course I forgot to put the light on before I went to work, and you know how dangerous that top step is."

Shaina just blinked at her.

"What?" Katie thanked the waiter for dropping off her new frozen margarita and sipped it. "These are so good."

Shaina shook her head. "You're telling me that that beautifully dressed, Maserati driving boss bitch that Pietro is terrified of drove you home in her fancy car, chivalrously walked you to your front door with a *flashlight*, and then helped you unlock your front door? This is the same woman who came in because you totally—one hundred percent—put her on every reminder call list, and Pietro nearly fired your ass over it. That woman?"

"She didn't help me unlock the front door," Katie corrected. "She broke in with my debit card. It was kind of amazing, actually."

"Well, damn." Shaina leaned back, cradling her margarita. "I don't even know you."

"Why?" Katie laughed.

"You had a total meet-cute with this woman and never even breathed a word about it. And after flirting with her at the desk tonight, now she's coming in on her birthday to get all naked and massaged by you." Shaina took a long sip of her drink. "I mean, good on you. She's gorgeous. And rich. And—wait, what was it like riding in a Maserati?"

Katie's head was spinning. "Meet-cute? What are you talking about?"

Shaina looked at her like she had three heads. "Listen. My roommate in college was gay. I'm hip to it. I totally get it, too. Men mostly suck. I guess you and I never talked about whether you were into women, too, because you and Asher were always off and on so much. I just never thought to ask."

"I'm not into women," she replied, distracted by the mention of Asher. They had dated off and on for a little over a year and a half, but when things got serious with her mother, Asher pretty much ghosted her.

Shaina gave her a look. "Okay. Fine. Is she?"

Katie considered the kiss she saw in the parking lot this morning and what little she knew of Ellison. "Yes. She was married to a woman at some point. And today I saw her giving an extremely hot and heavy good-bye kiss to a female friend."

"Kissing her *friend* on the mouth?" Shaina was leaning in now, like she couldn't get enough.

"Her use of the word *friend*, not mine. Because it was totally more than a friendly kiss in my opinion." Katie had never kissed a friend like that. Not ever.

"At what point did you two discuss her ex-wife? Like, how did that even come up?"

Katie sipped her drink, pleased that she'd gone with her favorite mango flavor again. "Sometime during the ride home from the bar. We were commiserating about how shitty a day we'd each had. I won, though—putting your mom in a home will do that."

Shaina frowned. "How are you doing with that?"

"Mostly okay." Katie dragged her finger along the top of her glass for something to do with her hands. "She seems happy, I think. She's adjusting well, anyway. And I can tell that the regular physical therapy and occupational therapy are working. She's moving her arms more and engaging a bit. She smiles more now."

"That's great, Katie Cat."

She nodded. "It is. I think it was the right choice. I just wish I could afford to keep her there for more than a few months. But unless some miracle lands in my lap, by the end of the summer I'll be flat broke no matter how many massages I give between now and then. I just hope she's made enough progress by then to move back home," Katie said the words but didn't believe them. The doctors had warned her that her mother would likely never return to her pre-stroke condition—not that she'd been independent then, either. But she was certainly more of her *mom* then. Not just a stranger that smiled at her from time to time.

"You'll figure something out. I know you will," Shaina said.

"Yeah, maybe." Katie toyed with the napkin under her drink, hopeful but not foolish. "Maybe you're right."

"I am," Shaina said with such confidence that Katie wanted to believe her. And for tonight, at least, she would.

CHAPTER EIGHT

Ellison pulled into her usual spot with a sigh. She powered down her car and rested her head on the seat back for a moment, contemplating the day. It was her birthday, and her day was filled with work engagements and meetings until tonight's massage with Katie. Which she was sure she'd need after her post-lunch appointment at the surrogacy center that was already making her shoulders tense with stress. She'd finally made the call with Faith's support over the weekend and spoken to a lovely woman who'd set up the appointment. At first, she'd been hesitant to agree to it, but Faith had made her promise to keep the appointment. And she wasn't one to break promises, even if this time she really wanted to.

She looked over at Tranquility Indulgence Spa and thought of Katie. She liked her. She was funny and captivating, and beautiful. And probably straight. But that didn't bother her in the least. She'd bedded plenty of nominally straight women in her life. Though she felt like her draw to Katie wasn't just physical. She was physically attracted to her, yes. But what's more, she was charmed by her, curious even. She felt like they had a magnetic chemistry, but she couldn't figure out why.

She stepped out of the car and considered this further. Maybe it was because *she* wanted a distraction, and a beautiful woman was perfect for that. And Katie was plenty beautiful. The fact of the matter was that though she enjoyed her time with Faith this weekend at the beach house, Faith wasn't a reliable source of physical affection. And Ellison knew that in times of great stress, she craved touch more and more. This weekend with Faith had been a great recharge, but it also amplified Ellison's need for self-care. She'd been working out with an increased ferocity of late, which she knew was an attempt to quell some of life's little anxieties, but she'd been neglecting her wellness routine. And seeing Katie the other day had reminded her of that. Getting a massage as a birthday gift to herself was a step in the right direction. The rub here, of course, was her underlying attraction to Katie. When she caught Katie watching her and Faith kiss good-bye, she'd been a little turned-on. And she couldn't blame it on a dry spell, because her weekend with Faith had been anything but that. She knew it was because she was interested in getting to know Katie more. And being naked on a table under Katie's hands was about as intimate as she could get with her. Suddenly, Ellison started to reconsider her impulsive choice to make the appointment.

"Happy Birthday!" Jax cheered as she walked into her realty office.

Two party horns sounded, and a fistful of glitter confetti clouded her vision as Trina and Lauren started singing—off-key—their group rendition of "Happy Birthday."

Ellison laughed as she brushed glitter from her shoulders, sure she'd find that everywhere later. "Thank you."

"Woo-hoo, *paaartay*," Lauren said as she held up a tray of cupcakes.

"I can't believe you remembered," Ellison said as she embraced her crew.

"Oh, you know me and important dates," Trina said as she placed a kiss on her cheek. "You taught me that."

Ellison smiled at that. Certain dates were important. Anniversaries, weddings, birthdays—they all deserved a note somewhere, because to someone, those moments were special. That was one of the first things she'd told Trina when she came to work for her. The way to build a flourishing book of clients was to personalize things and celebrate them. Trina was uncanny at it. At the year anniversary of all her home sales, she sent the buyers an expensive bottle of wine or champagne to signify the occasion. She was selflessly generous. This was one of her finest traits—behind Trina's at times prickly persona was a woman with a heart three times the size of anyone else's. And without a shadow of a doubt, Ellison knew that this little impromptu birthday moment was all Trina.

"I'm going to put these in the conference room for now, but I am a firm believer that they'll get lonely out there and should be eaten immediately," Lauren deadpanned. "No cake, big or small, should be left unsupervised for long."

"Did you bring ice cream, Lau?" Jax asked, and Ellison wanted to know that answer very badly.

"Five flavors"—Lauren looked at her—"including Rocky Road for you. Some whipped cream, and a few pints of Maine blueberries from the farm share by the Boudreaux farm."

"My favorite." Ellison knew her smile doubled in wattage. The Boudreaux Family Dairy Farm was an institution from Ellison's past, and some of her fondest childhood memories were there. It was also where she had her first ever job, so it held a special place in her heart. The near sale of the century old farm last summer was the project that introduced Lauren to her girlfriend, Thea Boudreaux, and helped Ellison to rekindle her connection with Faith. Saving the Boudreaux farm legacy had taken most of their summer last year, but it had been worth it. Especially since now she regularly got her favorite flavors from her past since Lauren and Thea spent a weekend or two a month in Maine at the farmhouse.

"Kathleen sends her love and these cupcakes," Lauren said, mentioning the matriarch of the Boudreaux family. "The ice cream is in the staff freezer." She paused, lowering her voice to add, "I hid your pint in the back and labeled it *broccoli* to keep people's grubby hands off it."

"You're too good to me," Ellison said.

Lauren gave her a wink before disappearing into the conference room with the towering stack of multicolored cupcakes.

Jax followed her toward her office, updating her on the goings-on of the morning as they went.

"Mrs. Fratelle called to inquire about the status of her vacation home listing. Barney Closterman left you a voice mail and asked that a written message be handed to you regarding the Newbridge on the Gardens apartment that's available. The plumber came by to fix that slow leak in the employee bathroom sink. And I dropped the mail off on your desk," Jax said, nearly out of breath.

"It's barely nine in the morning, and all of that already happened?" Ellison sighed.

"Ruby also briefly disappeared but was recovered without bloodshed, although the thief was not identified," Jax replied, referencing Lauren's BeDazzled stapler.

Trina gave Ellison a Cheshire cat grin. "And the thief won't ever be identified because I'm not saying boo, even though I saw the culprit in action."

"You did?" Jax's eyes widened.

"Mm-hmm. But I won't tell a soul, because I plan to employ blackmail tactics instead," Trina said.

Ellison watched as Jax swallowed heavily.

It was no secret that Lauren had the best stapler in the whole office. Even though Ellison had gone over and above to procure six more of the exact same staplers, Ruby was still the most coveted. She would bet it was the bright red accents Lauren had added, but she had no scientific proof to support that theory.

Ellison stepped into her office and nearly dropped the mail Jax had handed her. "Wow."

"Just something small from all of us," Trina said.

On Ellison's desk sat the tallest, most ornate bouquet she had ever seen. The colors were vibrant, the roses sky-high, and the cascade of flowers and greens down to the desk offered a textured and multilayered extravagance.

"They're beautiful," Ellison said as she caressed the velvety petal of one of what she estimated to be two dozen roses before her.

"We're glad you like them," Jax said, blushing. They were adorable.

"I've got a showing in a bit—when are we doing the cupcake thing?" Trina asked as she headed toward Ellison's office door in the direction of her own.

"Will you be back by noon? I have a meeting at one," Ellison replied.

"Oh, hell yes. I'm not missing Kathleen's cupcakes," Trina said. "I'll grab coffee on the way back. Let Jax know what you want."

"I'll see you around cupcake time," Jax said as they turned to go.

"Do you have a second?" Ellison asked. "I was hoping to chat with you about Talia."

Jax turned so fast, they nearly fell over. They cleared their throat, feigning nonchalance. "What about her?"

Ellison dropped the stack of mail and her purse on the chair across from her desk as she leaned against it. "I spoke with Faith this weekend."

"And?" Jax's foot was tapping nervously on the floor.

"And I asked her about Talia and how things were going with work and school. And I asked if she was dating anyone."

"And?" The tapping stopped.

"She said business for Talia was booming—which we know, since she's dressing me *and* Trina these days among a dozen other clients, yourself included. You look great, by the way."

Jax stood a little taller, adjusting the vest they wore as they said, "This is one of her original pieces."

"She's got an incredible eye."

"She does." Jax shifted. "Did you talk about anything else?"

"Oh yes. What was it?" Ellison tapped her chin playfully. "She mentioned that Talia's night school MBA classes are taking up a lot of time but were really helping her hone her brand. And…"

"And?" Jax's voice squeaked, and Ellison laughed.

"And that she had an on again-off again thing with someone named Johnny, but it seems to have recently fizzled out. For good."

Jax's face lit up at this revelation. "Really?"

"Really," Ellison replied. "And I'm told that she's planning a full website overhaul for some products she plans to launch and that she was looking for someone really tech-savvy to help her out with that. So I recommended that she call you."

Jax's joy was palpable. "Trina's right. You are the best."

"It's not a guarantee, but it's a chance to get to know her better," Ellison reasoned. "Maybe if she spends more time with you, she'll see what a great person you are."

Jax blushed. "Thanks for talking to Faith."

"Anytime."

Ellison watched Jax head out into the common area before looking around her office. She kept it quiet, almost understated in here. Her desk was large, but only because she used every inch of it, not because she had something to prove. The chairs and sofa that flanked the room were upholstered in a light gray herringbone pattern that she loved and hadn't changed since she opened this office so many years ago.

Her walls held a few framed articles about the company's success, but her favorite picture was the one of her with Trina, Lauren, and Jax at the LGBTQ fundraiser from a few years ago. That had been one of the happiest, most carefree nights of her professional and adult life. She knew that night that she'd struck gold with this group of employees. Because she'd felt like they were a family that night, and that feeling had never left.

As she looked at the overflowing arrangement at her desk, she felt that same way again. She might not have anyone left in the way of biological family, but she had the *best* chosen family. And that was something to be proud of—more proud of than any news article, award, or accolade. Because money and success didn't afford you the kind of close-knit chosen family she had built around herself over the years. And that was something she needed to keep in mind during the surrogacy consultant appointment today. She had a great life and so many things to be grateful for. She could do hard things. She could do this.

❖

Ellison's jaw was tight, and her neck was tense. The meeting with the surrogacy consultant went fine, but the whole thing put her on edge even though it was supposed to make her feel more comfortable with the process.

She had a lot to unpack and review from that meeting, but at least she'd gone. And she'd even managed to get a little work done at the office afterward, which was kind of a miracle because her head was swimming with information. But as the sun started to set and her massage time approached, the tightness from earlier seemed to amplify. She wasn't sure if that was psychosomatic or not, but the light pounding between her temples was certainly stress related. A massage sounded like the exact thing she needed at the moment.

"Hello, Birthday Girl," Katie said from behind the receptionist's desk as she walked in. "I'm happy to see you."

"I'm happy to be seen."

"Funny," Katie said with an eye roll. "You ready?"

"I guess so," Ellison said. "Lead the way."

Katie met her next to the desk and led her through a glass door toward a noticeably quiet and minimally lit hallway.

"There are a few other sessions going on at the moment, so we have to be hush-hush," Katie said, leaning in close. "I booked you the largest room in the back—it's got the most privacy, and it's the most removed from ambient noise and chatter. In other words, it's the farthest from the bathroom or break room."

"You spoil me," Ellison said. Katie's closeness revealed a light, citrusy perfumed scent. It was refreshing and subtle.

"Only the best for the birthday girl." Katie opened the last door on the left and ushered Ellison inside.

The room was spacious, containing a massage table draped in white sheets, a comfy looking chair nearby, as well as a small sink with counter space along the far wall. When Katie closed the door behind them, Ellison noticed the soft, fluffy-looking white robe on the back of the door. The lighting was low and the undermounts of the cabinets and sink had a soft glow, illuminating the floor and indirectly lighting the room. There were a few plants along the adjacent wall, green things that looked lush and healthy, though Ellison couldn't name them if she tried.

"Have a seat, and let's chat a bit," Katie said as she pulled up a rolling stool Ellison hadn't noticed before.

She sat in the plush armchair facing Katie and willed herself to relax, but her spine felt rod straight even though she didn't feel particularly anxious.

"You can take off your jacket," Katie said, standing to take it. "You'll be in much less very soon."

Ellison raised an eyebrow at that. "Will I?"

Katie nodded, accepting the jacket Ellison shrugged off. "We'll talk about your comfort level, but honestly the best massages happen when the client is naked. You'll be draped—of course—but still naked. If you're comfortable with that."

"Okay," she replied, rolling her neck to try to ease some of the tension there.

"Is your neck sore?" Katie asked, taking notes on a clipboard she'd taken from the nearby massage table.

"Tight. Not sore."

"What else is making you uncomfortable right now?"

Trying not to stare at your chest in those scrubs. Katie looked great in her spa wardrobe. She was in a slim-fitting black scrub set that hugged the generous curves of her chest and hips in a way that made

Ellison want to reach out and touch her. Though she was a few inches shorter than Ellison, she was curvier and had a gorgeous shape. Ellison tried not to think about that—she wasn't here on a date, after all. She was here for a service. One being rendered by a newish friend. Albeit a very attractive one.

"Nothing?"

"Sorry," Ellison said, shaking her head to ward off the lusty thoughts. "I have a bit of a tension headache. My shoulders feel like they are inundated with boulders, and my neck feels like cement. But I had kind of a stressful day, so I'm sure that's why. Everything else on me works just fine and feels good, though."

"What happened with work today?" Katie asked, her brow furrowed.

"Not work so much as some personal stuff," Ellison replied honestly. "It was just…something new I have to get used to."

"Change is hard," Katie said.

"As is relinquishing control." That was what was making Ellison so uncomfortable about the surrogacy route—losing control. Or at least, trusting someone else with something so precious to her. She didn't trust many people—her experience with Peyton had taught her to be careful. She'd been so burned by that relationship and failed marriage. She could trust her colleagues and her friends, but not until she'd weathered storms with them to see if they would let her down or not. She had yet to find that in a serious partner since her divorce. She needed the sense of control to feel safe.

"I get that," Katie said, her tone soft. She reached forward and put her hand on Ellison's knee. "I'm going to ask you to do your best to let me be in charge while we're together. Let me take control so you can let those angry and sore muscles take a break. I'll be your strength and your protection in this room. It's just you and me and whatever gentle background noise you decide on. I'll take that burden while we're together. That's my job. Your job is to let go and relax."

"I'll certainly try," Ellison said as she appraised the dazzling green eyes looking at her so intently. She could see tiny emerald flecks around her irises. She noticed a dusting of faint freckles on the bridge of Katie's nose that she hadn't seen before. The dark auburn curls that framed Katie's face made her look almost angelic in this moment in the subtle lighting. Her closeness was calming and her smile captivating.

Ellison let herself appreciate her perfectly straight white teeth and full, pouty pink lips.

"That's all I ask." Katie removed her hand from her knee as she added, "Well, that, and that you get naked."

Ellison laughed. "You're very forward."

"You only booked a sixty-minute slot, and I can tell from here we have some serious shoulder work to do."

Ellison rolled her shoulders and a loud pop made Katie laugh.

"Exactly my point." She stood. "I'm going to step out to give you some privacy. Please disrobe and lie facedown on the table. Drape that sheet over your legs and back, and I'll be back in a few."

"Thank you," Ellison said out of reflex.

"Don't thank me until you're no longer clenching that jaw," Katie said. "I'll make you feel good. I promise."

Ellison was a little afraid of just how good Katie made her feel already, but she tried not to dwell on that.

"See you in a bit," Katie said as she slipped out of the room and closed the door.

Ellison stood, stretching in place. She slipped out of her clothes, carefully folding her pants and blouse before placing them on the chair. It wasn't until she was in her bra and panties that she noticed the mirror that ran lengthwise along one wall. It was the height of the massage table and no more than a foot in width. From her vantage point she could see the toned stomach that she worked so hard on. Ellison ate clean and exercised regularly. Some of it was to keep up with Faith, but the rest was a combination of good genes and a healthy appreciation for the peacefulness that exercise brought her. She was competitive but not in a consuming kind of way. But exercise—running, swimming, Pilates—made her feel centered. She liked challenging herself to see what she was still capable of. And though her forty-three years on this planet had taken their toll in some way or another, she was proud that she'd managed to maintain the fitness of her youth. Improved upon it, even.

She finished disrobing and climbed onto the table and under the sheet, lying facedown. The sheet was warm, almost as if it had been heated before it was placed on the table. And the room was warm, too. She didn't feel cold even though she was naked.

A gentle knock at the door alerted her to Katie's return.

"Come in."

Katie closed the door softly as she entered. "I brought you a water and some towels for afterward."

Ellison turned her head to face her, watching Katie as she opened the cabinets by the sink, pulling out lotions and potions of varying heights.

"I never asked, but I assume you've had a massage before."

"I have."

"How long has it been?" Katie uncapped two containers and pulled them toward the edge of the counter, closer to the table.

"Oh, at least a year. Probably two."

Katie looked scandalized. "That's too long. We're going to fix that."

"You're the boss in here. Or so I'm told," Ellison teased.

"That's right," Katie said, giving her a look. "Now the real question is, are you going to be okay with that?"

"Do I strike you as someone that can't *not* be in charge?"

"You strike me as someone that's in charge so often, that maybe you don't even realize you're in charge anymore. Because it's so much of who you are, it's in the fabric of your very being. You're a boss bitch—there's nothing wrong with that."

Ellison smiled at that. "I see we've moved on to the name-calling portion of the evening."

"Oh no, far from it. I prefer to think of it as my acknowledging the awesomeness that is you. But that it can be burdensome as well. I imagine it's a double-edged sword at times."

"You minored in Psych, huh?" Ellison asked.

"Double-majored, actually." Katie reached out and touched Ellison's forehead. "I need you to put your face in the hole now, because this head position is not going to help your neck one bit."

Ellison complied, though she missed Katie's face.

Katie asked a few questions about allergies and scent preferences before turning on a sound machine nearby.

"How do you feel about ocean waves and sounds of the sea?" she asked.

"They're my favorite."

"Mine, too." Katie stepped up next to her and placed her hands on the skin of Ellison's upper back for the first time. "That's one of the reasons I went to school in California—I wanted to be able to get to the water all the time. But California waters and beaches are different than New England ones. In some ways, they're better. But it wasn't quite like it was here at home."

"I like the coolness of the water here. How it almost shocks you into living. Don't get me wrong, I love tropical bathwater-warm ocean water, too. But there's something about the crispness of the water here that makes me feel alive," Ellison said.

"Do you go to the beach often?" Katie's hands were kneading and gliding along Ellison's shoulders. Her hands were slick with something, lotion or oil. Ellison didn't care which, because Katie's touch was glorious.

"I used to go a lot. When my mother was still alive, I spent nearly all my free time with her by the water. She loved it, too. Where I grew up, we had a lake and these beautiful natural springs, but the ocean was a bit of a drive. It always felt like a treat to get to the sand and surf. That didn't change as I got older."

"I'm sorry about your mother." Katie's voice was soft, and Ellison felt sorry for bringing it up. She hadn't meant to broach the mother topic.

"We had a lot of wonderful time together at the end. I'm grateful for that. After she died, I bought a house at the beach. I guess in some ways I did it to honor her, but I don't spend enough time there. She'd probably chastise me for that."

"Why don't you spend more time there?" Katie's grip was firm but soothing. She worked over Ellison's shoulders and upper traps, pressing and releasing as she went. "I'd probably never leave the water if I had the choice."

Ellison exhaled as something popped in her upper back. A feeling of relief and a wave of warmth flooded the area, and as if she could sense it, Katie's hands chased the warmth toward her shoulders, easing the tissue with each calculated stroke.

"Is this too much pressure?" Katie asked. She was speaking softly, and though Ellison couldn't see her, she could feel that her lips were close to her ear. That made her shiver. Katie's hands paused on her skin. "I can use less pressure."

"The pressure is good. I like it. Don't stop." Ellison hadn't meant to let that last part slip out. But her headache was long gone, and she was feeling all warm and gooey in the best kind of way.

"All right." Katie worked along her upper arms, pressing her thumbs and fingers into Ellison's muscles before retreating. "Tell me about the beach house. Why don't you go there?"

"I'm busy. I work a lot." *The house is too empty.*

Ellison sighed as Katie's hands settled on the nape of her neck. The warmth of her palms pulled the truth from Ellison's lips. "It's a big house. Maybe too big. And it feels lonely."

"I could see that," Katie said, her voice sympathetic. She pressed into the vertebrae of Ellison's spine, eliciting another gentle pop as she worked up to the base of Ellison's skull. "I tell you what. Whenever you want to go, let me know. I'll be your beach buddy for the day or the weekend. You name it. I'll pack a sleeping bag and stay in the car for the night. Just tell me when and where, and I'll be ready."

"If you keep doing whatever it is you're doing, I'll even let you stay in one of the five bedrooms and not in your car." Ellison was in heaven. Katie's touch was magical.

"Five bedrooms? Damn, no wonder it feels empty."

Ellison chuckled. "There's a separate guest house over the garage, too. But that's not quite finished yet. I lost inspiration."

"Don't worry, I'll let you know what furnishings I like and don't like," Katie joked. Ellison liked that she was playful and easygoing.

"The guest house is for people I don't want in my space all the time. If you're keeping me company, you're in the main house."

"Sounds like a real deal-breaker," Katie teased.

Katie removed the clip from Ellison's hair to massage her scalp, and Ellison sighed as Katie ran her fingers through her hair.

"That feels amazing."

"I'll pay for my beach stays in your fancy house with scalp massages," Katie offered.

"Done," Ellison said. "That was the easiest deal I've ever made."

Katie worked her fingers into Ellison's scalp for a few more moments before tracing her hands along Ellison's shoulders to her midback. Ellison felt the sheet slip lower as Katie's hands replaced the fabric, working along her ribs and spine in that same rhythmic and glorious pressure she'd used at her shoulders.

"How's that headache?" she asked.

"Gone." Ellison exhaled as Katie's thumbs worked at her low back.

"Good." Katie moved the sheet lower until it was just above Ellison's ass. It was only then that Ellison thought to consider her nudity.

Katie continued to work along her lumbar spine, stopping just short of her glutes, which both disappointed Ellison and relieved her. She lifted her head out of the cradle and turned toward the mirror along the wall next to her. As her vision came into focus, she could see the concentration on Katie's face as she worked the tissue of her back. Katie glided her hands from Ellison's waist up to her shoulders, and Ellison felt Katie's chest press against her back before she saw it. The contact was brief but lasting.

"You're supposed to have your head in the cradle," Katie said softly.

Ellison made eye contact with her in the mirror's reflection. "I was curious."

"About what?" Katie's hands were resting on her naked upper back.

"What you were thinking. You got quiet."

Katie studied her face. "I was letting you relax. I forget sometimes that some people like silence during their sessions. I want to talk to you because I like talking to you. But I realized this isn't about me, it's about you. So I was checking myself a bit. Reining it in, you know?"

"I don't mind the talking." Ellison held her gaze. "I like it."

"Okay," Katie said as she rested her hand along Ellison's cheek. "In that case, head in the cradle please."

Ellison complied, and Katie moved from her upper back down to her legs, uncovering one at a time as she worked Ellison's hamstrings and calves with care and clinical expertise.

Ellison moaned when Katie took her foot into her hand, pressing her thumb into the sole of her foot.

"Your feet are tight," Katie commented. "Do you wear heels often?"

"I do," Ellison said. Even though she had no intention to, she still asked, "Should I stop?"

"You look great in heels," Katie said. "If you're comfortable in them, then that's fine. But you should work out some of the tension in these feet. Even just rolling a tennis or golf ball under your foot at your desk when you have your shoes off will help."

"You're assuming I take my heels off at work," Ellison replied.

"You don't?" Katie sounded surprised.

"Not often. I dated a dancer once that never took her heels off—except for sex, showering, and during some forms of exercise."

"Damn. That's impressive." Katie moved to her other foot, gently tugging on her toes before stretching her calf in her hand.

"She's very impressive in general—so it fit her."

"But it didn't work out with her?" Katie asked as she repositioned the sheet over Ellison's legs.

"I wasn't in the right space for a long-term relationship. We had fun, but it wasn't anything too serious. I see her from time to time now—she married a lovely matchmaker. They're perfect together. I'm happy for her." She was never jealous or upset when those in her inner circle found love or long-term companionship. Love was a beautiful thing, and she celebrated it in all forms. She just hadn't found her own yet. And as the years crept on, she wasn't sure that she would. But she had come to terms with that. Faith was the only person she had come close to feeling complete with. And though she once told herself she had found true love with Peyton, she knew now that that had been a lie.

"You're so positive about your exes. Good on you," Katie said.

"Queer circles are small. Getting along is better for the community as a whole," Ellison said with a laugh. "But I don't get along with all my exes, or everyone else, for that matter. It depends on the person and the situation."

"Yeah, people can suck," Katie said. She placed a hand on Ellison's shoulder. "It's time to turn over now. I'll give you some privacy."

Ellison rolled under the sheet, getting comfortable on her back. Katie was facing the sink, her back to her. When Ellison reached out and touched the outside of her hand, Katie jumped. "Sorry, I'm ready."

Katie turned and gave her a small smile. "You surprised me."

"By my stealthy rolling ability, or my touch?" Ellison hoped the touch wasn't unpleasant.

Katie laughed. "The touch. It was very gentle. Your hand is warm. Maybe you should consider a change in careers."

"I'd be terrible at this."

"Why's that?" Katie reached into the open jar next to her, her fingers emerging with a dollop of lotion.

"I'm not great at small talk. I mean, I'm a Realtor, so I am. But I'm not. Not really, anyway."

Katie took Ellison's left hand in hers and worked the lotion into her skin, pressing into her palm and soothing along her fingers as she went. "You're doing just fine right now."

"Somehow this doesn't feel like small talk," Ellison admitted.

"What does it feel like?"

Ellison could feel Katie's eyes on her. She met her gaze. "Getting to know you. Or getting reacquainted with you. I get this feeling like you're an old friend, even though you aren't."

"Is it because I'm holding your hand?" Katie asked with a sly smile.

"No, but I certainly don't hate that."

Katie manipulated her hand a bit more before adding, "Somehow, even your hands are tense." Katie moved up to her forearm and elbow. "But your neck wins for stress hoarding. That was remarkable."

Ellison let her head roll to the side, tracing Katie's face with her eyes. "I told you, I had a crappy meeting before this. I think I had my shoulders at my ears the whole time. I wouldn't be shocked if my hands were in fists, too."

"This was the not-so-much-work but more personal thing?"

"Yes," Ellison said, impressed Katie remembered her passing comment.

"Ah, meetings of the personal kind are the worst," Katie said with a nod. "Did you at least get a resolution at the end?"

"Maybe. Yes. No. Probably. The verdict is still out," Ellison said.

Katie made eye contact again. "Your eyes are supposed to be closed."

"You're much more interesting than my eyelids," Ellison replied.

"Why didn't you get a resolution to the personal thing?" Katie asked as she moved to Ellison's right hand and began toying with her fingers. "Is it a multistep thing? Because I was wrong before—complex personal issues that require multiple steps to reach a resolution are the worst."

"I went to a surrogacy appointment, to find out my options."

Ellison hadn't said anything to anyone yet. But saying it out loud to Katie didn't frighten her.

Katie soothed along her hand, cradling it between both her palms as she looked up at her. "How did it go?"

"Fine. It's a lot of money and multiple steps. And legal this and that. The process is not quick—by any measure—and it involves a lot of trust in someone I've never met." Ellison tried to articulate her anxieties around the meeting and the process. But she wasn't sure she was doing a great job.

"Relinquishing control is hard," Katie repeated from before as she stroked her thumb along Ellison's hand. "And new things can be scary."

"It is. They can. And you're right." Ellison appreciated the simplicity of Katie's statement. She didn't have to have all the words for the feelings she had about surrogacy and her own inability to carry—Katie's words were perfect.

Katie resumed her massaging and moved up to Ellison's elbow.

Ellison watched her intently as she asked, "How's your mom?"

Katie glanced up at her. "She's good. She's doing well there. I'm seeing a positive change in a lot of little ways. I think it was the right decision." She rested her hand on Ellison's bicep. "Thank you for asking."

"And you? How are you?" Ellison asked because she wished someone asked her that sometimes. She wasn't even sure how she would respond if someone did.

"I'm...okay. I think in a lot of ways I'm relieved that she's in the right hands, but also sad that I couldn't be that person for her." Katie moved Ellison's arm out to the side, stretching it before placing it back on the table. "But I think I'm lonely, too. Caring for her the last three years was a full-time job, and now that that's not the case, I'm lost. Maybe that's foolish. I don't know."

"That makes sense to me. I get it," Ellison replied. She'd felt that way after her mother had died. They'd spent almost every moment together in the end, and then there was nothing. Just emptiness and sorrow. So she filled it with work and relationships that didn't require anything too serious from her. She'd had her failed marriage, and she'd lost her mother. What else did she have but work to keep her busy?

"I'm going to work on your upper chest a bit before we go back to some neck and jaw work. Okay?" Katie asked as she moved away from Ellison's shoulder.

"Yes." Ellison closed her eyes, trying to hold on to the relaxed feeling she'd felt moments ago.

Katie placed her palm just under Ellison's right clavicle, gently kneading the tissue and stretching her arm out to the side. She repeated the motion on the other side, and Ellison wondered if Katie could feel her heartbeat race under her touch. She was still draped by the sheet, but the proximity of Katie's hand to her chest was all she could think about. Probably because her nipples were straining against the fabric of the sheet. Which she knew had everything to do with how good Katie's hands felt on her body.

"Let's work on that jaw you're clenching, and then we'll finish off with your legs before our session ends." Katie's hands left her body, and the sound of the rolling stool nearby drew Ellison's attention.

"I'm clenching my jaw?" She'd had no idea—although now that Katie pointed it out, the right side of her jaw ached slightly.

"You are." Katie's voice sounded just over her head. "I'm going to see what I can do about that."

Ellison exhaled as Katie cradled her head, moving down to press gently along her jaw. She calmed the angry muscles, rubbing them in a controlled, precise fashion that soon had Ellison's lips parted in nirvana. As she moved up to her temples, dipping into her hairline here and there, Ellison breathed out, "This feels unreal."

"Faces are important. The skin on your face is usually the first thing someone sees. But the muscles under your skin produce all the reactions you share with others—smiles, frowns, laughs—and they all require muscle work. Your face and skin should get just as much attention as the rest of your body," she said as she stroked her fingers along Ellison's cheek. "But I can tell you take great care of your skin. It's beautiful. I'd normally recommend a facial treatment with Shaina, but you don't need one. Your skin has a gorgeous natural glow to it."

"Well, now you're going to make me blush," Ellison said playfully.

"That would only enhance the radiance," Katie said, her voice soft.

Katie moved to her neck again, working along the bottom of her hairline before combing her fingers through her hair and massaging her scalp. Ellison had enjoyed all of the massage up to this point, but the scalp massage was probably her favorite. She could feel the tension lifting up and off her head with each stroke and glide.

"How long have you been doing this?" she asked as Katie stood and moved toward her left hip.

"Almost seven years now. I started doing it my senior year of college to offset some costs when waitressing wasn't cutting it anymore. I took night and weekend classes and built up a decent client base—so much so that it eventually became my full-time. I kept up with it when I moved back here three years ago. I like being around people, and I like making people feel better."

"Well, you're amazing at it," Ellison said, biting her bottom lip as Katie moved from her left calf up to her thigh. To get to the area, Katie had exposed the entirety of her left leg, and Ellison was more than casually aware of the thin sheet that barely covered her sex.

"Relax," Katie said, her voice whisper-soft again. "Let me do the work."

Ellison willed herself to let go, but Katie's magic hands were kneading and massaging her upper thigh, and that felt like an impossible request.

Katie pressed into the tense muscle at the uppermost part of her thigh, and Ellison groaned. "Your hip flexor is tight. I'd bet the other side is the same. You'll need to stretch this, or it'll lead to other issues down the road."

"I will, I promise," Ellison said, sure that she'd say just about anything under Katie's touch.

"Good."

Katie adjusted the sheet over her leg and moved to the right, repeating the delicious torture on that side, but Ellison was more prepared for it now. She managed to keep from squirming too much, even if her body fought her about it.

Katie returned to her upper shoulders and neck, running over the now relaxed tissue with choreographed ease, and by the time she placed her hand on Ellison's shoulder to let her know the session was complete, Ellison was a puddle on the table. Relaxed and mildly aroused but mostly in blissful calm.

"Well, you survived," Katie said as she laid a warm blanket over Ellison.

"I mean, I've mostly died and gone to heaven. So does that really mean I've survived?" Ellison asked.

"That means the massage worked because now you're on another plane of relaxation entirely."

"Wow." Ellison let out a sated sigh. "That was amazing."

"I'm glad you enjoyed it," Katie said as she swept her long, curly auburn hair behind her shoulder. "You're my last client for tonight, so take as long as you need to get up and get changed. Sit up slowly, and drink some of that bottle of water I left for you by your clothes. You'll need to hydrate a little more than usual tonight to help flush out the toxins and inflammation I mobilized with the massage." Katie paused with her hand on the door handle as she added, "I'll be at the front desk to check you out. It's just down the hall, straight through the frosted glass door."

"Thank you."

"Anytime." Katie slipped out the door, leaving Ellison in the quiet, soothing sounds of waves crashing.

She closed her eyes, enjoying the extra weight and warmth of the blanket Katie covered her with. She could hear her heartbeat in her ears and feel the gentle rise and fall of her chest with her breaths—she felt very, very present in the moment. And calm. Katie had certainly delivered in that department—this was the most serene and at peace she'd felt in a very long time. She thought of the green eyes that regarded her with so much kindness when she talked about the surrogacy appointment. And the soft, strong hands that knew all the right places to press upon and soothe. She was very attracted to Katie, and though her body had obvious reactions to her touch, she'd still managed to remain mostly relaxed throughout the experience. An experience that she already wanted to have again.

She sat up slowly, stretching her neck and shoulders as she stood from the table, letting the sheet and blanket fall by the wayside. She took a long slow sip of her water bottle, savoring the coolness of the water as she finished more than half in that first sip. She used the nearby towel Katie had left folded neatly to wipe the excess cream and lotion from her skin before dressing with care. She could have sworn she was standing taller now. Her heels felt inches higher, though not uncomfortable. And she felt lighter. Like the weight of the stress and discomfort of her body that had been there when she'd walked in was long gone.

She redid her hair and checked herself in the mirror, glad to see that her eye makeup had stood up just fine. She reapplied her favorite light pink lip gloss and pulled on her blazer, glad that she'd made this appointment for herself.

She was surprised when she found Shaina at the front desk and not Katie.

"Hi," she said before looking around. "I think Katie said something about checking out?"

"How was it?" Shaina asked.

"Great," Ellison replied honestly.

"Katie is sort of unbelievable, right? She's the best."

"She certainly is," Ellison replied. "Has she gone already?"

"No, she's on the phone with her mother's place. She shouldn't be too long if you want to wait for her."

Ellison couldn't think of a reason to justify sticking around other than she wanted to see her again, so she politely declined. "I can check out with you, that's fine."

"Okay, would you like to set up another appointment?"

Ellison considered this. She did. But she wanted to check her schedule first. And her libido. Because if she was developing a crush on Katie, then being naked while being massaged by her was sort of a not great idea. "I'll call and check Katie's availability once I check my work schedule."

"Got it," Shaina said as her fingers moved quickly over the keys. "Well, since Pietro put a credit on your account, today's session was free. So you're all set."

Ellison reached into her purse and pulled out her wallet. "I assume you ladies have a place to leave tips?"

"Yes," Shaina said as she pulled out a small envelope from the top drawer of the desk. She jotted Katie's name on the back of it. "You can put it in here, and I'll drop it in her staff mailbox."

"Thank you." Ellison put Katie's tip in the envelope and sealed it before handing it back.

"Thank you for driving her home the other night," Shaina said. "I never would have left her in that parking lot if I realized her car or her phone was dead. I really appreciate you making sure she got home safe."

"Anytime." Ellison gave her a wave. "Tell Katie I said good night, and thanks again."

"Will do."

Ellison stepped out into the cooler night air and breathed in deeply. She had one quick thing to finish at the office, and then she was free for the night. And though she was spending her birthday alone, she was feeling too good after that massage to be sad about it.

CHAPTER NINE

E verything okay?" Shaina asked when Katie reentered the room.
"Yeah. I guess Mom had a mild choking event during dinner tonight, but it was over quickly, and she was fine. Part of their protocol is to immediately report any incidents to the family. So I'm relieved. But I was totally a wreck for a minute there." Katie's heart rate still hadn't slowed down yet from seeing New Beginning's name flashing across her cell screen.

"Well, that's good that she's okay," Shaina said as she stood and stretched. "The log is closed. You and I are done. Let's blow this Popsicle stand."

"Did Ellison come out yet?"

"You just missed her." Shaina pulled on her jacket.

"Oh." Katie wasn't sure why she was so disappointed by that information, but she was.

"She left you this," Shaina said as she handed her an envelope.

"Thanks," Katie replied, slipping it into her bag.

"Oh, really? You're not going to open it?" Shaina looked surprised.

"Should I?"

"Katie Cat. You literally always open it as soon as the client leaves. And that envelope is *fat*. I'm just surprised is all."

Katie considered this. Why had she just tucked it into her bag? Because it was from Ellison. And for some reason, that felt like the right thing to do. Like she was respecting her privacy or something.

"What's going on with you two?" Shaina asked with a raised eyebrow. "I mean, first it's the exchange with Pietro, then the ride home. And now she leaves you an envelope full of cash, and you don't gossip about it with your work bestie? Secrets, secrets, secrets," she said, shaking her head.

"Nothing is going on. And I'm not keeping secrets." Katie pulled the envelope out and handed it to Shaina. "Here. You open it. That's how *not* secretive I am."

Shaina pretended to open it before handing it back. "I was just teasing you. But let it be noted that you immediately denied any goings-on with the gorgeous blond dynamo who happens to be gay and probably left you enough money in that envelope to buy you a new car. Or at least the first month's car payment."

Katie put the envelope in her purse and laughed. "It's probably a fistful of ones and a business card," she said, but she didn't believe that. Part of her wanted to be alone because she figured if Ellison left her something, it was for her eyes only. That was just a vibe she got from her—yes, she drove a flashy car, but Katie could tell that Ellison was a discreet person.

"Tell me I'm wrong later when you crack the seal," Shaina said with a smile. She ushered Katie out as she closed the door behind them. "I'm meeting up with Raul and his friends for drinks. You want in?"

Katie shook her head. "It's been a long day. I think I'm just going to go home and stay out of trouble."

"Smart lady," Shaina said as she gave her a hug. "I'll text you if any cute guys show up." She paused. "Or, you know, if I run into Ellison."

Katie gave her a look. "Good night, Shaina."

"Night, babe."

Katie reached into her purse to pull out her cell when she noticed the small box she'd stowed away in there to give to Ellison. She had meant to give it to her when she checked out, but seeing as she missed her...She looked across the parking lot and saw Ellison's Maserati parked in its usual spot. Maybe she hadn't missed her after all.

She took two steps toward the real estate office when she remembered the envelope. She tore off the end and thumbed through the bills, not believing what she found there.

"You've got to be kidding me." It was decided. She had to see her tonight. They needed to talk.

She'd never been inside Gamble and Associates, but the luxurious interior didn't surprise her. She could see Ellison all over the design aspects of the space: elegant, chic, expensive, and beautiful.

The front desk was manned by a handsome guy who Katie estimated to be about her age.

"Can I help you?" he said as he glanced at the clock.

"Yes. Sorry, I'm sure you're closing. But is Ellison in?" Katie asked, hopeful.

"Jax, did you print the Dawson file—" Ellison emerged from around the corner holding a leather portfolio. "Katie. Hi."

"Turns out she's in and available," Jax said with a smile before addressing Ellison. "Katie's here to see you. And the file is on the end of the conference table next to the cupcakes Lauren packed up for you. I'm under strict orders not to let you take work home without cupcakes, too."

Ellison laughed and Katie enjoyed the genuine sound of it. "Fine. Did you take some, though?"

Jax held up a small pastry box. "Two. And that's my limit. I'm working on my new beach body." Jax flexed in a cartoonish fashion, and Ellison laughed some more.

"Go home. Do some crunches. I'll see you tomorrow."

"Don't work too late—it's your birthday," Jax said as he grabbed his keys off the desk.

"Everything okay?" Ellison asked as she approached.

"Yes. Well, no. I meant to catch you before you left."

"Oh?" Ellison looked concerned. "Did something happen? Shaina said you were on the phone with your mom's place. Is she okay?"

"She's fine. Turns out it was nothing," Katie said, shaking her head. "I wanted to catch you to give you something. But now that I'm in your presence, I think we should talk."

Ellison leaned against the desk Jax had just occupied. "That sounds profoundly serious. I just left an extremely relaxing massage. And it's my birthday, you know. Stress and seriousness are off the table on birthdays."

"Is that so?" Katie asked, leaning against the desk as well.

"Yup. It's practically law." Katie could have sworn Ellison's blue eyes twinkled as she spoke.

"Okay. No serious talking then." Katie reached into her purse and pulled out the box. "I made you something for your birthday. It's nothing big, but I wanted you to have it."

Ellison looked touched. "Really?"

"Really," Katie confirmed as she handed it to her.

Ellison placed the leather portfolio on the desk, cradling the box delicately. "It's so light," she observed. "Is it empty?"

Katie laughed. "No, it's not."

Ellison pulled off the small gold ribbon that Katie had scrounged out of the holiday bin in the attic and opened the box as if its contents were prized.

"Oh, wow," she said as the box fell away once the ribbon was untied. In her hand sat the miniature origami bouquet of roses, tulips, daisies, and greenery that Katie had worked on the last two nights. "You made this?"

"My roommate in college was Japanese, and she taught me all kinds of cool things when we were procrastinating during finals week." Katie had found her origami paper stash when she was boxing up some of her mother's things for New Beginnings.

"Thank you," Ellison said, looking genuinely moved.

"You're welcome," Katie replied. "Now, about that talk."

Ellison gave her a wary look as she moved the bouquet out of reach. "I thought we agreed that there was no serious talk on my birthday. You just gave me flowers. We have a nice thing going."

Katie rolled her eyes at her. "They're origami flowers. They literally cost nothing."

"But you spent time and care making them, which makes them very, very special." Ellison held them up to her heart. "And I love them."

"You're easy to please," Katie replied.

Ellison looked at her. "Do you really think that?"

Katie considered this. "Yes and no."

Ellison waved her free hand. "Please feel free to elaborate."

"I think you're successful because you have high standards for quality, much like your decorating taste"—Katie motioned to the space around them—"so in that regard, no. But the people that work with you are playful and want to make sure you enjoy your birthday cupcakes. So you must also be very down-to-earth and somehow relatable under all that high fashion."

"I like to think I'm a good boss. So I'll take that as a compliment."

"It wasn't meant to be an insult," Katie teased.

"Have a cupcake with me," Ellison said.

"We need to talk first," Katie said, reaching into her bag.

Ellison put her hand on her arm, halting her progress. "Cupcake first, talk later."

Katie's stomach grumbled almost as if on cue.

"See? It's a brilliant idea," Ellison said, gently tugging Katie's elbow for her to follow. "You need sustenance. I have too much of it."

"We're still going to talk," Katie warned.

Ellison gave her a solemn nod. "After sugar."

Katie followed Ellison into the office area, taking in the space before her. There were multiple cubicle-like desks along the way, and what she assumed were larger offices behind the mostly closed doors along the corridor Ellison led her down. At the far end of the hallway was a large conference room with a gorgeous wooden table that had no less than ten different helium balloons tied to each chair around it. A dozen or so delicious-looking cupcakes sat in an open pastry box next to a stack of papers that Katie assumed were the Dawson file that Ellison had asked about.

"Chocolate or funfetti?" Ellison asked.

"Always chocolate."

Ellison handed her a cupcake with vanilla frosting and rainbow sprinkles. "I think those are devil's food cake."

Katie peeled back the wrapper and took a generous bite. "Mm, these are amazing."

Ellison looked pleased. She unwrapped a funfetti cupcake and took a bite. "My favorite."

"Funfetti over chocolate?" This amused Katie.

"Yes. I like my rainbows on the inside and the outside," Ellison said with a wink.

Katie closed her eyes as she hummed happily. This was one of the of best cupcakes she'd ever had. "Where are these from?"

"Maine," Ellison said.

Katie looked at her, unbelieving. "Maine? You got cupcakes all the way from Maine?"

"They were a gift," Ellison said with a shrug. "They also happen to be the best cupcakes ever, so where they came from doesn't matter to me."

"Well, they *are* amazing. I'll give you that," Katie said as she finished off the treat. Ellison handed her a small birthday themed napkin, and a thought occurred to her. "Who decorated the office for you?"

"My employees," Ellison said as she took Katie's used napkin and discarded it nearby.

"So I was right before."

"About what?" Ellison asked as she assembled a flat white pastry box that Katie hadn't noticed on the table. Katie watched as she loaded six chocolate cupcakes into it and pushed it in Katie's direction.

"About you being well-liked. Because you're easy and hard to please. But not about the little things. Your employees like you—why else would they go to all this trouble to decorate and celebrate you?"

"Because I pay their salaries?"

"Because you're probably too generous with them. Like you were with me," Katie said as she handed Ellison the envelope she'd had in her purse. "I can't accept this."

"Ooh," Ellison said, wincing. "That was some covert serious-talk ambush you just did."

Katie whined, "Ellison. I can't take this money. It's too much."

Ellison pushed the envelope back to her. "You can. And you should."

Katie put her hand on her hip. "This tip is more than three times what the actual massage would have cost, had it cost you anything."

"Which it didn't. A free massage means extra tip," Ellison reasoned, but Katie wasn't having it.

"It's too much," she tried again.

"Then…" Ellison paused. "Take me to dinner with it."

"Dinner?" Katie didn't hate the idea—she just didn't see the correlation.

"Look, you said so yourself. I'm easy and hard to please, right?"

"Right," Katie said, though she was still not following.

"So that should tell you that I'm not going to take the money back—"

"But—"

"But," Ellison continued, "I would be willing to negotiate a deal of sorts. You can take me out for dinner instead."

"With your own money," Katie said skeptically.

"It's your money because I gave it to you and I won't accept it back," Ellison said. "So take me out to dinner."

Katie could see she wasn't going to win this argument. "I'd be happy to have dinner with you."

Ellison smiled. "Then it's decided. When and where?"

"Well, it is your birthday this very moment," Katie replied.

"I like the sound of this," Ellison said.

"Do you have plans right now?" Katie was hungry, and that cupcake was fantastic, but it wasn't going to cut it in the dinner department. That and she was going home to an empty house. And the idea of spending more time in Ellison's presence was very appealing. She liked her. She was funny and charming, and surprisingly playful—which Katie liked the most.

"Suddenly it seems like I have dinner plans," Ellison said, clapping. "Where are we going? I'm starving."

Katie shook her head. "I don't know. What would you have had for dinner tonight had you not coerced me into taking you out?"

Ellison feigned offense. "Do you feel coerced?"

"No," Katie admitted. "But I do want to know what you planned to do later."

"Well, I was planning on getting take-out sushi, having a glass of wine, and soaking in my tub to make that relaxed feeling I've been floating on since your massage last all night."

That sounded heavenly. Katie would kill for a bathtub that didn't leak. "If I were you, I'd stick to that plan. That sounds amazing."

"But having dinner with you is not in that plan, and since the opportunity has arisen to be in your company, I'd much rather do that," Ellison said, and Shaina's words from earlier circled in her mind. Was Ellison flirting with her? She couldn't tell. But did she like it, whatever it was? Yes.

"Promise me you'll still take a bath after dinner. That will keep those muscles from stiffening back up," Katie replied, trying but failing at not imagining Ellison in a bathtub. What was coming over her?

"Deal," Ellison said, extending her hand. "Does that mean we're going to dinner?"

Katie took her hand and shook it. "It does."

Ellison looked pleased. "Great. Let me grab some work for home, and I'm all yours."

Katie nodded toward the cupcakes and the paperwork. "Jax said you're supposed to take the cupcakes with that file. He said it was a rule or something."

"They," Ellison corrected. "Jax uses they-them pronouns. And it was Lauren who made the rule. Jax was merely the messenger."

"Duly noted," Katie said, recording the Jax information to memory. "Who's Lauren?"

"She's one of my senior Realtors, and the deliverer of the Maine cupcakes." Ellison picked up the file and handed Katie the box she'd packed with chocolate cupcakes. "These are for you."

"You have Realtors all the way up in Maine? How far does this empire of yours go?" Katie asked, marveling at her.

"No, she's dating the daughter of my old boss. Who also happens to be the person that baked the cupcakes and sent them here as a gift."

Katie stopped short of following her out of the conference room. "Your old boss sent you cupcakes?"

"I kind of helped her out recently with her dairy farm. In a roundabout sort of way," Ellison replied.

"You worked on a dairy farm?" Katie's head was spinning. She sped up her pace to catch up to her.

"When I was a teenager, yes," Ellison said as she led Katie away from the conference room past the array of doors.

"Hold on," Katie said as she reached out to halt Ellison's progress. "You're telling me that your boss—from the dairy farm where you worked as a teenager—cared enough about you to send you cupcakes some twenty years later?"

"Twenty-nine years later, to be precise," Ellison said with a small smile. "And yes."

Katie shook her head, confused. "How old were you when you started working there? Five? Because I'm no Maine expert, but I think there were child labor laws in place twenty-nine years ago."

Ellison's laugh was carefree and hearty. "You need to stop complimenting me, or I'm going to think this dinner is a date."

Katie felt herself blush. Would that be so bad? She had to admit that since Shaina planted the seed in her head, she *had* noticed a more than usual chemistry between them. Or she could just be imagining it. Just because Ellison was gay and by her own report single didn't mean that she was interested in Katie. That's not how things worked—just because Katie was female didn't mean she'd caught Ellison's eye. Right? That thought made her a bit disappointed.

"I'm kidding," Ellison said, briefly touching Katie's arm. "I was fourteen when I started working there."

"What?" Katie was dumbfounded. There was no way the woman in front of her was forty-three. Not with skin and a body like that. Katie could only dream of aging so well.

"You're staring," Ellison said.

"I'm not," Katie replied, even though she was. "How? Do you—? Really?"

"Forty-three years on this Earth today," Ellison said with a small smile. "I've got good country bumpkin genes. My mother barely looked fifty when she passed at seventy-six."

"Wow," Katie said, not knowing what else to say. "I mean, congrats. That's…you look incredible."

"Thank you," Ellison said as they entered what Katie assumed was her office. Her eyes immediately landed on the bursting bouquet of real flowers that sat in an opulent vase on the table, next to a comfortable but chic looking gray sofa to her left.

"Those are beautiful," she said. "Are they from your friend from earlier?"

Ellison paused at her desk, watching her intently. "No. They're from Trina. And Lauren and Jax, but my money's on mostly Trina. She's as dynamic as that bouquet."

"And Trina is…?" Katie wanted to know more about Ellison. She figured the best way to do that was to ask.

"My most senior and successful protégé," Ellison said as she placed Katie's handmade origami bouquet next to the monitor on her desk, adjusting it once or twice before settling on its final position.

Katie watched as Ellison filled her leather portfolio with some paperwork before grabbing her blazer and purse and joining her by the couch. She pointed to a framed photo she was in that Katie had been looking at.

"That's Trina on the left," she said, identifying the Asian woman dressed like she was a fashion model for *Vogue* in a daring and slim-fitting red dress. "That's Lauren," she said, pointing out a tall dirty blonde with a dazzling smile. "And you've already met Jax."

Katie studied the picture. Together the four of them were an exceptionally attractive bunch.

"Where was this taken?" she asked. Katie noted that Ellison looked ageless here as well.

"At an LGBTQ fundraiser a few years ago," she said, looking nostalgic. "That was a fun night."

"You look happy here," she said, looking at her.

"I was," Ellison replied, holding her gaze. "I still am. I've had a really good life. I'm fortunate."

Katie found that the more time she spent in Ellison's presence, the more she wanted to know all about that life. "Ready to eat?"

"Yes, please."

Katie was in tears. Ellison was singlehandedly the funniest, driest, most sarcastic person she'd ever met. She couldn't remember another time she'd laughed so much. Her sides literally hurt.

"Anyway, that's the story of Stan the wooden moose and also why his legacy lives on in Casterville, Maine."

Katie took a sip of water in between gasping breaths. "Unbelievable."

"Fact is always stranger than fiction, right?" Ellison placed her napkin on the table. "Now, if you'll excuse me, my massage therapist insisted I drown myself in water today, and my bladder is protesting. I'll be right back."

Katie watched Ellison head in the direction of the bathroom as her phone vibrated on the table next to her. It was a text from Shaina: *Not coming out tonight was a smart idea. Guess who randomly showed up?*

Who? she texted back, though she didn't really care because she was having far too much fun with Ellison to have FOMO.

Shaina replied with a photo from the bar she was at. Two people down from Shaina's boyfriend Raul was Katie's ex, Asher.

Katie stared at the picture. She hadn't seen him in months, and though he was easily the most attractive guy she'd dated on this coast, seeing him brought her nothing but ugly thoughts.

"Uh-oh. Why are we scowling at the phone?" Ellison asked as she sat across from her.

"Was I scowling?" Katie didn't doubt it.

"Big-time. Or you've been secretly concealing a facial tic this whole dinner. But my bet is that's your annoyed face."

"It's certainly one of them," Katie said as she discarded her phone with probably more force than was necessary. The phone hit the center of the table and spun like a top until Ellison's hand settled on it, bringing it to a stop.

"Was it the text or the picture?" she asked as she glanced down at the still lit screen.

"Both." Katie hated how just seeing him put her in a mood. "Shaina went out tonight with her boyfriend and his buddies, and they ran into my ex. I could have happily lived my life without the photo evidence or the proof that, though he ghosted me, he is still very much alive."

Ellison picked up the phone, looking up at her for permission as she thumbed across the screen to keep it from locking. "Can I?"

"Sure," Katie said.

"Which one is he?" Ellison asked, turning the phone toward Katie.

"The tall dirty blond in the background. But don't worry, it's bottle blond. That's his secret. He's incredibly vain." Katie didn't have to see the screen to identify him—she was sure the picture was burned into her memory. Things involving Asher seemed to settle in her mind like a stone. Another annoying thing about him.

"Few blonds are true blonds," Ellison said, and Katie winced.

"Your hair is lovely. It complements your perfect skin and those incredible blue eyes. I didn't mean to knock all blonds. I just think I hate him, that's all. But that wasn't fair," Katie rambled. "Sorry."

Ellison placed her hand on Katie's. "Don't. You don't need to apologize to me." She placed the phone screen side down as she asked, "Do you want to talk about it? Or him?"

"Not particularly," Katie said, looking at the woman across from her that seemed to have infinite patience and kindness all at once. She decided that maybe she did need to get something off her chest. And Ellison seemed like the perfect person to vent to because, for whatever reason, she just didn't feel like she would be judged by her. For anything.

"We dated exclusively for a year and a half after I moved here. I met him at a bar and then again at a grocery store. He had those Hollywood good looks with that flawless jawline, you know? So even though I was taking care of my mom, I made time for him. And that was the truth of it. It was time for *him*, not time for me. Because the world revolves around Asher Collins." She hated how much she had played into his egomaniacal tendencies and catered to his every whim. But she'd needed a distraction from the pain of what was happening at home. And he was a warm body without too much emotional baggage, outside the regular ego-stroking he required. "Anyway, when Mom had her stroke, he ghosted me. Like, straight up disappeared."

She laughed angrily. "I guess he thought it was bad enough for his rep to have a girlfriend with a disabled, live-in parent. But when that situation worsened, the pity cred he was milking from his bros wasn't going to work because it was clear I was going to need more than the occasional shoulder to cry on and pat on the head here and there. So, that's Asher in a nutshell. Handsome—aesthetically gifted, really—and completely hollow."

"Sounds like him leaving wasn't the worst thing in the world," Ellison said.

"No. It was exactly the wake-up call I needed to redirect my focus." She took a sip of wine. "And the sex wasn't that good anyway. He was way too into himself and his needs."

Ellison raised her glass and clinked it with Katie's. "What I've learned in my years circling the sun is that life is too short for bad sex. Even mediocre sex. If you don't feel reborn afterward, you're better off doing it yourself."

Katie nearly choked on her sip, laughing so hard her eyes filled with tears. "O-M-G. You're so right."

Ellison gave her a broad smile as she finished her glass. "I usually am."

The waitress stopped by to gather the rest of their plates and thanked them for their patronage.

Katie looked up at Ellison to ask, "Do you want dessert? Or should we get the bill?"

The waitress—whose nametag read *Tina*—chimed in, "It's all set. Have a great night."

Katie watched her walk away, bewildered, before it dawned on her. "You already paid, didn't you."

Ellison's eyebrows were at her hairline. "That depends, are you going to yell at me?"

"Do you deserve to be yelled at?" Katie asked, crossing her arms in indignation. "I thought we had an agreement."

"We did." Ellison sat up, cocking her head to the side as she said, "But I decided to hedge my bets on you taking me out for dinner again. You know, like an IOU, except with wine and dining."

"I do like both of those things," Katie said, still not ready to forgive her yet.

"Mm, me too. See? We should do this again soon, then. We have similar interests."

Katie attempted to scowl at her, but only managed to smile. "You were never going to let me pay, were you?"

Ellison shook her head. "No. But you can take me out again and see if your luck has changed any. Besides, your company has been priceless. You can't compete with priceless."

"Is that a line you use to get women often? You tell them their company is priceless, and they just melt?" Katie asked, curious about the stunning creature across from her who never seemed to lack confidence, grace, or suavity.

Ellison leaned forward a bit, her voice lowered as she replied, "I don't have to use lines on women to get that result." Katie licked her lips because they felt dry, and she swore she saw Ellison's eyes flick down toward them as she said, "And I've never told anyone that their company was priceless before. That's special to just you."

Ellison's words made her stomach flip in a way she wasn't used to. She watched her for a moment, tracing her eyes along her face, considering what Ellison had said. What she meant. Was she flirting with her? She was, right? Katie wasn't sure if it was true flirting or if Shaina's words from earlier were lingering in her mind, making her second-guess what was happening between them. Which was nothing. Just friends having a friendly dinner. Right?

Ellison stayed there momentarily before leaning back. "I hope you don't mind that we skipped dessert, but I was kind of hoping you'd help me shave down the number of cupcakes in my car, so I don't end up with glucose intolerance at my advanced age."

"They are pretty spectacular cupcakes," Katie said, unable to forget the flutter in her stomach from moments ago.

"Good," Ellison said as she stood. "I was hoping you'd say that."

❖

"I know I said this before, but you buying yourself dinner and *then* going out of your way to drive me home sort of cancels out any and all birthday-ness to a birthday," Katie said as she lounged against the passenger seat of Ellison's Maserati, much more at ease in it this time than last time.

Ellison finished her cupcake with a shrug. "You're on the way to my place. And I wasn't going to let you hop on a bus home. Plus, it's my day, and I get to call the shots."

"Like you don't every day?" Katie teased.

Ellison gave her a coy expression. "How can you know me so well already?"

"How can I not? I've practically seen you naked," Katie said, smiling when Ellison howled with laughter next to her.

"Touché."

"Touchy, even." Katie waggled her fingers as she sighed a contented sigh. "I should probably go in now."

Ellison looked past her at the house they'd been sitting outside of for the last twenty minutes while they had been chatting and eating Ellison's birthday cupcakes. "I see that you put the front porch light on tonight."

"And I brought a house key," Katie said, holding up her keys. "But that's only because I knew I'd be working late, and I thought I was coming home alone."

Ellison raised an eyebrow in her direction.

Katie felt herself flush. "I wasn't…I didn't mean to suggest that you were coming in—" She palmed her face. "Ignore all the words that come out of my face. It's late. You fed me sushi, wine, and cupcakes. I can't be held accountable for any and all embarrassing statements I might have or will continue to utter."

Ellison laughed. "I knew what you meant."

"Good," Katie said as she shifted in her seat. "Because I do want to have dinner with you again. And I don't want you to get the wrong idea."

"About what, exactly?" Ellison's attention felt like a spotlight.

"That I want anything more than friendship from you."

Ellison's face was unreadable.

Katie tried again. "Let me pay next time. Really. I don't want this to be some pity thing where you buy things and do things for me. I want to do my part. I want to contribute to this." She motioned between them. "That's what I meant."

After a long pause, Ellison acquiesced. "Okay."

"Okay?"

She nodded. "Just make sure there is a next time, and I'll behave."

Something about that statement made Katie feel warm all over. "Good."

She put her hand on the car door before pausing. "Just know that we might be going to McDonald's because my budget is certainly tighter than yours. Especially while I try to keep Mom in New Beginnings, which looks like I can maybe swing for another two and a half months before I have to start selling organs."

Ellison gave her a small smile. "Can I ask you something?"

"Anything," Katie replied.

"This house…what does it mean to you?"

"It feels like an albatross," she said candidly.

Ellison seemed to consider this. "I can't speak to your financial situation. And I don't know enough about your mother or you to make any assertions about anything, but I can tell you this—this home is unique and special. And would sell for a small fortune to the right buyer."

"What are you saying?"

"I'm saying that you could probably dig yourself out of debt and keep your mother in that facility for a long time if you sold that house. Not that I'm trying to Realtor schmooze you or anything. It's just an observation, really."

Katie shook her head. "I have no love for that house, and the reality is that it's not ever going to be the right layout for Mom and her needs. Nor could I ever afford to make that a possibility. Hell, I can't even afford to patch the boot-sized hole in the top step or fix the leaky second floor bathtub that has started to drain into the kitchen ceiling. Or even afford to get an electrician in there to tell me why I keep blowing the power on the first floor when I use a hairdryer. Life is hard enough without living in a house that seems like it's trying to kill me," she said with a laugh. Because laughing kept her from crying. And talking about this house and her financial woes was a surefire way to get the waterworks to start. "I could never get this house in any condition to have it sell for what it *might* be worth. Never."

Ellison gave her a sympathetic expression. "There are lots of realty offices that offer a concierge service to help fix up homes to get them ready to sell."

"I just told you I have to take you to McDonald's on our next dinner adventure," Katie deadpanned. "I can't afford concierge anything."

Ellison scrunched her nose. "I like McDonald's. Their fries are the best. Don't knock it."

"I'll even splurge on getting you a meal with a toy, if you want," Katie replied.

"Well, if I wasn't sold before…" She nudged Katie's arm with her elbow before continuing, "Seriously, about that concierge thing, though—the cost is covered by the agency that represents you and is deducted from the sale price after the closing. There are no upfront costs with that, just design input, that sort of thing. There are lots of options if that's something you're interested in."

"I guess I never realized it was an option," Katie said, knowing she'd have to give this a lot of thought.

"There are always options," Ellison said, stifling a yawn.

"Go home, get to bed. It's almost no longer your birthday," Katie said as she pointed to the dashboard clock.

"Okay," Ellison said, yawning again. "You win."

"So, I can buy next time?" Katie said as she opened the car door.

Ellison handed her the cupcake box she'd packed her earlier. "If you take these, then yes."

"Twist my arm," Katie said. "Oh, wait."

"What?"

Katie placed the cupcakes on the roof before scurrying over to Ellison's driver's side window. She motioned for Ellison to lower it, then leaned in to give her a hug once it was down. "Thank you for dinner, and the tip."

"Thank you for an awesome birthday." Ellison wrapped her arms around her, and Katie felt herself melt.

"I see what you mean about not needing a line to get women to melt," she said, still staying in Ellison's embrace.

"Oh?" Her voice was soft next to her ear.

"Yup. It's your hugs. You give great hugs."

Ellison chuckled. "That's most certainly it."

Katie pulled back but not before Ellison gave her a brief kiss on her cheek.

"Let me know when it's time for that next dinner," Ellison said.

"Okay." Katie stepped back from the car, resisting the urge to touch the place where Ellison's lips had been on her cheek just to see if the skin was as warm as it felt.

"Don't forget the cupcakes," Ellison said, motioning toward the top of her car.

"I won't," Katie said, but she already had. "You're going to sit here and watch me get into the house, aren't you?"

"It's like you live inside my head," Ellison said.

Katie really wished in that moment that she did because her own head was feeling very foggy at the moment—foggy with a myriad of thoughts about Ellison, it seemed.

"Good night, Katie," Ellison called as she walked to the house, and Katie smiled because it already had been.

CHAPTER TEN

E llison answered the call without checking who was on the line.
"Ellison Gamble."

"You're a hard lady to reach." Faith's voice sounded across the line.

Ellison winced. Faith had left her two messages this week, but she'd been busy. And avoiding her. "Is that why you called my office line?"

"You're never not working. I should have called this line first."

"Things have been—"

"Excuses waste oxygen, Ellie. Are you ready to stop wasting oxygen and everyone's time? I got things to do, too. Just because you're a natural blonde doesn't mean you're the sun and the world revolves around you." Faith always was no-nonsense.

Ellison leaned back in her chair. "You're right."

"I know I am. So, have you turned in the paperwork?"

"Uh, not yet," Ellison said. She'd filled out the application and gathered the materials the day after her initial surrogacy appointment. She'd just been sitting on it.

Faith sighed. "Let's do a check-in."

Ellison rolled her eyes. "I'm fine."

"You're not. Otherwise, you would have submitted the paperwork, and we would already be picking a sperm donor for eggie one and two. So check in with me. What's going on? What are you worried about?"

"Everything," Ellison said. For once, she had a semi-clear direction in place. She needed a surrogate if she wanted to try to have a genetic baby—this was a fact. And yet that fact made her feel less secure than anything else in this process thus far.

"Explain," Faith replied patiently.

"This isn't about meds and ovulation tests anymore, right? I mean, it is. But it isn't. Prior to this it was all on me. If I got pregnant and had a child, that was on me. But it's not like that anymore. This is a contract with another human being, and once the train is set in motion, it's in motion. There's no backing out once she's pregnant. That's it. I'm on the way to momhood."

"Let's back it up a bit. Do you want to be a mother?"

"Yes."

"Do you feel emotionally capable to raise a child, most likely on your own, within the next year?"

"I mean, did you have to say the *on your own* like that?"

"Answer the question," Faith replied.

"Yes." She did. She'd been slowly changing her work-life balance to make sure she would be more present and more available if children did come into the picture. Yes, she worked a lot, but gone were the late-night showings and hustling of the past. She was a multi-business owner now. Most of her work was phone calls and managing her Realtors or investing in new business opportunities. The business was a well-oiled machine. She could take a step back and still be successful. She'd put that into the plan. And the plan was perfect, minus the hostile uterus part.

"Then what's the point of waiting? It's not going to happen overnight. You still have months of stuff in between. You need to see if your eggs even fertilize before you can start going back and forth about all the other stuff."

"You came with all the truth bombs today, huh?" Ellison knew she was right, but she wasn't about to roll over for it.

"Send in the application. And pick a donor this weekend. Go to the beach house, clear your head, and pick a handsome specimen to give me the cutest little nieces and nephews. Do the work on your end, and stop stalling," Faith said, and Ellison knew better than to argue with her.

"Fine. I'll send the forms over tonight."

"Do it now before you change your mind. I know they're in that beloved leather portfolio next to you on the desk. You know you've been carrying them around this whole time."

Ellison looked around the room to see if Faith was actually in there with her. "How did you know that?"

"Because I've known you as long as dirt. That's how."

Ellison laughed. "I'll send it now."

"Good."

Ellison heard some shuffling in the background. "What are you up to today?"

Faith paused. "I had a guest over—they're leaving. Loudly, it seems." She sounded annoyed.

"Ooh, that's exciting," Ellison said, though a little part of her deflated. If Faith had a new bedroom partner, that meant their most recent rekindling was over. Which was probably for the best if Ellison was going to be more emotionally and physically needy as this surrogacy thing got underway. She'd be better off finding some respite closer to home and maybe with less emotional connection than with Faith.

"We'll see. It's new." Faith cleared her throat. "I'll be in town in a few weeks for Talia's photo shoot. Maybe we can grab lunch?"

"I'd like that," Ellison said as she double-checked the calendar. Talia was launching her new clothing line and had requested a few of her regular clients—Ellison, Trina, Lauren, and Jax—as well as Faith to be in some of the photographs she was taking for her website and webstore launch. Jax had been working with her on some of the IT stuff and had been excited when she'd asked them to model some of her clothes. The photo shoot was a big conversation topic around here. Ellison had even used her real estate contacts to secure a warehouse for the night to make sure there was plenty of space and privacy for this to go off without a hitch.

"All right, send in that application. I'll talk to you soon."

"Yes, Mom," Ellison said before disconnecting.

She drummed her fingers on the desk for a moment before opening her portfolio and pulling out the stack of paperwork.

"Send it in. Pick a donor. Leave it up to the fertility gods. Go from there." Ellison opened her laptop and pulled up the electronic copies of the documents in front of her. She almost always had paper copies of her documents at hand, because she was so used to reviewing contracts that way, even though paper was becoming more and more a thing of the past.

She scanned through the documents one last time before uploading them to the secure server at Full Circle Surrogacy. She fired off an email letting her designated counselor Tammy know the files had been uploaded, and she closed the laptop with a sigh.

It was done. She'd pick a sperm donor tonight and call Dr. Brinkley about getting those last two eggs fertilized. Then she'd just wait and see if her luck had finally run out, or if she had a little left to preserve her biologic tissue.

Her phone buzzed on the desk and she reached for it. She smiled at the text from Katie on the screen.

Free for a quick salad lunch? My next client canceled, and I was hoping to chat with you about the house thing.

Ellison checked her planner. She was free until a three o'clock call with Zander Alter, the architect she had grown friendly with during the undertaking of the Newbridge on the Gardens project from last year. He'd helped her make that dream become a reality, and she was eager to work with him and his new independent design firm moving forward.

I'd like that. What kind of salad?

Katie sent back a screenshot of the deli a block away, and Ellison sent over her order.

Be by in fifteen, Katie replied.

Ellison smiled. This was an unexpected but welcome addition to her day. Her dinner with Katie last week had been the highlight of her week. Well, after that life-changing massage, of course. She'd hoped she hadn't overstepped when she'd made the comment to Katie about selling her home. It appeared as though maybe she hadn't.

Trina knocked on her doorframe as she poked her head in. "We're ordering lunch. Do you want anything?"

"I've got some on the way, actually," Ellison said.

"Cool. We're going to eat in the conference room if you want to join," she said with a wave.

"Sounds good," Ellison said as she glanced down at the phone that vibrated in her hand. It was a confirmation email from Tammy.

Got your application. We'll start working on this right away. This is exciting!

"Well, I guess that's that," she said, feeling a mixture of relief and anxiety. The train was in motion. Now it was time she stopped dragging her feet on the sperm donor. Maybe she'd take Faith's advice after all.

"Beach house. Shop for sperm. Do my part. I can do it." And she knew she could.

❖

Katie stepped into Gamble and Associates feeling a little nervous. Was she really about to do this? Could she do this?

"Hey," Ellison said with a big smile. "How are you?"

"Good," Katie said as she stepped into her embrace. "I come bearing food."

"Then you are very welcome," Ellison said as she stepped back, motioning her toward her office.

Laughter sounded behind her, and she turned to see what the commotion was about. She recognized the faces immediately: Jax she'd met before, but the other two were in the photograph that Ellison had shown her in her office.

"Don't mind them—they know not of their volume," Ellison said with a playful smile. "You know Jax already, but this is Trina Lee and Lauren Calloway. And the three of them together are a step above hyenas."

"The insults we have to endure," Trina said, looking mischievous. "It's no wonder we're practically feral."

"We all know you're a biter," Lauren said to Trina, which garnered her a swat.

"And we all know you're a back-seat moaner," Trina said as she untied the belt around her incredibly fashionable trench coat. Katie thought Ellison was a great dresser, but Trina looked like a cutout from a fashion magazine.

"I'm staying out of this," Jax said wisely, and Katie had to laugh. It was clear they were the closest of friends. "Hey, Katie. How's it going?"

"Oh, you're Katie," Trina said, directing her attention to her. "It's nice to meet you."

"Have you been talking about me?" Katie asked Ellison, amused.

"No," Ellison replied, giving her employees a look. "But it seems they have."

Jax's hands went up in defense. "Nothing bad. I promise."

"Yeah, Jax just said you swung by the other night around closing," Lauren said, nudging past Trina in the direction of the conference room Katie had tried the cupcakes in.

"Mm-hmm," Ellison hummed. "Go to lunch."

"On it, Boss." Lauren saluted Ellison, and the friends whisper-laughed down the hall before disappearing behind the conference room door.

"They're talking about us right now, aren't they?" Katie asked.

"Probably," Ellison said, looking unbothered. "More likely they're just teasing each other until someone gets pinched."

Katie laughed. "They seem nice."

"They're the best," Ellison said, and Katie could tell she meant that. "Shall we?"

"Yes, please."

Katie followed Ellison into her office, taking a seat at the chair in front of Ellison's desk as she closed the door behind them. "Can I sit here? Or do you prefer the couch?"

"Here's fine if you don't mind the desk between us," Ellison said, as she sat across from her.

Katie's eyes fell to the origami bouquet she'd made her. Ellison had kept the flowers front and center on her desk.

"They're the perfect cheeriness for an otherwise stress mess of a desk," Ellison said, though Katie thought this was the cleanest desk she'd ever seen. Nothing was out of place, and the few papers out were labeled and in folders.

"I'm glad you like them," she said as she pulled out Ellison's salad. "Grilled shrimp, Caesar with olives, and extra croutons."

"You're the best," she said as she took the container. "How are you?"

Katie drizzled her dressing on her salad, stirring it as she replied. "Good. Fine. Well, I've been thinking a lot about last week, and I was hoping we could talk about it."

Ellison paused, the fork hovering by her mouth as she asked, "What about, specifically?"

"My house."

Ellison looked relieved. "Sure. Of course. What's on your mind?"

Katie shook her head. "What did you think I was going to say?"

Ellison shrugged. "I had no idea."

"You looked worried," Katie argued.

"Did I?" Ellison asked, seemingly nonchalant. "I didn't feel worried."

Katie nodded, not quite believing her. Or maybe not believing herself. Because she *had* wanted to talk to Ellison about the house. She'd been thinking about it since Ellison had brought it up. But she'd also been thinking about the hug, and that cheek kiss, and how she hadn't been able to stop thinking about their dinner together. So maybe she was projecting. "I saw my mom today, and I talked to her about it."

"How is she?"

Katie loved that Ellison inquired about her. "She's good. She's doing really well there. I'm seeing strides I haven't seen in months. I want her to get the best care she can get, and I think that's happening there. So maybe it's time we talk more about how I can make that happen. I want to know more about what selling the house might entail. And if it's even a possibility."

"Everything is a possibility. And that house—if returned to its prior glory—would sell in a weekend."

"Wow, you really think so?"

"Yes," Ellison said as she pushed aside her salad. Katie watched as she booted up her computer and began typing quickly along the keys. "Here are a few comps in the neighborhood."

She turned the screen toward Katie as she selected a few houses. "There are a few Tudors, a few single familys, and this is an antique Victorian, like yours."

Katie's jaw dropped. The sale price couldn't be right, could it? "You're kidding me."

Ellison laughed. "I'd have to see the inside to be sure, but"—she pulled up an aerial view of Katie's home and began highlighting areas around it—"your house has a better location. And its proximity to this school and this park here make me think we could probably get more than that person did for theirs."

Katie frowned. "I'm in a vulnerable place. I'm seriously

considering selling my childhood home and only family legacy. Don't tease me."

Ellison touched her hand. "I know. And I wouldn't. I promise."

"Wow."

Ellison squeezed her hand before picking up her fork again. "You said that already."

"I mean it more this time around, I think." Katie was speechless. "How do I—? Where do I even start?"

Ellison chewed for a moment before sipping the iced tea that Katie had brought her. "Well, you should find a Realtor you trust and have them do a walk-through of the property. If the house needs as much work as you say it does, and you don't have the liquid assets or credit to make that happen, then you should find a realty company that will offer that upfront concierge service I mentioned to you."

"You mean where they cover the cost of renovations and cosmetic improvements and take the cost of those improvements out of the final sale price as a reimbursement," Katie said. She'd been online researching some of this stuff, so she didn't seem like a complete buffoon in Ellison's presence. Not that she thought Ellison would judge her or anything. But still.

"Exactly. It's like a loan. It benefits everyone, really, because the Realtor will usually get a higher sale price, and their commission will go up, and the seller can usually recoup the rehab deduction because the house sells for more. It's a win-win."

"Okay. So, when are you coming by?"

Ellison choked mid-sip. "What?"

"Well, you said I should find a Realtor I trust to do a walk-through. I trust you. And I checked your website—you offer that concierge rehab service thing. So you're hired. I want you. Take pity on me and say *yes*."

Ellison laughed. "You don't have to contract with me or Gamble and Associates. That wasn't the point of me telling you all of this."

"I know. But if you hadn't, then I wouldn't have known this was even an option, and I would have lost that house to tax liens. And my mother would be out of New Beginnings the next day," Katie said, fighting back some of the emotion that threatened to bubble up. "Please. I know I'm sort of a mess. But can you at least do a daytime walk-through and give me your honest opinion? Even if I can't reach the sales numbers of that last house, I could maybe secure a few years for my mom at a decent rehabilitation place. And that would be enough to let me sleep at night."

"Of course," Ellison replied without hesitation, and the unexpected relief that came with that reassurance broke Katie's final resolve.

"Thank you," she said as she tried to stifle the sob without success. She covered her face, embarrassed by her lack of composure.

"Hey, it's okay." Ellison's voice was soft but the arms that wrapped around her were strong and comforting. "We'll figure it out."

Katie nodded, leaning in to Ellison's embrace. She let herself feel the complex emotions that rushed through her. This was scary and exciting at the same time. Selling the house would unburden her in so many ways, and yet it was the last piece of her mother and her family history that she had any contact with. There was so much to unpack about all the things in her life that had brought her to this moment, this decision, and yet she felt oddly at peace with it right now. Because something about Ellison's touch—her embrace—felt like a shield. She felt protected and safe—two things she hadn't felt in a very long time. Long before her mother's accident. Long before her life changed forever.

"How do you do that?" she asked, resting her head on Ellison's shoulder. She could smell the light, slightly floral perfume on her neck. It was lovely.

"Do what?" Ellison brushed a hair behind her ear, and Katie's skin tingled in the most amazing way.

Katie was quiet for a moment, just appreciating the thrum of emotions that her body felt from the close physical connection. It occurred to her that outside of Shaina giving her an occasional friend hug, Ellison was the only person to touch her in an affectionate or caring way in months. Her body ached for it. She felt starved and fulfilled all at once.

"Make everything better. Even if just for this moment." She pulled back, not because she wanted to, but because she wasn't sure she could rationalize being this close to someone she was about to go into a business agreement with. Even if she was the Best. Hugger. Ever.

"I'm glad you feel that way, but I assure you I haven't done anything yet." Katie was surprised to find Ellison kneeling in front of her. It hadn't occurred to Katie how she had managed to completely wrap herself around her. Ellison had literally knelt before her to get on her level. To fix things. In what were most certainly the most expensive slacks Katie had ever set eyes on.

"You listened. You're patient. And you have the kindest and bluest eyes of anyone I have ever met," Katie said. She'd thought about those eyes this past week. She felt like she'd subconsciously dreamed about them. Her hand moved, seemingly of its own volition, toward Ellison's jaw, missing the contact they'd just shared.

Ellison intercepted her hand, clasping it between hers as she said, "My job as your Realtor is to help you close one chapter and begin the next new adventure with as little stress as possible." She stood, placing a hand on Katie's shoulder as she said, "And my job as your friend is to help you hash out the hard stuff that gets in the way of the good stuff. And having financial security for your mom, and yourself, will help you find more good stuff."

"It's that easy, huh?" Katie wiped away the last of her tears. She accepted the tissue Ellison offered her before she retreated behind her desk, too far away for Katie's liking.

"No. It's stressful, and you'll probably want to quit a thousand times. But I won't let you."

"You promise?"

"I promise."

CHAPTER ELEVEN

Katie was nervous. Like, blind-date nervous, butterflies in her stomach doing Cirque du Soleil kind of nervous. And she knew she shouldn't be. But she was. So. Nervous.

After her breakdown in Ellison's office the other day, she'd managed to pull herself together long enough to have a nice lunch with her. And they'd texted back and forth quite a bit the last few days leading up to today, but this was it. The moment she'd dreaded most. Ellison was going to be here—any second—for the first of what she assumed would be many walk-throughs of the house.

Katie had cleaned ad nauseam, but she swore there wasn't a change inside at all. Everything looked sad and tired and hopeless. But dust-free, at least. Katie knew she had nothing to be ashamed of. She kept a tidy space and had next to no belongings or clutter of her own, but her mother's things remained largely untouched. Her mother's bedroom was the way it had been the night of her accident—lived in and slightly disheveled. Her grandparents' antique furniture lined the hallways and long abandoned guest rooms, representing nothing of Katie's taste or even her mother's.

The house was like a time capsule to the past in a lot of ways, and Katie imagined that Ellison lived very differently. She was embarrassed about the simplicity of her space. She'd done the very best she could with it, but it didn't represent her. This house was too much of a mausoleum to be a space she felt attached to. Even as a child she'd felt like a temporary inhabitant within its walls.

The knock at the door told her it was time.

"I see you didn't fall into the hole in the top step," she said as she opened the door.

"I managed. But just barely."

"You look nice," Katie said, trying not to stare but failing miserably. Ellison was in a sheer, flowy top with high-waisted flat-front wide-leg slacks that she'd paired with blood-red heels. Her hair was half up and half down with those oversized designer sunglasses positioned at the crown of her head. This was a look that Katie hadn't seen on her yet. She liked it.

"Summer is my favorite season. I like the opportunity to pair bright colors with different textures and fits," Ellison said.

"I've never seen you not look nice. Which I feel like I should also mention." Katie knew she was rambling.

"I can't take the credit for that. I have the great fortune of having a personal stylist."

Katie appreciated that though Ellison said that aloud, she didn't look shy about it. She really was a boss in every sense of the word. "Well, he or she"—Katie paused—"or they have a great eye and know what will look great on you."

"She does," Ellison said with a small smile. "And I'll tell her that the next time I see her. I'm sure you'll meet her sometime. She'll be by the office quite a bit in the coming weeks. She's working on a clothing line launch, and she strong-armed the office into modeling some of her designs."

"Oh, wow."

Ellison gave her a once-over before reaching out and gently tugging on one of Katie's loose curls. "You know, she'd love to dress you, too. You're beautiful, and that auburn hair with those green eyes of yours would look stunning in her ad campaign. I'll introduce you two."

"Th-thanks," Katie stammered. She was positive that this time Ellison *had* just checked her out *and* called her attractive.

Ellison held her gaze for a moment before asking, "Can I come in?"

"Yes. Sorry," Katie said, annoyed with herself for being a garbage host. "Just promise not to judge me too harshly. And remember that I moved back here under duress that really hasn't lessened much."

"No judgments. I promise," Ellison said as she stepped past, and

Katie recognized the perfume she'd smelled on Ellison from when she was a blubbering mess in Ellison's office a few days ago.

"Do you mind if I wander a bit?" Ellison asked, looking back.

"Help yourself." Katie held her breath as Ellison looked around.

Ellison walked through the first floor, opening doors and looking up at the ceilings in a way Katie assumed was deliberate. She asked a few questions here or there but mostly just observed the space in quiet.

Katie led her up to the second floor up the grand front staircase, pointing out bedrooms and bathrooms until they reached her own.

"This is my only real space in the house." Katie opened the door and stepped back as Ellison stepped in.

Ellison walked into the modest guest bedroom that had once been her childhood room. She'd stripped the posters off the walls and thrown away most of her knickknacks her mother had kept from her childhood. The queen bed she'd put in here was almost too big for the space, but she'd refused to sleep on the full-sized bed of her youth. She watched as Ellison traced her fingers along the duvet at the foot of the bed before glancing into her cramped and cluttered closet.

"This space is nice. Very cozy and welcoming," she said.

"Thanks," Katie said, feeling a modicum better about herself. "This is the only room I spent any time on. I painted the walls and cleaned up the windows. Just gave it a little makeover."

Ellison walked to the windows, pushed back the curtains, and looked outside. "This room gets a lot of natural light, huh?"

"Yeah. Honestly, that's the main reason I stuck with it. This was my childhood bedroom growing up, and though it's not the largest in the house, it's got the best light. For sure."

"Natural light makes all the difference," she said.

"The windows are a bit drafty, though, probably because this side of the house is the most exposed to the elements."

"But the light is good," Ellison said.

"Exactly, so I sleep under extra layers," Katie replied. "No sleeping naked in this room."

Ellison gave her an amused look.

"I said that last part out loud, didn't I?" Katie felt her cheeks redden.

"It's your bedroom, your rules," Ellison said with her hands up.

"I didn't mean like no nudity ever. I'm not—" Katie pressed her hand to her forehead, embarrassed by her awkwardness.

"You're not what?" Ellison asked, and Katie had a hard time focusing because Ellison chose that moment to sit at the edge of her bed and cross those long legs in that effortlessly fashionable pose that she seemed to always have.

"Um, a prude? Celibate? I mean, I'm willfully single. It's not like I can't get lai—" She shook her head. "You know what? I think it's time to admit the downward spiral and stop before I bury myself in a hole." She took a breath. "Yes, the windows are drafty. But the room is worth it."

"Sounds reasonable to me," Ellison said as she stood. Katie was aware how much taller those heels made Ellison than her. She liked it. She liked just about everything about Ellison, which she was beginning to realize was maybe sort of a problem. Or not. That was unclear just yet.

"Anyway, let's see the rest of the house. Shall we?"

Katie led her out into the hall toward the third and final floor that had served as her grandfather's office and writing room. Although there was an attic, Katie almost never went up there anymore since they'd had multiple leaks in the roof over the years. Out of precaution and a desire for preservation, her grandfather's office space held most of the holiday decorations and storage boxes that previously resided in the attic.

"This space is lovely," Ellison said, running her hand along her grandfather's hand-carved wooden desk.

Katie frowned at the finger streak in the dust on the wood. She hadn't thought to dust up here. "My grandfather retreated up here often. He said it helped him clear his head to be so high up." She pointed to the stained-glass window at the end of the lofted space that faced the front yard. "My grandmother picked the colors for that glass and helped design it. She used to say it was her way of watching over him when he was up in his belfry."

"She had great taste," Ellison said, taking in the cluttered room. Katie wondered what she was thinking.

They headed back downstairs, making their way through the kitchen toward the backyard. Ellison opened the pantry door, and

Katie winced—the shelves were mostly bare. As usual. She never kept anything in there because she'd had an issue with mice for a long time. If she couldn't keep it refrigerated or in airtight containers, she didn't buy it.

Ellison stopped short, looking at the doorframe of the pantry.

"I almost forgot that was there," Katie said, watching her as she traced her fingers over the height marks her mother had made over the years. Katie reached out and tapped one starred entry. "This was the year I was finally taller than Mom."

"Who are these other names?" Ellison asked, peering closely at the fading script.

"My grandparents, my uncle, and my mom. She grew up here, and we moved back in when I was in elementary school when my grandparents' health started to decline."

"And aside from your life in California, has this been your only home since?"

Katie nodded. "It was too much house for Mom by herself before the accident, and after the accident it was too much house for us both," she replied. "But there's no mortgage, and it's the only thing left from my mother's family. My uncle died of a heart attack when I was young, so when my grandparents passed, my mother inherited the house uncontested."

Ellison leaned against the opposite doorframe, looking out at the kitchen as she asked, "Who had the rooster obsession?"

Katie laughed as she imagined what it must look like to an outsider. Every few tiles of the kitchen backsplash featured a rooster—in varying colors and positions—across the entire room. "My grandmother. Bless her heart. I'll have you know I removed all the ones that weren't attached to the wall or nailed down. And it was a significant amount," she said.

Ellison pointed to the faded rooster-print curtains over the sink. "Couldn't part with those, huh?"

Katie shrugged. "The tiny raptors freak me out. I was afraid if I disturbed too much at once, they'd come back and haunt me. Plus, that's an oddly small window, and I'm no seamstress. I'd never be able to find a curtain that fit."

Ellison walked over to the sink, looking out as she said, "Whoa. Tell me we can get outside from here."

"Through here," Katie said with a smile. She knew what Ellison wanted to see. It was the best part of the house by far—her mother's garden.

They stepped out onto the small back porch and onto the flagstone path her mother had slaved over to make just right. Though it was slightly neglected, her mother's garden oasis was still breathtaking.

"This is unbelievable," Ellison said as she looked around the overflowing lush garden space.

"You should see it at night," Katie said, leaning against the large maple that designated the start of the garden area. She pointed to the oblong shaped stones that flanked the flagstone path. "Those are solar LEDs. They light up at night and illuminate the space. Mom spent a lot of time painting them with multiple grays and blues and playing with texture to make them look like actual stones. So they seemingly glow from within when they light up."

"Wow," Ellison said as she walked around the flagstone circle her mother had woven between varying heights of raised earth and flower beds. She stopped at the stone bench Katie had had made for her mother on her fiftieth birthday. Her mother had made that the focal point of the garden, surrounding it with strings of fairy lights that connected back to the maple tree and ran up to the back porch of the house. "This place must be magical at night. Because it's breathtaking during the day."

"I'll send you some pictures of the way it looks at night," Katie said. "Maybe you could use them in the marketing materials."

"Or have me by and let me see it in person," Ellison said, as her eyes traced Katie's face.

"I'd like that," Katie said, because she would. Though she had a feeling Ellison's proposition had nothing to do with gathering marketing photos.

"So would I." Ellison's voice was soft, but her face was unreadable. Katie wanted nothing more than to know what was going on in her head in that moment.

Katie felt that nervous butterfly feeling from before return. The feeling intensified when Ellison stepped closer, reaching out to take her hand.

"This space is fantastic. The house is beautiful and has such a rich history and celebrates the original architecture of the Victorian style. It will sell fast. Are you sure you want to put it on the market?"

Katie looked down at their joined hands, wondering if Ellison usually touched her clients like this. She hoped that wasn't the case. She hoped she was special. Ellison made her feel special, after all. And safe.

Ellison seemed to reconsider their contact, releasing her hand and moving back.

Katie stepped forward and rejoined their hands again before intertwining their fingers. She felt like the decision would be easier if she was touching Ellison.

"I am. I'm ready." She stroked her thumb along Ellison's. "The house needs so much work, though. Do you really think you can fix it up and get top dollar for it?"

Ellison nodded. "The bones are good. Your family clearly loved this home and treated it with reverence. There's a respect for history within those walls. The work will be cosmetic. Some new electrical and plumbing—maybe a roof. Nothing big."

"You make it sound so easy," Katie said.

"It *is* that easy. It's just hard to see it when you're in the thick of it."

"Okay, I trust you."

"Good," Ellison said ducking her head to meet Katie's eyes. "I won't let anything bad happen to you. Or this house. I promise."

"I know," Katie said without hesitation. She looked back at her mother's bench, knowing she'd miss this part of the house the most. "Do you think, maybe, we could just sit here for a while?"

"Of course," Ellison said, guiding her by her hand toward the bench and waiting for her to sit before joining her. "We can sit as long as you'd like."

Katie cuddled up next to her, placing her head on her shoulder as Ellison cradled their hands in her lap. She breathed in the warm spring air and the scent of Ellison's perfume as she looked at all the dazzling colors of her mother's garden. She felt calm in this moment and at peace with her decision. She knew deep down it was the right one. And she also knew that this connection she had with Ellison was bordering on more than friendship. And she was more than fine with that as well.

CHAPTER TWELVE

E llison had been sitting in her car for over five minutes, contemplating what to do next. Which was stupid, because she knew what she had to do next, but she also knew that things felt like they were careening in a different direction than previously planned.

She'd spent the last few days running numbers and calling in favors, and this morning the email she'd been waiting for came in: Zander Alter and his design firm agreed to take on Katie's house reno project as a discounted favor to Ellison, ensuring that Katie would have a bigger piece of the pie when the sale was finalized. And by sheer luck, Ellison had caught Zander between major projects, which meant they could get started right away. Now all she had to do was tell Katie. Which didn't worry her, really. All this meant was that the timeline was going to be accelerated, which would most likely work in both Katie's and Ellison's favor. Katie would benefit from a quick reno and sale, and Ellison would be able to list the house by the end of the summer when the sale prices were still at their highest. Zander promised her he could have the place finished in eight weeks or less. That timeline was perfect in every way.

What wasn't perfect—and what was keeping her in this car, second-guessing herself—was her undeniable attraction to Katie. The businesswoman in her told her to pump the brakes and assign anyone else to this project because the lesbian in her was into Katie *big-time.* And that was a problem because Ellison didn't mix business and pleasure. Well, at least not until the deal was done. Then it didn't matter who she bedded if the conquest happened after the payday. No. She knew better than to get into bed with a client before the sale was secured. And yet she couldn't stop thinking about Katie in very nonplatonic ways.

There had been at least three instances during the house tour that Katie gave her when Ellison found herself too close, too comfortable, and too casual in Katie's presence. Moments that Ellison knew if Katie had taken the touch a step farther, she would have, too. Because Katie had the most incredible smile and the most beautiful mouth. Her laugh was a symphony of sounds that made Ellison's heart sing in all the right ways. And she was so fucking sweet while somehow also managing to be sexy. And smart. Ellison loved that Katie was as smart as she was beautiful. She had a creative approach to problem-solving and processing things, not unlike Ellison's associate Lauren. The pragmatist in Ellison was impressed by that, again and again. There was a whimsy there that intrigued her and enticed her. The fact was Katie was exactly the type of woman Ellison would pursue in any other situation was the problem here. Because Katie was just a handful of signatures away from being her client on paper and not just in theory.

She reached for her coffee, knowing this would be one of many today, since she'd been jarred awake by the early morning construction of Mr. Stetler's place. It had been a long four days of vibrating and pounding noises, and this was only the beginning of what she could look forward to all summer.

She sighed. Sitting here had not helped her sort out her growing feelings for Katie, and she knew she had a mountain of work to get done before the day was over. It was time to leave the shelter of her car and face the world, even though she would rather go home and try to get more sleep. Especially since her dreams seemed to be filled with a charming auburn-haired beauty these days.

Her phone reminder chimed. She groaned. Tonight was the self-imposed deadline she'd set to pick a sperm donor. She'd let herself get distracted by Katie and her house, but she knew part of that was because she was avoiding the sperm thing. She couldn't move forward with Full Circle Surrogacy until she had a fertilized egg to implant into someone. And she wouldn't know if she did until she tried. But she needed sperm. And not reviewing the catalog of potential donors wasn't doing her any favors.

"Go to work. Pick some sperm. Get your life together, Ellison," she said, briefly dropping her head back on the headrest before slinking out of the car. She'd only made it two steps from her car when Pietro's voice ruined her already sluggish and unnecessarily contemplative morning.

"Ellison," he called.

She turned in his direction, not bothering to remove her sunglasses. "Pietro."

"I was hoping you'd had a chance to pass on that proposal to GM Enterprises. I'm eager to hear their thoughts." Pietro was taller than her from his place on the curb, but that height quickly vanished when she stepped onto the surface next to him.

She literally looked down at him when she replied, "It's still in the box where you left it. I'm sure it'll be reviewed shortly."

"Oh," he said, sounding disappointed. "I was hoping they might consider it a priority. Perhaps you can—"

Ellison raised her hand, stopping him. "Rental correspondence is typically reviewed at the end of the week or rental period, which in your case is the first of the month. So I would say it's fair to expect that you'll have some sort of answer around that time."

"Great, thank you," Pietro replied, sounding inconvenienced and ungrateful in Ellison's opinion, but she knew why. He wanted something, and he felt like red tape was standing in his way.

"Have a nice morning," Ellison said with a nod, ending the exchange. She needed to get to her office to make sure the lawyers had updated Katie's paperwork with Zander's most recent renovation projections. This needed to be buttoned up by the weekend if she had any hope of securing Zander's timeline and availability.

She hustled to her office and was glad to see Jax by the front desk when she walked in.

"Jax. You're just the person I was hoping to see," she said.

Jax froze with a half-eaten pink frosted doughnut in their hand. "Oh?"

"Are you busy right now?"

Jax shoved the rest of the doughnut into their mouth, shaking their head.

"It's not that dire. You could have enjoyed those last two bites that you made into one," Ellison said, as she pushed the Nalgene bottle in Jax's direction. "Don't choke. I need you alive for the next few minutes."

Jax laughed after taking a big swig. "Just the next few minutes?"

"No. Of course not. I need you alive for a very long time if you're going to take over my black book someday," Ellison said.

Jax's mouth dropped open comically. "Seriously? That's even an option?"

Ellison pushed Jax's jaw shut. "I'm old. I can't do this forever."

Jax scoffed. "I don't believe that for a second."

"That I'm old? Or that I can't do this forever?"

"Both. Especially the first part. And the second." Jax seemed to consider this. "Honestly, there are flaws in both statements, but I'm too nice to point them out. Because you're my boss."

"And you're afraid of me?"

"Healthily, yes," Jax replied.

"This is why you're my favorite," Ellison said, playfully nudging their shoulder. "Don't tell Trina and Lauren. It'll devastate them."

"Don't tell us what?" Trina asked as she and Lauren sashayed through the door behind them.

"That Ellison is giving me her client list when she retires," Jax replied cheekily.

"Ellison's never retiring," Lauren said, feigning a yawn. "This is fake news."

"She's right. If you were informed otherwise, you've been duped," Trina said with a confident nod.

"You all really want me to work until I'm dead, huh?" Ellison asked with a smile.

"I mean, who else will keep us in line?" Trina asked with a shrug. "It's not like we can be trusted to our own devices."

Lauren nodded. "Speaking of devices, did you see what Super Jax did to Talia's mobile webstore app? This is next level."

Ellison looked at Jax. "You've been working your magic on the app, too?"

Jax's face was flushed in embarrassment. "It's nothing. It needed a little tweaking. All I did was smooth out some wrinkles. No biggie."

"Talia might forgo dating and just propose at this point," Trina said with a sly smile.

Jax looked like they might melt on the spot. "Don't you think that's putting the cart before the hor—"

Lauren clapped. "Oh! Can I be in the wedding party? I've always wanted to be part of the I Do Crew."

"Is that a thing?" Ellison asked.

"It is now," Trina replied. "I mean, it's genius. I might steal it first, Jaxy."

"Is it finally wedding bells time?" Lauren looked at Trina with a gleefulness that was so genuine that Ellison literally *aww*ed.

"I was joking," Trina said, backtracking. "Things are good between me and Kendall. Let's not rush anything."

Lauren rolled her eyes, and Jax looked relieved that they were no longer the topic of wedding conversations. Trina and Kendall were so perfectly paired that it was ridiculous that they hadn't gotten engaged yet. Ellison had even added to the secret wedding pool they had going on behind Trina's back, because she was so confident they'd be on their way to the altar by now.

"What *are* you waiting for?" Ellison asked. "I already lost a hundred dollars to Lauren last month. I was planning on doubling down next time, but this doesn't give me much confidence in winning back my losses."

Trina looked scandalized. "You three have a wedding pool going for me?"

Lauren scoffed. "I mean, the whole office is in on it. We're not the only people invested here."

Trina was speechless, and it occurred to Ellison that she wasn't sure she'd ever seen her that way.

"It's because we love you and we *love* love, and we are just really excited about the open bar at your wedding," Jax added, patting Trina's shoulder.

Trina cocked her head at Ellison as she asked, "You only put a hundred dollar bet on me?"

Ellison raised her hands in defense. "That was just the buy-in amount. I'm about to be in almost a grand if you don't get your ass in gear."

Trina shook her head. "You people are a mess. A mess. Messiest mess I've ever seen."

"But we're your mess," Lauren said, kissing her cheek.

"Ugh. How lucky am I?" Trina asked with a wink. "I'm going to brood in my office about the secret shenanigans no one included me on."

"The shenanigans are literally about you," Lauren reasoned. "Without you there would be no shenanigans."

"This is true," Ellison confirmed.

"Fine. I still love you all." Trina headed toward her office before stopping to add, "But I'm not going to accelerate my engagement plans just because you're on the hook for some money, Ellison."

"I'm not the only one," Ellison challenged.

"Wait, does that mean there *are* actually engagement plans?" Lauren asked as she hurried to catch up with Trina.

"Oh, sweet Jesus," Trina said, shaking her head.

Jax waited until they were out of earshot to ask, "That totally means there are *plans*, right?"

"Oh, definitely."

"Awesome," Jax replied.

"So, before we were hijacked, I was hoping to borrow you for a bit," Ellison said.

"I'm all yours. What's up?"

"I need help organizing and double-checking Katie's file. And I need to scrounge up that letter Pietro submitted to the management company. Have you seen it?" Ellison knew he'd dropped something off, but in the craziness that had been this week, she'd lost track of it. She didn't have an answer for Pietro because she hadn't even opened his envelope.

"On it. Doubly." Jax was already out of sight before Ellison could thank them.

She let out a relieved sigh. She might not have an answer to her growing feelings about Katie, but at least business as usual was running without delay.

Katie sat in the recliner next to her mother's bed, waiting for her to return from her group exercise class.

She looked out the window at the sunny but deceptively chilly spring day before her. Though it was closer to the start of June than

May, it was unusually cold today, and there was a threat of freezing temperatures later tonight. Katie shivered just thinking about it.

Her mind searched for warmer thoughts, and she smiled as she thought of Ellison calling earlier. Ellison had told her about Zander and his design firm, even going as far as to send her some screenshots of his prior work with her and links to his firm's website—as if Katie needed anything other than Ellison's recommendation. She trusted her eye for design and luxury as much as she trusted her and her mother's future to her. There was nothing about Ellison that made Katie hesitate, even for a moment. Which she was realizing was something that she hadn't experienced from a woman before. And though she'd initially ignored Shaina's observations, she had to admit there was validity there. At least on her part.

Thinking of Ellison anytime—even recalling a mostly business conversation on the phone earlier—made Katie feel all warm and fuzzy. Well, warm and *something*, that was for sure. She had no idea if Ellison felt the same way or not. But something about the other night at her house, the way Ellison had looked at her in her childhood bedroom and the way she'd sat with her and held her hand, something about that felt like maybe Ellison was feeling more than friendly feelings for her, too. And that excited the hell out of her.

But it also scared her a little. And not because Ellison was an attractive, successful, kind, and thoughtful *woman*. She was scared because she needed Ellison's help, and the last thing she wanted to do was complicate that with also maybe having romantic thoughts about her. Like kissing her. And wondering how soft her lips would feel against her own. Or how she couldn't help but remember how pert Ellison's nipples were under the massage table sheet. Or how soft yet strong her body had felt under her touch. Things like that. Things that made Katie feel a little bit—okay, a lot bit—gay. And the excitement of that beat the scaredness every time.

But before she could decide what to do with this realization, she had to talk to her mother about the house more seriously. Which she had been avoiding like the plague, but Ellison had moved mountains to find the right architect and designer to get the work done fast and during peak sales season, so she had to stop dragging her feet and woman up. It was time.

"Here she is, Super Mae in all her glory," Dennis said as he wheeled her mother into the room. "She did awesome today."

Her mother smiled when she saw her.

"I love that she greets me that way now."

Dennis nodded. "She's really coming along. I feel like she's more engaged every day."

Katie agreed. Her mother had even been speaking a little bit lately. She nodded from time to time when Katie talked, and she had been speaking, simple words like yes, okay, no, good. And as amazing as that was, it was her nonverbal communication that Katie thought had improved the most. She had started reaching for Katie's hand with her right hand when she was nearby. She squeezed her fingers in response to Katie's words, as if to show she was following along. And her eyes seemed so much clearer now. Sometimes she was still lost, her thoughts seemingly elsewhere. But more and more she seemed to be present, and Katie was thrilled.

"I'll leave you to it," Dennis said with a wave as he slipped into the hall, closing the door behind him.

Her mother smiled at her again.

"Hey, Mom," Katie said as she scooted closer, extending her hand. Her mother took it immediately. "How was your exercise class?"

She nodded. "Good."

Katie felt herself get emotional. She seemed so clear. "Do you like it here?"

She squeezed Katie's fingers. Katie took that as a yes.

"Good." She wiped a tear from her eye with her free hand. "I think I found a way to make sure you can stay here and get the best care you can, Mom."

Her mother held her gaze.

"But I have to sell the house to make that happen." Katie had been dreading this, but this was the last step in the process before she signed on with Ellison. She wouldn't feel right without telling her first.

"I'm working with a wonderful woman who's going to help me fix up the house before it goes on the market, so we can get top dollar for it. I'll be able to pay for anything that you need. Maybe we can even get a smaller place in the future as you get better. Maybe we can live together again if you'd like."

Her mother squeezed her fingers, and Katie let the tears fall uninterrupted.

"Is that okay, Mom? If I sell the house?" Katie felt like she needed to give her mother some say, even if she didn't see any other option.

"Yes," her mom said with a nod. "Okay."

Two words. She'd given Katie the gift of two deliberate words, and Katie's fears melted away. She brought her mother's hand to her lips, grateful.

"We're going to be okay." And for the first time in a long time, Katie believed that.

❖

The drive back to work—and to Ellison's office—was automatic. Which was good because Katie, though relieved by how things had gone with her mom, still felt a little foggy. Her head and heart were a mess of emotions, but she was unafraid of the next step.

She eased her leased Corolla—a car that she'd only been able to afford due to Ellison's generous tip from her massage—into the spot closest to Ellison's Maserati. She'd been joking about the tip being the equivalent of a car payment, but it had been true. And now getting back and forth to work and to visit her mom was significantly easier since she could drive herself again. This was just one more thing she was thankful to Ellison for, it seemed.

She looked around the parking lot as she exited her car. Dusk wasn't far off, and the lot was mostly empty on this unusually cool night. She could see that the spa lights were on, but she wasn't working tonight, so there was no need to investigate who was. She had one goal tonight, and that was to sign everything and anything Ellison put in front of her before she backed out.

A gentle chime sounded as she opened the door to Gamble and Associates. The front desk was unmanned, but she could hear voices coming from Ellison's office.

"I'll check," Lauren said as she popped her head out from Ellison's doorway. "Oh, hey, Katie."

"Hi." Katie took that as an invitation and headed toward her.

"I know you two have a meeting. I'll see myself elsewhere," Lauren said as she pointed every which way.

"Good night, Lauren," Ellison called out.

"Night," Lauren called out as she gave her a wink. "I heard you are signing on with Gamble and Associates. Ellison's the best. You're in good hands."

"Thanks," Katie said as she waved good-bye to her. She closed the distance to Ellison's office, leaning against the doorway to watch Ellison for a moment because she could. And because she looked amazing in that blazer and blouse combination.

Ellison moved a few files around her desk before dropping her pen and looking up at her through long eyelashes. "Hey."

"Hey," she echoed.

Ellison leaned back in her chair, crossing her legs, and Katie got a glimpse of bare skin. Ellison was wearing a skirt today.

"Are we ready to make this official?" she asked.

"Hmm?" Katie was distracted by how high the fabric settled on Ellison's thighs.

"The house. Working together. To sell it," Ellison said, sounding amused.

"Yes. Yeah, totally," Katie said, shaking her head to focus. "Absolutely. I'm ready."

Ellison's light pink lips formed a small smile, and Katie was sure she'd caught her staring.

"I'm ready," Katie repeated as she stepped into the office. "If you are."

"Always," Ellison said, uncrossing her legs and gliding forward in her chair. Katie missed the view of her bare skin immediately. "Sit"— she pointed to the chairs across from her—"get comfortable."

Katie wasn't sure she could since she seemed to be battling butterflies again. What was it about Ellison that made her so delightfully uncomfortable?

"So, I'll walk you through the paperwork, but I can't promise you it won't be boring," Ellison said. Once Katie sat, Ellison stood and joined her on her side of the desk, sitting across from her, their knees almost touching in the process. "We need a few signatures on multiple copies of the same document. One goes with you, and the other is filed here and with the necessary agencies."

"Okay," Katie replied, not concerned in the least. She held up the pen Ellison had handed her. "You point and I'll sign, initial, date, whatever."

"You're so amenable," Ellison said with a smile.

"That's a nice way of calling me easy, isn't it?"

"And somehow, we end back up there, don't we?" Ellison said, referencing the night of her birthday. "Easy isn't a bad thing."

"Then yes, I'm easy. But only for you," Katie replied, instantly regretting the double entendre that she'd walked into. "I mean—"

Ellison held up her hand. "No need. I know what you mean."

Did she, though? Katie sighed. She was tongue-tied, butterflied, and brain-fried with Ellison this close, looking and smelling that good. She should be focused on the forms Ellison wanted her to sign, but she only noticed her lips and the way she smiled so genuinely in her direction. And those eyes. They rivaled the ocean on a clear day. Eyes that were watching her intently right now. Shit. She must have missed something important.

"What?"

"Where'd you go just then?"

Swimming in those perfect oceanic orbs. "Nowhere. You have my full attention."

"Oh, I know I do," Ellison said, her voice velvety soft. "But I still want to know what you were thinking."

"That your eyes are dazzling. They are the bluest blue I think I've ever seen." Katie was candid.

Ellison watched her a moment. "Thank you."

Katie nodded, breaking eye contact because she knew if she didn't, this paperwork would never get signed. She cleared her throat as she shuffled the stack before her. "So, care to translate these for me?"

"Of course." Ellison shifted closer. "Ready?"

"As I'll ever be."

Time flew, and before Katie knew it, she'd been there nearly two hours. A few of Ellison's Realtors had poked their heads in to say good night over the course of their meeting, and Katie was acutely aware that they were alone now.

"Sorry, I had to replace the toner in the machine," Ellison said as she handed an embossed, expensive-looking folder to her. "All your copies of the documents are in here. You'll want to hang on to them in case you need to reference them at any point. If you have questions, though, you can just call or text me, and I'll save you the papercuts of looking back through them."

"Thanks," Katie said, taking the folder and slipping it under her arm. "So that's it?"

"That's it." Ellison powered down her computer. "The next step will be a formal walk-through with Zander and his team to ensure my projections line up with his, and then the demo begins. We'll have movers handle the objects you want to save and put them into storage. Anything you want to go to auction or to be donated will be sorted at that time. Zander's design team will give you a few design options that are neutral and will sell well, which I'm happy to weigh in on, and then they get to work. Once the project is complete, the stagers will come in, and the house will go on the market."

"And sell in a weekend?" Katie said it more to put it into the universe than because she believed it.

"That's the goal," Ellison said as she came to Katie's side of her desk, leaning her hip against it. "I'll start promoting the space as soon as it looks finished. We'll hire a drone photographer for the marketing specs, and I'll start advertising the property to Realtors and agents a few weeks before it goes to market. I'll have that open house packed before the project is even complete, I promise."

Katie didn't doubt that. "Great."

Ellison motioned to her desk as she said, "I'm done here for tonight—are you heading over to work? Or are you done, too?"

"No work today. My only agenda was to see Mom and sign my life away to you," Katie replied.

"How is your mom?"

"She's great. Like, really great. There's been so much progress in such a short period of time. She likes New Beginnings, and she's clearly benefiting from it. I'm glad to know that with the home sale she'll be able to stay there longer," Katie said.

"No pressure," Ellison joked.

"None at all."

Ellison cocked her head to the side as she asked, "Do you want to get coffee with me? I'm done with work for the night, but I have some personal projects to attend to, and I'd rather be caffeinated when I take them on."

"Sure, I'd love that."

"Good," Ellison said as she stood.

Katie waited in the lobby as Ellison finished packing up her briefcase. Her phone buzzed, and she glanced at the screen. It was Shaina. *Are you here? I see the new whip in the parking lot.*

Yes, busy, Katie typed back before slipping her phone back into her bag as Ellison approached.

"Is Starbucks okay?" Ellison asked as she held open the door to the parking lot.

The incoming gust of the wind from outside made Katie gasp. She'd forgotten how cold tonight was supposed to be.

"Fuck," she said as she pulled her jacket tighter around her. "Anyplace with heat that's indoors will suffice."

Ellison laughed, playfully looping her arm around Katie as they walked outside. "I'll keep you warm for the walk across the parking lot."

"Aren't you cold in that?" Katie asked, motioning toward Ellison's long coat, knowing damn well Ellison was only in a skirt underneath. "There's no substance to that thing."

"It's wool. Wool is very warm. Plus, I run hot," Ellison said.

"Well, share some of that hot with me, please," Katie said as she snuggled closer to Ellison, guiding Ellison's hand into her jacket pocket.

"Got that thin California blood still?" Ellison teased.

"I mean, if it means you'll hold me this close while we walk to coffee together, then yes," Katie said, slipping her hand into her pocket.

Ellison intertwined their fingers as she asked, "Is this an elaborate way to get me to hold your hand?"

"It's to ward off frostbite, but the hand-holding certainly doesn't suck," Katie said, bumping her hip.

Ellison laughed as she held open the door to Starbucks, and Katie was sad they'd gotten there so quickly. Especially since they had to disconnect their touch as she walked through the door.

The Starbucks was busy, like it always was. Katie would bet this was the busiest Starbucks in the city. It was one of the few twenty-four-hour ones, and the gym rats next door kept this place bumping at all hours. You could never get a seat, and the wait was never short of ridiculous. She and Shaina had had to resort to using the Starbucks app fifteen minutes ahead of their break just to ensure they could get a coffee and get back before their next clients.

"What would you like?" Ellison asked as Katie headed toward the end of the line.

"Chai tea with milk and honey," Katie replied. "Coffee will keep me up all night, but I need something to warm me now that you're so far away."

Ellison gave her a small smile. "You're flirting."

"Yeah, maybe," Katie replied.

"I'll be right back," Ellison said as she slipped out of sight.

By the time she'd returned to Katie's side, Katie had only moved forward three steps. The line was at a standstill.

"Here, it's piping hot, though, so be careful," Ellison said as she handed Katie a cup.

"How did you do that?" Katie said in disbelief.

"Do what?" Ellison asked as she sipped her own drink.

"Get these drinks." Katie pointed to the teenager in the hoodie in front of her who was nodding his head to whatever was playing in his Beats headphones. "I'm still behind High School here."

"Oh," Ellison said, looking shy. "I'm friendly with this franchise's owner. I never have to wait in line."

"Wow," Katie said, giving Ellison an exaggerated once-over. "I mean, you are incredibly impressive on the regular, but knowing that you have special cut-the-line privileges brings my respect for you to a whole 'nother level."

Ellison laughed.

Katie's jaw dropped as a thought occurred to her. "Did you even have to pay for this?"

"Of course." Ellison paused. "Well, I will."

"When?" Katie had to know.

"At the end of the month. I have a tab."

"Who has a tab at Starbucks?" Katie said, not believing her.

"The woman who collects the rent checks," Ellison said with a shrug. She walked toward a tall two-seater table that had opened and motioned for Katie to sit.

"You're magic. That's it. I cracked it. You're a unicorn under that designer wool, aren't you?"

"I mean, you've seen me in just a sheet, so…" Ellison teased.

"You're right. I didn't notice any horns or hooves, but no one gets a table in here. Ever. You didn't have to wait in line *and* a table suddenly opens up for you and only you? Witchcraft must be at play."

"You're at the table, too. It's not just me. Did you ever think that maybe you're the good luck charm here?"

Katie shook her head. "Never once has a table been available in here. Not ever. And I come in during all hours of the day. Just admit it. You have superpowers."

"Well, I have been accused of melting people," Ellison said, and Katie smiled at the reference to their birthday dinner together. "Speaking of which, are you warmer now?"

Katie had been cradling the cup, savoring the warmth between sips. "Much."

"Good." Ellison leaned back, circling her fingers around the lid of her cup as she did.

"So, what's the personal project that you needed to be on the bean for?" Katie asked.

"Hmm?" Ellison seemed surprised by her question.

"You said you were finished with work but had something to do that was personal. I was just curious what it was." Katie reconsidered her question. "I mean, I'm not trying to pry."

"Sperm."

"What?" Katie nearly choked on her tea.

"I have to look over the donor bank and pick some sperm," Ellison replied.

Katie slow blinked. "I can honestly say that was the last thing I thought you would say right now."

"Me, too," Ellison said, sipping her drink. "But if I plan to move forward with this building a family thing, then I need to purchase a few vials to try to make that happen."

"Does that mean the surrogacy appointment you went to went well?"

Ellison looked surprised again. "You remember that?"

Katie nodded. "I never forget the things my clients tell me when they're naked and vulnerable. They almost always speak their deepest truths in those moments. But you described that meeting as personal, too. So your word choice reminded me."

Ellison seemed to consider this. "They say it takes a village to raise a family, but having infertility of any sort feels deeply isolating. And *personal*. So I guess that's just where my mind goes."

"Can I—?" Katie wasn't sure how to ask the whole question.

"Go ahead," Ellison said, with a wave of her hand. "Ask away."

"How do you decide on what kind of a donor to pick? Like, what criteria do you use?"

Ellison was quiet for a moment. "I suppose you look for qualities that you find attractive. Like someone who's kind. Or thoughtful. Someone who's smart and creative."

"It sounds like you've done this before," Katie noted.

Ellison gave her a small nod. "This isn't my first venture down this path. But it is my last. I have two eggs left, and I've been told those are it for me. So I suppose other qualities that I should be looking for are strong swimmers and plentiful numbers."

Katie laughed at Ellison's sarcasm. "Do you want someone tall?"

Ellison shook her head. "That doesn't matter much to me. I suppose there's a part of me that wants the baby to look like me, if I even get that far. So maybe someone with lighter hair and eyes, I guess. But I'm not super picky about it, no."

Katie used the forefinger and thumb of each of her hands to make a frame around Ellison's beautiful face. "For you I see a strapping multilingual Scandinavian doctor with sandy colored hair and blue eyes who likes to knit in his spare time, when he's not volunteering to walk the elderly dogs at the nearby pet shelter."

"Oh, my. And is he athletic?" Ellison asked, looking fascinated.

"Oh, definitely. Maybe he's a triathlete. Or into crew. He's got nice shoulders and a strong back," Katie replied.

"And how tall is this Norse demigod you speak of?" Ellison asked.

"Six feet, minimum. Probably six two, though. He needs to be taller than you." Katie added, "And he has to be a sharp dresser."

"I'm not sure these sites are *that* specific," Ellison laughed.

Katie waved that off. "That can be taught, I suppose. Taste is acquired, right?"

"Some, surely." Ellison swirled the contents of her cup. "What qualities would you be interested in?"

Katie considered the myriad of men she dated, unpacking their best and worst qualities as she went. "Now that I think about it, the only man who has been in my life who had qualities that I'd maybe want to see in a child is someone I wasn't even romantically involved with." She thought of Billy Balmer, her high school science partner for freshman and sophomore year. "He loved plants and poetry. He was incredibly smart and a total math and science genius who wore dark-rimmed glasses and always had a shoe untied. I'm pretty sure he wouldn't eat orange vegetables because they freaked him out," she said with a laugh. "He was woefully unpopular and had braces, but he was a great listener, and when my father left, he was the only one that understood how it felt to be abandoned. So I guess I'd want a donor like Billy—someone gentle and patient."

"He sounds lovely. Is he still in your life?" Ellison asked.

"No. I haven't seen him in a long time," Katie said, vowing to find him on social media later.

"So that's what you'd look for in a donor. What about in a romantic partner?" Ellison asked.

"I've done the vain, shallow type. It didn't work out. I guess I'm looking for someone like my ideal donor candidate—gentle and patient. But also someone who's smart and kind, funny and sensitive. If full lips and beautiful skin are an option, I'll take that, too."

"Taller or shorter than you?" she asked.

"Taller. I like to look up when I kiss," Katie said, not sure why she added that last part.

"Dark hair or light?"

"I seem to have a thing for blondes," Katie said, holding her gaze.

"He sounds perfect," Ellison said, licking her lips.

"I'm not so sure he's a he," Katie replied softly.

Ellison opened her lips to speak when she was interrupted.

"Late night coffee break?" Shaina's voice sounded to Katie's left.

"Shaina," Katie replied, trying to hide her annoyance at the poorly timed interruption.

"I was wondering who had you so busy," Shaina said. "I see that it's Ellison."

Katie glanced at Ellison, afraid to see the look on her face. She was relieved to see a small smile there.

"It's true. I was completely hogging all her free time. Guilty," Ellison said as she stretched.

"How did you two manage to get a table?" Shaina asked, motioning to the full café behind them. "It's a madhouse in here."

"Just a little luck, I guess," Ellison said as she shrugged on her coat.

"Are you leaving?" Katie asked, reaching across the table to halt her progress. Ellison leaving right now was the last thing Katie wanted.

Ellison gave her a small nod. "You should catch up with your friend. I have catalogs to peruse."

Katie couldn't stop the frown if she tried.

Ellison touched her hand briefly before pulling back. "Thank you for the coffee and the company."

This was not how Katie envisioned the night ending. Not that she'd planned to admit to Ellison that she was developing feelings for her, but now that she'd basically laid it out on the table, she was feeling a little exposed. And confused. Because weren't they sort of having a moment?

"Enjoy your night," Ellison said to Shaina as she started to leave.

"Sit here and don't move," Katie said, shoving Shaina into the now open seat. "We need to talk."

"Okay," Shaina obliged, but Katie barely heard her as she rushed after Ellison.

The icy air hit her lungs with a shattering sharpness. She'd been in such a rush to catch Ellison that she'd left her jacket, like a fool.

She coughed, her throat tight from the cold. "Ellison. Wait."

Ellison turned to face her, and Katie was stunned by how bewitching she looked in that moment. She had the collar popped on her jacket, framing her face, and the dozen or so closed buttons pulling the wool fabric against her tall, lean form made it look like it was tailored to her. The overhead light from the outside of the café shone down like a halo over the golden strands of her hair, which managed to still look flawless despite the sharp wind cutting through the night. But her eyes were what rooted Katie on the spot, bright and vibrant and captivating.

"Where's your coat?" Ellison rushed back to her, rubbing her hands up and down Katie's arms.

"Inside." Katie shook her head, trying to ignore the shivers that swept through her. "I forgot something before. When you asked me about qualities I was looking for in a romantic partner—I forgot to mention generosity of touch. And quiet confidence. And the ability to give me butterflies by just being near me."

Ellison slowed the movements up her arms, and Katie stepped into her space.

"And also, that I'm not looking. Because I think I've already found that person." Katie bit the inside of her cheek to keep her teeth from chattering.

"You're freezing," Ellison said, wrapping her arms around Katie's shoulders.

"I'm warming up by the second," Katie argued, as she shivered.

Ellison leaned in, placing a far too chaste kiss to the edge of Katie's mouth before whispering into her ear, "Next time we have coffee together, let's make it more official."

Katie savored the warmth of Ellison's cheek against hers. "Dinner. A date," Katie corrected. "Have a dinner date with me."

Ellison pulled back, and Katie swooned at the fullness of her lips paired with that smile. "Are you sure?"

"No. The entire thing makes me incredibly nervous and supremely unsure. But I still want to try it. If you're interested. Unless I'm totally misreading all of this"—she motioned between them—"which I could be because there's a lot of big stuff happening in my life at the moment, and yet this is the only thing I can't stop thinking about, and maybe I'm imagining this chemistry I feel between us—"

"You aren't." Ellison's hand found her jaw, silencing her panic. "I would very much like to have a dinner date with you."

"You would?" Katie asked, not quite believing it.

"I would," Ellison said, leaning closer.

Katie felt breathless at how blue Ellison's eyes were. And how full and pink her lips looked. She would bet they were as soft as they looked. She licked her own lips as she imagined feeling Ellison's pressed against her mouth. She watched as Ellison's eyes followed the action, and Katie ached to close the distance between them.

"You're making not kissing you right now sort of impossible," Ellison said, caressing her jaw.

"Then maybe you just should," Katie reasoned, desperate to know if Ellison kissed as well as she dressed. Because that feeling she had in her lower abdomen told her she did and more.

Ellison smiled before rewarding Katie's forwardness with the softest, fullest, hottest kiss she had ever experienced. The contact was electric. Ellison's lips were warm and plump and oh-so-confident against hers. Katie sighed at the warmth of Ellison's hand cupping her jaw and her thumb massaging along her cheek as her lips parted against Katie's, teasing her to follow suit. And Katie did, opening her mouth for Ellison and moaning in ecstasy at the way Ellison deepened the kiss.

Katie felt this kiss everywhere, and as Ellison's tongue glided against hers, she shivered again, but this time not from the cold. She pressed her palms to the front of Ellison's jacket as Ellison's mouth made her start to melt in the most delightful ways. That's when it dawned on her.

"That's how you do it," Katie said, breathlessly pulling back.

"Do what?" Ellison asked, staying close. The heat radiating off her body made Katie mostly forget that she was outside and dangerously underdressed. And the heat Ellison was stirring within her was certainly a delightful distraction as well.

"Make women melt. It's not a charming pickup line. Or even those incredible hugs you give. It's that mouth of yours," Katie said, reconnecting their lips to see if she felt that same electricity a second time. She did, even more than before.

Ellison smiled against her lips. "Mmm, do you feel like I'm making you melt?"

"You're making me feel a lot of things, and melty is certainly one of them." Katie moaned when Ellison sucked on her bottom lip, making her clit throb.

"You should go inside before you freeze," Ellison said, nuzzling her nose.

"If you keep kissing me like that, I'll be an inferno in no time. I promise," Katie replied, not ready to be away from those lips yet.

"Shaina's probably watching," Ellison said as she rubbed her thumb along Katie's jaw.

"I don't care." She didn't. "Do you have to go?"

Ellison surveyed her for a moment, her face unreadable. "I probably should. You've had a day filled with big decisions already, and I don't want to complicate that—"

"By being your amazing self? Because you're failing at that," Katie joked as Ellison rested their foreheads together.

"By giving you more things to stress about," she said.

"Kissing you doesn't stress me out. Picking out an outfit to wear to our dinner date does, but that's a worry for another day." Katie looped her arms around Ellison's neck, standing on tiptoe in the process.

"I'm excited about this dinner you keep talking about." Ellison gave her an easy smile.

"Wait until dessert," Katie replied, connecting their lips once more.

Ellison hummed against her lips, and Katie felt that all the way to her core.

"Go inside. Talk about me with your friend. Just know I'll be thinking about these lips of yours all night," Ellison said, kissing her slowly.

"I'll die out here," Katie said, not moving an inch. "I don't even care."

"Go. It's cold." Ellison put some distance between them, and the absence of her warmth reminded Katie of the unusual brutalness of this spring night. "Text me when you get home."

"I will," Katie said as she stepped toward the café doors. "Good luck tonight."

Ellison adjusted the collar Katie had flattened slightly. "So far it's been the best night I've had in a long time. I don't think I could get much luckier, but thanks."

"Good night, Ellison."

"Night, Katie."

Katie floated inside, pulling the door shut behind her as the wind threatened to take it out of her hands. She walked back to the table, finding Shaina waiting for her with her mouth open in disbelief. And even though Katie knew she was about to be bombarded with a thousand questions that she might not have the answers to, she wasn't worried. Because Ellison Gamble had just kissed her stupid outside of a Starbucks, and life was fucking great.

CHAPTER THIRTEEN

"When did you two—" Shaina started.

"I think we need to talk," Katie blurted out.

"*I* need to talk after that," Shaina said, fanning herself. "Damn, girl. That was some kiss. I can't believe you're alive right now. If someone kissed me like that, I would probably die on the spot."

"I might be dead right now. I can't tell." Katie reached for her jacket, slipping it on before she sat across from Shaina. The internal temperature that Ellison had stoked was still burning hot, but externally she was legit freezing.

"I mean, that goofy grin looks very much alive, but maybe I'm still vicariously living through that Hallmark make-out session I just witnessed." Shaina shook her head. "I leave you alone for one night, and you get a girlfriend and don't tell me. Unbelievable."

"I think I'm going to faint," Katie said, dropping her head to her hands. She felt dizzy.

"Are you okay?"

"Yes. No. I mean, yes in theory. But no. I need help sorting out some shit." Shaina had this incredible ability to put things into perspective, and she needed some perspective right now.

"Is this about the kissing? Because I'm mostly interested in that."

She lifted her head long enough to give Shaina a look. "Yes, it's about the kissing. And the house."

"What about the house?" she asked.

"Well, when you texted earlier, I was in Ellison's office. I finalized the contract to go forward with selling the house."

"Oh," Shaina said with a nod. "I'd forgotten today was the big day. Did you have a chance to see your mom first?"

"I did," Katie replied. "She took it surprisingly well."

"That's a relief, I'm sure."

"It was. Yeah," Katie said. "But it was kind of emotional, too. Like, good emotional, but emotional."

"You mean like that kiss I just saw?"

Katie felt herself blush. "I mean, kind of. Yes."

"Well, get on with it," Shaina said, waving her hand. "Talk it out."

Katie thought for a moment. "The meeting with Mom was emotional because for the first time in forever, I feel like there's some resolution on the horizon. Like, selling the house will secure her future in a way that I never could have. And also, it's like the end of this big chapter in my life. But also, there's a freeing feeling. It's complicated."

"And Ellison?" Shaina asked as she sipped her iced coffee.

"I can't believe you're drinking anything with ice in it. Didn't you see me almost freeze to death out there?" Katie pointed to the dark parking lot on the other side of the glass.

"It's the end of May. Regardless of a cold snap, I refuse to drink anything hot. We're moving into summer, baby." Shaina pointed at her. "Also, you seemed to be plenty warm all wrapped up in Ellison's arms and lips. Which you still need to talk about, by the way."

Katie laughed. "So, there's that part, too, right? Because Ellison has just been so amazing during this whole process, and today at the office was no different. She makes everything so seamless and *easy*. I wasn't worried about signing off on the house sale because a lot of that relief I felt when Mom agreed to the sale was because I knew Ellison would make sure we get the best possible outcome." She toyed with her now lukewarm tea. "I don't know how to explain it. It's like, when she's around, everything seems so much more manageable. Like she calms me. And yet also really excites me, too."

"There it is," Shaina said with a clap. "Finally."

"Finally, what?"

"You finally admitting that you two are totally into each other. I mean, the kissing sort of told that same story with way fewer words, but I'm glad you're aware of it now."

Katie rolled her eyes. "I didn't deny it before. I just wasn't sure."

"Oh, because you had your straight girl goggles on, you mean," Shaina teased.

"It's not like I have extensive experience flirting with women," Katie said in defense. "She might have just been really nice. You know?"

"I mean, no. I don't know. Because I've never seen her once look at you like I look at pretty girls—like they're people that exist in a space, and not people I want to bone. But I mean, whatever."

"She does not look at me that way," Katie argued.

"She did tonight under that spotlight," Shaina said.

"That was tonight," Katie replied.

"That's every time since she drove you home and you two have been in my presence, but okay." Shaina gave her a playful smile. "I'm just teasing you. I think it's great. She's gorgeous, and clearly she has excellent taste because you're great, too."

"Thanks," Katie said, finishing her tea.

"So, tell me the truth. Was that kiss as hot as it looked? What was it like? Will there be more kissing? Can you tell me when and where, so I can watch again? Because that made my whole freaking night."

Katie laughed. "I can say with all honesty that you witnessed the best first kiss of my life. Hands down."

"I knew it," Shaina cheered. "That makes me feel much better about being a voyeur."

Katie let her mind wander to the way Ellison's lips felt against hers. They were as soft and luscious as they looked, and Katie wanted to feel and taste them again. Soon.

"So, will there be more kissing?" Shaina asked.

"I hope so," Katie said, making a note to text Ellison tonight. "I have a feeling that was just a taste of the kind of kissing she is capable of. And I can tell you I'm already hooked."

Shaina gave her a broad smile. "I know today was a heavy emotional day in a lot of ways, but I'm excited for you. This is exciting stuff, Katie Cat. All of it."

"It is, isn't it?" Katie glanced down at the table as her cell buzzed. It was a text from Ellison.

Thank you for tonight and for following me out into the cold.

Katie smiled as she replied. *Thank you for keeping me warm and for melting me with that kiss.*

Ellison sent a kissing emoji with the words *Chat soon?*

Yes, please. And maybe more kissing, too. With chatting. But also kissing, Katie replied.

I think we can make that happen.

"Damn, you two are super cute. Like it's ridiculous," Shaina said from over her shoulder, and Katie covered her phone screen.

"Spy," she said as she flipped over her phone.

"I said like three things to you right now. You were just in Lustville, USA, not hearing a word. So I figured Ellison must be flirting." Shaina pointed to her phone. "I wasn't wrong."

"You weren't," Katie said, leaning back into her seat, feeling all warm and fuzzy as her body temperature finally seemed to normalize.

"Just like I said, exciting stuff," Shaina said with a stretch. She yawned. "I have to head home, but I expect updates."

Katie saluted her. "Will do and same. I'm exhausted."

"I bet you are," Shaina said with a knowing smile. "You going home alone? Or to Ellison's?"

Katie scoffed. "Alone. Obviously."

Shaina shrugged. "It was worth asking. But don't think I don't know you'll be thinking about her all night."

"Oh, I'm sure I will," Katie replied honestly.

Shaina just smiled. "Go home, you nut."

"See you tomorrow?"

"You bet."

❖

Ellison's heart was racing. Her palms felt sweaty as she gripped the leather, so she tightened her grasp on the steering wheel to maintain control.

She glanced at the speedometer and contemplated slowing down, but that thought quickly passed. She knew the Maserati could handle the high speeds, and she trusted her own reaction time—what she wasn't so sure about was what she'd see when she got to Katie's house.

She'd only been asleep about an hour when the call came in. The insistent vibrating on the bedside table woke her up instantly, but she was completely unprepared to see Katie's name on the screen. And though she wasn't alarmed by that per se, the sounds on the line did scare her—Katie was sobbing, and there were sirens in the background. There'd been a fire.

She slowed as she pulled into Katie's neighborhood. She could see the flashing lights and emergency response vehicles from the end of Katie's street, blocking her view of the house. She pulled over and was out of her car in a flash, jogging toward the chaos and past sleepy onlookers in bathrobes and slippers.

A police officer stopped her on the sidewalk in front of Katie's house. She could see remnants of smoke coming out of Katie's bedroom window. Panic started to seep in.

"You have to stay back, miss," the cop said, holding up his hand.

Ellison ignored him, waving to the familiar face beyond him as she shouted, "Sasha!"

Captain Sasha McCray of Boston's Engine Company 28 adjusted her helmet as she looked in the direction of Ellison's call. Ellison had never been so relieved to see the dark-haired firefighter and long-term girlfriend of her philanthropic friend Abby Rossmore than she was right now. She knew Sasha would help.

"Ellison?" Sasha trotted over to her. "What are you doing here?"

"Katie called me. The homeowner, she's a friend. Is she okay?" Ellison was afraid to ask as a huge puff of smoke came from Katie's bedroom window.

"She can come through," Sasha said to the police officer as she lifted the caution tape for Ellison to slip under.

"Where is she? Is she okay?" Ellison scanned the many faces of the first responders, but Katie was nowhere to be found.

"She is. She's over there at the bus." Sasha pointed toward the ambulance at the end of Katie's driveway, and Ellison's stomach dropped.

"Oh God," Ellison said, covering her hand with her mouth.

"It's okay. She's going to be okay," Sasha said as she took her elbow, guiding her past the emergency personnel standing around. "She's smart. If she hadn't acted as quickly as she did, the whole house probably would have gone up."

Ellison meant to reply but her eyes were locked on the bandages the EMT was wrapping around Katie's forearm. Katie was reclined on the stretcher with an oxygen mask on, her eyes wet with tears as she nodded in response to something the EMT was saying to her.

"What happened?" Ellison asked, standing just out of Katie's sight.

"A space heater in the bedroom shorted the wiring, and the outlet caught fire. Katie managed to control most of the fire with some blankets until we got here to put it out, but she got a few burns in the process."

Ellison felt sick. "That must have been terrifying."

Sasha nodded. "I'm sure. But like I said, she probably saved the house. The wiring is a mess in there, and the house would have gone up like a match if she hadn't called us and tried to stop the spread. She's a total shero."

"Ellison," Katie called out, and Ellison ran to her.

"Hey," Ellison said, putting her hands up to slow Katie's descent from the ambulance. "Are you supposed to be coming out of there?"

"She can go," the short-haired EMT said in a gruff voice. She added, "Just watch that arm."

Katie took Ellison's hand and gingerly stepped down from the back of the ambulance before crumpling into her arms.

"I'm sorry. I didn't know who else to call. I know it's late," Katie gasped between sobs.

"Shh. It's okay. You did the right thing. I'm glad you called," Ellison said as she tightened her embrace around her. She kissed the side of her head as she rubbed her back. "Shh, it's okay. You're okay."

Katie cried against her chest. "The house. I'm so sorry. It's all my fault."

Ellison shook her head. "What about the house? It's no one's fault. Sasha here tells me you saved the block by trying to put the fire out with your arm. Though not the wisest approach, it does seem to have worked some."

Katie laughed then coughed. "Ouch. Don't make me laugh."

Ellison pulled back to look at her. "Are you hurt somewhere else?" She brushed the hair off her forehead and searched her face. She had some black specks round her nose and what looked like soot along her cheek. But besides the tears, her face appeared fine.

"She has a little smoke inhalation, and she's a little bruised. So she'll need to rest those lungs a bit," Sasha added.

"So no laughing," Katie said, poking Ellison in the stomach.

"For me or you?" Ellison teased, glad that Katie was okay. Katie gave her a look, and she pulled her close again. "I'm glad you're okay."

Katie nodded against her shoulder. "But the house, Ellison. It's ruined."

"It's a house. It can be fixed." Ellison turned Katie's view away from the debris being tossed out of the second-floor window. "You are irreplaceable. The house is not."

"But the sale—" Katie tried.

"I'll worry about the house. You worry about that arm." She stepped back, holding out her hand. "Let me see it."

Katie raised her arm with a wince. The UC Santa Barbara sweatshirt she had on was covered in soot and damp with water. The sleeve of her left arm had been cut away above the elbow, but Ellison could see bloodstains along the inside of Katie's left torso. Katie's forearm was bandaged from the wrist to just below the elbow.

"Does it hurt?" she asked as she cradled Katie's hand.

"A little. But I'm sure it'll hurt a lot more tomorrow when the endorphins wear off." Katie intertwined their fingers before groaning and releasing her hold on Ellison's hand. "Okay, that hurt."

"No holding hands. Got it," Ellison said.

"I have this hand. This one still works," Katie said, holding it toward her.

Ellison took it with a smile. "Well, that's a relief."

"I didn't realize you were seeing anyone," Sasha said. "Abby usually tells me all the juicy gossip. Which means this is either super new or you've been keeping secrets."

Katie looked between them. "You know each other."

Ellison smiled. "The queer world is small."

"How small?" Katie asked adorably.

"Small-small." Ellison teased, "Are you jealous?"

"Maybe." Katie wiped at her cheek, smudging the soot a little. Ellison was glad to see some levity in her face.

Sasha laughed. "Ellison is a very generous donor to my girlfriend's family's nonprofit. And she's a good friend." Sasha held up her hands. "That's all, I promise."

"I meant to tell you—congrats on your promotion, by the way," Ellison said. She turned to Katie to catch her up. "Sasha is the youngest female fire captain in Boston's history."

"Thanks," Sasha said, giving her signature playful grin. "I'll tell Abby you send your regards."

"Please do," Ellison replied. "Oh, when do you think we'll be able to get back inside?"

Sasha frowned. "We have to make sure it's safe. Once the fire marshal clears the scene, you can send in your insurance adjuster. But you're going to need some structural review, too. So be prepared for that."

Katie's eyes got big, and Ellison squeezed her hand. "We'll call the insurance company in the morning, and Zander will figure out all the structural stuff."

"Any chance I can grab my toothbrush? Or how about some shoes?" Katie asked, looking overwhelmed. Ellison glanced down at her lower half for the first time—she was in loose-fitting sweatpants that were equally as dirty and wet as her sweatshirt, but her feet were bare.

Sasha hesitated. "You can't go back in there. They're still tossing debris."

Katie looked like she might get sick.

"But I tell you what," Sasha offered, "why don't you tell me where some of the stuff you need is, and I'll throw as much into a bag as I can fit. Cool?"

Katie looked relieved. "Thanks."

"Don't tell anyone, though." Sasha leaned in to whisper, "I'm only doing this because Abby is going to ask Ellison for a shit-ton of money next quarter, and she's hoping for a blank check."

Ellison laughed. "Get her shoes, and I'll seriously consider it."

Sasha gave her a thumbs-up.

Ellison dialed Sasha's number and handed the phone to Katie. She walked back to the ambulance to borrow a blanket for Katie, as Katie talked Sasha through the rooms. In less than five minutes, Sasha returned with a gym bag from Katie's closet, overflowing with items including Katie's sneakers and the winter jacket that Ellison overheard her tell Sasha was just inside the front door.

"Thank you," Katie said, reaching for the bag.

Ellison intercepted it, slinging it over her shoulder. "I'll take this."

Katie braced herself on Ellison's shoulder as she slipped her sockless feet into her sneakers. Ellison draped her jacket over her shoulders when it became apparent that Katie was not getting that bandaged arm into the snug-fitting sleeve.

"So, you won't be able to stay here tonight. I'm sorry," Sasha said with a frown. "And we're going to be here for a bit to make sure everything is out inside. So heading to a hotel for a few nights isn't a bad idea. I'll make sure they get the place checked and cleared ASAP. We'll have someone call you when it's safe to come back."

"I really appreciate all your help," Katie said, looking tired.

"I'll call Abby in the morning about that check," Ellison said with a wink.

"Sounds good. Nice to meet you, Katie. I'm sorry it isn't under better circumstances," Sasha said.

"Me, too. But thanks again. For everything."

After Sasha walked away, Katie looked back up at the house. She shook her head with a heavy sigh. "I can't believe this is my life right now."

"Come on, let's get out of here," Ellison said, taking her hand again.

Katie looked back at her with fresh tears in her eyes. "Where do I go from here?"

"To bed. I have a guest room that is desperate for a purpose outside of storing my old files. You can stay with me while we figure out the house thing. Rest. Recover. Tomorrow is another day. We'll tackle the big stuff then." Ellison tried to reassure her.

"Bed sounds nice," Katie said with a yawn.

"Let's get you cleaned up and in fresh clothes and tucked in," Ellison replied.

"Yes, please."

Chapter Fourteen

Katie loved Ellison's heated seats. They were toasty warm before she even got in the car, and now that she was nestled into them, they were lulling her to sleep. She glanced out the window at the empty streets and bright streetlights when something occurred to her.

"Where are we going?" she asked.

"My place," Ellison replied.

"Which is nowhere near where I live, it seems," Katie pointed out.

"Hmm?"

"You told me driving me home those times was no big deal because I was on the way to your place," Katie replied. "This is the exact opposite direction of my house."

"Oh," Ellison said, looking bashful. "I lied."

"You lied?"

Ellison nodded. "Your house was not on the way to mine."

"I can see that," Katie said with a laugh. "So why *did* you offer to drive me, then?"

"Because you needed a ride. And I enjoy your company," Ellison replied matter-of-factly.

"Do you still enjoy my company? Even after I got you out of bed in the middle of the night to rescue me?"

"Especially because of that," Ellison said, smiling at her sweetly as they pulled up to a light. "And I already told you not to worry about that. I'm happy to help."

"You say that now, but what if I like your guest room so much I never leave and become a squatter. What then?" Katie asked.

"I'm sure my limited domestic skills will drive you out long before that happens."

"Are you messy?"

Ellison gave her a look. "Do I strike you as messy?"

"Not at all. I bet your place is clean enough to eat off the floors," Katie said, smiling for the first time tonight at the thought of Ellison cleaning the house.

Ellison scrunched her nose. "I have cleaners, and they came by today. So you're right."

"I'm very intuitive," Katie teased. She looked up at the building they were approaching slowly. "Where are we?"

"Home," Ellison said as she eased into the brick-paved front of a luxury condominium.

"Well, damn." Katie wasn't sure what to say. It made perfect sense that Ellison lived in a fancy apartment building. She'd just never considered it before.

A gentle-faced valet opened Katie's door, startling her.

"Sorry, miss."

"It's okay," she said as she took the white gloved hand he offered to help her out.

In a moment Ellison was by her side, taking her uninjured hand and guiding her toward the entrance. Katie looked back at the car to grab her bag, but she could see Mr. White Gloves carrying it for her.

She rode the elevator in silence as Ellison made small talk with Mr. White Gloves, who it appeared was also known as Pavel.

Pavel held open the door of the elevator when they got to Ellison's floor and took Ellison's keys to open her apartment before placing Katie's gym bag in the foyer. In a flash, he was gone, and they were all alone in the most expensive-looking apartment Katie had ever stepped foot in.

"Come in, get comfortable. Let me get you something to drink. Are you hungry?" Ellison shrugged off her jacket, hanging it in the closet next to the front door before helping Katie shrug off the one draped over her shoulders.

"Um, I think I just really want to wash my face." She looked down at her clothes and sighed. "And maybe get changed."

"Of course. I'll take you to the guest room." Ellison scooped up her bag and waited for Katie to join her. "Your room is right through here. Just off the kitchen if you change your mind. I'll make a quick snack just in case."

Katie followed Ellison into the spacious guest room. The walls were off-white, and the queen-sized bed looked plush and welcoming. Ellison placed the bag on the bed as she shuffled some files off the duvet and into a box. Katie watched as she moved the box next to a small desk on the far side of the room, before tidying the surface a bit.

"I sleep in a tiny ball on my side," Katie said. "You can leave the files. I don't want to screw up your life."

"You aren't. And you don't have to share the bed with old charitable donation documents." Ellison flicked on the bedside lamp before walking to the far left of the room. "This is your en suite. It's nothing fancy, but you'll have it all to yourself."

"Your guest room has an en suite?" Katie asked.

"It does. But it only has a shower. If you want to take a bath, you'll have to use the hallway bathroom. Or the soaker in my en suite. Which is far superior to the hallway tub, if you want my opinion."

Katie laughed. "I'm too tired to do anything more than towel off my face right now, but thank you."

"I totally get that." Ellison reemerged from inside the bathroom with a stack of fluffy white towels. "There's soap and face wash in the linen closet behind the door here, and I think I even have a couple of toothbrushes if Sasha wasn't able to find yours. Whatever you need, just make yourself at home."

"Thanks."

Ellison hesitated before saying, "I'll be just out there in the kitchen if you need me."

"I'll be okay," Katie replied. Ellison was looking at her bandage and seemed anxious about leaving her. "I promise."

"Okay. But if not, just call out, and I'll come right back," Ellison added before slipping out the door and closing it behind her.

Katie looked at the bag on the bed and felt the emotion bubble up inside her chest. She'd been so freaked out by everything that had happened. She wasn't even sure what she'd asked Sasha to grab for her.

She sat on the comfy duvet and slowly unpacked the contents of the bag. She was surprised by how much she found in there. Sasha had grabbed her laptop and charger, the clothes she'd left in the dryer on the first floor but had never bothered to fold, a fleece hoodie from the downstairs closet, the products from the upstairs bathroom counter, including her toothbrush and night retainer, and the extra cell phone charger she kept on the kitchen counter.

She reached into her pocket, wincing at the condition her cell phone was in. The glass front was cracked, and the bottom left of the screen was completely blacked out. This was the only thing she'd managed to get out of her bedroom before they'd ushered her out of the house. But it must have been damaged at some point during the fire or the evacuation. She wasn't quite sure. It was mostly a blur.

She grabbed the wrinkled pajamas she was glad she'd forgotten in the dryer and headed into the bathroom. She nearly dropped her toothbrush when she saw herself for the first time. Her eyes were red from crying and her tear-streaked cheeks were smoky and dirty. Her hair was a frizzy mess, and she looked as exhausted as she felt.

"Wow," she said to her reflection. "You look like shit."

The linen closet was full of travel-sized products of all kinds. She pulled out a bar of soap and some toothpaste that looked like less work than trying to squeeze out the final dollop from the Tom's brand Sasha rescued from her bathroom.

After some vigorous one-handed washing and primping, she felt almost human. Damn, this left arm hurt to move. As she pulled off the ruined sweatshirt and sponge-bathed her naked chest and neck, she glanced down at her body. She had a significant bruise forming along her left flank that she'd forgotten about. The EMT had noted it in the ambulance, but it hadn't hurt at the time. Now that she was looking at it, though, it ached, like her arm. She still wasn't sure where it had come from, but she was too tired to try to figure it out. She grabbed an equally wrinkled pajama shirt to pair with her plaid pants and was glad it was a loose fitting T-shirt. She had no idea how she was ever going to get this Frankenstein monster's mummy-wrapped arm in a sleeve.

When she finally exited the guest room, she found Ellison perched on a stool at the kitchen island. She had two mugs of something steaming in front of her and a plate of fresh cut fruit.

"Hey," Katie said as she approached.

Ellison turned and smiled. "You look great."

"I look like I'm wearing the pajamas I forgot were in the dryer from last week's laundry day, but I don't think I smell like smoke as much," she said as she looked up. "No promises about the hair, though."

She lifted her bum arm with a wince. "I didn't want to get my bandages wet."

"We can wash your hair in the sink tomorrow if you want. I'll help," Ellison offered. "Here, I made some caffeine-free tea. And cut some fruit. I can also make you some toast, but you're soon going to exhaust my kitchen talents."

Katie laughed. "I doubt that you can't cook. There isn't anything you can't do, is there?"

Ellison smiled as she sat beside her. "I'm terrible at folding the fitted sheet on a bed. The worst."

Katie scoffed as she sipped the delightful chamomile tea. "Lucky for you the tea is perfect—otherwise that little factoid would certainly drive me out."

Ellison pushed the fruit plate toward her. "The EMT told me to feed you and give you some pain meds. She told me that you'd be feeling awful right about now. What do you think? Ready for some Tylenol?"

Katie nodded. "Yes, please."

"Be right back."

She nibbled on the strawberries and blueberries from the plate as she looked around. Ellison had a chef's kitchen with the highest end appliances and furnishings, everywhere she looked. The white marble countertop before her was almost as massive as the dining table just off the kitchen that could easily seat twelve. The place was large and luxurious, but Katie was surprised by the warmth here, too. Ellison had photographs and paintings all throughout the walls. Her living room—which was just beyond the dining area—had a plush, soft-looking sofa and a love seat, with two comfortable-looking side chairs that faced the large, flat-screen television that was mounted above a gas fireplace. Though the curtains were drawn, Katie had a feeling that beyond them was a beautiful view of the city, one she was sure would flood the living room with light in the morning.

"Your place is incredible," she said as Ellison returned with a bottle of pills.

"Thank you," she said as she grabbed Katie a glass of water. "It's probably more than I need, but I like the retreat it offers me from life. I feel like an island up here by myself, and in a lot of ways that's comforting."

Katie took the pills Ellison offered her and chased them with a swig of cold water. Ellison sat quietly beside her, and before she knew it, she'd finished the fruit plate and the Greek yogurt that magically appeared by her side.

"I guess I was hungry after all," she said, sagging in her seat as the fatigue settled heavily on her shoulders.

"It's late," Ellison said as she cleared their empty cups and plates. "Let's get you to bed."

Katie yawned before following Ellison to the door of the guest room.

"I'm just down the hall," she said as she pointed to the slightly ajar door. "Call out if you need anything."

"Thank you," Katie said.

"You can stop thanking me," Ellison replied. "Just get some sleep."

"Okay," Katie said as she reached for her. "Wait."

Ellison looked at her, and Katie felt that emotion from before stir in her chest. She tried to stifle it, but Ellison must have noticed it before she could.

"Come here," Ellison said as she opened her arms. Katie stepped into them, glad to feel Ellison's embrace again. "I'm glad you're okay. You really had me worried."

"Me, too. And ditto," Katie said against Ellison's collarbone.

Ellison placed a kiss on her temple, and Katie shifted to connect their lips.

The kiss was gentle, almost cautious. Katie nodded in understanding. "I'm not trying to start anything, nor do I expect anything. I just…I just needed to be reminded of the good part of tonight, just a little."

Ellison stroked her cheek. "Kissing you is never a burden. You can remind yourself on my lips anytime."

"Good." Katie cuddled close, grateful for Ellison's world-class hugs. She didn't want to be out of these arms. Especially not tonight. She looked up at Ellison and scanned her face as she asked, "Can I sleep with you tonight? I don't want to be alone."

Ellison didn't hesitate. "Of course."

She took Katie's hand and led her down the hall. Ellison's room was spacious with a sitting area off to the left by the large floor-to-ceiling windows. There was a fan above her king-sized bed that hummed quietly, circulating the air slowly. The bed was like the guest room's, though larger and somehow more luxurious looking. The duvet was fluffy and white with matching pillows in embroidered cases. Ellison's bed looked like a fancy hotel bed you'd see in ads for a destination vacation in Bali.

"Make yourself comfortable," Ellison said as she rested her hand on Katie's hip. "I'm going to freshen up, but I'll be quick."

Katie watched Ellison as she opened a massive walk-in closet and pulled out a silk robe. She carried the garment into the en suite bathroom that, from Katie's vantage point, looked to be as large as the entire guest room. She could see the edge of Ellison's soaker tub, but the glittering chandelier above it was what caught her attention. She could say in all honesty that she'd never seen a chandelier in a bathroom before.

Ellison disappeared behind the door, and Katie sat at the edge of the bed, unsure of what to do with herself now. She looked toward the left bedside table. She assumed this was Ellison's preferred sleeping side since there was a book and a glass of water there.

She ran her hand along the smooth surface of the matching table next to her, admiring the construction, when the bathroom door opened, startling her. She groaned in pain, gripping her side.

"Sorry, I didn't mean to frighten you." Ellison rushed to her.

"It's okay," Katie said, cradling her side. "I'm just waiting for the Tylenol to kick in."

Ellison stood over her, looking concerned. "Why are you holding your side? What's wrong?"

Katie shrugged. "I think I bruised it. It'll be fine, I'm sure. I'm just tired."

Ellison was having none of that. "Lie back, let me see."

"I'm fine. I just spooked a bit. I'm jumpy, I guess." Katie didn't want to be any more of a bother than she already was.

Ellison helped her up and made short work of the comforter, pulling it back with the sheet and motioning for Katie to get in. "Lie down."

Katie did as she was told, gingerly scooting up the bed until she rested on one of the many pillows Ellison had around. She watched as Ellison discarded the silk robe she was wearing, exposing a soft-looking tank top and loose-fitting sleep bottoms. But hers weren't flannel like Katie's—these were some fancy pants, cashmere maybe. Whatever the fabric was, Katie could tell they were as smooth as silk and softer than anything she'd ever felt.

"Can I?" Ellison knelt beside her with her hand on the hem of Katie's shirt. Katie could tell Ellison was braless by the sheerness of her top. She let her eyes linger there for a moment.

"Are you going to overreact?" Katie asked, resting her good hand on Ellison's. "Because if you are, then no."

Ellison frowned. "That means there is something to be concerned about under this shirt, and not only are you aware of it, but that you'd rather conceal it."

"*Conceal* feels sneaky. Maybe *not make a big deal out of it* is a better explanation of my actions," Katie reasoned.

Ellison gave her a look. She sighed and nodded, closing her eyes as she felt the fabric slide up to just under her ribs.

"Katie…" Ellison's voice was filled with worry.

"Are you overreacting?" Katie asked, keeping her eyes closed.

"Are you underreacting?" Ellison challenged.

Katie felt the coolness of Ellison's touch against the hot bruise. It felt nice.

"Did the EMT see this?" Ellison caressed along her side.

"She did. She told me I might have a bruised rib or two and that I should see my PCP ASAP." Katie opened her eyes to find Ellison studying her face.

"We can call them tomorrow." Ellison watched her.

"Tomorrow is another day, right?" Katie parroted Ellison from earlier.

"It is," she said with a small smile. She went to pull down Katie's shirt, but Katie stopped her.

"That feels nice. It's making the heat and ache recede a bit. Can you—?"

Ellison nodded. "Get on your side."

Katie sat up first, her rib cage screaming in defiance. She tried to prop herself up on her left elbow, but that howled as well, and she cringed in pain.

"Lie back," Ellison said, pressing against her collarbone gently.

"But I want to remember again," Katie said, looking at her lips.

"I'll come to you," she said, and Katie settled back.

Ellison maneuvered the blankets over them, bracing herself on her elbow as she leaned forward and connected their lips.

Katie sighed against Ellison's lips, grateful for the affection and distraction. Ellison kissed her slowly, but Katie wanted more. She opened her mouth, tentatively licking along Ellison's bottom lip until Ellison's tongue danced with hers.

Ellison's hand was at her jaw again, like before, caressing her cheek and angling her mouth to deepen the kiss. Katie loved how passionately yet tenderly Ellison kissed. She had this wonderful way of sucking and licking while teasing at Katie's lips that had Katie lifting off the bed once more, just to get closer.

"Easy," Ellison said against her lips. "There will be plenty of kissing if you want. But you have to take it easy tonight."

Katie hated this idea. "My ribs and arm don't hurt when my lips are busy."

Ellison laughed, sucking on her bottom lip briefly before adding, "And yet you're also not going to get better if you keep resisting rest. And I need you better."

"Why's that?" Katie asked as she reconnected their lips.

Ellison kissed away from her mouth to nibble on her ear as she whispered, "Because you make me want to do a lot more than just kiss you, and that's not going to happen until you're less bruised and bandaged."

Katie moaned at the feeling of Ellison's lips on her earlobe and the promise of her words.

"I want that," Katie replied. All of that.

"Then rest," Ellison said, nuzzling her earlobe. "And I'll make it worth the wait."

Katie let out a shaky breath. Partly because her breathing had picked up and her rib cage was burning, and because the anticipation of *anything* Ellison wanted to share with her was, well, breathtaking.

"Roll to your side. Let's get you propped up with pillows and get you some rest." Ellison pressed one last kiss to her lips before pulling back.

"Fine. But only because I'm a guest in your house."

"And my bed," Ellison noted.

"Do you mind that?" Katie asked, curious.

"Not at all. I would have told you if I did," Ellison replied. "Truthfully, I'm glad to have you close. I feel better knowing I can keep an eye on you."

"Because you're afraid I'll burn your house down, too?"

Ellison brushed a hair off Katie's forehead as she replied, "Because I like it better when you're with me than when you aren't."

Katie smiled. "Okay. Fine. Sleep now. More kissing later, though. Okay?"

"Okay," Ellison said as she helped Katie onto her side.

After a few moments of shuffling pillows, Ellison had Katie resting on her right side, with her bandaged arm cradling a pillow. To her delight, Katie felt Ellison scoot up behind her, spooning her. Her hand slipped under Katie's shirt again, gently caressing along the tissue around the bruise, and Katie felt herself start to relax into Ellison's touch and the warmth of the bed.

"Thank you for everything," Katie said, closing her eyes at the gentle, rhythmic strokes.

"Good night, Katie."

CHAPTER FIFTEEN

Ellison shifted, groggy from sleep when the humming began nearby. She blinked as the insistent noise increased slightly. What time was it? She reached for her cell phone, but her progress was halted by the weight on her chest.

Katie was asleep in her arms as she had been for most of the night. She'd struggled after the first few hours of sleep on her right and only seemed to be peaceful when Ellison held her. Which meant Ellison hadn't slept particularly well, but she wasn't bothered by it. She'd messaged Jax during the night to reschedule her day, so she knew she'd have the chance to catch up on sleep. Plus, the company was nice. She'd forgotten how much she enjoyed touching and being touched by someone.

The humming escalated again, and this time there was a banging sound every few moments. Ellison internally groaned. Fucking Mr. Stetler and his fucking construction. They'd gotten barely any sleep last night, and the last thing she wanted was for Katie to wake up to the sounds of a jackhammer the night after a trauma.

Katie stirred in her arms, cuddling closer. Her hand slipped underneath Ellison's tank top and rested on her stomach. Ellison closed her eyes at the sensation. She'd been honest with Katie last night. She did want to do more than just kiss her. Sure, this wasn't the time, but it wasn't like she could just shut off her attraction to her.

Katie shifted again, murmuring in her sleep. Her hand moved up, and Ellison's breath caught as it settled just beneath her breast. Katie's hand was warm—that sleepy kind of warm that comforts but also excites. Ellison looked down at her. Katie was so beautiful. She had that faintest dusting of freckles on her nose and long red-brown eyelashes. Her complexion was fairer than Ellison's, and she had the luscious thick auburn hair that Ellison constantly wanted to thread her fingers through. She was as exquisite asleep as she was awake.

An intrusive banging sound from behind Ellison's headboard caused Katie to jerk in her sleep. Ellison bit the inside of her cheek when Katie's palm found its way to her breast. She squeezed her eyes shut trying to think of anything other than the delicious weight of Katie's hand on her chest, but she was failing miserably.

Thankfully, a louder bang—this one so aggressive that it shifted the picture on the wall to the left of the bed—jarred Katie awake. Which was fine, except she sleepily massaged Ellison's breast as she woke up, which was not helpful. At all.

"Ugh," Katie whined, burying her head into Ellison's shoulder. "What is that banging?"

"Construction in the unit next door," Ellison replied. "I'm sorry it woke you."

"I'm not really awake," Katie said, not bothering to open her eyes. "You are the softest person I've ever slept on."

Ellison's laugh was cut short when Katie flexed her fingers. She attempted to stifle the reflexive moan, but she wasn't as successful as she hoped.

Katie lifted her head with a start, her eyes wide as the realization set in. "Oh my God. Ellison. I'm so sorry."

Katie's hand was off her chest and almost out of her shirt by the time she stopped it. She pressed against the back of Katie's hand through her shirt, holding Katie's palm against her abdomen. "It's okay. I didn't mind."

Katie blushed. "Well clearly, *I* didn't mind since I was having the best dream of my life, and blissfully unaware that I was also groping you."

Ellison traced circles through the part of her shirt that Katie's hand was under. "What kind of dream was it?"

Katie looked up at her. "Um, I'm not really sure. But I know it was a good one, and I remember waking up just now feeling satisfied and happy."

"Well, in that case, I'm glad my breast helped you achieve dream nirvana."

Katie buried her head into Ellison's shoulder. "I'm so embarrassed. I don't think I can even look at you. Ever. Just leave me here to die."

"In my bed? On these sheets?" Ellison scoffed. "The thread count is far too high to also serve as a body bag. That's blasphemy."

"The sheets are awfully luxurious, I'll give you that," Katie said, peeking up at her.

"Would you describe them as soft and supple?" Ellison teased.

"You're mocking me. I get that," Katie said with a laugh, tickling Ellison's belly as she added, "but that's making me feel less and less bad about the wandering hand."

Ellison squirmed before gripping Katie's wrist to stop the onslaught. "Oh?"

"Mm-hmm." Katie withdrew her hand, toying with Ellison's fingers. "Yup. The embarrassment has passed. I'm now in the Sleep Katie is a badass stage of the incident."

"Because Sleep Katie decided to run the bases and Awake Katie wouldn't dare?" Ellison asked playfully.

Katie shook her head. "Sleep Katie has fewer inhibitions, that's all. But you'd best believe that Sleep Katie is inspired by Awake Katie's thoughts. She just forgets to ask for consent in all her enthusiasm."

"Awake Katie wants to fondle my chest?"

Before Katie could answer, a sharp vibration shook the wall, dislodging the previously crooked picture to the floor with a thud.

"I'll kill them," Ellison said, reaching peak annoyance.

Katie covered her ear with her one good hand as the sound rang out again, somehow louder. "Is this how you wake up every morning? Because I have to say, I'm sure it's not cheap to live here, but your neighbor sucks."

Ellison groaned. "I'll be right back."

She slipped out from beneath Katie's warmth, careful to tuck her in before heading to her closet. She stripped out of her pajama pants and pulled on a pair of her favorite jeans, shrugging on a loose cashmere sweater to hide the nipples that had been erect since Katie's hand started wandering. She cast one quick glance in the mirror by the door as she clipped up her hair. She was going to have a chat with the people next door, but there was no reason to look like a mess even if she felt like one.

"You have a look of determination on your face that is making me worried for the owner of whatever that tool is." Katie had to yell to be heard over the incessant banging and clanging.

"I'll be nice, I promise," she said, and she meant that. Mostly.

❖

Katie stretched out in the bed, but not before she scooted over to the warm indentation Ellison left behind. She tried to close her eyes and savor the feeling of Ellison's body heat still in the sheets and the smell of her perfume and shampoo on the pillow, but all she could focus on was the sound of breaking glass and smashing tile through the wall behind her. What were they doing over there?

She looked up at the slow-moving fan blades, and though she was still tired—and sorer than she had been when she went to bed last night—she wasn't nearly as stressed out as she expected to be. Sure, there were a million things to get done, and she was temporarily homeless, but here, in this bed, she felt surprisingly calm. And she knew that had everything to do with Ellison.

Ellison. Whose touch soothed her and whose lips made every part of her body thrum with excitement. And who she found herself unable to stop openly flirting with. Even in her sleep, it seemed.

"Sorry about that," Ellison said as she walked back into the room.

"That was fast." Katie paused, only just now noticing that the noise had ceased. "Where's the banging?"

"Temporarily halted for an extended coffee break," Ellison said with a coy smile.

"How did you manage that?" Katie asked, amazed.

"I didn't wear a bra," she joked, pointing to her chest, which Katie obviously looked at, but to her disappointment the sweater hid what her hand knew existed beneath. "And I gave them each a hundred dollars to stop the madness for the next two hours."

Katie laughed.

"But unfortunately, the noise will resume. So I had a thought. How would you feel about relocating to the beach?"

"The beach?" Katie asked, sitting up and wincing in the process. "Ouch."

Ellison sat at the edge of the bed, taking her hand. "Remember that beach house I told you about? I think we should spend a few days there while everything gets sorted out here. You'll be able to rest and recuperate, and there won't be anyone trying to drill through my bedroom wall."

"Sold. Sign me up. I'm in." Katie froze. "Shit. I can't. I have clients."

Ellison frowned at her. "Katie, you can't work on a client with your arm like that. Or with your side that bruised. You're going to have to take some time off."

Katie tried not to panic. Why hadn't she thought about work? "I have to work to pay for New Beginnings. I can't miss a shift, I can't—"

"Shh. You can. We'll figure it out. You need to heal, and that's going to take some time. It'll be okay," Ellison said, far too calm for Katie's liking.

"I can't, it's not like I—" Katie huffed.

"Can randomly hand out hundred-dollar bills to the construction people next door to buy some much-needed silence?" Ellison asked, and Katie felt guilty.

"I wasn't going to say that," Katie replied.

"But you thought it, right?" Ellison didn't seem bothered. "The reality of the situation is this—you need to get better, and no amount of worrying about money coming in or out is going to fix that. Let's get cleaned up and get out of here before the jackhammering resumes. We can make all the calls we need to on the way."

Katie wasn't so sure about that. Sure, the beach with Ellison sounded amazing. But it wasn't like she could just up and leave, right? Not that she had anywhere else to go, but still.

"I guess I should call Pietro, then." She reached for the cell phone she had left on the opposite bedside table, but her splitting side stopped that action real quick.

"I'll get it," Ellison said as she retrieved it for her. "Oh, Katie." She held up the cracked and broken phone with a frown. "Will this even make outgoing calls in this state?"

"I called you with it." Katie shrugged.

"And I'm glad you did." Ellison handed it to her. "Okay. Call work. Then we'll get you a new phone. Then we'll head to the beach."

Katie began to argue about the phone thing, but Ellison stopped her.

"You have insurance on the house. I know you do because you

included all that information when you signed on with Gamble and Associates to renovate and sell your home. Insurance will cover reimbursement for purchasing a new phone. We'll take a picture of this poor guy and put it in your claim file. It's going to be fine."

"Is it? Really?" Katie felt overwhelmed.

"It will be. Yes." And Katie decided there was nothing else to do but believe her.

❖

"Thanks, Dennis," Katie said into the receiver of her new cell phone.

"Sure thing. Get well soon," he said before disconnecting the line.

Katie was glad Dennis was working with her mother today. She didn't dare show up burned and bruised at the facility for fear of worrying her mother, but she didn't want her to think she'd forgotten about her either. Dennis helped Katie engage with her over the phone and had promised to pay her extra attention until Katie could get back there to visit.

"It's so weird that I don't have to press a home button to get back to the main screen," Katie said, staring at her new phone. The salesperson at the phone store had politely tried to hide his shock that Katie's phone model was so old. And he was very kind when he informed her that they didn't carry that model anymore. So Katie now had a much newer generation device to relearn and figure out. "This is going to take some getting used to."

"You'll adjust quickly. You're bright," Ellison teased as she drove.

"I just want you to know that this is the first claim I'm filing, so I can pay you back," Katie replied. Ellison had offered her charge card to get the phone issue resolved, and Katie had only accepted on the condition that Ellison agreed to let Katie pay her back.

"I know where you live. It's okay," Ellison said with a smile.

"Well, I currently live with you, and all my worldly belongings are in your trunk."

"Exactly," Ellison replied. "How's the arm?"

In addition to getting Katie a new phone today, they'd also managed to get an emergency visit with her PCP. She'd had the injuries evaluated, and Ellison was trained to help dress the arm burn. Between that and the phone call she'd made to Pietro, letting him know she had to take a brief leave of absence, Katie couldn't remember having a more productive day in, well, ever.

"Okay. The ointment helps. That hot, tight feeling is going away." Katie had been relieved to find that the burn was a mix of first- and second-degree only. A topical treatment and regular dressing changes should have her mostly back to normal in no time at all.

"And the ribs?" Ellison asked. "Do they feel better since you took the Tylenol?"

The ribs were another story. Although the in-office X-ray didn't reveal any fractures, she did bruise them pretty good. She was told to rest and refrain from any unnecessary exertion until her next follow-up.

"Much," she said as she shifted toward her right out of reflex. "I hope they heal soon. They're significantly more uncomfortable than the arm I torched."

Ellison winced. "I still can't believe you had the wits about you to try to stop the fire. I don't know what I would have done."

"I was probably stupid, but your friend Sasha was too nice to say anything about it. Plus, I need that house to not burn down until after it's sold. Please and thank you."

"That room needed a skylight. You were just increasing the value of the home in a creative way," Ellison replied.

Katie smiled. She loved that Ellison never seemed worried and that she found a way to lighten the heaviness of everything. Always.

"Well, here we are."

Katie had been watching Ellison and admiring the way her swept-up hair looked with those oversized sunglasses, making her look effortlessly chic, as usual. She was too busy appreciating Ellison's profile to acknowledge their surroundings, until now.

"Oh. Wow."

Ellison eased them onto a long driveway made of intricately laid pavers toward the largest beach house Katie had ever seen. The two and half stories before her were classically shingled in the Cape Cod style with a gambrel roof, but that was where all other beach house comparisons ended for her. Ellison's house was massive, stretching left and right with a circular gazebo-like porch at one end and a clear view of the private beach and water Katie could see just beyond the railings. To the right of the elaborately masoned driveway was a three-car garage with the same shingled aesthetic, with three large white barn doors. Above the garage was another entire floor that completed Ellison's house in a L-shaped fashion.

"Excuse my reach," Ellison said as she leaned over, slipping her arm between Katie's legs to open the glove box.

Katie watched as she pressed a remote, and the garage door to their left opened, revealing one bay. They pulled in, and Ellison cut the engine.

"Ready?" she asked as she opened her driver's side door.

"Uh, yeah," Katie said, not quite believing the pristine garage in front of her. There were storage bins along the wall, all neatly organized and labeled. This was the cleanest garage she'd ever been in.

She stepped out of the car and noticed for the first time the bright orange Jeep Wrangler in the next car bay. "Whose car is that?"

"Mine." Ellison popped the trunk of the Maserati, pulling out their luggage as she spoke. "I prefer to use the Jeep when I'm down here. It draws less attention, and it's easier to drive onto the beach."

Katie pointed at the Jeep with a laugh. "That draws less attention?"

"Are you criticizing my color choice?" Ellison asked playfully. "The Maserati makes enough of a statement on its own in black, but the beach should be fun and flirty. Orange is a very flirty color."

Katie ran her hand along the leather roof of the Wrangler. The car looked brand-new. "I suppose you're right. Have you ever even driven this thing? Be honest."

Ellison looked shy. "I told you—I don't come down here a lot. Well, more in the summer, but not as much as I probably should."

"I'm so impressed by your garage that I don't think I can handle seeing the rest of your house. Just leave me here with my bag of smoke-smelling clothes. I don't want to depreciate your house's value with my charred scent."

Ellison put her glasses into her hair, rolling her eyes. "Shut up. Let's go."

Katie could see that the garage was attached to the house by a small hallway, but Ellison took her back across the driveway to the pillar-encased front door of the house. The small porch off the front entrance ran along to the left, connecting to that wedding-venue of a porch on the far end—which Katie was dying to see up close. But Ellison took her through the ornate glass doors into the house instead.

"Holy shit." Katie's jaw dropped. Before her was a massive living room filled with soft-looking gray and white couches and chairs that were positioned across from an enormous square driftwood coffee table in front of a gorgeous stone fireplace and mantel. But what took Katie's breath away was the entire wall of glass that faced the beach beyond them. The back of Ellison's first floor was a picture of perfection. Katie could see a few hundred yards of precisely manicured grass edged by a white picket fence that led to a small wooden staircase. Beyond that fence, no more than fifteen feet below the line of Ellison's property, was an expanse of white-sand beach and the bluest ocean Katie had ever seen. "This is a dream, right?"

"It's a reality now. But it started as a dream, yeah." Ellison's voice was soft.

Katie turned to face her, surprised by how close Ellison was standing to her. "What do you mean?"

Ellison studied her face for a moment. "The real treasure here is the land, and the view, obviously. But the original house here was uninhabitable. I had this place built from scratch, but it took longer than I expected. We ran into a lot of delays and issues with building materials not withstanding the elements as well as we'd expected. But it's perfect now. My dream home."

"That you never stay in," Katie said, still not believing it. She would never leave this view. Not if she didn't have to, that was.

Ellison shrugged, her smile sagging. "It's a big house. Too big for one person."

Katie remembered their conversation before. "Looks like I made good on my promise to keep you company here, though. Yay, me."

Ellison's smile returned to its usual brightness. "You didn't have to burn down your house for that to happen. You could have just asked."

"Ha-ha," Katie said, nudging her arm. "I like to really commit to things, you know?"

"Seems that way," Ellison said as she stepped farther into the house. "Make yourself at home. But let me manage the fireplace, 'kay?"

"The jokes never end, do they?"

Katie followed Ellison to the right of the living room through the open-concept dining area. Ellison had a huge dining table whose surface matched the coffee table. Katie estimated the table could comfortably sit twelve, like the one in her apartment, though it only had chairs for eight.

"I have two more benches in the loft above the garage, but I've never had the opportunity to use them," Ellison said as Katie ran her fingers along the grooved wood of the table.

"So you're saying we need to throw a party? Because that's what I'm hearing," Katie replied as they headed into the kitchen area. "This island is big enough for another twelve people. That's two dozen butts between here and there. Don't even get me started on all those couches and chairs by the fireplace. Whew."

"Oh?" Ellison looked amused. "I don't know if I even know that many people."

Katie gave her a look. "Lies."

"Or rather, I don't know if I like that many people enough to share this place with them," Ellison corrected.

"Thank you for sharing it with me," Katie said, touched. As warm and welcoming as Ellison had always been with her, she was surprised by how private she seemed to be with others.

Ellison pulled two tumblers from the glass-front white cabinets next to the sink. She filled them with ice and water from the double refrigerator nearby and handed one to Katie as she said, "I have a feeling I'd share just about everything with you."

Katie sipped the water before stepping into Ellison's space. "I appreciate that, too."

Ellison lowered her head, kissing her slowly as she leaned against the counter. The marble was cool against her skin.

"Let's get your stuff upstairs and get settled. I'll give you a tour of the grounds before we get dinner," Ellison said against her lips.

"Grounds? Dinner?" Katie chased her lips to kiss her once more. "You are so fancy."

"The fanciest."

To Katie's delight, Ellison held her hand for the remaining tour of the first floor. Off the chef's kitchen with the double sink and the view of the beach beyond was a side-entrance mudroom, equipped with a full washer and dryer. This connected to the walkway to the garage and the rear staircase to the upstairs.

Once on the second floor, Ellison pointed out a small living room with a balcony facing the beach that was flanked by two guest rooms and a full bath. Across from the living space was a similarly sized third guest room, this one with a small en suite. At the end of the hallway to the right was another room that in Katie's opinion was palatial, though Ellison assured her it was merely a smaller main bedroom than the one at the other end of the hall.

"I figured this might be your room. Though, you can have your choice," Ellison said with a casual wave. "This one has a private balcony facing the water and a larger bathroom than the other guest room with the en suite. Plus, it gets great light. Which I know you appreciate."

Katie looked around the space in awe. The queen-sized four poster bed had delicate sheer sheets draped along the frame and faced the balcony Ellison mentioned. "This is outrageous."

"Good or bad outrageous?" Ellison asked, looking concerned.

"Good. So good," Katie said, shaking her head. "It's like a photograph from a vacation magazine."

Ellison laughed. "Thank you."

She placed Katie's bag on the edge of the bed and showed her where the toiletries and towels were in her bathroom. Katie noticed that the bottles in the cabinet and the towels were the same as the ones at Ellison's city apartment. She would bet the incredibly lush-looking comforter and sheets were as soft as Ellison's were at her other home as well.

That got Katie thinking. "Can I see your room, too? Or is that off-limits."

"Nothing's off-limits," Ellison replied. "My room is this way."

Katie followed her to the other end of the house, past the sitting area. Ellison pointed out a full second-floor laundry room to the left, across from the entrance to her room. Although *suite* was a better descriptor for it.

Ellison's space was twice as big as Katie's, maybe more. She had an entire sitting area to the left of her enormous king-sized bed, much like the bedroom of her city apartment. And where Katie's room had windows with a porch door, Ellison's porch was flanked by panoramic glass doors that nearly took up the entire sea-facing wall.

"Ellison," Katie said as she walked up to the glass doors of the balcony. "This is unbelievable."

Ellison stepped up beside her, opening the door and gliding it out of the way. The sounds of the ocean waves crashing below were music to Katie's ears as the warm sun hit her face, and the smell of the sea breathed life into her lungs. She closed her eyes, basking in parts of New England beach life that made her senses come alive.

"The tide is low right now—it's good sea-glass hunting conditions if you'd like to take a walk with me," Ellison said.

"I'd love that," Katie said, turning to her.

"Then let's go."

CHAPTER SIXTEEN

Ellison hadn't held hands with someone walking along this beach in a long time. Probably since her mother was alive. When she was still able to walk before she got too sick, that was. The only real houseguest she had ever had here was Faith, but Faith preferred to run on the beach than walk it. Which always made Ellison laugh because she was sure that Faith got plenty of exercise in the bedroom with her. But Faith was militant in her exercise routine, and she never missed a chance to run.

"Ooh, check this out," Katie said, releasing her hand to bend down carefully and scoop up a small piece of purple sea glass.

"Purple is a rare find," Ellison said, slipping it into her pocket and retaking Katie's hand as they continued on at their leisurely pace.

"It's lovely here," Katie said, looking out at the water.

The late day sun was reflecting off the surface before them, and the air was starting to cool down, but thankfully, that cold snap seemed to be behind them. Still, the cool in the air reminded Ellison that they should head back.

"We should drop off these treasures you've found and think about dinner. I don't have much in the way of groceries at the house right now."

"Dinner sounds nice," Katie said, rubbing her thumb along Ellison's as Ellison guided them back in the direction of her house.

They watched two little kids in lifejackets wrestle in the shallow water nearby as a mom lounged in a beach chair with an old golden retriever on a leash that was snoozing by her side. Ellison waved to her when she held up her hand in acknowledgment.

"Is it always like this? Or does it get busier as the weather warms up?" Katie said, smiling at the gleeful screeches of the kids.

"It's certainly busier midday and when the weather gets hot, but there's always plenty of space and privacy. The nice part about this stretch of beach is that the beachgoers are primarily owners. The only people that have access to it are the people that own the houses along the seashore here," she said, pointing to the houses that lined the beach for the mile or so before them. "So everyone is your neighbor, of sorts."

"Wow," Katie said as she stepped over a small piece of driftwood. "Do you know many of them?"

Ellison shook her head. "No, not by name. I recognize the families with kids the best." She didn't bother to mention that was because she coveted what they had.

Katie squeezed her hand, looking up at her. "I forgot to ask in all the chaos, but did you end up picking a donor like you'd planned?"

"I did," Ellison replied.

"And was it a Norse god with a fondness for puppies and knitting?" Katie asked with a smile.

"Close," Ellison replied. "He's a pediatric physician that plays jazz and enjoys painting and woodworking in his spare time."

"Smart, musically and creatively inclined, *and* good with kids? Home run," she replied approvingly. "Is he also tall, blond, and built like a Greek god?"

Ellison laughed, putting her arm around Katie's shoulders. "Six foot one, athletic build, and a redhead."

Katie stopped short. "A redhead? Get out."

Ellison pulled her back to her side. "He had a poem in his file about a sock monkey he had all through med school, and he had the cutest baby photos in the world." She ran her fingers through the ends of Katie's long, curly red hair. "Plus, redheads are pretty great."

Katie nuzzled her nose, kissing her sweetly. "I won't argue with you there."

Ellison breathed in Katie's scent, loving the way she fit in her arms. She let herself enjoy Katie's lips on hers as the waves crashed behind them. This was her happy place—near the sea and kissing a beautiful, charming woman.

"You're smiling. Why?" Katie broke the kiss to look up at her.

"I'm happy. In this moment, I'm happy." Ellison had no trouble being candid with her. She found it freeing.

"Me, too." Katie shivered, tucking her head under Ellison's chin.

"I see a cozy blanket, some couch time, and pizza in our future. You in?" Ellison asked.

"You had me at cozy blanket, but the couch and pizza really complete the package."

"Good. How do you feel about shrimp?" she asked.

"Love it. How do you feel about duck?"

Ellison paused. "I'm a fan but only certain times of the year. Why?"

"You asked me about shrimp. I figured we were playing a get-to-know-you food game," Katie teased.

Ellison shook her head as she led them up the private staircase to her backyard. "I asked about the shrimp because there's a restaurant not far from here that specializes in shrimp scampi pizza, and I'm more than a little obsessed with it."

"Sounds delish," Katie said, stifling a yawn.

"And since no one got much sleep last night," Ellison said, closing the gate to the beach behind them, "I figured ordering in was a wise choice."

"You are very wise," Katie said, feigning seriousness. "The wisest."

"Ha. That comes with my advanced age," she replied.

"If you hadn't told me how old you were, I never would have guessed," Katie said as they walked through the sliding door into Ellison's kitchen. She attempted to help Ellison close the door, but she gasped and clutched at her side in the process.

"That's very kind of you. And very chivalrous of you to help with the door, but like I told you ten times this morning when we loaded my car to get here—you are strictly prohibited from lifting, pushing, pulling, or exerting yourself. You're lucky I let you pick up sea glass." Ellison closed the door, engaging the lock as she pointed toward the living room. "That blanket is the softest and warmest thing on the planet. Crawl under it. I'll be there shortly."

Katie pouted. "I'll have you know that I very carefully engaged in sea glass gathering."

"You did," Ellison admitted as she emptied Katie's treasure onto the island in the kitchen. "And you found some good ones, too."

"Thank you." Katie beamed as she hurried toward the gas fireplace Ellison turned on via an app on her phone. "You were right about the time of day to go looking. I can say in all honesty I've never had such a bountiful search."

"Low tide after a cold weather front or a storm is the best time," Ellison said as she pulled out her phone and dialed the restaurant. "Salad?"

"Sure," Katie said, already wrapped up in the blanket and mid-flop to the couch.

Ellison placed the order and made Katie a cup of tea to help her warm up, but when she brought it to her on the couch, she found Katie fast asleep and snoring lightly.

"You've had a busy two days, love," she said as she settled on the adjacent couch, sipping Katie's tea.

She watched her, her face barely visible while she was wrapped up like a burrito in Ellison's favorite fluffy white throw blanket. It dawned on her that this was the second time today that she'd had the opportunity to watch Katie sleep. She felt honored by that.

Her pocket buzzed, and she fished out her phone. It was an email from David Brinkley letting her know that her donor sperm was already en route to the embryo storage facility—that sperm bank moved fast. David's team would thaw her eggs. If the thaw failed, then her bio-mom journey was over. But if one or both survived, then they would try to inseminate. Then the waiting game would begin, and they'd wait for a healthy cell division. And if the embryo survived until the end of the week, she could move forward with Full Circle Surrogacy and have another meeting with Tammy. This was the last step. She'd done her part—now all she had to do was wait and see. Soon enough she'd know if she'd have a genetic embryo to implant in someone else, or if she'd be taking a different route entirely.

She dropped her phone on the couch, hugging the mug between her hands. So much about this process made her feel insecure and chaotic. Yet even with the whirlwind of the last few days, Katie had helped her feel grounded. Choosing a donor after she'd been dragging her feet had been easy, following their coffee session together. Particularly after Katie revealed that she had been thinking of Ellison the way Ellison had been trying not to think about Katie. And that kiss. That incredibly sensual and electric first kiss was everything. Ellison wanted to live in the moment, especially the moments with Katie in them. So, suddenly, choosing a donor hadn't felt as daunting as it had before. Because even though she was doing this alone, she didn't feel lonely like she had before. She felt happy. And excited. And that had everything to do with the sleeping burrito beauty stretched out on her couch.

❖

Katie could hear the faint sounds of ocean waves as she stirred. She'd intentionally left the curtains open at the foot of her bed because though she knew her body needed sleep, she didn't want to miss her first morning waking up here. She wanted the sun to rouse her as the light poured into the guest room. Because she didn't want to miss a moment of today.

She sighed contentedly as she rolled onto her back. She'd slept well last night. This bed was as soft as it looked, and as luxurious as any she'd ever slept on. She shifted, her left arm protesting slightly as her ribs reminded her that they weren't quite in fighting shape yet. But she felt better already, and she knew that was a good sign.

She looked up at the slow-moving fan blades above her head, breathing the clean scent of linen in as she stretched, being careful not to irritate her left side. This space was peaceful and tranquil. Ellison had chosen such beautiful colors and shades to make it feel welcoming without distracting from the real beauty of the room: the view just beyond the foot of her bed.

She sat up against the headboard, looking out at the endless blue beyond the edge of her private balcony. So much of this felt like a dream. A dream cultivated and curated by Ellison Gamble.

Though Katie slept deeply last night, she had a feeling she'd dreamed as deeply as well. And if the first thing that she thought of this morning was any indication of her mind's nightly wandering, Ellison was the star of her subconscious.

Katie brought her knees up to her chest, wrapping her arms around them as she rested her chin on her knees. Her low back stretched slightly, and her ribs initially ached, though the longer she sat like this, the less they bothered her. She rolled her shoulders and rocked side to side, stretching her body this way and that before slowly unfurling her limbs and settling into a lotus position. She closed her eyes, listening to the fan above her and the waves beyond her, and instead of visualizing the sea or clouds, or the blank space she usually focused on when she meditated, all she seemed to be able to focus on in her mind's eye was Ellison. And that smile she shared with Katie that felt like it was reserved for just her.

She thought of last night when the smell of pizza had pulled her from her slumber. She hadn't meant to fall asleep, but that blanket was so warm, and that fireplace was so welcoming. Ellison was sitting adjacent to her on the other couch. She was in the same loose-fitting sleep pants from the night before but with a cozy-looking top she had rolled up at the sleeves. She was reading some documents, silently shuffling papers as she nibbled on a piece of pizza. She managed to look sexy and adorable at the same time as her brow furrowed in concentration.

"You're working," Katie had said with a yawn.

Ellison immediately discarded the paperwork. "I'm always sort of working."

"We're having a pizza party," Katie said as she sat up, pulling the blanket around her more in the process. "There's no working at a pizza party."

Ellison took another bite of what looked like the tastiest pizza Katie had ever seen as she said, "You were having a slumber party. I was holding up the pizza torch all on my own."

Katie yawned again. "I suppose I'm not much company if I keep falling asleep on you."

"You're the best company," Ellison said. "I'm only teasing you. Ready to eat?"

"Yes, please," Katie said. The hunger had crept up on her, but now that she could see the pizza in addition to smelling it, she was a goner.

Ellison handed her a plate with two generous slices on it before sliding a bowl of salad in her direction. "No pressure on the greens, but I figured it was easier to divide it up this way."

Katie inhaled the garlicky shrimp pizza, and her mouth watered when it touched her lips. "It's still warm," she said, before taking what was probably an obnoxiously large bite.

"I heated a pizza stone and slipped it underneath it to keep it warm," Ellison said, like that was a normal thing someone did with delivery pizza.

"Oh my God." Katie was in ecstasy. The pizza was gooey and cheesy. And even though it was a white pizza, the crust was crispy and not too buttery or soggy. The garlic and seasonings were perfectly blended, highlighting the freshness and expert doneness of the shellfish. "This is amazing."

Ellison nodded. "I literally dream about this pizza. If Reeled In ever closes, I'll have sleepless nights forever."

"Reeled In?"

"Isn't that the best name for a seafood place? Sheer genius."

"I'll say." Katie quickly moved on to her second piece. "Is all their food this good?"

"It is," Ellison confirmed. "They have a great grilled seafood menu, plus the standard fried fare that's popular on the Cape. But their pizza and their cocktails are out of this world. Truthfully, I've never had a bad *anything* there, but I pretty much stick to the calamari and the pizza because I'm a creature of habit."

"Calamari?" Katie's ears perked up.

Ellison smiled, nudging a covered dish that was on the table before them. "Help yourself."

Katie moaned. "It's like you read my mind."

Ellison leaned back, looking amused. "I have a feeling I could lose myself in that mind of yours and never get bored."

"It's a confusing place at times, but I'm never not entertained," Katie admitted.

"We can swing by the restaurant and grab dinner in-house one night if you'd like. The atmosphere is great, and they have outdoor seating that's wonderful during the warmer nights. My favorite bartender, Chelsea, works on the weekends, and she makes a watermelon martini that is to die for."

"Outdoor seating and cocktails? I could absolutely get down with that," Katie said, suddenly feeling parched.

"Oh, right." Ellison put her empty plate on the table, shifting forward. "Can I get you something to drink? I have water, wine, beer, iced tea, and"—she rubbed her chin, deep in thought—"I'm pretty sure the liquor cabinet is stocked, but I'm not sure with what or how much."

"Water is fine." Katie started to stand but Ellison stopped her.

"I'll get it. You rest."

Ellison returned with a pint glass full of ice water for her.

"I'm not fragile, you know," Katie said as she sipped the beverage. "You don't have to do everything for me and baby me."

Ellison raised an eyebrow in her direction. "Do you feel babied?"

"No," Katie said, considering her words more carefully. "I just don't want you to be going out of your way for me. I mean, you're already housing me and feeding me."

"Does that bother you?" Ellison asked, looking curious.

"What?"

"Accepting my generosity?" Ellison asked. She crossed her legs as she leaned back, and Katie let herself admire the length of them.

"No," Katie replied. Because in truth, it didn't. "I just want to contribute in some way." She ran her hand through her hair. "I've never not done for myself. You know? I'm used to working for what I have, and I can't match this," she said, waving around them, "but I'd like to do what I can to help. That would make me feel better."

Ellison seemed to consider this. "What do you propose?"

"I'm a great cook." She pointed to the pizza. "Not this great, but I have a good palate, and I spent a lot of time working in restaurants in college to help offset tuition costs before I got into massage work full-time. So if you're okay with it, I'd like to be in charge of dinner while I'm here."

"A personal chef?" Ellison sipped her water. "That sounds lovely."

Katie laughed. "Well, don't get too excited. I might have oversold my talents."

"Too bad. I accept." Ellison clapped. "But only on one condition."

"What's that?" Katie asked.

"You let me be as generous as I want without challenging me," Ellison said. "I won't tread on your independence or intentionally step on your toes, but if I want to pay for groceries and buy dinner on the nights you don't cook, I don't want to catch any flak for it."

Katie narrowed her eyes, feeling like there was more. "And?"

"And you are a guest in my house, so forgive me if I seem overly formal at times. But a guest is a guest. And I want you to feel welcome here," Ellison replied.

Katie put down her glass. "You've been so welcoming. And open. And you share without any expectation of something in return.

There isn't a thing about you that doesn't feel genuine or attentive. And I didn't mean to offend you by verbalizing my desire to cook for you. I *want* to cook for you. Because I want to show you some of that graciousness back in the only way I know how." Katie scooted forward to place her hand on Ellison's knee. "You know, until this arm is better. Then it's a lifetime of free massages and scalp rubs."

Ellison placed her hand on Katie's. "Then we have a deal."

Katie turned her hand over, pleased that Ellison intertwined their fingers. "Come sit with me on my sofa?"

Ellison easily complied, cuddling next to her. "Your sofa, huh?"

"Yeah," Katie said, draping the blanket across both their laps before she reached for the calamari to share with Ellison. "Because this is where my blanket lives. With my sofa. They're a package deal."

"Your blanket?" Ellison feigned offense. "I told you that was *my* favorite blanket."

Katie shrugged. "You also told me I was a guest and that I should feel welcome here. I feel very welcome sharing my blanket and sofa with you," she said, resting her head on Ellison's shoulder.

"That's all I care about, then." Ellison placed a kiss on her temple before reaching for the nearby television remote. "Shall we mock poorly matched couples on HGTV?"

"Oh yes, please," Katie said. "Best. Night. Ever."

And it had been. At least the best night she'd had in a while. Everything about last night had felt like a date to her, and the kiss Ellison gave her at the guest bedroom door last night was surely the inspiration for her dreams. She instantly regretted not inviting Ellison in, and she had a feeling she would keep regretting that moment until she acted on the feelings that were becoming too obvious to ignore. She liked Ellison a lot. And kissing was great, but she wanted more.

Katie's phone buzzed on the bedside table next to her, pulling her from her reverie. It was a text from Ellison.

Are you up?

Katie texted back with a smile. *I am.*

Ellison replied instantly. *Are you decent?*

Barely ever, she replied before looking down. She was wearing a tank top and flannel pants, so yes. Though she should probably put on a bra, but that felt like a lot of work right now.

She heard a soft knock on her door. "Come in."

Ellison stepped in looking refreshed and sun-kissed. "Good morning."

"Morning," Katie said.

"I brought you some coffee, but I realized halfway up the stairs that you might prefer tea. But I'd already committed to it, so here we are." Ellison was effortlessly charming.

Katie reached for the cup Ellison was holding. "Caffeine in any form is accepted."

Ellison laughed, handing her the mug. "It's got milk and sugar in it. I wasn't sure how you took it."

"Like this," Katie said, wiggling in place as the robust dark roast ignited her senses. "Mm, this is great."

"All that's in the house is cereal and oatmeal, so I'm planning on hitting up the grocery store in a bit if you want to tag along," she said as she sat at the end of Katie's bed.

"I'd love that," Katie said, already planning out dinners in her head. "Do you have to work today?"

Ellison shook her head. "I cleared the day. The only thing on my agenda is to fill the fridge and stay by the phone in case anyone calls."

Katie frowned. She'd temporarily forgotten that her house had nearly burned down, and that was why she was here. "Oh, right, the house fire. How could I forget?"

Ellison pointed to the bandage on her arm. "How are you feeling?"

"Better," she said as she turned her hand over and back. "It just feels like a bad sunburn at the moment."

"And the ribs?"

"Like I fell over a piece of furniture." Katie laughed. "Which I vaguely remember happening. But I can't be sure."

Ellison winced. "We should pick up some Tylenol, too."

"I'll make a list," Katie said, whipping out her phone. "Siri, can you start a list for me?"

"Sure thing," her phone replied.

"Thank you."

Ellison laughed.

"What?"

"You are so polite to Siri. It's cute."

Katie swung her legs over the side of the bed, scooting down so they were closer. "I'm polite in everything that I do."

"Oh yeah?" Ellison asked, eyeing the shortened distance between them.

"Yes." Katie scooted closer still. "For instance, I was going to thank you for this coffee, but I got distracted by my list-making task. So I'd like to start over and say thank you."

"You're welcome," Ellison replied, but Katie wasn't interested in that kind of exchange.

She leaned into Ellison's space, placing a tender kiss just to the right of Ellison's full, pink lips. To her delight, Ellison turned to meet her mouth.

"Thank you for my coffee," she said against what were quickly becoming her favorite lips.

"Thank you for the kiss," Ellison replied.

Katie kissed her again because she could. And she would have stayed there forever had her stomach growling not totally killed the moment.

"I have to be honest with you," Ellison said, pulling back. "The cereal is stale, and the oatmeal is expired."

Katie laughed. "Damn."

"Let's go get breakfast at the diner down the street. They probably have better coffee," Ellison offered.

Katie cared less about the coffee and more about the company. "I love this idea."

"Then let's go."

CHAPTER SEVENTEEN

Ellison was smiling ear to ear, and she didn't care. Because this week and a half had been some of the best days in her life, and the news from Dr. Brinkley was the icing on the cake. Both of her eggs had survived the thaw, and both successfully bonded with the sperm, before dividing and growing appropriately. She had two fertilized embryos ready for implantation, and she could scream she was so excited.

She fired off a text to Faith to update her since she'd been hounding her. Then she checked off as many menial tasks she could before she couldn't avoid the most important call she had yet to make—it was time to call Tammy at Full Circle Surrogacy.

To Ellison's great displeasure, Tammy answered on the first ring.

"This is Tammy," she said.

Ellison had been hoping to leave a voice mail, but she figured this was probably a better alternative in some universe. "Tammy, hi. It's Ellison Gamble."

"Ellison! We just heard the good news from Dr. Brinkley's office. I assume you're calling to start the process of finding the right surrogate?"

Ellison took a breath. "I am."

"Excellent. As you know, we have a wonderful portfolio of possible surrogate matches for you, and now that we have definitive embryos—congratulations again, by the way—we can narrow our search to gestational carriers only. I've been personally working on your file, and I feel as though I have the perfect woman for you."

"Oh?" Ellison wasn't sure what that meant. Who exactly was the perfect woman for her? The more time she spent with Katie, the more she thought she might fit that bill.

"Yes, I'm confident about it." Tammy shuffled some papers. "So, coincidentally, I have an opening this afternoon. Would you be free to meet around two? We could get a jump on this right away."

"Today?" Ellison panicked a bit.

"At two. Yes."

Ellison pulled up her calendar. Her morning had been busy—this was only the fourth day she'd been in the office since she and Katie had retreated to the beach house ten days ago. But she'd worked fast today and was ahead of schedule. With some creative maneuvering, she could be free. If she wanted to. The question was, did she want to be? Fortune favored the bold, she reminded herself.

"Yes, I'm available." Ellison pulled the trigger. Things had been fantastic, and the embryo news was even more fantastic. What did she have to lose, going to the meeting?

"Great. We'll see you this afternoon."

She disconnected the line, feeling a little out of breath. But excited. At least she thought that was what she was feeling.

A rap at her office door interrupted her.

"Yes?"

Jax opened the door and gave her a wave. "Just checking to see if you need anything. And to find out how the remote work is going. Because I have been nerding out about Wi-Fi signal repeaters, and I think I might have found a good one for you to try."

"Hi, yes. Come in. Tell me all about your nerd findings," Ellison said, as she motioned for Jax to sit.

"Cool," Jax said before diving into tech talk that was above Ellison's head but that she was glad to be privy to. "Anyway, I think it's worth a shot if you plan to work remotely more often. I'm not trying to pry or anything—but do you think you will?"

Ellison had been considering this herself. She knew that part of the reason the week had been so fantastic was because she'd been by the water and the beach. But she knew the majority of the credit went to Katie. She loved her company. She enjoyed her humor and learning about her life and just getting to know her better. Katie constantly surprised her and revealed parts of herself in such a vulnerable and candid way that continued to endear her to Ellison, over and over. There wasn't a thing about Katie she didn't like. Which was making some things increasingly more difficult. Like keeping her hands to herself. Though Katie had spent every night in her own room, Ellison had a feeling that if she extended the invitation for Katie to join her in hers, she would. And she knew this because their daily flirtations and encounters—of the mental and physical kind—were escalating: the small touches, the cuddling on the couch, the making out that seemed to keep happening for longer periods and without any provocation other than Katie's lips in close proximity. All of it was making Ellison vibrate with want. The want for more. And though they'd danced around the topic, Ellison wasn't ready to go there until Katie was feeling better. And until she explicitly asked. Because kissing and holding hands on their nightly beach strolls was one thing, but the things Ellison wanted to be doing with and to Katie were another thing entirely.

"Is that a no?" Jax asked.

"Sorry," Ellison said, shaking her head. "Got distracted there. Yes, send me a link for the repeater thing, and I'll give it a try. I think I'll be working from home more often for the next few weeks. My plan is to be remote at least a few days a week until the end of the summer."

"Sounds good," Jax said as they stood to leave. "How's Katie?"

"Hmm?" Ellison stalled, hoping it wasn't obvious she was daydreaming about her.

"Katie. I know the fire set things back a bit, but I saw that you're scheduled to go out to her place at the end of the week with Zander. So that's good, right? Has the house been cleared?"

"It has. And she's good. Better every day." Ellison loved that Jax asked about her. In fact, all of her employees that knew about Katie had asked about her. Trina and Lauren both popped their heads in earlier asking the same questions. She appreciated that.

"That's great."

"Jax?" Ellison asked.

"Yeah?"

"How's Talia's website and upcoming launch prep going?"

Jax smiled. "Awesome. So awesome. She's gonna kill it. We have all the social media platforms running promotion, and I've stress-tested her Shopify link a half dozen times. It's going to be great."

"I have no idea what you said or what that means, but you're happy, so I'm happy," Ellison said. "Now all we have to do is dress up and smile pretty for the camera. Then the rest is up to you to make sure the site can hold all that hotness without burning up."

Jax laughed. "I'm more nervous about the photo shoot than the product launch."

"Why?"

Jax looked down at their feet. "I don't know. I want to do a good job, you know? I want to represent Talia's style right. And not look like a goof."

"You won't. You told me she hired the best photographer in the city, right?"

"She did. Sydney James is supposedly a phenom," Jax confirmed.

"Then all you have to do is wear the clothes and take direction. Can you take direction, Jax?"

Jax saluted her. "You know I can."

"Then relax. Talia asked you to be involved because you have the look she wants to represent her brand. You should feel honored. I know I do." Ellison had been looking forward to Talia branching out, even though she knew this might be the end of her personal stylist's availability. This was what Talia wanted. And she wanted her to be successful.

"You're right." Jax stood up a little taller. "You are all right. Trina. Lauren. All of you. Do you ever get tired of being right?"

"Never," Ellison said. "Oh, can you organize that paperwork for Pietro Ferrazi's spa? I'd like to process his expansion request."

"Sure thing," Jax said before jogging to their desk.

Ellison had weighed the pros and cons of Pietro's request versus the numerous other applications she had gotten for the commercial space and decided that with a two-year rental agreement, the expansion of Pietro's spa was the wisest business move. If Pietro was as successful in this new endeavor as he was proposing, then that would generate more business for all of the shops and cafés in the complex. Which was good for everyone. Including Gamble and Associates. The more foot traffic, the better.

Her phone buzzed. It was a text from Katie.

Do you have an oyster knife?

Ellison laughed. She'd messaged her after Faith to tell her they would be celebrating tonight, but she'd intentionally kept it vague. She wondered if this had anything to do with her text.

Do you have oysters? she asked.

I took Sunny out for a spin. So yes.

Ellison laughed again. Katie had taken to calling her orange Jeep Sunny after Sunkist, the orange-flavored soda. She didn't hate it, so she let it continue.

Do you know how to shuck?

Katie wrote back immediately. *This feels like an interrogation.*

Top drawer to the left of the dishwasher. There's a chain mail glove in there, too.

Katie sent back a thumbs-up and a smiley face emoji. *I'm making dinner. We're having oysters. Don't be late.*

Sounds great. I can't wait.

Ellison could get used to someone making her dinner every night. Katie had amazed her with her culinary prowess thus far. The oyster information excited her.

She looked at the clock on her desk. If she put her nose to the grindstone, she could even squeeze in a quick trip to the florist before her meeting with Tammy.

❖

Katie heard the chime alerting her that someone was pulling into the driveway, and she smiled. Ellison was home.

Today had been a good day. Ellison had called to tell her that the house had finally been cleared and that they could go there at the end of the week with Zander to check it out. She'd had a telehealth appointment with her MD about the arm and the ribs, and she was given the go-ahead to resume more strenuous activities as long as she kept up with her hydration and had plenty of rest. After breakfast she'd had a FaceTime sesh with her mom and Dennis. And she'd taken Sunny out to pick up some goodies to surprise Ellison with at dinner, long before she'd gotten the text from Ellison telling her that they were celebrating.

She knew that Ellison was waiting for news about her egg fertilization, and Katie hoped that this was the good news they were celebrating and not delayed excitement about the house thing. Sure, she wanted to get back into her house to see how things were, but this week had really opened her eyes to what Ellison had said—a house could be replaced. People couldn't. And the idea of Ellison getting something that she wanted—a child of her own—was something they'd talked about often. And Katie wanted that for her. She deserved it.

She opened the front door and leaned against the doorframe as Ellison pulled into the open garage bay. She watched Ellison open the trunk of the Maserati and load a pile of flattened boxes into Sunny like she had every day this week. They'd be taking Sunny into the city during their house tour with Zander, since she had more room in the back than Ellison's Maserati. The plan was that after the walk-through, they would pack up whatever was salvageable and mark all the furniture Katie wanted placed in storage versus those pieces she wanted to send off to auction. Which—just thinking about all that that would entail— made Katie's head spin.

"Hi," Ellison said, looking amazing as usual. Her hair was up in a french twist with her sunglasses on the top of her head. She wore a silk blouse and those black slacks that made her long legs look endless. She had on her signature heels again today. Her elegance never seemed to fade.

"Hey." It wasn't lost on Katie how much she owed this woman her life. In so many ways, it seemed. But especially for how incredible she had been during this whole process. If something needed to get done, Ellison did it. Or had a friend that was somehow connected to it. And suddenly, it was handled. She'd helped Katie wade through the insurance filing process, the fire department communication, setting up the appointment with Zander, and even securing a storage facility for the items Katie wasn't sure what to do with.

But more than just being an unbelievably organized multitasker, Ellison was lovely in every sense of the word. She was wonderful. Every morning she greeted Katie with a fresh cup of coffee and a bowl of cut fruit when she wandered down from her guest room. And Ellison spent every minute that she didn't have to be in the office working from the beach house, in case Katie needed something. Had Katie not been healing from her injuries, the entire stay thus far would have felt like a vacation. With a lot of kissing and couple-y behavior, which she really enjoyed.

Ellison gave her a broad smile before pulling an enormous bouquet out from the back seat of her Maserati.

"Damn," Katie said. "Who's sending you flowers like that?"

"Why? Are you jealous?"

"Yes," Katie said.

"Because you think someone sent me flowers? Or because you're under the impression that these aren't for you?" Ellison asked as she walked up to her, balancing the vase on her hip.

"For me?" Katie was blown away. She'd only ever seen a bouquet this ornate in magazine photos, not in real life. "You're kidding."

"I'm not," Ellison said as she stepped up onto the porch. "How was your day?"

"Fine. Great. Getting better by the minute, it seems," Katie said as she reached for the bouquet.

"You feel up to carrying it?" Ellison asked, watching her carefully.

"Arm and ribs are in good shape. The doctor cleared me to do all the things," Katie said, flexing a bit. "I want to cuddle the flowers. Let me cuddle them."

Ellison laughed, handing her the bouquet.

"God. These smell amazing." Katie held them close as she breathed in their scent.

"I'm glad you like them," Ellison said as she leaned on the opposite doorframe to Katie.

"I do." Katie stepped into Ellison's space, as close as the overflowing bouquet would allow, to add, "I like you, too."

"Oh yeah?" Ellison asked, her blue eyes shining in the late day sun.

"It's true," Katie said as she rose up on her toes to place a chaste kiss on Ellison's lips. "And I missed you today."

"Mm, the feeling is mutual. All around," Ellison said, reconnecting their lips. Though this kiss was brief, it was anything but chaste.

Katie bit her bottom lip to keep from moaning. She opened her eyes to find Ellison watching her. "Do you kiss everyone like that to say hello?"

"Just you," Ellison said, giving her a small smile. "And that was more than a hello kiss. That was an *I'm happy to see you* kiss. It was a *your lips have been missed* kiss. And a *this is the best part of my day so far* kiss. You know, all of the above."

Katie toyed with the hem of Ellison's silk shirt before reaching out to caress along Ellison's side. She could feel how warm her skin was beneath the thin fabric. She wanted to touch her without the barrier between them. "I'll have to always meet you at the door, then."

"I wouldn't hate that," Ellison said, her eyes tracing Katie's face. "You seem better."

"I feel better," she replied. Today was the first day that she felt like she was back to her old self. And that old self wanted more kissing, like Ellison had just teased her with. And more than that.

"I'm glad," Ellison said, sweeping an errant hair off Katie's forehead.

"So, I could just stand here and stare at you all day, but did you want to come in? To your own house?" Katie asked, after she realized they were still standing in the doorway. "Because dinner is almost done, and those oysters aren't going to shuck themselves."

"I would hate to be late for dinner. Let me at least put these on the counter since you're doing everything else. It'll make me feel useful." Ellison took the flowers from her as she headed in toward the kitchen.

Katie laughed as she followed her. She watched her arrange the bouquet in the center of the island and head to the sink to wash her hands before taking in the many stations Katie had going throughout the kitchen.

"I promise you it's organized chaos." Katie pointed to the dozen oysters resting on ice chips. "That's the shucking station." She motioned toward the covered pan on the stove top with a wave. "And that's dinner. Well, most of it. I have to finish the rest."

"What *are* we having for dinner?" Ellison asked as she leaned against the sink. "Because everything smells amazing."

"First oysters. Then lobster and mushroom risotto with garlic herb butter crostini."

Ellison looked shocked. "Seriously?"

"Seriously," Katie said as she stepped into Ellison's space again. "But if you want to make sure nothing is overcooked, then I need to shuck these oysters."

"Oh? And am I somehow impeding that?" Ellison looked amused as she rested a hand on Katie's hip.

"You are rather distracting," Katie said as she mirrored Ellison's touch.

"Sorry not sorry," Ellison said. She lowered her head, and Katie had to resist kissing those lips again. Dinner would never happen if the kissing continued. And she wanted tonight's dinner to be special.

Katie nuzzled her nose, avoiding her lips to say, "But besides that, you're blocking the drawer with the oyster knife."

"Oof," Ellison replied, feigning hurt as she moved aside. "My apologies."

"You can make it up to me later," Katie said, sparing her a quick kiss before grabbing what she needed from the drawer. She slipped on the chain mail glove and began wielding the oyster knife with the practiced ease of someone who'd spent more than a handful of summers working at seaside restaurants.

"And how shall I do that?" Ellison asked, stepping up behind her and resting her hands on Katie's hips.

"Well, first you can tell me about your day." Katie stilled the knife when Ellison swept the hair off her neck. She closed her eyes when Ellison's lips gently kissed the newly exposed skin and nearly dropped the oyster she had in her other hand when she felt the swipe of Ellison's tongue between warm, wet kisses.

"And after that?" Ellison was by her ear now. Her lips teased along Katie's neck before drifting away. It was one of the most sensual and maddening things anyone had ever done to her.

"After that"—she exhaled when Ellison's lips closed around her earlobe, making her clit throb—"you can help me with dessert."

Ellison bit down gently before soothing her earlobe with her tongue. "And what is for dessert?"

"That's a surprise." Katie stifled a shudder as Ellison's breath skated across her ear. The warmth of her body made Katie feel like she was on fire in the best way possible.

"I like surprises." Ellison's grip on her hips loosened as one hand slid to Katie's abdomen, holding her close. The grasp was intimate and somehow also possessive in the sexiest way.

"Good." Katie dropped her head back onto Ellison's shoulder as she pressed her ass into Ellison's front.

Ellison rewarded her by sucking on her jaw, as her free hand grazed the front of Katie's upper thigh. "I like this, too."

Katie was beginning to pant, and she was surely about to drop the knife or the oyster, or both. She had to regain some control here, or there really wouldn't be any dinner. Which seemed to bother her less and less the more Ellison's mouth showered her with affection.

Ellison spread her fingers out, sliding up and down Katie's thigh without stopping the kissing and sucking, and Katie was going to explode.

"You're supposed to be telling me about your day," she said shakily as she rested the heels of her hands on the counter in front of her to ground her.

"My day was not nearly as exciting as helping you with meal prep is," Ellison replied between kisses.

"Are you helping me? Or are you distracting me even more than before?" Katie turned her head to catch Ellison's lips. She moaned as Ellison's tongue slipped into her mouth. That was all she could take. She dropped the knife and oyster to spin in place. She held her hands up, for fear of ruining Ellison's shirt, but Ellison just pressed her against the counter with her body—meeting her kiss with a deeper, sex-destroying tongue glide that had her hips bucking forward of their own volition.

"Sorry not sorry," Ellison repeated as she slowed the kiss, and Katie whimpered when Ellison's hand found her ass.

"Me neither," Katie said, resting her elbows on Ellison's shoulders and accepting defeat. Dinner could wait.

The doorbell rang, imploding their moment, and Ellison swore.

"Are you expecting someone?" Katie asked, trying to catch her breath.

Ellison shook her head, looking as frustrated as Katie's sex felt. "No. Yes. Sort of."

Katie wasn't sure what to do with that information. "Should I have picked up more lobster?"

The doorbell rang again, and Ellison gave her an apologetic look. "No. I'll be right back." She hesitated before leaning in to give Katie a softer but no less passionate kiss than the ones that had truly taken Katie's breath away a moment before. "Don't go anywhere."

"I'm not sure my legs even work anymore."

Ellison looked pleased. "Good."

Katie used the space from Ellison's lips and hands to calm the fuck down. She steadied her hands on the cool surface of the marble countertop before forcing herself to focus on the task that was literally in her hand before Ellison made her forget how to function.

By the time Ellison came back into the kitchen, she'd finished shucking the oysters and had started the mignonette sauce. All that was left now was warming the lobster tails and stirring in the remaining lobster chunks with the mushroom risotto, and she was done. Well, besides the seemingly impossible task of sitting across from Ellison at a table without being connected to her mouth, that was.

"Sorry about that," Ellison said as she held up a bottle of champagne and an ornate cheese and meat basket that was wrapped and displayed on what appeared to be a hand-carved cutting board.

"Were you worried that oysters weren't a filling-enough appetizer?" Katie teased as she put the finishing touches on the crostini before placing them in the oven to warm.

"These are a gift," Ellison said, placing them both on the counter. "And I was more than willing to sacrifice the oysters to have you as an appetizer. Just FYI."

Katie nearly dropped the spoon into the risotto. How was she supposed to make it through dinner if this kind of verbal seduction continued?

"I spoke to Faith earlier, and she told me she was sending me something here, but she didn't specify what it was or when it was arriving. But I don't hate that chilled champagne arrived at my doorstep."

"Faith sent those?" Katie asked over her shoulder. She tried not to feel jealous even though she knew Ellison and Faith had a history.

"She did." Ellison's hands were on her hips again. "Does that bother you?"

"No," Katie lied as she stirred the risotto with more force than was necessary.

Ellison turned her, pulling her close. Katie could see that the playfulness from before was gone as she said softly, "We're just friends. Really. And I know you saw what you saw in the parking lot—"

"Kissing. I saw a lot of really hot and passionate kissing," Katie replied, failing to keep her tone light.

Ellison gave her a small smile. "We have a complicated and—

yes—physically close history. But that's over now. She met someone. But more importantly, so did I."

Katie blinked, not sure what to say to that.

"*You*. That someone is you. In case you were wondering," Ellison said as she massaged Katie's lower back. "I can assure you I only have eyes and hands"—she dipped down to give Katie's ass a gentle squeeze—"for you."

Katie reached up and ran her finger along Ellison's lower lip as she asked, "And what about this mouth?"

Ellison's lips parted, and her tongue swiped against Katie's finger before disappearing behind her sexy smile. "All yours."

Katie grabbed her chin, pulling Ellison's mouth to hers as she replied, "Good." She let herself get lost in the ecstasy that was Ellison's kiss until the faint smell of burning broke her away. "Shit. The crostini."

"Here." Ellison handed her the nearby oven mitts, and she pulled out the forgotten baguette slices.

She sighed. About half of them were charred.

Ellison lifted one of the burnt toast slices and shrugged. "I'm sure we can scrape some of the singed parts off."

Katie laughed. "This is all your fault."

Ellison looked rightfully guilty. "You're right. I'll do the scraping."

Katie shook her head. "It's fine. There's enough salvageable for dinner. I made extras anyway."

Ellison looked relieved. "There you go, putting out fires again."

"Only fires that I seem to start, though. I'm two for two now. You should dump me," Katie replied, not meaning to put a label on what they had, but it was out there now, so it wasn't like she could take it back.

"No, thanks. I'll keep you, if it's all the same to you," Ellison said as she took over stirring the risotto.

That was music to Katie's ears. She dressed the crostini as she asked, "Can I ask what the gift is for? Because if it's for your birthday, she's super late."

Ellison laughed. "Oh, it's about the good news I mentioned before."

"The reason we're celebrating," Katie replied, annoyed that she'd forgotten to ask Ellison what she'd been alluding to before. But in her defense, there had been a lot of kissing and groping. "Is it the eggs? Tell me it's good news in the baby department."

Ellison's smile broadened as she nodded, and Katie squealed with delight.

"How many? Say it's both," Katie replied, hopping from foot to foot before stilling her movements to add, "but it only takes one. So tell me it's at least one."

"It's two," Ellison said, and Katie wrapped her arms around her as she bounced with joy.

"Two! It's two," Katie said, pulling back to look at the teary blue eyes in front of her.

"Two healthy, strong embryos just waiting to be implanted."

"And then it's baby time," Katie said, thrilled for her. "This is the best news."

Ellison wiped at her eyes, a small smile on her lips as she replied, "I know. It really is. Isn't it?"

"I'm so excited for you," Katie said, kissing her lips and brushing the tears off her cheeks. "Clearly choosing the redhead with the best swimmers was the right choice. Redheads rock."

"That they do," Ellison replied, looking at her with such genuine sincerity that Katie thought she might tear up as well.

"So, champagne?" Katie asked as she looped her arms around Ellison's waist.

"Might as well, while it's cold, right?"

"Hell yes," Katie replied, glad that tonight was the night she'd decided to make her secret signature meal. There was so much to celebrate, it seemed, and it all had to do with the woman in her arms who was positively glowing right now.

❖

Katie had planned the dinner as a thank-you for all the hospitality Ellison had shown her since they'd met. But she would be lying if she hadn't purposely integrated aphrodisiacs into every course because besides showing her gratitude to Ellison, she wanted to show her something else—that she was ready to move things along in the bedroom department.

And if the way Ellison never seemed to be more than a touch or kiss away the entire dinner was an indication—her message was received loud and clear.

Katie pulled out the dark chocolate and pomegranate seed tart she'd specially ordered from the local bakery as Ellison cleared the plates, but her progress stopped there when Ellison appeared at her side, hungry for something besides dessert.

"That looks delicious," she said as she glanced at the next course. But her eyes quickly returned to Katie. "But you look better."

Katie leaned against the counter, facing her. She loved the look of desire in Ellison's eyes. That was a look she'd been seeing more often this week, but it hadn't left Ellison's gaze all night. She was emboldened by it. "Is that so?"

"Dinner was incredible, but the company was what has made tonight so memorable thus far." Ellison placed her hands on the counter on either side of Katie's hips, as she moved closer. "You look beautiful tonight."

"I've been in the same four outfits all week. You must be bored by now." Katie spoke directly to Ellison's lips. Not that her brain could work beyond this moment, but there was a part of her that was looking forward to getting into the house tomorrow, if just to spice up her wardrobe alone. Assuming her clothes had survived the fire.

"I don't think that's possible." Ellison's hands moved to her hips, and before she knew it, Katie was being boosted up onto the island as Ellison said, "Though I wouldn't be opposed to you being out of those clothes. If you felt so inclined."

Katie spread her legs, and Ellison stepped between them while her hands still gripped at Katie's hips. In those heels, Ellison was as tall as Katie was sitting on this counter, which turned Katie on like nothing else. She reached out and looped her arms around Ellison's neck as she pulled her closer. "Are you asking me to get naked?"

Katie's heart was already racing, but the look on Ellison's face as she licked her lips made her feel like it might beat right out of her chest.

"Yes."

"I thought you'd never ask." Katie scooted forward, bringing her sex to Ellison's front. She moaned at the contact as Ellison leaned in and connected their hips and chests. And lips. That mouth was on hers again, and any anxiety Katie had felt about what would happen next dissolved into the blissful puff of an afterthought as Ellison's hands moved over her body, claiming her.

Ellison had her out of her shirt in an instant, but Katie was too preoccupied with how soft and warm Ellison's hands were on her naked back to worry about whether or not her shirt had been ripped in the process.

She wove her fingers through Ellison's hair, bringing her mouth back to her neck as she hooked her legs around Ellison's hips, searching for friction.

Ellison's hand left Katie's body long enough to free her hair from the elegant french twist, and Katie luxuriated in the luscious blond locks that tumbled down around her fingers.

She massaged Ellison's scalp as Ellison's mouth returned to hers. Ellison's hand worked over her ribs before one cupped her breast, causing her to cry out in pleasure.

Ellison's fingers found her nipple through her bra, and Katie shuddered, bucking forward against her. And though she was more than enjoying all the licking and sucking and groping, she hit her threshold when Ellison's tongue swiped across the aroused nipple, soaking her bra and panties in the same moment.

"Bed. Take me to a bed," Katie said, pulling Ellison's lips back to her own.

"Any bed?" Ellison asked as she sucked on her bottom lip and made her even wetter.

"Yours. Now," Katie growled. She clutched at Ellison's hair and pulled her lips away from her skin. "Or I'm going to make an even bigger mess of your kitchen island than I already have."

Ellison seemed unfazed by this, but she nodded in agreement. "Fine, but don't expect me to keep my hands off you on the walk. That's an unreasonable request."

"Please don't." Katie had no desire to be away from Ellison's touch.

Ellison's bedroom door was open, which made walking over the threshold backward, with Ellison undoing her bra while kissing her, much easier.

When the back of her knees hit the bed, she smiled against Ellison's lips. She was happy to be at their destination and desperate to be out of her pants.

"You're gorgeous," Ellison said, as she discarded Katie's forgotten bra and put enough space between them to appreciate Katie's form in an unhurried fashion.

Katie couldn't remember another time someone had looked at her like that. Like there was a reverence to seeing her nearly naked.

"Let me see the rest of you," Ellison said softly, toying with the button on Katie's jeans. "I want to see all of you."

Katie trembled at the attention and the bubbling of her desire that had never seemed quite so intense before. She reached out to touch Ellison's chest through her blouse. She could feel her breaths coming fast, and Ellison's hand closed over hers, encouraging her to cup the tissue before her. She did, and it was Ellison's turn to moan as she stepped closer again.

Katie savored the wonderful weight of Ellison's breast in her hand as Ellison unbuttoned her jeans and eased them off her hips. Her lips were never far off as she helped Katie out of her panties and encouraged her to sit on the bed.

Katie obliged and leaned back on her elbows as Ellison stepped back and looked down at her sex as her tongue moved over her bottom lip.

"You're incredible," Ellison said as she shrugged off her blouse. And any hesitation Katie might have felt faded at the view of Ellison's naked and toned torso.

"Be naked with me," Katie practically begged as she spread her legs for Ellison to step between them again.

"Gladly," Ellison replied, her voice thick with lust that Katie felt like a lightning bolt, down to her clit and back.

Ellison disrobed with the same gracefulness that she seemed to do everything, and in no time, Katie was out of breath again. This time from the confirmation that all her wildest dreams didn't compare to reality. Ellison naked was unreal.

"Fuck," Katie exclaimed as Ellison knelt before her, massaging up her thighs and inside her legs as she moved closer.

"All night. Until you beg me to stop," Ellison said, licking her lips as she looked up at her. "Can I taste you?"

"I might die if you don't," Katie said, gripping the comforter to keep her ass on the bed, because her instinct was to press her pussy into Ellison's face.

"Well, we can't have that." Ellison spoke directly to her sex, and Katie vibrated with anticipation as Ellison stopped just short of her destination to ask, "Are you sure?"

"Please." Katie abandoned her death grip on the blanket to palm the back of Ellison's head, guiding her mouth closer. "I can't wait anymore."

"Me, neither," Ellison replied, but Katie barely heard her because all sounds stopped besides the deafening beating of her heart in her ears when Ellison's mouth connected with her wet and swollen lips.

Ellison moaned against her, and Katie felt the vibration all the way down to her soul. Ellison's lips and tongue moved over her in a precise, practiced ease that soon had her whimpering and bucking against her face. Ellison slowed her ministrations, and Katie gasped for breath, but she was too wound up to slow the climb.

"Ellison," she warned as she lay back on the bed, clawing at the bedsheets beneath. She had never felt this turned-on for anyone before, nor had oral ever gotten her this close, this fast. She was too excited to appreciate that right now, but she knew she'd think about this moment for a very long time.

"Good. Come hard, so we can do it again," Ellison said. And when Ellison slid her tongue deep inside her, Katie's inner walls spasmed, and her body flushed with warmth and ecstasy.

She cried out as her body tremored under Ellison's touch. Ellison held her hips down as she continued to lick and lap at her until Katie released her hold on Ellison's hair, sated and buzzing. And when Ellison's lips left her body, she breathed in deeply, filling her lungs and willing her heartbeat to slow, but Ellison didn't give her much recovery time. Before she knew it, she was being guided up the bed by strong hands and insistent lips.

She laughed as Ellison pulled the comforter out from underneath her, rolling her a bit in the process. She lay on her back on the fresh sheets below, and Ellison moved over her, caressing her side as she nuzzled at her neck.

"You taste incredible," Ellison breathed across her ear, and Katie felt her already overstimulated clit throb once again.

"That was amazing," Katie said, turning her head to connect their lips. "I've never, not like that. I can't—"

Ellison shook her head, kissing her slowly. "We're not done yet."

"We aren't?" Katie asked, but she lost all words when Ellison kissed down her chest to pay attention to her breasts. Ellison's lips and tongue teased and sucked on Katie's nipples, causing goose bumps to spread over her naked skin.

She panted and moaned in ecstasy as Ellison's hand massaged and pinched at the soft skin of her breast, while her mouth worked over her other nipple. Everything felt so unbelievably sensitive and stimulating that she reached out to grip at Ellison's strong upper back to ground herself and focus on what felt good. Which was all of it.

Ellison slid lower, kissing along her left side as she dragged her thumb over Katie's swollen pink nipple. "Does this hurt?"

"Does what hurt?" Katie gasped out between the flashes of pleasure Ellison was eliciting from her nipples.

"Your side. Did I hurt you?" Ellison asked between hot, open-mouthed kisses to her left side.

Katie closed her eyes at the gentle touches and caresses Ellison showered her side with. "No. That feels good. You make me feel so good."

Ellison placed one long, slow kiss to the healing bruise at her side before settling beside her.

Katie turned her head to face Ellison and was struck by her beauty yet again. Her long blond hair was a tousled mess thanks to Katie's wandering hands, but the deep blue of her eyes was what Katie found so captivating. Ellison looked at her like she was the most important person in the world, and under her touch, she felt like she was.

Ellison traced a hand between her breasts to encircle her navel, and Katie bit her bottom lip to keep the moan she wanted to release restrained. She wasn't sure she could climax again, but she certainly was willing to try. And if that meant she could feel Ellison's fingers inside her, then that was more than fine by her.

"I want to feel you," Ellison said, as she resumed her affections at Katie's breast.

"Please," Katie begged again. It seemed she wasn't above begging in bed with Ellison.

She felt Ellison smile against her breast as her hand slid between her legs. Ellison teased at the soft flesh on her inner thighs, moving up only to then reverse course just before running her fingers through Katie's lower lips. Katie whimpered as she clawed at Ellison's back before guiding Ellison's mouth back to hers.

"Kiss me while you fuck me," she said against Ellison's lips. She smiled at the pleased noise Ellison let out in response.

"Are you tight for me?" she asked.

Katie nodded and kissed Ellison deeply as Ellison slipped through her wetness. Ellison rubbed along her lips and caressed her clit before moving lower yet again. Katie spread her legs, beckoning Ellison closer, and sighing when Ellison finally slid one finger inside her.

"More," she gasped as Ellison slid out, before filling her with a second finger and starting a slow, agonizing rhythm that Katie could feel winding her up again.

"I thought licking you was my favorite thing," Ellison said against her lips as she flexed her fingers inside her. But as Katie cried out, grinding against her hand harder, Ellison added, "but this is pretty heavenly. Being inside you might be my favorite thing."

Katie continued to grind against Ellison's hand while she alternated between kissing her and gasping for breath, but when Ellison moved Katie's hand from her back to cup at Ellison's breast again, that growing crescendo Katie felt in her lower abdomen started to peak.

"Are you ready again?" Ellison asked in a tone that told Katie she was well aware that she was.

"Kiss me." Katie lifted her head to connect their lips as she massaged at the flesh of Ellison's chest. Ellison increased her thrusts before rubbing her thumb over Katie's clit and bringing her to a spine-tingling second orgasm.

Her cries of pleasure were silenced by Ellison's mouth, and she rode out her orgasm by slowly continuing to grind against Ellison's hand until she was too sensitive. She wrapped her hand around Ellison's wrist and squeezed gently. In an instant, Ellison's arms were wrapped around her as she came back down.

After a few long moments of silence, Katie covered her face with her forearm and laughed. She laughed until her ribs hurt, and tears spilled from her eyes onto the pillow below. All the while, Ellison kept a hand on her stomach, reminding her of her touch. As if Katie could ever forget.

She let out one last exhale before turning to face Ellison. She cupped her jaw as she shook her head. "I get it now. I really, truly get it."

"Get what?" Ellison asked, looking amused.

"What you said at your birthday dinner. What was it? Something like life is too short for bad sex, or even mediocre sex. And you told me that if you don't feel reborn after having sex, then you're better off doing it yourself. Right?"

"That sounds like something I would say. Yeah," Ellison replied.

"Well, you were right. Because I can honestly tell you that in all my years of having sex, I have never once experienced anything quite like that. And if this blissed-out, happy thrum running through my whole body is a sign of rebirth, then I am all for it." Katie felt alive. She felt tired but energized. She felt like she finally understood what Ellison was talking about because she could tell that nothing short of *that* would ever be good enough. And she had a feeling she was just scraping the surface of what pleasure truly could be.

"Is this a roundabout way of you saying that you've stumbled into a sexual awakening? Because I think I get a toaster or something if that's the case," Ellison said with a wink.

Katie looked at the woman beside her that had changed everything in so many ways, and her fatigue slipped away. She wasn't done experiencing things tonight.

"Oh, you've certainly awakened something." She pressed her hand on Ellison's shoulder, pushing her flat onto the bed as she leaned over her. It was Ellison's turn, and Katie was more than ready to find out what made her come undone.

CHAPTER EIGHTEEN

Ellison moaned at the sensation of Katie's lips on her chest. She was still on such a high from fucking Katie that she hadn't really considered her own aching sex. She hadn't had any expectations for tonight, yet she'd been pleasantly surprised. Which was happening again in this moment as Katie's knowledge of the body and its erogenous zones was frustratingly evident in the best way.

Katie's touch was otherworldly. She applied the perfect amount of pressure everywhere she went, and Ellison was panting and writhing from the attention she was paying her chest alone. And those lips. Katie had the fullest, sexiest lips. And the way she kissed…there was something magical about it.

Katie climbed over her, and Ellison loved the weight of her against her. She reached up into Katie's thick auburn hair, pulling her mouth to her as Katie slipped a leg between hers. Ellison moaned again as Katie's thigh pressed against her clit. She rolled her hips up for more friction, and Katie pressed her thigh against her more fully.

Katie reached down and gripped her ass, pulling her against her harder, and Ellison saw stars. She was plenty turned-on from their foreplay and the first two rounds with Katie—she didn't need much priming to climax. This would do just fine.

"I want to touch you," Katie said against her lips, and Ellison's breath caught. She wanted that, too, but she wasn't about to rush Katie into any other new experiences tonight.

Ellison slowed her movements and spread her legs. She guided Katie's hand off her breast to her hip as she replied, "Then touch me."

Katie broke their kiss to look down at her. She studied Ellison's face before giving her a small smile, almost as if to double-check that she'd been given the green light. It was adorable.

She wasted no time, and soon Ellison was writhing again, this time from Katie's teasing near-touches along her swollen lips.

"Tell me how you like it," Katie said, licking her lips and looking between the apex of Ellison's hips and her eyes. "No. Better yet, show me."

Ellison's arousal surged at Katie's request-turned-command. She nodded before reaching down to touch herself, spreading her lips and collecting wetness as she rubbed along the edge of her clit. She dipped inside and moved through the familiar routine again, this time with the unfamiliar experience of having a voyeur. Which did nothing to dampen her arousal in the least bit. In fact, when Katie began toying with Ellison's nipple and licking down her stomach, Ellison nearly lost that last bit of control she'd been holding on to.

"My turn," Katie said, guiding her hand away, and Ellison threw her head back in ecstasy as Katie proved herself a quick study. Katie stayed with her, studying her face and kissing her lips as she dragged Ellison's orgasm out longer and longer.

After what felt like an eternity of tremors, Ellison switched their positions. With Katie underneath her and her hand still between them, Ellison guided two of Katie's fingers inside her as she climbed on top. Katie's free hand went to Ellison's chest, and Ellison dropped her elbows beside Katie's head. She ground down on Katie's hand as she kissed her until the friction and the position brought her back to climax again.

She rested her forehead against Katie's before slipping off to her side, and she smiled as Katie wrapped her up in long limbs and gentle caresses. Katie tucked her head under Ellison's chin as Ellison guided the blanket over them.

She felt a tender kiss to her collarbone as Katie stifled a yawn. "That was amazing."

"Which part?" Ellison teased.

"All of it," Katie replied, her voice sounding sleepy. "Being reborn is tiring."

Ellison laughed as she kissed the top of Katie's head. "Then we should get some sleep."

Katie looked up at her, hopeful. "So we can do it again tomorrow?"

"Maybe even later tonight," Ellison replied.

"Deal," Katie said, and Ellison held her close, breathing in her scent as she let the warmth of Katie's naked body wrapped around her lull her to sleep. Sated and so, so happy.

❖

"Remind me again why I agreed to get out of bed this morning?" Katie asked from the passenger seat.

"Because we have things to do today. Like get you into your house so you can spruce up your wardrobe—your words, not mine. Because I prefer you in nothing at all," Ellison said, sparing her a playful glance.

"I can't just be naked all day in your beach house," Katie said, reaching out to take her hand.

"But can't you?" Ellison teased. The last few days had been a dream. And waking up with Katie—naked and cuddled close—was the best way to wake up. Hands down.

"The evening beach walks might draw a bit of attention," Katie said with a smile. "But having clothes on around you has been a struggle since the oyster night."

"The oyster night," Ellison said with a laugh. "I barely remember those."

"I worked hard on shucking those beauties. You were no help, by the way," Katie replied.

"I was helpful in other ways." Ellison hadn't thought to ask, but now seemed like an okay time to do so. "But you haven't had any regrets, have you?"

"Only that we have somewhere to be today," Katie said. "Because I certainly could have been convinced to stay in bed and listen to the waves all day."

"I'm not working this weekend. I promise to dedicate an entire day in bed to you," Ellison replied.

"You spoil me," Katie said, squeezing their joined hands. "So, remind me what's on the agenda today. My head is a little foggy from all the rebirth sex I've been catching up on and the naughty dreams that seem to follow."

"You've been having naughty dreams?" Ellison asked.

"I think so? I can't be sure. All I know is I woke up today really turned-on and already amped up."

"Maybe that's because you woke up with your hand on my breast again," Ellison teased.

"It's not my fault my body—my hand, specifically—gravitates toward you. It should be a compliment. My subconscious thinks your tits are hot. My conscious agrees." Katie shrugged.

"I didn't mind it."

"I figured as much when you dragged me back to bed before coffee," Katie replied.

"I'm not going to turn down a chance for quickie morning sex with a beautiful naked woman. Coffee can wait fifteen minutes," Ellison reasoned.

"Fifteen minutes?" Katie scoffed. "Kissing you hello takes fifteen minutes. So far the least amount of time sex with you has taken is an hour, minimum. And that was this morning when we had a timed deadline to get on the road." She laughed. "If this is the standard to expect, I need to start making room in my calendar."

"Hey, we still managed to get breakfast," Ellison said. "And it's even hot."

Katie held up the bag from Dunkin' with a nod. "I'm not mad about orgasms and wake-up wraps before nine a.m. I'm just making a point."

"Which is?" Ellison asked.

"Nothing. There is no point. So far today has been awesome," Katie said, giving up. "No regrets."

"Same." Ellison laughed. "Okay, to answer your initial question— we have to stop by my office to pick up a few things for our meeting with Zander."

"And I'm going to pop in to say hi to Shaina, in between her clients," Katie replied.

"Right. Then we're swinging by your mom's place for you two to visit while I take a quick conference call in the parking lot before we head to your house to meet Zander."

"Are you sure you don't mind?" Katie asked.

"Not at all. And look, if you decide you want to stay, I can do the meeting with Zander alone. I'll just leave Sunny with you and take a cab," Ellison said. She knew Katie had FaceTimed her mother every day since the fire, but that she hadn't seen her in person in a long time. She didn't want Katie to feel rushed. But she couldn't cancel with Zander, either. So she was willing to do the walk-through alone if that was easier.

"There is nothing I want to do less than walk through that house and see how bad things are," Katie admitted. "But I have to. I need to see it."

"I understand," Ellison said, rubbing her thumb along Katie's as she turned Sunny onto the exit. "The good news is, after we get in the house and find your car keys, you can get back in your own car again."

Katie frowned. "I'll miss Sunny."

"She's not going anywhere. You can still tool around with her if you want. It'll save mileage on your lease. And it's not like Sunny was getting much action before you came along. I literally only drove her on weekends, and mostly only in the summer. I'm sure she loves having a purpose." Ellison had had to have Sunny jump-started every year since she'd gotten her three years ago. She loved coming home from work now and seeing the top down, and knowing that Katie had taken Sunny out for a spin.

"Oh, thank God," Katie exclaimed. "I was already having withdrawal."

After a pause, Katie asked, "So, with Zander, we do a walk-through and grab whatever is salvageable, right?"

"That's the plan," Ellison said, nodding to the stack of boxes in the back. "We pack up what we can and mark the rest for storage or auction. Then the movers will come and relocate whatever we don't take to the storage facility you rented for the time being."

"You mean the one that *you* rented," Katie corrected. "Because none of this has cost me a dime yet."

"Gamble and Associates rented it, yes. That's par for the course. The three-month rental is included in the contract you signed. When the house sells, you take over the rental contract and decide what to do after that. That way we ensure that the house is cleared out for Zander to work his magic."

Katie looked out the window and was silent for a while. "Tell me something to take my mind off how scared I am about what we're going to find today."

Ellison thought for a moment. "I forgot to mention it to you on oyster night, but I did more than just get news about the embryos that day."

"Oh?" Katie turned to face her. "What else happened?"

"Well, after I got the embryo update, I called the surrogacy agency."

"And?" Katie asked, leaning forward. "What did they say?"

"They had a last-minute opening, so I went in for a meeting."

Katie rolled her hand, motioning for Ellison to get on with it. "And? You're killing me here."

"And they have a few matches for surrogates for me. But there's one woman in particular that they think would be a good fit for what I'm looking for."

"Which is what?" Katie asked.

"I want someone who's had a child before. Someone in a partnered or married relationship with a strong support system. Someone with a varied palate who likes lots of different foods and textures, so the baby can be exposed to tastes and flavors. I want someone that likes music or who sings, because I want the baby to hear sounds and be surrounded by art." Ellison paused. "I want someone who wants to do this for someone else because they know how important that role is. Not just someone that wants a paycheck. Because I want that person to be as invested in this baby as I will be. I need that. I need someone that knows how hard this process has been and will continue to be until that baby is in my arms and is mine. And that's the hardest," Ellison said. "Trusting someone else with your most valuable, precious part."

Katie watched her for a moment. "The way you talk about this could-be baby, with such passion and devotion already—it's beautiful. It's poetic and deep and clearly so genuine. You're going to be a great mom, Ellison. This baby will be lucky to have you."

"I hope so." Ellison thought about it often. Would she be a good mom? She thought she would be. She wanted to be. She was willing to do just about anything to get the opportunity to try.

"What's her name?" Katie asked.

"Whose?"

"The possible surrogate match."

"Terry. She's a mom of two boys—ages seven and nine. She's been married to her wife for fifteen years, and she works from home."

Ellison added, "Now I just have to wait to see if Terry agrees to meet with me and if we feel like it's a good in-person match. Then we can start the rest of the process."

"And when she sees how freaking awesome you are, then it's time to put that super cute baby in there," Katie said matter-of-factly.

"That's the plan. Though there are a few steps in the middle," she said with a laugh. "You think the baby will be cute, though?"

"I mean, you're gorgeous. And redheads are amazing—"

"And stunning in their own right," Ellison said, squeezing Katie's hand.

"Exactly. And charming. And hysterical. And brilliant, I might add."

"Well, you're certainly a fast learner. I'll give you that," Ellison said.

"I was and continue to be extremely motivated. I have much to learn still, but thank you," Katie said. "Plus, selfishly, I'm becoming obsessed with the sounds you make in bed. So my intentions are equally self-serving."

"I'm keeping you," Ellison said.

"Good."

Ellison thought about what Katie had said, and she asked, "Do you think you'd ever want to have kids? I mean, you *are* the total package."

"Me? Oh, I'm nowhere near stable enough to even consider that," Katie replied. "Sure, they'd be Gerber Baby adorable. I mean, look at these freckles," she said, pointing to the bridge of her nose. "But I'm a mess. And the idea of that kind of responsibility terrifies me."

That surprised Ellison a bit. All her experiences with Katie showed her to be a healer and to have truly maternal and caring instincts. She imagined Katie would be a fun and loving parent. "Why's that?"

"Well, for one, I'm living in your house because I burned my own place down. And I can't drive my own car because the keys are locked in the burned-down house that until today was only safe enough to be entered by trained professionals. And then there's the issue that I can't afford to take care of my mother until I sell the house that I almost burned down." Katie sighed. "I could go on and on, but I'm just making myself depressed."

Ellison frowned. "I think you're being a little hard on yourself."

"Am I, though?" Katie rested her arm against the passenger

window. "I'm twenty-eight and I live—well, I *lived*—in the house I grew up in. I have two psych degrees I never use, and my attempts to get through physical therapy school to better myself and my career while helping my mother rehabilitate after her accident stalled when she had her stroke. And though I love what I do at the moment, it's not exactly changing the world. Plus, there's the added fact that I'm alone. I have no family outside of my mother, and I remember what it was like growing up with a single parent. It was hard even on the good days. I can't take care of my adult mother as an adult myself—how could I take care of a child?"

"I'd be raising this child as a single parent," Ellison said. "And I was raised by a single mom, too. And it wasn't easy, but there was a lot of love in that house. I know that's not always the case, but it was for me."

"You're lucky then. And you're also established in your life and work. You're going to be an extraordinary mother because you *want* to be one so badly. And you can do for this child like no one else can," Katie said. The sigh that followed was heavy. "Me, on the other hand… I'm a disaster. Life is in total flux right now, and I'm in no place to even consider it."

Ellison understood that. And she'd been Katie's age once. Admittedly, her life was very different back then. But she'd known she wanted kids. The only difference was that she put that dream on hold when Peyton pumped the brakes. Something she was glad she did because the idea of co-parenting with someone that didn't want children sounded like a nightmare. And yet Peyton seemed to be singing a different tune these days. Try as she might to forget, she knew that Peyton and Ilaria's baby shower was coming up soon. And she could already feel herself getting irritated about that.

They drove in amicable silence the rest of the way with Katie quietly singing along to the radio. Ellison thought about their conversation and about their time together. It made her think about the future of things. She hadn't planned to get into a romantic relationship with anyone, and certainly not someone as young as Katie. Especially since she had so many big things happening in her own life. It was early still, and they were still figuring things out, but Ellison felt a little bit of unease start to creep in about the baby plans on the horizon. She liked what was happening between her and Katie, and she wanted it to continue. But she wouldn't push off her plans to be a mother, not again. She hoped that she could have both and hold on to this happiness she felt as long as she could. But time would tell, she supposed.

As they pulled into the parking lot of Gamble and Associates, Katie turned to her. "Are you okay?"

"Hmm?"

"You got a little quiet," Katie replied, and Ellison felt bad.

"I just got in my own head about some work stuff," she lied.

"Is that all?" Katie asked, watching her closely.

"Yes." *No.*

Katie seemed to consider this, though she said nothing.

Ellison turned off Sunny and stepped out of the driver's side door, surprised to find Katie there, waiting.

"I meant what I said about you and your baby journey. I'm excited for you, and I do think you're incredible in every single way. I can't wait for Terry to be as blown away by you as I've been," Katie said, looping her arms around Ellison's neck. "Because you are nothing short of extraordinary."

Ellison smiled at the compliment, pulling Katie close and dipping her head to connect their lips. "Flattery will get you everywhere."

Katie sucked on her bottom lip before deepening the kiss, and Ellison moaned in response. "I'm hoping it gets me your undivided attention in the bedroom this weekend. Because there are some things I want to try."

"What things?" Ellison asked, already getting turned-on again.

"Well," Katie said as she dropped one hand from Ellison's neck to slip inside her blazer and massage along her side. "I was hoping maybe *I* could be on my knees next time."

Ellison ached at the instant visual Katie's words brought on. "I think we can make that happen."

"Good," Katie said, ghosting her thumb across Ellison's nipple before removing her hand from under her blazer. "Because I've been thinking about that a lot."

"Now it's something I'm going to be thinking about all day," Ellison admitted.

"Sorry not sorry." Katie parroted Ellison's seemingly new favorite phrase.

"You're the worst." Ellison sighed. "The absolute worst."

Katie merely winked.

The sound of someone clearing their throat caused Katie to jump in Ellison's embrace.

"Morning, ladies," Trina said from just to Ellison's left.

"Trina," Ellison said, giving her a brief nod.

"Hi," Katie said, waving with her eyes adorably squeezed shut. The light blush on her cheeks was equally lovable. "Good morning."

Trina laughed. "I guess I'll see you inside, huh?"

"Probably," Katie said, dropping her head to her hand.

"I'll have Jax add an extra coffee to the morning order," Trina replied, looking as though she was enjoying herself. "How do you take your caffeine, Katie?"

"Embarrassed with a side of mortification," she replied.

Ellison laughed. "With cream and a little sugar. A dash of cinnamon, too."

"On it, Boss," Trina said with a wave. "Carry on with your, uh, morning routine."

"Go away," Ellison said, and Trina chuckled as she typed furiously into her cell phone while heading toward the office.

"She's already texting about this, isn't she?" Katie peeked up at her through her fingers.

"Oh, she probably already posted it on social media," Ellison said, not at all concerned.

"I'm so sorry," Katie said, wringing her hands. "If I knew your employees were…I never would have…"

"Relax," Ellison said, placing her hands on Katie's and intertwining their fingers. "I've walked in on just about every one of my employees doing something borderline scandalous. Remind me to tell you about the time I caught Trina making out with her archrival turned girlfriend and how she almost lost the bet of a lifetime while also putting my realty office's reputation on the line. Or the many times I've unintentionally stumbled upon Lauren and her girlfriend hooking up in the back seat of Thea's car, since that seems to be their particular type of kink. It's comical at this point, really."

Katie looked less overwhelmed. "And Jax?"

"Ah, well, Jax is a little more modest than those two. And they're trying to win over the girl of their dreams at the moment. But I'm sure they'll embarrass themselves in front of me eventually. I seem to be a magnet for it."

"So you aren't mad?" Katie asked.

"Only that I'm going to be thinking about what you said all day and not be able to experience it," Ellison replied.

Katie gave her a secret smile. "Think of it as something to look forward to."

Ellison took her hand as she closed Sunny's door, pulling her toward the office. "Come on, let's get this show on the road, so we can get back to the beach and out of these clothes."

"You're so sexy when you take control," Katie teased.

"Oh, baby. You haven't seen anything yet."

Chapter Nineteen

Shaina squealed when she saw her. "Tell me this tan isn't from the house fire," she teased.

Katie smiled, glad that Shaina had caught her before she'd gone into Ellison's office. She was hoping to see her today, but Shaina hadn't texted her back yet. "That's from all the beach walks I've been taking." And the naked postcoital sunbathing she'd been doing on Ellison's bedroom balcony, but she left that part out.

Shaina shook her head. "Lifestyles of the rich and well-heeled girlfriend life, huh?"

Katie nudged her. "Shut up. I already feel out of place there. She lives like a literal celebrity."

"A celebrity that has the hots for you. How are things going with Ms. Maserati?"

"Great, so great," Katie replied. She couldn't downplay her happiness if she tried.

"Oh, damn," Shaina said with her eyebrows raised. "You slept with her."

"How did you—?"

Shaina gave her a look. "Well, I watched you personally float over here from the entrance to her office. Where you two were holding hands and smiling like lovebirds. But mostly you gave it away with the moony, far-off gaze when I asked you how things were going. And your face told me life was sextastic."

"I'm not sure that's a word."

"So I'm wrong, then?" Shaina challenged.

"I didn't say that," Katie hedged.

"Tell me everything," Shaina said, grabbing her arm before second-guessing that and pulling back. "Oh, sorry. Did I hurt you?"

Katie shook her head. "No, I'm pretty much back to one hundred percent. But don't tell Pietro that. I plan to take next week off as scheduled. Just to make sure I can do a full day's work without getting too wiped out."

Shaina made a zipper motion to her lips. "My lips are sealed. But yours better not be about the sex. Spill." She checked her watch. "I have ten more minutes before Mrs. Erickson's facial."

Katie ran her hand through her hair. "I don't know what to say, exactly."

"Tell me it was phenomenal. Because I know it was."

"It was more than phenomenal." Katie wasn't sure how to put the last few days into words just yet. If she wasn't able to reach out and touch Ellison as often as she could, she would have thought it was all a dream. "It's like, I never experienced true pleasure before. Like *true* pleasure. Like the kind that keeps happening over and over, even though you're sure it can't possibly happen again. It does. A lot."

"Wow," Shaina said. "I need to dump Raul and get a girlfriend."

"How are things going between you two? Any better?"

Shaina shrugged. "I don't know. I'm getting a lot of mixed signals from him lately. I think maybe we're spending too much time together. I'm going to spend fewer nights at his place over the next week and see if that changes things at all." She shook her head. "It's not like we're having the kind of sex you two are."

"I mean, I'd be jealous if I were you," Katie said.

"Oh, I am," Shaina said with a smile. "I'm glad you're doing okay. I was really freaked out when I heard about the fire."

"I am okay. We're heading over there for the first time today, to see how bad it all was."

"It's going to be okay, remember? It's all going to be okay," Shaina said.

"I love you." Katie wasn't sure she'd ever told Shaina that. But she felt like now was as good a time as ever.

"I know, Katie Cat. I love you, too." Shaina gave her a hug. "Now go be with that hottie with a body while I go back to work. I'm sure Ellison is wondering what's taking you so long."

"I'm just giving her a chance to miss me," Katie joked.

"Uh-huh. Sure." Shaina gave her another hug as she added, "Call me sometime when you come up for air. Just so I know you're still alive."

"I'll be back to work in a week, I promise."

"If you can still walk by then," Shaina called out with a suggestive hand motion as she headed back toward the spa. "I'd be sure to tire myself out this week, if I were you. Just remember some of us plan to live vicariously through you."

"Bye, Shaina."

"Bye."

Things were abuzz when she walked through the entrance of Ellison's office. There were Realtors working that she'd never met before and a lot of laughter from the conference room toward the back, where she and Ellison had shared cupcakes.

"Katie, hey," Jax said, as they juggled some paperwork. "Sorry, it's a madhouse here. Does Ellison know you're here?"

"I was just looking for her," Katie replied.

"Come in, come in," Jax motioned for her to enter, nearly dropping the files in the process. "Crap. I really can't multitask. I should stop trying."

"Give me those before you make a fool of yourself in front of another pretty girl," Trina said, swooping in and catching the top file that slipped from Jax's grasp.

"Rude," Jax said, though they looked grateful.

"Don't worry. We all know this pretty girl is taken," Trina said, giving Katie a wink. "Ellison is in the conference room with Talia, finishing up some fitting stuff."

"Talia?" The name sounded familiar, but Katie couldn't remember why.

"Yeah, the *original* pretty girl Jax can't seem not to make a fool of themself in front of," Trina teased, and Jax blushed.

"I hate you," Jax said unconvincingly.

"You'll love me when you finally realize that you're worth it and that you should ask her out already. I'm just pointing out the obvious—you're a stud. Go do studly things and get her on the same page. Please. I'm dying over here." Trina feigned death.

"Oh, why are we stage-dying?" Lauren appeared holding a coffee.

"Jax is suffering from imposter syndrome in front of Katie," Trina said, taking the coffee from Lauren and handing it to Katie. "This is yours. Cream and sugar, with a touch of cinnamon."

"Thanks," Katie said, before she whispered to Jax, "I get imposter syndrome around these people all the time. I totally get it."

"One normal person, finally," Jax cheered. "You all walk around here like deities. It's nice to meet a human being."

"Oh, Jaxy, you should know better than to talk to demigods like that," Lauren said, as she tickled Jax. "We might curse you in your sleep."

Jax wiggled away, dropping two more files. "I'm being sabotaged."

Katie picked up the files before adjusting the papers within them and shrugging. "Sounds like they just love you a lot and have a funny way of showing it."

"I like you more every day," Trina said to her with a broad smile, and something about that told Katie that was high praise from her.

"Come on, I'll take you to Ellison," Lauren said, looping her arm in Katie's. "And you can tell me all about the parking lot make-out sesh."

Katie rolled her eyes. "It's like you two have a mental hotline," she said, motioning to Trina.

"I heard about it, too," Jax said, their voice cracking a bit. "I mean, not to blow up your spot or anything."

"Too late," Katie said.

"You and Ellison, huh?" Lauren asked, seemingly genuine. "That's great. She's great. And we already thought you were great. So the greatness floweth over, it seems."

"That's Lauren-speak for welcome to the circus. Where the popcorn is free, though occasionally stale, but the clowns are always entertaining," Trina said, holding open the conference room door. "We're happy to have you."

"Katie," Ellison said, looking up with a smile. "I was hoping you could meet Talia. I'm glad you made it before she left."

The woman Katie assumed was Talia was sitting at the conference table, looking over a series of photographs. She looked up and gave her a small wave. "Hi, I've heard so much about you."

"You have?" Katie gave Ellison a look.

"All good things, mostly," she said, and her smile was mesmerizing. Her gorgeous natural brown hair had hints of blond highlights, and she was so stylishly dressed that she made Trina look almost casual. Her skin was a rich brown, and she had a subtle gold shimmer on her cheekbones that brought out the flecks of yellow in her dark brown eyes. She was just one more exquisitely magnificent creature in this group.

"Oh, I can't wait to hear this," Katie said, leaning against the doorframe.

"I'm kidding," Talia said as she stood. "She's been mostly mum about you except to tell me that you might be a great model for our little internet campaign. Which I can see she was dead-on about. Love that curly auburn hair, girl. And those emerald eyes." Talia leaned in. "Tell me those freckles are natural."

"One hundred percent," Katie said, feeling a bit shy by the attention.

"Well, I was sold before I met you because we all know Ellison has great taste—"

"Because you dress me. Which is probably going to change when you become super famous and too big to deal with me," Ellison said, pretending to pout. Katie thought it was adorable.

"Ha. As if Auntie would ever let me. I'll be dressing her well into the grave and the great beyond. We all know you're part of that package deal, too."

"Auntie?" Katie asked.

"Talia is Faith's niece," Ellison replied.

"Oh, I see it now. Stunning looks must run in the family," Katie said.

"Thank you." Talia gave her a curious look, and Katie wanted to know what she was thinking. "Say you'll let me dress you in a few outfits for the campaign. We're doing a photo shoot at the end of next month, and I'd love for you to be involved. I'll make sure Ellison buys you dinner for your troubles."

Ellison laughed.

"Dinner, eh?" Katie pretended to consider this. She knew this was a big deal to Ellison, and she wanted to support her since she'd done so much for her already. She loved playing dress-up, and she'd seen most of Talia's work. She knew she'd look amazing. "I'm sold. But make it two dinners."

Ellison made a bowing motion. "Done."

Talia clapped. "Awesome. I've got Ellison's measurements down pat, but I'll need to get yours so I can get to work on some outfits for you before the shoot. Any interest in getting into your underwear real quick?"

"Now?" Katie asked.

Talia shrugged. "I mean, I can come back. But I already got Trina, Lauren, and Jax done today. Ellison hasn't had a size change in the entire lifetime I've known her. So you're all that's left." She clasped her hands and made a begging motion. "Pretty please?"

Ellison's hand was on her low back in a flash—her face unsure. "You don't have to. I didn't mean for you to be put on the spot."

"Is dessert included?" Katie asked, locking eyes with her.

"Included in what?" Ellison asked.

"The dinners." Katie gave Ellison that secret smile again, and Ellison loosened up.

"Absolutely. You can even have it first. Your call."

Katie held her gaze for a moment. A silent agreement passed between them before she nodded to Talia. "I'm in. Let's get semi-naked."

"Yes," Talia cheered as she pulled out a tape measure and some pins. "I'll be quick."

"Just don't poke me with those," Katie joked.

Talia crossed her heart. "I swear. If I do, Ellison can be on the hook for three dinners."

"Ellison is buying a lot of meals all of a sudden," Ellison said, feigning annoyance. "Anything else to add to the tab?"

Katie looked at her as she pulled her shirt over her head. "I wouldn't turn down champagne and oysters again."

"I can make that happen," Ellison said, and Katie noticed the way she checked her out as Talia's back was to her.

Talia had her bust measurements done in no time, and when it was time for Katie to drop trou, Ellison excused herself, disappearing behind the closed door.

Talia knelt in front of her, measuring this and that and putting a pin here and there. She stood up and stepped back, looking at Katie before she moved on to measure her inseam. "So, Ellison, huh?"

Katie glanced down at her. "Hmm?"

Talia stood, tossing the unraveled tape measure over her shoulder as she jotted down some numbers on the small notepad in her hand. "I was honest about what I said before—she didn't say much about you except to mention you'd be a great model for my clothes. I've only ever seen her that quiet when talking about one other person. Not that she's super chatty on the usual, but this quiet felt discreet."

"Who's the other person?" Katie asked, but she had a feeling she already knew.

"Auntie," Talia said. "And I take it from your comment before that you know about them."

"A little. But only per Ellison's report. I've never met your aunt. Not really, anyway," Katie said, leaving out the make-out session she interrupted so many weeks ago.

Talia handed Katie back her pants. "Ellison and Auntie were an item long before I was born. And though they keep it pretty carefully under wraps, I know they've gravitated back to each other over the years." She packed up her materials as Katie buttoned her jeans. "But Ellison acts around you and talks about you like she does with my aunt. Like you're special. And like she's keeping a secret. But the good kind of secret, not the bad kind. You know?"

"Maybe?" Katie wasn't quite sure.

"She likes you. And Ellison doesn't give off that vibe in a romantic way very often. I've known her since birth, and I've only ever seen it once before." Talia grabbed the photographs off the table and picked up her purse. "It's nice. I'm glad for you both. She's a special woman."

"I know," Katie said. Ellison's friend circle—her family—were all as remarkable as she was. And they cared about her deeply. That was easy to see.

"Well, thanks for coming on board and for getting almost naked with a stranger," Talia said, shaking her hand. "And good luck with whatever you two have going on. I hope it works out."

"Thanks," Katie said, feeling touched. "Me, too."

Talia gave her a nod before stepping into the corridor. Ellison was waiting—adorably—just outside the door.

"Everything go okay?" she asked Katie after saying good-bye to Talia.

"Fine," Katie said, stepping closer but making sure to keep a socially acceptable distance since they were in Ellison's office. "You good?"

"Well, I mean, you just took your pants off in front of my quasi-niece. But aside from that, I'm fine."

"Does that mean you were jealous? Because from what I hear, she's family."

Ellison raised an eyebrow at that. "Oh? And what did she say exactly?"

"That you like me, and it's super obvious to everyone with eyes."

Ellison paled. "She said that?"

"Not exactly. But the fact remains." Katie reached for her before deciding that would be crossing the line and pulling back.

"Well, she's not wrong," Ellison said, her gaze on the hand Katie extended in her direction. "I seem to like you more and more each day."

"I'm very likeable," Katie said. "It's a superpower of mine."

"One of many, I'm learning," Ellison said, and Katie got the feeling they were talking about bedroom things now.

"Do you have much more to do here? Because this distance thing we're doing right now sucks. And I want to make out with your face," Katie said.

"I'm done. Let's go," Ellison said, giving her that flirty smile she loved so much.

"Just one thing," Katie said, holding up her hand. "Since you owe me all these dinners and desserts—"

"And now champagne and oysters," Ellison supplied.

"Right. Since I'm volunteering for Talia's campaign—which I know is important to you—maybe that means you'll let *me* drive Sunny to our next destination? Because, you know, we have a good thing going on."

"You and Sunny? Or you and me?" Ellison asked.

"Both. Although Sunny and I have a solid sisterly bond. And what I have with you...well, there's nothing wholesome about that."

Ellison stepped into her space, breaking the unspoken social distance rule to whisper, "I plan to do many very unwholesome things to you tonight. So you can be the lead and drive Sunny all you want, as long as you know that I'll be taking the lead with you later."

Katie swallowed thickly. "Is that a promise?"

"Cross my heart," Ellison said, and Katie couldn't get out of there fast enough.

CHAPTER TWENTY

Katie had been floating all afternoon. After Ellison's office, they visited her mother and even sat in on a group exercise class. Ellison's conference call ended early, so she came in from the car once she texted to see if it was okay. Katie nearly cried at how seamlessly Ellison got on with her mother. She sat right down and talked to her like she'd known her her whole life. In no time, her mom was holding Ellison's hand like she did with Katie and smiling along—even speaking a few words here and there. Katie had only seen that interaction with Dennis and a few physical and occupational therapists' sessions she'd sat in on. The Ellison magic seemed to know no bounds.

She was holding on to that memory as they pulled up to the house. Katie was anxious about this, bracing herself for what she might see.

Zander Alter was waiting for them by the front porch, ready to survey the damage and give his impression of how much this might delay the renovations they'd planned to complete to get the house ready to sell. Katie found out quickly that, like Ellison, he was calm and kind. He had a softness to his voice, and the skin around his eyes crinkled when he smiled.

"Watch your step on the porch," Ellison said to him. "There's a hole there."

Zander looked down at the porch, frowning. "Is this from the firefighters?"

"If only I could blame that on the fire," Katie said, feeling embarrassed.

Zander gave her a sympathetic look. "Old houses like this sometimes fall apart. That's no one's fault."

Ellison's hand at her low back told her not to worry, so she didn't. No matter what they found inside, she knew Ellison and Zander would figure out what to do.

Ellison and Zander pulled down the caution tape that crossed the door before Katie tried the key. When the key failed to open the front door, Zander used his shoulder to help unstick it, and the smell of stagnant smoke-filled air rushed out as the door flung in.

The foyer and living room were disheveled, and there were muddy, dirty boot prints from the firefighters all over the floor and the edge of the carpet, but otherwise the only sign of the fire was the lingering smell of damp burned wood. As they made their way through the first floor, Ellison and Zander chatted quietly, and Zander took pictures with his phone while scribbling notes on his clipboard.

The water damage from extinguishing the second-floor fire was evident on the kitchen ceiling and along the walls that encased the back door to the yard and garden area. Once Zander had checked the pipes under the sink and reemerged from the basement to check what was left of the electrical panel, he announced it was time to go upstairs.

"Are you ready?" Ellison asked, watching Katie's face closely.

Katie wasn't really sure. On the one hand, yes—she had to know what it looked like up there and if there was anything salvageable in her bedroom or the rooms around it. On the other hand, the idea of seeing the place where the fire began made her uneasy.

"I can stay down here with you, if you'd like," Ellison said, gripping her hand. Katie didn't realize it was shaking until Ellison held her hand still.

"I'm fine. I'll be okay." Katie's desire to know overpowered her fear.

"Okay, I'll head up first. Just to make sure it's safe," Zander said, ascending the stairs a few steps in front of them.

Katie knew that the house was safe enough to enter—that's why they were here. Sasha had pulled some strings and got the house cleared quicker than usual, but she'd warned them to enter with a structural integrity professional. She said the second-floor bedroom and roof were irreparably damaged, and that some areas would remain roped off until they could be repaired.

The hallway to the bedrooms was eerily quiet, save for the occasional sound of the wind that fluttered the plastic sheets someone had put up. Katie assumed it was the firefighters' work. The off-white flowered wallpaper of the hallway had smoke lines along the ceiling, a tarry substance that thickened as they got closer to Katie's room.

Zander slipped in and out of the other bedrooms and bathroom, making notes and nodding his head. Katie saw that her mother's room was mostly fine save for some water damage from the ceiling along the wall that bordered Katie's room.

Zander pulled back the drop sheet covering the doorway to Katie's room, before glancing back at her. "Can I?"

"Please do," she said, clutching Ellison's hand as he pulled back the barrier for her to look in.

The far wall was completely gone. Her bed and dresser were tossed against the wall closest to them, and the desk that formerly occupied the space that used to exist between the windows was a pile of burnt rubble by the entrance to her closet. The floor was charred where the space heater had been, and the black shadow of a fire racing up the wallpaper to the ceiling looked ominous and ghastly. The ceiling above where the wall had been was scorched, with chunks of plaster and insulation hanging down. And the faint smell of water still lingered in the air, though it was easily overpowered by the smell of an extinguished inferno that seemed to radiate out of every surface.

Ellison handed her something, and she took it blindly as she watched Zander step carefully along the floor toward her closet. He pulled out his own caution tape and attached it to the door handle of the closet, stretching it back toward them and marking off the portions of the floor that sagged or creaked, or weren't connected to anything at all.

Katie felt Ellison take whatever she had given her back. "Here," she said, turning Katie's chin in her direction. "Let me."

Katie closed her eyes as Ellison wiped the tissue along her cheeks—collecting tears Katie had been too distracted to feel.

"All set," Ellison whispered, and Katie blinked her eyes open to find what were quickly becoming her favorite blue ones looking back at her. "We're almost done here, I promise."

Katie nodded, taking Ellison's hand again as Zander talked to her about what he saw. She zoned out for most of it, but it sounded like he was echoing what Sasha had said—the room was a total loss, and he could see up through the portions of the roof that were missing. This was a mess.

Katie waited in the living room as he went up to the third floor and attic spaces. She'd seen enough, and the smell on the second floor was making her nauseous and dizzy. Ellison handed her a glass of water from the kitchen before leaving to retrieve some boxes from Sunny.

"How are you feeling?" Ellison appeared at her shoulder. She hadn't noticed her re-entering the house. She was too lost in her own thoughts.

"Tired," she admitted.

"This is a lot," Ellison said, sweeping an errant hair from Katie's forehead before offering her another sip of the glass Katie had abandoned on the nearby coffee table.

"It is."

Ellison sat next to her on the sofa. "We don't have to do this today. We can come back another time."

"It's fine. I need clothes, remember?" Katie said, putting on a brave face.

"I love a reason to shop," Ellison said. "We can get you new clothes."

"I know. But I have to get this done. For Zander to get started. To not delay this any longer. For Mom. I need to keep to our timeline for Mom. The sooner we sell the house, the longer she gets the best care money can buy." Katie finished the glass of water. "I can do something that makes me uncomfortable for a short time if it improves her life for a long time."

"Well, I have all the pictures and notes I need to move forward," Zander said as he joined them in the living room.

"Just from first glance, what do you think?" Katie asked, scooting to the edge of the sofa.

"The damage is extensive, but luckily not involving a whole lot more than we were already going to fix. We were planning on redoing the roof, plumbing, and electrical anyway. So now we just have to add a few structural supports and an extra wall or two on top of that." Zander didn't seem as worried as Katie felt.

"And will this delay things?" Ellison asked.

"Maybe by a week, two tops," Zander said, checking his notes. "We have to order some more materials, but that's not an issue. It's more about whether you want to wait until the insurance adjustment comes in."

Ellison looked to Katie and Katie shrugged. "Should I?"

Ellison seemed to consider this. "I wouldn't. Whatever they decide doesn't resolve the fact that you're missing a wall on your house right now and leaving it open to the elements. If I were you, I'd start the process with Zander like we'd already planned. We'll just incorporate the insurance payment into paying Zander's final bill."

"Works for me. That will keep us on our timeline," he said. "I love when a calendar works out."

"Then let's do it," Katie replied.

"Great. I'll start pulling permits now." Zander headed for the door.

They said their good-byes to Zander, and Ellison stood. "Why don't I order us lunch? Maybe food will help us get these boxes filled."

"Is that what you've learned about me this last week and a half? That I'm food motivated?"

Ellison sat on the coffee table across from her, so their knees were touching. "Well, yes. And I also learned that you're an amazing cook. You're super good at crossword puzzles and the frustrating middle section of jigsaw puzzles. You're a whiz at fixing a spotty Wi-Fi connection. And you are hands down the best sea glass finder in the world."

Katie leaned forward, placing her hands on Ellison's knees. "Anything else?"

"I also learned that you cannot stay awake during any movie, regardless of the genre or how many deafening action scenes are in it. And that I've officially lost my favorite throw blanket to your clutches."

"The blanket and I have bonded. We are one. I make no apologies for that," Katie said, leaning in closer still. "That all?"

"No," Ellison said, closing the distance between them as she spoke against Katie's lips. "You have the most kissable lips I have ever encountered, and I am greatly enjoying their frequent proximity and willingness to let me suck on them. Plus, you make me want to stay in bed all day, and I can say as a lifelong workaholic, that is a considerable feat."

Katie hummed. "These lips always make things seem less scary. They're my favorite way to remember the best parts of the day."

Ellison nuzzled her nose. "And what was the best part of today so far?"

Katie leaned back. "Seeing you with my mom."

"She's lovely," Ellison said, her sincerity endearing her to Katie even more.

"And waking up next to you," Katie added. "That was my second favorite part."

"Let's fill these boxes and get back to the beach," Ellison said. "And just so you know, those were my two favorite parts of today, too."

Katie knew that things felt more than a little out of control in her life right now, but what she had with Ellison grounded her like nothing else. It felt so right. And she was so, so happy about that.

❖

Ellison knocked on her bathroom door to make sure Katie was okay. She'd been quiet since they'd finished up at her house. After dinner, she'd asked to take a bath in the soaker tub in Ellison's main bath, citing fatigue and soreness from the day. Ellison knew she was emotionally drained from the house tour. And she surely was physically exhausted—they'd filled Sunny and Katie's car with boxes of clothes and personal items that Katie wanted to keep near. Ellison counted no fewer than a dozen box-laden trips for each of them. And though everything else was organized and left for the movers to worry about, it hadn't been a small task.

"Come in," Katie called out.

Ellison poked her head into the room. "I brought you a glass of wine. And I wanted to make sure you hadn't fallen asleep."

Katie was submerged up to her neck in bubbles, with her long red curls in a clip on top of her head. Her smile was genuine, but her eyes looked tired. "I'm awake, but very, very zen. This tub is heavenly." She reached for the wineglass, caressing Ellison's fingers as she took it from her. "And the waitstaff around here are spectacular."

"Rose water and coconut milk, huh?" Ellison pulled over the small wooden bench she kept spare towels on and sat down on it. "That's a favorite of mine."

"I assumed as much since that jar was significantly more depleted than the other three luxury bath mixes you have. Really, though, who has that much bubble bath?"

Ellison shrugged. "I like options."

"I almost chose the citrus and lavender, but I second-guessed myself at the last minute." Katie held out her hand for Ellison to take it as she sipped her wine.

"Why's that?" Ellison traced her thumb along Katie's palm.

"I figured your taste hadn't disappointed me thus far. So why not go with it?"

"My taste, huh?"

"Mm-hmm." Katie handed her the wineglass as she rose and brought her lips to Ellison's. "It's very distinctive."

Ellison broke their kiss to steal a sip of Katie's wine before abandoning it on the floor nearby. "What's it like?"

"Let me double-check." Katie reconnected their lips, opening her mouth for Ellison to deepen the kiss.

"What's the verdict?" Ellison asked, breathless as Katie began unbuttoning her shirt.

"Hot, wet, delicious," Katie breathed out against her mouth. "Get naked and get in here, so I can taste more of you."

Ellison felt her lower abdomen ache with want. The visual from Katie's earlier promise flashed in her mind.

"What are you thinking about?" Katie asked as she helped her out of her bra.

"You on your knees."

Katie moaned. "On second thought, help me out of here."

"In due time," Ellison said, gently pushing Katie back into the bubbles. "I'm enjoying this too much to rush it to an end."

"Me naked under a blanket of bubbles, too far away to put my mouth where we both want it?" Katie's words made Ellison grip the tub harder than was necessary. "Because that seems silly."

"What if I like you vulnerable and at my whim like this?" Ellison moved closer, leaning forward until she could comfortably submerge her right arm.

"I did promise to let you drive later," Katie said, leaning back.

"We both know how I like to be in control," Ellison whispered as she walked her fingers down Katie's sternum to caress her chest. "And we both know how much I love touching you."

"And how much I love to be touched," Katie said, closing her eyes as Ellison walked her fingers lower.

Ellison smiled as she felt the water move when Katie bent up both her knees, spreading her legs apart. She rubbed along the inside of Katie's thigh as she brought her lips to Katie's mouth. "I'd say I was waiting until you were wet enough to fuck you, but I suppose I can't really know, can I?"

"Jesus. Ellison." Katie gripped at Ellison's jaw as her hips chased Ellison's retreating fingers. "If you keep this up, I'm going to flood this tub."

Ellison gave in to Katie's canting hips and massaged her lower lips with her fingers. "How badly do you want me inside you?"

Katie's free hand found Ellison's bare chest, tugging on her pert nipples and making her hiss in ecstasy. Katie held her mouth close as she panted out against Ellison's lips, "How badly do you want to come in my mouth?"

"So bad," Ellison said, loving that Katie met her every step of the way.

Katie pulled back, her dark pupils framed by the brilliant green of her irises as she said, "Then hurry up and fuck me, so I can find out how expensive you taste."

Ellison licked across Katie's lips as she stroked along her sex. She gripped the edge of the tub to steady herself as Katie continued to toy with her chest. Each swipe of Katie's fingers over her nipples caused Ellison's clit to pulse, making it harder and harder to focus on the very important task in her hand.

She teased Katie a few moments longer before she slipped inside, loving how tight Katie was. Ellison curled her fingers as Katie's inner walls pulsed around her and deepened her thrusts—dragging her thumb along Katie's clit as Katie's moans echoed louder and louder.

The movements of her fingers along Ellison's breasts got more erratic as Katie cried out, and some bath water splashed out of the tub as her body shook with pleasure.

"I sure am glad you came to check on me," Katie said as Ellison withdrew her hand from the water to toss a towel on the wet bathroom floor.

"Me, too," Ellison said, holding Katie's hand as she stepped out of the now draining tub. She watched unabashedly as Katie toweled herself off before she handed her one of the plush cotton robes that she'd brought in from Katie's long-forgotten guest room.

Katie unclipped those luscious red curls, letting them cascade around her face as she stepped up to Ellison. She toyed with the waistband of her pants as she said, "I like this topless look on you. You have the sexiest collarbones." She tugged on the fabric in her hands as she added, "But I'd like these off now. Please."

Ellison undid the clasp on the front of her slacks and let them fall off as she stepped out of them. "Well, since you said please."

Katie's eyes fell to the lace panties that concealed the last bit of Ellison's nudity. "And if I say pretty please, will you let me take those off with my teeth?"

"I might," Ellison said as Katie's hand settled on her stomach, pushing her toward the bedroom. When she felt the bed hit the back of her knees, she stopped, grasping Katie's wrist to command, "Ask."

Katie looked up at her, the robe open and resting on her shoulders as her full chest heaved with short breaths. "Pretty please?"

Ellison nodded and Katie knelt, licking along the skin just above the top of her panties. She licked across the fabric, running her tongue up and down the crotch of Ellison's panties as she let her nose bump against Ellison's still clothed clit.

"Mmm," she moaned as she dragged the flat of her tongue up Ellison's panties. "Did the bath get you wet, too?"

"That's all you, baby," Ellison said, bringing her hips forward as Katie leaned back. "Take those off."

"Gladly." Katie nipped at the skin of her lower abdomen before soothing it with her tongue. She moved lower and took the lace between her teeth, pulling it down a bit before using her hands to guide them off and away.

Ellison was more than turned-on already, but the visual of Katie looking up at her and licking her lips before bringing her mouth to Ellison's pussy was nearly enough to make her climax. She gasped at the sensation of Katie's mouth on her sex. The wet heat of her tongue moving over her, exploring, and lapping at her made her knees feel weak.

Katie's hand pressed on her stomach, encouraging her to sit, and Ellison did with as much grace as her legs could muster. Which wasn't much.

She eased back on the mattress, moving up to make it easier for Katie to lick her fully. She spread her legs as Katie sucked on her swollen tissue, and she shuddered when Katie caressed along her inner thigh before lazily circling her opening.

"That feels amazing," Ellison said, giving in to her desire to weave her fingers into Katie's hair.

"I like that," Katie said when Ellison massaged her scalp. "Show me how fast you want it."

Ellison increased the movement of her fingers on Katie's scalp— she pressed down harder before gliding away slightly and repeating it again and again. She moaned as Katie mimicked her fading pressure with her tongue by running over her clit with the flat of her tongue before moving away slightly.

"You keep that up, and I won't last long," Ellison admitted, already feeling herself climb.

"Good," Katie said before redoubling her efforts.

Ellison's legs began to quake on either side of Katie's head, and Ellison gripped her hair to pull her mouth closer. She ground her hips against Katie's mouth and was nearly at climax when Katie slipped a single finger inside her, sending a surge of pleasure through her body that catapulted her across the threshold.

She dropped back on the bed, breathless, as Katie continued to lap languidly at her sex. She squirmed as Katie kissed up her stomach and tickled her sides as she climbed over her.

Katie let the robe fall from her shoulders as she straddled Ellison's stomach, looking down at her like a sex goddess with a wicked grin.

"You look very pleased with yourself," Ellison said as she wiped clean Katie's bottom lip.

"I'm feeling very pleased. Among other things." Katie rested her hands on Ellison's breasts.

Ellison closed her eyes as she savored the ripples of her climax still washing over her. She smiled as Katie leaned forward, and the pressure of her hands was replaced by the soft skin of Katie's full breasts.

Katie nuzzled her nose before kissing her cheek. "Thank you for that."

Ellison opened her eyes to watch her. "Why are you thanking me? I should be thanking you."

"You're right. You should," Katie teased as she shifted with Ellison, scampering under the covers Ellison pulled back for them both before cuddling up to Ellison's side. "But still. Thank you for sharing yourself with me. And for being patient while I figure out what you like best."

"You. I like you best."

"Then we're on the same page," Katie said, stifling a yawn.

"Good night, Katie," Ellison said, wrapping her arms around her.

"The best night, Ellison."

CHAPTER TWENTY-ONE

"Hey, babe?" Katie called out from upstairs.

"Yes?"

"Can I put some of my stuff in the guest room's closet?"

"Of course," Ellison called back, laughing. Katie asking if she could take up space in this house was ridiculous. It amused Ellison no end that she insisted on keeping her things in the guest bedroom that she hadn't spent a night in since her first week here. After the oyster night, she'd spent every night in Ellison's bed. But she respected Ellison's space and had made a little stop-off zone in her old room, even though Ellison never requested that of her. Ellison found it adorable.

It had taken multiple washes and two trips to the dry cleaners to get the smell of smoke out of Katie's clothes. And even then, she had to part with some of the things she had previously held dear. So little by little she had filled Ellison's guest closet with her de-smoked clothes as she sorted through the many boxes that they'd brought back with them. Katie assured her that she was just about done, not that Ellison minded. She enjoyed going through the old photo albums and seeing papers from Katie's days in grade school that her mother had kept. The nostalgia seemed to be good for Katie, too. It helped to offset some of the house stress they'd run into with Zander.

Now into their sixth week of renovations, things seemed to have smoothed out a bit. Katie had been involved in all the design decisions and proved to have quite an eye for it as well. Zander had been his usual incredibly accommodating self and had fixed all the problems they uncovered once the walls came down, without so much as batting an eyelash. Now that they'd finalized a design and look, Ellison was ready to start taking pictures and generating buzz for the house. In no time, the finish work would be complete, and she could have the stagers come in. Once that happened, the house would fly off the market.

She finished washing her hands as she looked at the window ledge over her kitchen sink. Katie's presence was everywhere she looked. There were multiple tiny little origami figurines along the ledge, in various poses. Two little origami flower bouquets bookended the large panoramic window over the sink, and three clear mason jars of staggered heights were centered on the windowsill, all filled with the brightly colored sea glass that she and Katie—mostly Katie—had found on their daily beach walks.

Ellison touched the little origami giraffe that she loved so much and moved her closer to the origami tree Katie had created to give her something to pretend-snack on. She smiled. Katie brought such a playful effervescence to everything that she did. Ellison loved it. She loved the life and sounds Katie brought into this house. And into her days.

She'd struck a nice balance of working three days in the city and the rest home at the beach. Katie was back working at the Indulgent Tranquility Spa, and on the days that their schedules overlapped, they rode in together—those were some of Ellison's favorite commutes. She looked forward to them, oftentimes reorganizing her day to match Katie's.

She was amazed how seamlessly living with Katie had happened. Well, besides the fire and the drama around that. There was a part of her that felt like Katie had always been a part of her daily routine, something that Ellison realized she was becoming more and more protective of. As the timeline for finishing the house approached, she wondered what would happen to them. Would Katie take the sale money from the house and move out? And when the summer ended, would this summer fling end with it?

Ellison doubted that. Because nothing about this felt like a fling anymore. Sure, they were still sort of in the hot and heavy, lust-filled beginning of a relationship stage. But this felt different from relationships she'd been in in the past. This felt real. And lasting. Like it could endure the test of time. Maybe even endure the test of adding a baby to the mix.

That worried Ellison the most. Her in-person meetings with Terry and her family had gone swimmingly. Her wife and two sons were lovely, and Ellison could tell immediately that Tammy had been right—Terry was the perfect person to be Ellison's surrogate. The paperwork and legal stuff went off without a hitch, and though her personal bank account balked, the entire process had been swift and mostly painless. Any day now, Terry would be ovulating, and Ellison's embryo would be implanted. Then they'd wait. If the pregnancy was a success, Ellison would be on a new roller-coaster ride all over again. One that had a very real life change at the end of it. A life change that she had wanted and planned for, for a very long time. But not one that she'd planned to coincide with a new relationship.

Having a child was not a small undertaking. And expecting someone like Katie to just go along with it, when she'd verbalized her concerns about her preparedness for children, seemed like a dead end. So even though they talked about Ellison's process to motherhood, Ellison kept it light. She wanted to enjoy what she had with Katie for as long as she could. Terry wasn't even pregnant yet. She didn't have any answers. This could go nowhere or somewhere, very soon. But weighting down what she had with Katie wasn't something she wanted to do.

She'd worry about what their future—if there was one—would look like once she had a more concrete timeline to work from. But she hoped that there was a future for them. Because every minute she spent with Katie was another moment she fell in love with her. And coming to terms with that was another issue entirely. She was more than just falling for her—she was practically head over heels for her. And that was scarier than the prospect of finally being a mom.

She headed upstairs to see if Katie needed help with the last few boxes she'd been fooling around with. As she reached the top of the stairs, she saw Katie's bedroom door open and Katie sitting at the edge of her bed. She was flipping through a photo album. Ellison's wedding album, more specifically.

"Find something interesting?" Ellison asked.

Katie smiled up at her, patting the space beside her on the bed.

"I found this in a box at the top of the closet in the back. A box that I totally dropped like a klutz trying to get it down, so sorry about that." She pointed to the box Ellison had forgotten about—its contents were strewn about inside. "I wasn't snooping. I promise. I was just trying to fit my suitcase up there."

"And if you weren't snooping, then what do you call this?" Ellison asked good-naturedly.

"I would call this gathering intel," Katie reasoned. "You're so magical here. Look at you."

Ellison looked down at the photo Katie was referencing. It was a posed picture by the gazebo of her and Peyton's wedding venue. There was a weeping willow tree in the background with one of the most beautiful natural ponds Ellison had ever seen. They'd chosen that venue because of that pond and tree. It had reminded Ellison of the natural beauty of her home in Maine.

She noted that she was smiling there and that the smile had been genuine at the time. Peyton was looking at her, equally smitten. In many ways, Ellison felt like that picture was probably their best ever together, both in image and in relationship status.

"You look happy," Katie said, studying the photo before slowly turning the pages.

"I was your age there," Ellison said, the irony not lost on her. "And I was happy. For a little while, at least."

"My age? You say that like you're ancient," Katie said, nudging her shoulder. "You look as ageless now as you did then. Past Ellison was as hot as present Ellison. Though, I think you look better now if I'm being honest."

"You're sweet. I'll keep you."

"Please do," Katie said, turning a few more pages.

"I'm not sure why I still have that," Ellison said. "I'd forgotten it was up there."

Katie gave her a funny look. "Why wouldn't you?"

"Because that part of my life is far in the past. What do you do with memories you don't need anymore?"

Katie watched her, seeming to consider this. "Memories don't fade, regardless of whether you have pictures or not. And sure, your life is different now. But this, these"—she flipped through the pages—"are moments that made you who you are."

Ellison stopped the pages to point to one picture in particular. "This is my mother, Lorelai. This was one of the last formal pictures I have of her. She got sick shortly after my wedding, and I lost her within a year of that."

Katie looked up from the page, her eyes scanning Ellison's face. "You look just like her."

Ellison nodded, having heard that all her life. "She was my best friend. I miss her."

Katie took her hand.

"My life fell apart when she died. My marriage fell apart. My heart felt broken for a long time. I filled my days with work and hid behind my successes like a shield. But I don't think I was really over her passing until recently."

"Really?"

"Yeah. I think finishing this house helped in a lot of ways. It was the distraction I needed after my divorce to be reminded of how important my mom's final days at the beach with me were. My heart is here at this beach. I know that now."

Katie turned to the next page, and Ellison groaned. Peyton had smashed a slice of wedding cake into her face, even though they'd collectively decided against that.

"Not into cake-face smashing?" Katie asked.

"Not particularly. At least not with Peyton. We'd agreed against that, but she had a different plan on the day of. I found out over the course of our marriage that a lot of things we'd talked about and agreed upon weren't really agreed," Ellison said, trying to contain her bitterness.

"Like having a baby," Katie said, closing the book.

"Exactly." Ellison took the book from her and placed it back in the nearby box, covering it with a lid and pushing it aside. "Her baby shower with her new wife is tomorrow. I've been trying to forget I know about it, but I'm failing."

Katie seemed to consider something before standing. "Are you finished with work today?"

"I am. What did you have in mind?"

"Some much needed canoodling on the sand and a quest for more turquoise sea glass. We are seriously lacking that hue."

"Sounds heavenly. Especially the canoodling part."

Katie looped her arms around her waist. "I know tomorrow might feel frustrating for you, but I promise to help you keep your mind on other things."

"Oh?" Ellison liked the sound of that.

"Mm-hmm." Katie nodded. "I have to work tomorrow for part of the day, but I'm thinking maybe we should take Sunny out when I get home and go on an adventure."

"Tomorrow is Saturday," Ellison said. "That's shrimp scampi pizza night."

Katie massaged Ellison's low back with her hands, and Ellison moaned in appreciation. Katie's touch never got old. "Don't worry. I have no plans to disrupt our weekly Saturday night routine. But I was thinking that maybe we could eat out, instead of in."

Ellison raised an eyebrow at that comment.

Katie slapped her arm. "We can do that, too. Lots. But maybe since the weather is supposed to be perfect tomorrow, we could do a date night on the town. Before we come back here and do…other stuff."

"If shrimp scampi pizza and other stuff are in my future, then I'm good," Ellison said with a smile.

"You're so easy," Katie said, rising up on tiptoe to kiss her.

"Only for you," Ellison replied.

"So shall we beach it then? Because I need a break from this boring view," Katie joked, motioning toward Ellison.

"I don't know how you put up with it," Ellison replied, dropping her hands to cup Katie's ass.

"I'm a saint," Katie replied.

"That's fine as long as you promise to be a sinner with me on the beach," Ellison said.

"On the beach, on the counter, in the bed, in the bath, on the balcony, anywhere you want," Katie said. "As long as we find more turquoise sea glass first."

"You have a one-track mind."

"Two tracks," Katie corrected. "Sea glass, and you. Is that okay?"

"More than okay."

❖

Katie yawned as she checked the clock over the front desk. Mr. Albertson had five more minutes to show up before she canceled his appointment and left. She paced, trying not to be annoyed, but that seemed impossible.

She had never minded working weekends before, but now that she was dating Ellison, she hated it. Sure, Ellison occasionally worked on the weekends, but since she could work remotely, she spent fewer and fewer weekends in the office than when Katie had initially moved in with her. Which was probably good because that meant Ellison had some alone time without Katie in her space, but Katie missed her when she wasn't around. And she hated being in this parking lot and not seeing Ellison's Maserati a few spaces away.

"Albertson just called—he's going to reschedule," Shaina said, appearing from the back room.

"Sonofa—" Katie grunted. "Wait, I didn't even hear the phone ring."

"That's because you were staring out into the distance and grinding your teeth in annoyance."

Katie frowned, releasing the subconscious jaw clench. "I was not."

"Liar," Shaina said as she leaned against the desk. "So, are you headed to paradise now, or what?"

Paradise was what Shaina had started calling Ellison's beach house. She'd come down a handful of times and spent a few nights there as well. She had unofficially claimed the guest room closest to the one Katie never spent any time in as her own. Katie loved it. She also loved how well she and Ellison got along. That was an added bonus.

"I saw Mom before work, so yes."

"How's Mom?"

Katie smiled. "So good. She's standing with the help of her new leg brace, and she's helping with her transfers. The physical therapist thinks with some more intensive training, she'll be able to take steps in the parallel bars in the gym soon."

"Oh, Katie Cat," Shaina said. "That's amazing."

"I know, right?" Katie felt herself get emotional. "It's just so encouraging that New Beginnings is working for her. It was a real gamble, but it's paying off. And with the house going on the market soon, I can even afford a private therapist to supplement some of her treatments there. More therapy, more gains." Katie didn't let herself verbalize her hope that her mother's progress might one day bring her back to some form of independence.

"And how's the house coming?" Shaina asked.

"Good, I guess. Ellison made me promise not to go back there until everything is done. We're getting close. Zander estimates he'll be done in a week and a half. She wants to have the place staged before I set foot back inside. As a surprise of sorts."

"Are you good with that?" Shaina asked.

"Oh yeah. I'm all for just seeing the final product. I asked her to keep me out of it once the tile choices and hardware options nearly put me over the edge." Katie had no problem agreeing to this. She had been totally freaked out by seeing the house in varying stages of construction. The whole thing made her anxious.

"When is the open house? I'm dying to see what you guys did with the place."

"Two weeks, assuming Zander doesn't run into any last-minute delays. Which won't happen since Ellison is so involved in everything. Between the two of them, I wouldn't be surprised if they finish earlier than planned."

Shaina laughed. "A boss bitch gets shit done."

"That she does," Katie said, thinking about just how much Ellison was capable of.

"There's that dreamy far-off look again," Shaina said, poking her in the arm. "Still in seventh heaven, huh?"

Katie smiled. "We have plans tonight. It's the two-month anniversary of me moving into the beach house, and I want it to be special."

"You two are obnoxious. I love it," Shaina said, and Katie felt bad. She and Raul had split not long after Katie had moved to the beach. She seemed to be doing okay, but Katie hadn't been as present and available to her as she would have been in the past.

"Are you okay? I mean, I know things with Raul didn't go as planned…"

"I'm good. Really. I needed to be apart from him to see that what we had was toxic. It wasn't going anywhere. And I'm okay being on my own. Hell, maybe now I'll be someone's sugar baby like you soon."

Katie gave her a look. "I'm not Ellison's sugar baby."

"I'm just teasing you. I think it's super cute. And you two really are perfect for one another."

"Yeah," Katie said. She'd been thinking that more and more herself.

"Where is she on the baby mama front?" Shaina asked.

"She's just waiting for the call for the surrogate to be ovulating—then it's go time," Katie replied. She hadn't told Shaina about Ellison's infertility issues. Ellison had freely brought it up one of the weekends that Shaina had stayed with them at the beach house. Since then, Shaina asked for updates regularly. It was sweet.

"That's so exciting. Babies are the cutest," Shaina said as she wiggled in place. "Ellison is going to have the cutest baby ever."

"She is," Katie agreed.

Shaina gave her a look.

"What?"

"Nothing, it's just…"

"What?" Katie asked again.

"You seem really happy is all. Like the happiest I've ever seen you since I've known you. And it looks good on you. Happy is good for your skin," Shaina replied.

"I'll take that as high praise from my bestie and resident aesthetician. And I am." Katie thought about that and why that was. "I think I love her."

Shaina nodded. "I think you're right."

"Really? You're not even a little surprised? I'm going through an epiphany here," Katie said, waving her hands.

"Maybe you are, but I've known for a while now. I just wasn't sure if you were going to admit it anytime soon or not."

"When did you know?" Katie asked.

"That first weekend I spent down there. I could just tell," Shaina said. "You were different. Like, you were you—the *real* you—when you're in her presence. You know, the you I get on girls' night. Except now you have girls' night every night," she said with a nudge.

"Shut up." Katie pushed her.

"Well, when did you know?" Shaina asked, turning the tables.

"When she was sitting with my mother, talking to her and laughing. When my mother freely took her hand and smiled. I knew then, I think.

I just haven't said it out loud until now." Katie felt like a weight had been lifted off her shoulders.

"So, are you planning on telling her that? Or just me?" Shaina teased.

Katie worried her bottom lip. "I was trialing it out on you. I didn't faint, so that's a good sign."

Shaina shook her head. "You're a fool if you think she doesn't feel the same way about you."

"You think so?" Katie was hopeful.

"I saw a lot of things that weekend. And a *lack* of love was not one of them."

Katie smiled at that. "I'm going to surprise her with a special date tonight."

"Then maybe tonight's the night."

Katie thought she might be right. "Maybe it is."

CHAPTER TWENTY-TWO

E llison looked across the outdoor table of Reeled In at Katie, and her heart skipped a beat. Katie's smile was mesmerizing. Her bright green eyes glowed in the candlelight, and her full pink lips captivated Ellison's imagination.

"You're staring," Katie said as she sipped her champagne flute before placing the half-full glass down near the empty oyster shells on the table.

"You're beautiful," Ellison replied, circling her finger on the rim of her own flute.

"Are you having fun?" Katie asked, leaning back and looking delicious in that flowy black sundress.

Ellison allowed herself to appreciate the ample amount of cleavage the dress exposed in this position. "The most fun."

"Good." Katie had come home from work and jumped into the shower, leaving Ellison with strict instructions to "get dressed up for an adventure and some upscale casual outdoor dining." Which made Ellison laugh because casual wasn't really a thing she did, but she'd try. They'd started the afternoon with some touristy sightseeing in Sunny and meandered in and out of some local seaside shops while Katie snapped a few dozen photos of them together. The day had been wonderful, and she'd been enjoying Katie's company so much that Ellison had completely forgotten she was supposed to be annoyed about anything today.

"You never did tell me—how did you pull this off?" Ellison asked, motioning to the table.

Katie had somehow arranged for them to get a private table removed from other diners in the outdoor seating area of Reeled In, with a fancy candlelight dinner, white tablecloth, and a bottle of champagne. All of which was romantic and lovely, but not at all the kind of place Reeled In was.

"You're not the only person that knows people," Katie said.

"I'm beginning to see that."

Katie blew her a kiss. "I told our favorite bartender, Chelsea, that her best regular—the woman who orders shrimp scampi pizza with all the necessary date-night accoutrements every Saturday, rain or shine—needed to have a special night with her girlfriend."

"Oh? And she just agreed?" Ellison asked as she waved to Chelsea, who happened to look up from her post behind the bar.

"Well, I might have told them you would be booking an end of summer party at your place and needed it catered."

"Did you now," Ellison said, raising an eyebrow in amusement.

"No," Katie said with a smile. "I just told them that I wanted to do something special for someone who is very special to me. And then I told them my house almost burned down and that I was pathetic. And Chelsea felt bad, so she pulled some strings. And here we are," Katie said as she motioned to the table. "Happy date night, Ellison."

"Happy date night, indeed." Ellison finished her last sip of champagne. "Tell me this is just the start to a really wonderful, sleepless night."

"This is barely an appetizer to the evening," Katie said, uncrossing her legs in a devastatingly slow fashion before she scooted forward. "I was hoping you'd help me out of this dress soon."

"Let me get the check," Ellison said, already raising her hand.

Chelsea showed up with a pizza box and a broad grin. "Ladies. This is the rest of your pizza—all boxed up and ready for you. Now, are we having dessert?"

"I think we're good," Ellison said.

"Are we?" Katie asked, her voice full of torment.

Chelsea looked between them, laughing. "Seems like maybe you two aren't sure. How about a dessert cocktail? Two Watermelon Sugars, on the house?"

"A free drink," Katie said, touching the back of Ellison's hand. "Surely we have time for that."

"I'll pass—I'm driving. But I'll have a few sips of hers," Ellison said with a wink.

"Yes," Katie cheered. "Bring on the martini."

Chelsea saluted her before disappearing behind the bar.

"You're torturing me," Ellison said.

"I'm just helping you build anticipation," Katie reasoned. "Plus, we've never come here and not had a Watermelon Sugar martini. They're your favorite."

Ellison loved that they had a dinner date place. And Katie was right—they never left without her favorite martini. "But we've also never had champagne here," Ellison added.

Katie shrugged. "They made an exception for me since you tip every time like you just won Powerball. Though I do admit to swiping this from your wine fridge the other day and dropping it off."

"That explains why they had my favorite brand and vintage on the menu," Ellison said. "You're the best."

"I know."

❖

Ellison let out a shaky exhale as she watched Katie unzip her dress and step out of it. She'd gone without panties tonight, it seemed. Which Ellison was glad she didn't know before now, because she surely wouldn't have been able to keep her hands to herself.

Katie kicked off her heels and crawled on the bed, kneeling with her legs spread as she beckoned for Ellison to come to her. "You're so far away."

Ellison stood, making the short trip to Katie's outstretched arms. "Hello, beautiful."

"Hello," Katie purred against her lips as she helped her out of her clothes. "Come to bed with me."

"Gladly," Ellison said as Katie guided her by her jaw up the bed and over her.

"Today was magical," Katie said between lazy, openmouthed kisses to Ellison's chest. She sucked on Ellison's nipple as she tickled up her side.

"Your mouth is magical," Ellison said, licking her lips at the sensation of Katie's warm tongue circling her other nipple.

Katie bit down slightly, and Ellison hissed. "You know what I was thinking about the entire day?"

Ellison moaned as Katie soothed the skin with another languid lap of her tongue. "What?"

"How badly I wanted to be under you," Katie said, spreading her legs as Ellison shifted between them, pressing her thigh to Katie's naked sex. "Yes. Like that."

Ellison smiled as Katie's hand rested on her ass, encouraging her to start grinding against her. "Is that all?"

Katie shook her head as she kissed across Ellison's chest to her other nipple. "I wondered if you were as excited as I was about our date. Are you excited for me?"

Ellison's breath caught as Katie's thigh pressed up against her. "Can't you tell?"

Katie laughed, kissing up her sternum and licking along her jaw as she reached between them, gliding her fingers along Ellison's lower lips and collecting her wetness.

Ellison cursed when Katie brought her fingers to her lips, tasting her. That turned her on every time.

"Seems like it." Katie made a show of licking her fingers, and Ellison was getting short of breath watching that pink tongue flick in and out. "What are you thinking?"

"That your tongue is too far away from where I want it," Ellison replied honestly.

"In your mouth? Or in your pussy?" Katie asked, and Ellison's clit throbbed. Katie gripped her ass more forcibly as she encouraged Ellison's grinding pace to pick up.

"Either. Both," Ellison panted out as she felt herself start to climb from all the friction and the dirty talk.

"I can make that happen." Katie licked at the shell of Ellison's ear as she continued to roll her hips against Ellison's thigh. Ellison tried to match her pace, but Katie's teasing touches on her chest were sending flashes of pleasure that were making it hard to focus. "Kiss me while you come undone with me, and I'll lick you clean afterward."

When Katie finally brought those full lips to hers, Ellison was achingly close. And from the noises Katie was letting out between gasping breaths, she was, too.

Ellison slipped an arm under her, pulling Katie flush to her chest while she rode Katie's thigh. Katie started to whimper as Ellison deepened their kiss. She slid her hand down Katie's stomach and slipped into her between thrusts. Katie cried out, climaxing hard and fast into her hand, while bringing Ellison right there with her.

Katie smiled against her lips as Ellison slipped out of her. She continued her gentle rolling hip movements, to drag out Katie's pleasure. And her own. She was in no rush to put any space between them.

"I love being under you." Katie dropped her head back on the bed, looking up at her. "I love how kissing you makes my lips feel like they have a purpose. And your touch"—Katie intertwined their fingers—"your touch makes me feel so desired. And so safe. I love the way you touch me, even just casually." Katie ran her free hand up Ellison's back, caressing the skin beneath her fingers. "I love how vulnerable you are with me, how nothing is off-limits. And I love how every moment I spend with you makes me feel alive. Like, truly alive. Like, I didn't know how to live before you entered my life."

Ellison propped herself up on her elbow, smiling down at her. "That's a lot to love."

Katie nodded. "And yet, still not what I love most."

"Which is what?" Ellison asked, her heart beating faster.

"Not a what. A who." Katie brought their joined hands to her lips as she kissed along Ellison's knuckles. "You. I love you. And I'm so, so happy about it."

Ellison shifted, rolling them on their sides so she could hold Katie's face in her hands and kiss her lips as she breathed out, "I love you, too."

Katie laughed, kissing her sweetly and hugging her close. Ellison couldn't remember a time she had felt happier.

They stayed wrapped up in each other's limbs for a long time before Katie spoke again. "Do you know what today is?"

"The happiest day of my life?" Ellison teased.

Katie nipped at her bottom lip. "It's the two-month anniversary of me moving in to the beach house with you."

"A reason to celebrate, then, for sure," Ellison said, touched that Katie had made note of that. "Thank you for moving in."

"Well, you did rescue me from a house fire and not get mad when I felt you up in my sleep," Katie replied.

"Now that you've professed your love for me, can I ask you something?"

"Anything," Katie replied, her green eyes sparkling.

"Were you really asleep that morning? Or were you just trying to cop a feel and got caught?"

Katie laughed. "I wish I could be that smooth, but I assure you, Sleep Katie was way gayer than Awake Katie was at the time. Luckily that seems to have changed."

"I happen to be very fond of both Katies, so we're good." Ellison ran her hand along Katie's side before gripping her ass and pulling her closer again. "But—admittedly—gay Katie is my favorite."

"Mine, too." Katie gave her a devilish look as she started to kiss down Ellison's abdomen. "Speaking of really gay things, I do believe I made you a promise that I need to make good on."

"Best. Girlfriend. Ever."

CHAPTER TWENTY-THREE

Ellison was vibrating with excitement. And nerves. But mostly excitement. It was finally happening—Terry was going in for the embryo transfer any minute now, and in less than two weeks' time, they'd know if the transfer was successful.

"You look happy," Faith's voice sounded from her office door.

"I am," Ellison said giving her a broad smile. "I just got word that Terry is headed in for the embryo transfer."

"Yes!" Faith cheered as she rushed Ellison's desk. "It's happening."

Ellison stood, giving her a hug. "I'm cautiously optimistic."

"I'll be recklessly optimistic for the both of us," Faith replied. "It's your time. I just know it."

"Thanks," Ellison said, resting her head on Faith's shoulder. "I'm glad you're here."

"It's because I give the best hugs, right?" Faith cuddled her close.

"You do give great hugs," Ellison said, letting out a contented sigh. She'd missed her friend.

"I'm great at other things, too," Faith said, leaning back to look at her. "Do you have plans after the photo shoot this afternoon? Because I'll be in town for another day or so."

Oh. They needed to talk, it seemed.

"I'm seeing someone," Ellison said, slipping out of her embrace.

"You are?" Faith replied, curious. "Since when?"

"A few months, actually. I didn't mention anything because I thought you had something going on, too," Ellison replied, feeling bad that she hadn't mentioned Katie to Faith. It hadn't been intentional—it just hadn't come up. They didn't usually discuss their intimate relationships with other people, except to communicate if they were free to be with each other for any stretch of time.

"It was short-lived. Burned quickly, but petered out." Faith appraised her. "So maybe that glow you have isn't just the transfer news, is it?"

"Probably not, no," Ellison said.

A knock at her door drew her attention.

"Katie," she said with a smile. She could feel Faith's eyes on her as she stepped toward the office door.

"Oh, I didn't realize you had company. Jax neglected to mention that," Katie said with a frown, looking between Faith and Ellison and seeming unsure.

"Katie, this is Faith. Faith, Katie." Ellison touched Faith's arm as she walked past.

"It's nice to meet you," Faith said with her usual charm, though Ellison could tell she'd connected the dots right away.

"Hi. I've heard great things," Katie said as she took her hand.

"Have you?" Faith asked, giving Ellison a look.

Katie nodded. "And Talia speaks the world of you, so there's that, as well."

"Ah, you're the friend of Ellison's she mentioned would be joining in on the photo shoot today," Faith said, giving her a once-over. "That explains a lot. Today should be fun."

"Are you riding there with me?" Ellison asked Katie, taking her hand.

"Yes, I just promised a quick coffee date with Shaina first. But I wanted to stop by to congrat—" She paused, looking back at Faith as though she wasn't sure she should continue.

"She knows, it's okay," Ellison said, touched that Katie was trying to be discreet.

"Oh, good. I won't keep you. Let me know when you're ready to head to the photo shoot, and I'll breeze over," Katie said. She gave Ellison her private smile. "I'm excited for you. Congratulations."

"Thank you. Say hi to Shaina for me," Ellison said, leaning in to give her a quick kiss. "I'll text you in a bit."

Faith had the decency to wait until Katie had left the building before she said, "She's young, huh?"

Ellison gave her a look. "Don't start."

"What? It's an observation, that's all." Faith's hands were raised in surrender. "I'm not taking any digs or anything."

"Good. Because we both know age has never been a problem in your dating history before," Ellison said with an eyebrow raised.

"Not in mine. But in yours it has. I've never seen you date anyone younger than yourself. At least not that much younger, anyway." Faith leaned against her desk. "And what does Miss Pretty Young Thing think about you being someone's mama? You know, besides hers."

Ellison narrowed her eyes at Faith. "Get it all out of your system now, please. I'm not going to play defense to your snark all night."

Faith looked offended. "I'm not being snarky."

"You're right. You're being ageist," Ellison said, none too pleased.

"Whoa. Back up. You don't need to play mother for that cub of yours," she said with a sly smile. "I was teasing about how old she is. I don't care about that."

"Good, since it's none of your business," Ellison said, still bristling.

Faith took a breath. "Let's start over. And do a check-in."

Ellison huffed. "I don't want to do a check-in."

"All the more reason to do one, then." Faith crossed her arms, making it clear that she wasn't about to back down.

"Fine." Ellison waved her hand. "Check-in away."

"Is this thing serious between you two?" Faith asked, her tone gentle.

"Yes. I think so," Ellison replied, her anger receding.

"Then I'm happy for you. Because you deserve to be happy. Does she make you happy?"

"She does. Or rather, I feel like I'm a happier person with her in my life," Ellison corrected, knowing too well that it wasn't anyone else's job to help you find your own happiness.

"Then that's the answer." Faith crossed the room to give her a hug. "Can we start over?"

Ellison sighed, stepping into her friend's embrace. "Yes."

"I love you. You know that. And I really was just teasing you about the age thing. We both know that growing up in the exquisite nature of rural Maine and all that time we swam naked in the lake locked us both in an ageless vacuum. We're still the best-looking people in the room, even at fortysomething," Faith teased. "Not to mention the richest."

"I know." Ellison stepped back with a laugh. Faith always did have a way of lightening the moment. But she felt like she should explain herself. "I think I was more upset about the baby mama thing."

Faith nodded. "Have you talked about that much?"

"No," Ellison replied. "I've been waiting on a deadline, I guess. Like it didn't seem worth having a life plan discussion over hypotheticals."

"But an embryo transfer into a surrogate isn't hypothetical anymore," Faith said.

"Right. So I suppose we have a conversation on the horizon," Ellison replied, dreading it. She knew where Katie stood on having kids—she'd told her she wasn't ready. And it wasn't like Ellison expected her to become an insta-family with her or anything, but she knew a child would change things. For both of them.

"Well, what do you want?"

"In a perfect world?" Ellison asked.

"Sure, we can start there," Faith said. "Lay it on me."

"I want to live at the beach with her and watch the waves from bed with her every morning. And I want to design a nursery—at the beach house and in the city apartment—and I want her to weigh in on the color choices. And I want to have a little family with her," Ellison replied. "Because it feels right. Like in my soul, it feels right."

Faith gave her a small smile. "She's special, huh?"

"She is," Ellison said, afraid to say it out loud even if she knew it in her heart. Because as good as the transfer news was, it was also the start of a countdown that might or might not start very soon. "But she doesn't want kids right now. And I can't just stop what's in motion already. Nor do I want to. I lived on someone else's timeline for long enough. I won't do it again."

"So have the conversation, then. And see where you two are on the baby topic. She might surprise you," Faith offered.

"Maybe," Ellison replied. "For now, I'll choose to remain cautiously optimistic about the transfer and my relationship status with my P-Y-T."

Faith snorted. "You're a dork."

"I'm okay with that," Ellison said.

❖

"Are you ready to be a cover girl?" Shaina asked as she stood from her seat at the little front table in Starbucks.

"Ha. No, I'm actually a little anxious about the whole thing." Katie gave her a quick hug before sitting across from her. "How did you score a seat?"

"Lucky, I guess," Shaina said with a yawn. "But I'm thrilled about it, because I'm wiped. Today has been busy. It's a good thing you're off today—the spa is a madhouse."

She'd spent the morning with her mother, just catching up. "What's happening there?"

"Pietro started his construction on that space out back, and he's working with some wacky designers to try to join the two spaces without losing treatment area to—quote—*maximize his bottom line*," Shaina said, miming air quotes.

"I thought he wasn't starting until next week?" Katie took a sip of the iced coffee Shaina had ordered her.

"He wasn't supposed to, but he moved things up, it seems. I think it has something to do with that new laser hair removal place across the street. They have a plastic surgeon on staff, and I hear they're generating buzz by giving out half-price Botox shots with laser hair packages." Shaina shrugged. "It's above my pay grade. All I know is that there are way too many people wandering around today for any visit to be relaxing for anyone. So steer clear."

"Done and done," Katie said.

"So, tell me everything. What's new?"

"Uh." Katie traced her finger through the condensation on the outside of her cup. "I just formally met that hot woman Ellison was making out in the parking lot with that one time."

"You mean that one time months ago before you two started playing house?"

"Exactly," she replied, though the *playing house* comment reminded her about the other thing she had wanted to tell her. "She's going to be in the photo shoot today since her niece is the designer, but she was in Ellison's office when I stopped by to congratulate her."

"Congratulate her on what?" Shaina asked.

"The embryo transfer is today," Katie said, smiling.

"Hell yes! It's baby time." Shaina applauded.

Katie laughed. "Not yet. There's still a wait to see if the transfer was successful and then, you know, nine or so months of gestation."

"Party pooper," Shaina whined. "Fine, I'll be quietly excited by myself over here."

"I'm not *not* excited," Katie replied. "There's just some time still."

"Have you thought about what's going to happen after?"

"After what?"

Shaina looked unsure if she should continue. "Uh, after the baby comes."

Katie frowned. "I hadn't thought that far in advance. Though I suppose now is about the time to start thinking about that."

"Well, you're right. There's still time. I suppose you have to tackle the first issue before that happens, anyway," Shaina said.

"What issue is that?" Katie asked, feeling blindsided.

"The house sale. What are you going to do when the house sells? Are you going to formally move in with Ellison? Because she's great. And it seems like it's going well, right?"

"It is," Katie said, starting to feel anxious. There seemed to be a lot of big decisions looming suddenly.

"I just wasn't sure if you'd talked about that yet." Shaina palmed her forehead. "Here I am asking you about the baby coming and what your role would be, and I have no idea where you'll even be living. Sorry. I just assumed you'd move in with Ellison and—"

"Become a mom?" Katie felt the color drain from her face. Why had she not thought about that before? She hadn't given much thought to life after the house sale because she would be in a different financial position and would have options. Also, she was in no rush to end the most perfect summer of her life. But what was going to happen after the sale? And what about the baby?

"Are you going to faint? Because you look like you're going to faint." Shaina looked alarmed.

"No. I'm good," she lied. "I just...you present some valid points that I should probably start to seriously consider."

Shaina sighed. "Shit. Katie, I'm sorry. I was just gossiping with you and catching up. I wasn't trying to deflate your lust bubble or anything."

"You didn't," Katie said. Not even believing herself.

"I did. You were all giggly and heart eyes and now you look like I broke your favorite toy." Shaina touched her forearm. "I'm sorry. Really. I'm sure you two have a plan or will have a plan. Or it doesn't matter, Shaina, mind your own damn business."

Her phone buzzed on the table. Ellison was ready to head out. She stood as she said, "You didn't do anything wrong. It's smart for me to get my head out of the clouds and have some semblance of a plan. First, the house has to sell. The rest happens after that."

"Good point." Shaina looked relieved.

"Gotta get through that first," Katie said, forcing a smile. "Now, if you'll excuse me, I have to go be beautiful with Ellison and all her gorgeous colleagues."

"Love that for you," Shaina said, giving her a thumbs-up. "Take pictures for me."

"Will do," Katie said.

CHAPTER TWENTY-FOUR

The warehouse Talia had rented for the photo shoot was massive, but there were stations set up everywhere, so they could lounge and chat between shots. Hair and makeup were done off to the left, and the lighting and physical shoot area was off to the right. The photographer, Sydney James, was dressed in all black, her leather pants and boots covered in metal studs. She moved quickly, changing positions often as she called out cues. Trina and Lauren were modeling looks for her when Ellison and Katie walked in.

"Trina looks great in red," Katie said, as they walked past.

"That's sort of her signature look," Ellison replied as they waved to Talia.

"Oh, good. You're here," Jax said, looking exasperated.

"We're right on time," Ellison said, pointing to her watch. "We're even a little early."

Jax wiped their brow. "I know. I just want to make sure everything goes smoothly."

"It will. You're an expert planner," Ellison said with an affectionate pat to their shoulder. "How's Talia?"

Katie could see her standing behind Sydney, making notes and occasionally speaking, though she couldn't hear what she was saying.

"She's perfect," Jax said, looking smitten.

Ellison fluttered her hand in front of their face. "And with the shoot? How is she with the shoot?"

"Oh, right." Jax cleared their throat. "All good. A consummate professional. She's already done three livestreams, and we started dropping some accessories onto the webstore to test the Shopify link. So far, so good."

"That's great." Ellison looked proud.

"I think she needs you," Katie said, motioning in Talia's direction. She was waving to Jax and pointing toward something.

"Oh, shit. The clipboard." Jax pulled the board away from their chest, shaking their head. "Anyway, I have to go." They turned to Ellison. "Talia needs you in wardrobe—your station is over there." Jax turned to her. "Katie, you are needed in makeup, and then you two are supposed to swap. Your station is next to Ellison's."

"Good luck," Katie called out, but Jax was already halfway across the studio space.

"I hope Jax finally asks her out after this," Ellison said with a sigh. "It's time."

"They'll do it when they're ready," Katie said. "Sometimes big things take time to think over."

Ellison looked at her but said nothing.

"Katie?" one of the makeup artists Talia had booked called out.

"That's my cue." Katie gave her a smile before walking to the chair.

While she had her hair and makeup done, she watched the reflections in the mirror. One by one, Ellison's friends took their photos, while chatting animatedly in between sessions. Faith was with Talia, looking over photographs on the monitor nearby, and Jax—who had been buzzing around—was now in wardrobe trying on their second outfit. The slim-fitting suit with subtle pinstripes was beautiful. They looked so dapper.

While she zoned out, Shaina's words circled in her head like a shark in seal-infested waters. She stopped noticing the sounds around her because her mind was so loud it was already deafening. What did she want for the future? How had she gotten this far involved with Ellison without some sort of plan? What kind of person goes through their life without a fucking plan? Her. That's who.

She loved Ellison—there was no doubt about that. So why was she so blindsided by Shaina's very appropriate and legitimate questions? Was she just going to keep living with Ellison indefinitely? Like, when the summer ended, was she just going to move into Ellison's fancy-ass apartment as her sugar baby? Was that what she was? And what if this transfer worked out? Was she ready to have a girlfriend with a newborn? Children had not been in her plans, not after her mother's accident. She was just getting her life in order, by ridding herself of her past.

She wondered if that was why she struggled so much with seeing the house in stages of renovation. A part of her felt like she was abandoning the life she once had. But another part of her felt like she was finally taking the first step toward freedom. A freedom from a house she couldn't manage. A freedom from a caregiving position she wasn't well enough equipped to do alone. The house sale fixed both of those issues. But that didn't fix her. She wasn't focused or driven or put together. She liked her job—she knew she was damn good at it—but was that enough?

She looked out at the reflection of the people around her again. Everyone seemed so at ease with each other. They fit together: beautiful, wealthy, charming, hilarious, career-focused, and *stable*. Each and every one of them was a diamond in their own right. Katie felt like an imposter among them.

"Are you ready?" Ellison's voice sounded from her shoulder.

"Hmm?" She looked up and was caught off guard at what she saw. Ellison's makeup was already done, and she was in the most amazing off-the-shoulder blue gown Katie had ever seen.

"It's your turn for wardrobe." Ellison placed a hand on her shoulder.

"You're stunning," Katie said to Ellison's reflection in the mirror.

"You say that like you aren't, too," Ellison said, effortlessly charming as usual. "Go get dressed. I'm dying to see you in what Talia picked."

Katie was surprised to find three outfits waiting for her, but her favorite was a form-fitting vibrant green dress that Talia had set aside for last. She headed to Sydney and was pleased at how easy she was to take direction from. Jax and Lauren were nearby being their hilarious selves, so Katie had no trouble smiling and laughing on cue. She let herself live in the moment, enjoying the uniqueness of the situation, even though she felt like an outsider…a bit.

The makeup artist made a small adjustment to her makeup when she donned the green gown. Talia came over to make some suggestions, and once she was finished, Katie was blown away.

"Wow," Ellison said, looking up from the nearby monitor. "Tell me she gets to take that dress home."

Talia shook her head. "No one is taking anything home. These are originals."

"You sure you can't be bought?" Ellison gave her a nudge. "Because that dress is—"

"Holy shit, Katie. You're hot," Trina said. "I mean, you're always hot. But damn. This is…wow. Talia, A-plus, girl."

Katie knew she was blushing as all the attention in the room turned to her. Sydney snapped a few pictures, and Katie covered her face out of reflex.

"Bashful is a good look," Sydney said, showing Talia something from her screen.

"I didn't mean to embarrass you," Ellison said as she approached. "I just think you should own that dress—you know, like the way you're owning it right now."

Katie scrunched her nose. "People can probably hear you."

Ellison shrugged. "I don't care what people hear."

Talia and Sydney were looking at the monitor, so Katie stepped off the floor marker toward Ellison, who had perched on a tall white stool nearby.

"I like this sheer shirt thing," Katie said, reaching out to run her fingers along the lapel of Ellison's shirt. This outfit of Ellison's was her favorite. The sheer white top gave her pirate vibes in a super sexy way, and the high-waisted deep blue pants brought out the oceanic hue of her eyes. Her makeup was minimal, since she never needed any, but she was breathtaking, nonetheless. "It's kind of impossible not to stare at you."

"Stare all you want," Ellison said, reaching out for her. "As long as you don't mind me staring right back at you."

Katie stepped into her space, loving the way Ellison's hand rested on her hip.

"Spin for me. I want to see the whole picture," Ellison said, as she guided her in a tight, slow spin.

Laughter off to their left drew her attention, and Katie saw that Trina, Lauren, Jax, and Faith were doing some sort of silly dance while still managing to look chic. Faith cackled, and Jax snorted in response, which brought the other two to near tears. They were all so vivacious.

"What?" Ellison asked as she intertwined their fingers.

"Your friends—they're all so sure of themselves. Like it's totally normal to stand in front of a noted photographer and have hair and makeup done."

Ellison laughed. "They're all Realtors. We do photos and media blitzes all the time. Half their job is posing and posturing. The extravagance of this isn't foreign to them."

Katie looked at her, loving those blue eyes that watched her so closely. "Your life is so interesting and complex. I've never met anyone quite like you."

"And yet I've never been so captivated by anyone else like I am with you," Ellison said, and Katie felt herself melt a little.

"I love how easily you can unwind my insecurities." Katie reached out to caress her face.

"You have nothing to be insecure about." Her voice was soft, and her lips looked as kissable as ever. Katie wasn't sure what their future would hold, but she was sure those lips would always be a part of her dreams.

With Katie in these heels, and with Ellison perched on the tall stool, they were about the same height. Katie stepped between Ellison's legs, cradling Ellison's jaw as she placed a delicate but lingering kiss on Ellison's lips.

"I love you," Ellison breathed out.

And Katie nodded, resting her forehead against Ellison's. "So much."

"Now that's the photo series you want," Sydney said, jarring them apart. "The passion, the sincerity. The closeness and the delicate touches. All of it. Perfect. Those two will sell your clothes, and sex right with it. Excellent."

Katie looked back at Ellison, bewildered. "Did she just—"

"Take photos of us having a private moment that will undoubtedly get uploaded somewhere? Yes."

Katie dropped her head. "Well, shit."

Ellison laughed, pulling her into a hug as she stood. "Come on. They want to do group photos. And I'm sure it's time for us to get razzed by the crew."

"I'm forever embarrassing myself around your friends," Katie said.

"They're family to me. So, really, you're embarrassing yourself in front of my family. Which is probably worse, but...meh," Ellison teased.

Trina wolf-whistled when Katie accepted the playful nip Ellison gave her bottom lip. "It's already begun," she said, conceding.

"Oh yeah." Ellison put her arm around her shoulders, leading them toward the group of people slow clapping as they approached. "We're going to be in hell the rest of the night."

CHAPTER TWENTY-FIVE

By the time they made it back to the beach house, it was late. Katie slept soundly at first, but a nightmare jarred her awake. In it, she was running down the halls of her house, opening door after door and not recognizing what was behind it. Each door led to more hallways and unfamiliar surroundings. She was racing to find the exit, and all the while a growing feeling of dread was in her chest, that she'd chosen the wrong door. She'd chosen the wrong path.

She woke up in a pool of sweat, gasping for breath. Luckily, Ellison remained asleep nearby, the slow, rhythmic sounds of her breathing never changing. Katie slipped out of bed, heading to the guest room she never used. She looked out the window at the darkness over the water. It was before sunrise still. And though she tried to calm her thoughts, her heartbeat still hadn't returned to normal.

After deciding that a hot shower would calm her nerves, she slowly undressed. The water felt good on her neck and shoulders. She braced herself against the tiled walls and breathed in the steamy air, clearing her mind and her lungs with soothing breaths. She closed her eyes and thought about the photo shoot and Ellison's found family. She thought about Shaina's words and her own fears of inadequacy. She thought about Ellison's changing life and the one she was leaving behind.

She moved as if in a fog, dressing and wandering downstairs as the sun began to rise. She stepped out onto the back porch and walked down to the water. Cradling a cup of coffee in her hands, she sat in the sand and watched the high tide slowly recede. She didn't want to give this up. She didn't want to give up this view or this life. And maybe she didn't have to, but she had to do a few things first. She had to talk to

Ellison and find out what was happening between them. And figure out if that could withstand the amount of change that was on the horizon. She thought it could, but she didn't trust herself either. Because panic had started to creep in. That same panic that had taken over her life after she received the call about her mother's accident. The panic that her life was over. That an irreversible change was looming. And she wasn't sure she could handle that again. Not until she had some closure.

She headed back into the house, leaving a note for Ellison next to the fresh pot of coffee she left warming. She knew Ellison would be up soon, since she was an early riser. But Katie knew she had to be gone before that happened, or she'd lose her nerve. She had to do this on her own, or that dream about the doors would come true—she'd be searching for a way out and not be able to find it.

The drive to her house was lonely. She missed Ellison's company and her fancy car. She tried talk radio, but she'd bored of it quickly. As she pulled up to the house, she was speechless. She'd avoided coming by until now, and what she saw showed her just how much had changed.

The entire front lawn had been landscaped. The driveway was pavers where it had once been asphalt. The walkway to the front porch was wider and more luxurious than it had been, with intricate designs in the stonework. The porch was completely brand new, and the lighting complemented the old Victorian style and grandeur it once had. The house had been painted a new color, with bright accents on the trim and intricate woodwork that Zander's team had remastered.

Katie stepped up onto the new porch, marveling at the view before her. From up here, the stonework was even more incredible. The freshly laid sod was bright green and lush, and the overflowing flower beds separating the porch from the grass mimicked her mother's garden out back. She was sure that was not a coincidence. The eye for detail so far was too precise to be accidental. This was all Ellison, and she knew it.

She looked at the new hand-carved front door with accents of stained glass. She recognized the colors and patterns from the window that was on the third floor in her grandfather's old office space. She touched the glass, smiling at the history Ellison had brought down to the ground level.

The door was locked, but Ellison had given her a key a few weeks ago, so she could check on the progress at her leisure, though until today, she never had. She turned the key in the lock and noted how easily the door opened. Not anything like the previous mechanism and door.

As the door opened and revealed the interior that was once her living room, her jaw dropped. The floors had been redone, and the walls were newly painted. The windows were new, and the fireplace had been reconfigured and lined with marble and expensive-looking wood trim. Long gone were the rickety old couch and mismatched high-backed chairs. They had been replaced with comfortable, luxurious-looking furniture in bold hues that highlighted the newly designed space. As she wandered from room to room, her surprise grew. The company Ellison had hired to stage this house was incredible. Every room had a consistent and elegant theme that ran through the first floor, culminating in the most exquisite kitchen Katie had ever seen. There were no more roosters here, only clean lines and white cabinets with a stunning marble countertop. The pantry had been renovated and made more efficient, and the window to the backyard was twice as large over the extra-deep farmhouse sink.

The upstairs was equally impressive. Each bedroom held a comfortable-looking but grand bed, and her mother's old bedroom was staged as an office. Katie's old room boasted a new, oversized window with window bench, capitalizing on the incredible light that side of the house got. Her closet was custom now, affording a better use of the space. And where the fire had burned its hottest, a door now stood. To her surprise, behind the door was small, three-piece bathroom.

"That would have been nice while I lived here," she said aloud to no one.

She went up to the third floor and saw they had staged a workspace there. She noted the stained glass that had inspired the entryway downstairs. As she made her way down the new front stairwell, she took in the way the lighter colors on the walls reflected light. The house felt airy and bright. And nothing like the house that had existed here before.

She made her way through the kitchen to the backyard, anxious at what she would find there. A large back deck met her that hadn't been there before. And the stonework to her mother's garden area had been redone, though she could see that the original stone her mother had put in had been repurposed along the raised beds. The flowers had been maintained and weeded. The bright colors of summer were everywhere. The only thing missing was the stone bench she'd given her mother, which Ellison had told her she'd had moved to storage. In its place was an artfully designed wrought iron bench that was flanked by two Adirondack chairs and a small stone firepit. The fairy lights her mother had strung had been reimagined and updated. This garden would be a heavenly oasis for the person that purchased this home. She had heard Ellison say, time and time again, that a space to escape the hustle and bustle of the city was priceless. With the new landscaping and sod back here, Katie was sure this fit that bill.

She walked back through the house, casting one last glance at it before closing the door and heading back to her car.

"That life is gone now," she said as she sat in the driver's seat, looking at the somewhat familiar but drastically different home full of memories—both good and bad.

She felt herself get emotional as she pictured her mother waiting on the porch to greet her after her first day of elementary school. And she could see her grandfather tooling around by the maple tree, affixing a birdhouse that had long ago crumbled over the years. She saw her grandmother being helped up the stairs by the hired aide that became a confidant in her dying months. And then her own mother being lifted into the house by stretcher after the accident. After returning from California, she had spent many a night sitting on that top porch step crying, so overwhelmed by how much her life had changed. And mourning what she thought she had lost. She'd mourned her mother's loss of independence and cursed the house that she couldn't afford to make livable. So much of her life had happened within those walls, and in no time at all, the house would belong to someone else.

Katie felt sad. And lost. So very lost. Like a balloon untethered in a storm, she felt out of control and like a passive observer. But at the same time, she wanted this. She wanted to be free of the things that made her feel tied down, and this house was certainly that. But was she ready to be freed? Freed to do what, exactly? Just start a new life with Ellison? Was that something she could do? And did she even want to? She wasn't quite sure. Her brain felt murky and sluggish. She needed to get away from the house she barely recognized and think. There was so much to think about.

❖

Ellison checked her cell again. She was worried about Katie. She'd found the note by the coffeepot, but her texts checking in on her had gone unanswered all day. She was annoyed at herself because she had seen that at times last night, Katie seemed uncomfortable at the photo shoot. And try as she might to make her feel loved and cared for, she wasn't sure she'd succeeded. Katie just seemed...distracted. Ellison worried that she had pushed her too hard to be involved. It hadn't been her intention to make her feel overwhelmed. She just wanted to share parts of herself with her. But maybe that was a step too far.

She stepped out of her car and wandered past the little shops, absentmindedly looking through the windows when something caught her eye. There was a little white baby onesie with three multicolored pastel seashells on it and the words *Shell-o, I'm New Here*, which for some reason made Ellison laugh uncontrollably. The adorable absurdity of it was impossible to ignore.

She found herself walking into the children's boutique, looking at crab hats and lobster footie pajamas. She had no business looking at baby clothes, yet she didn't want to leave the store either.

"Can I help you find something?" a sweet, young-looking twentysomething asked her.

"The onesie in the window, do you have any more?" Ellison heard herself ask.

"We do. That just came in," she said as she walked to the window display, reaching under the white shelf and pulling out a few different sizes. "What would you like? We have newborn, zero to three months, and three to six months."

Ellison took the newborn size, marveling at the softness of the material. She held up the tiny article of clothing and smiled. Some baby, someday, would fit in this and be adorable. She wondered if that baby would be hers.

"I can gift wrap it, if you'd like," the saleswoman said.

"That won't be necessary," Ellison said, handing it back to her. "A regular bag will be fine."

"I'll check you out whenever you are ready," she said, resuming her post behind the register.

Was she really going to do this? Was she going to buy a baby onesie for a child she wasn't sure would even happen? And was that bad luck? She'd considered the beginner's bet mistake she'd made when she had the beach house built—she'd designed it with her heart, not her head. Her heart wanted a massive house to fill with kids, but her head knew that probably wasn't possible. And until this summer, she'd stayed there infrequently because the vastness of it was painful for her. But that had changed when Katie had entered her life. And suddenly the house didn't feel too large—it felt perfect.

She wondered if she'd still feel that way when one of the bedrooms was a nursery. Would she be glad she had a washer and dryer on the first and second floors after a midday diaper blowout? Would her oversized kitchen sink be the perfect place for nightly bath time? Or would she crawl into her soaker tub with her little cherub for bath time fun together?

She handed the woman her credit card, accepting the bag with a smile as she let herself get lost in her thoughts. Could this really—finally—be happening? She hoped so. She really did.

❖

Katie was at the house when she returned, and Ellison breathed a sigh of relief. Until she noticed the boxes in the back of Katie's car.

Katie walked out of the house with her gym duffel on her shoulder, her eyes red and swollen.

"Katie?" Ellison asked as she stepped toward her. "Is everything okay?"

Katie froze, seemingly unsure what to do. After what seemed like an exceptionally long moment, she dropped the bag by the driver's side door of her car. The unzipped top flap flipped up at the force of the bag dropping, and Ellison could see Katie's clothes thrown in haphazardly. Like she was in a rush.

"What's going on?" Ellison asked, alarmed.

"We need to talk," Katie said, sounding exhausted.

Ellison shifted the boutique bag to the hand farthest from Katie so she could reach to her.

"Baby Barn?" Katie asked, reading the bag's label.

Ellison nodded. "It was an impulse buy," she replied, not sure why she was justifying shopping when they clearly had other things to talk about.

"What is it?" Katie asked, her voice small.

"A onesie," Ellison replied, afraid to make any sudden movements or deflect Katie's questions. Katie seemed fragile for some reason.

"Can I see it?"

Ellison handed her the bag while stepping closer, but Katie stepped back once it was in her possession. Ellison watched her peek into the bag and smile, her eyes now red *and* wet.

"That's beyond cute," she said, handing the bag back to her. "I'm sure she'll love it."

"She?"

"Oh. In my head, you're having a girl," Katie said, wiping her eyes. "She'll be smart and sassy and have big blue eyes. And she'll like to hold hands and walk the beach in the evenings before bed, but she'll never want to leave the water. And she'll fight you, every night."

Ellison had intentionally not found out the sex of either embryo. She wanted to be surprised. She would have been amused by Katie's imaginary baby narrative if she wasn't so worried about all the crying and the packed bags.

"What is happening? Is something wrong?" Ellison wanted to reach for her again, but she remembered how she'd stepped back. "Did I do something wrong?"

"No," Katie said, shaking her head as fresh tears fell. "You didn't do anything wrong. You've been perfect. You *are* perfect. You have this beautiful life with lovely friends, and you're going to be the best mother in the world. I have no doubt."

"Why does this feel like a breakup speech, then?" Ellison asked, her heart starting to race.

Katie motioned to the house behind her. "Because this is your life, Ellison, not mine. And there's too much happening in my life for me to be any good in that life of yours. I don't belong. You deserve someone that's not a mess. You deserve someone that's stable. And more like you."

"What are you saying?" Ellison said, not believing what she was hearing.

"I love you. I think I will always love you. But I can't do this." She pointed to the Baby Barn bag and the house with a heavy sigh. "It's too much. I just...I can't."

"Katie, wait," Ellison said, stepping toward her again. This time Katie didn't step back. Instead, she started to sob.

"Just let me get in this car and go," Katie pleaded. "Don't be perfect. Don't say all the right things. That'll only make this harder."

Ellison stopped, stepping back. "I won't force you to do anything, ever. To stay. To go. I don't have that power, and I wouldn't dare. But I wish you'd reconsider. I wish you'd stay to talk."

Katie shook her head, wiping at her cheeks. "I need some space from all of this."

Ellison felt her heart breaking fiber by fiber with every beat, as Katie tossed the duffel bag into her car and closed the driver's side door. Ellison watched through eyes blurry with tears as Katie backed out of the driveway, and out of her life. In a split second, the woman who had made her the happiest she had ever been broke her like no one ever had before.

CHAPTER TWENTY-SIX

Ellison was waiting for Terry's call. Today was the day they'd find out if the transfer worked. She adjusted her sunglasses before exiting her Maserati—it had been another silent drive to work with plenty of useless tears. To say she was a mess would be an understatement. The last week and a half had been brutal. She'd had no correspondence from Katie at all. Nothing. Katie had literally just gotten into her car and driven away.

Ellison had respected her request for space and not tried to reach out to her, but she had hoped to hear from her. On her terms, if she was ready. Which didn't seem to be the case. She cracked her neck, stretching it after another restless night. The beach house felt so empty without Katie there. And her bed...it felt vast and cold. She'd tried moving back into her city apartment, but that asshole Stetler's place was behind schedule, and her bedroom still shook with construction noise and vibrations. After one failed night's sleep in the city, she'd trudged back down to the multi-million-dollar beach view that offered her little comfort. Everything reminded her of Katie there, and that felt like torture.

She tried to chill the fuck out so she could go into work and be civil with everyone, but that seemed unlikely. She was agitated—she knew that. She'd been sleeping like shit. She was anxious about Terry's call, and she could see Katie's car parked by the spa. Sharing a parking complex with someone you loved who'd left you as abruptly as Katie did was not fun.

She was two steps from her Maserati when Pietro's voice rang out.

"Ellison, I was hoping to catch you," he said.

"Sounds like you were waiting for me to get out of my car," she said dryly. "That's waiting, not hoping."

He ignored her reply. "I wanted to know if you could contact GM Enterprises for me. I've sent them a few emails and left a message, but they haven't gotten back to me, and I'd like an answer today."

Ellison stifled the snarl that threatened. Pietro had messaged with a ton of new requests for his space expansion. He seemed to be trying to renegotiate after the fact. Ellison was already annoyed with him since he'd started construction early, prior to the start of his permit window. Which resulted in her having to put out no less than three rage fires, when the nearby businesses complained about construction trucks blocking their spots. And then there was the less than pleasant exchange she'd had to have with him regarding permits and regulations and the legality of them both. The reality was she'd been too busy with Katie's house sale and all her other responsibilities to worry about Pietro's annoying emails. This expansion was supposed to be easy, but he was making it anything but.

"You'll hear from them," she said curtly. She didn't have time or patience for this today.

"That's why I'm talking to you. To make that happen faster," he said, pushing back. "You're their contact person. Surely you can move my concerns along."

"It's a busy season, Pietro. They'll get back to you," she replied.

"Now. I want them to get back to me now. Why is that so hard?" he said, dropping the semipleasant facade. "You move the papers and make the connections, right? So why can't you move them? Put them right under their noses, and get them to answer my questions."

Ellison felt her temper flare. "We're done here."

"This is why I hate dealing with women. You can never tell when it's their time of the month," he growled as he turned away from her.

"Excuse me?" Ellison's minuscule threshold for the day had hit its max.

Pietro replied with gritted teeth, "Just put me in touch with the man that's in charge. I'm tired of dealing with overly emotional women who can't get the job done."

Ellison laughed. "The *man* in charge? That's what you want? You want to talk to who's in charge?"

"That's what I said," Pietro snapped back, showing his true colors.

"Well enjoy the view, Pietro," Ellison said, removing her sunglasses and giving him her best razor-sharp smile. "I'm in charge. GM stands for Gamble Metro. GM Enterprises is me."

"What?" Pietro looked stunned.

"Should I spell it out for you? I own the building complex. All of it. You pay rent to me. I don't just handle the checks—I cash them. I'm sure it's hard for you to comprehend that someone so overly emotional and *female* as myself could bankrupt you ten times over, yet here we are." She took a half step in his direction, making him step back. "But don't worry—the urgency of your complaints has been heard. As well as your incredibly tactless rudeness and sexism. You can be sure your concerns will be addressed in a timely fashion. Or not at all. I guess we'll see if I'm on my period or not."

Pietro said nothing, his mouth agape as Ellison turned toward her office. Jax was standing nearby, with a similar expression as Pietro's while they held out Ellison's coffee.

"I, uh, got you this," they said.

"Thank you." Ellison spared a glance back at Pietro. He was still standing here, with a mix of anger and confusion on his face. She spoke loudly enough for Pietro to hear her when she said, "Pull the permit register for Indulgent Tranquility Spa, and make sure everything is on the up-and-up. If it's not, shut them down."

"Yes, Ellison," Jax said, looking freaked out.

Ellison touched their forearm. "Thank you for the coffee. I appreciate that."

"Sure," they said, swallowing hard. "Let me get the door for you."

Ellison gave them a small smile before slipping through the door and heading straight to her office. She closed the door with more force than was necessary, as she shut out the rest of the world.

"Fucking misogynistic motherfucker," she hissed as she placed her leather portfolio on the desktop. "I'm raising his fucking rent."

She paced the office for a moment before sipping the still hot coffee Jax had brought her. This was lovely, and it had appeared without any request at all, which was always nice. Jax had been thinking about her. She took another long, slow sip even though the last thing she needed was more caffeine. She was plenty jittery already. And evidently short-fused.

There was a knock at her door, and she sighed. She didn't want to see anyone today—but being the boss and all, that seemed unlikely.

"Yes?"

"Do you have a second?" Trina's voice sounded from the other side of the door.

"I do," she said, copping her best understanding and patient boss voice.

The door opened to reveal Trina and Lauren standing there. From where Ellison was perched at the edge of her desk, she could see the very top of Jax's hair behind Lauren's shoulder.

"Is something wrong?" Ellison asked, surprised that her top three employees all needed her attention at the exact same moment.

"You tell us," Trina said, ushering the other two in. She had to shove Jax a little to get Ellison's office door closed. Jax seemed to be the least interested in being in an enclosed space with Ellison, which didn't surprise her if they'd overhead any of her exchange with Pietro.

Ellison raised an eyebrow in Trina's direction.

"Jax tells us you just dressed Pietro down so aggressively in the parking lot that he died of exposure," Lauren said with a smirk. "Which I'm all for since he leers like a cretin, but well, that's not usually your style."

"And you've been extra quiet since the photo shoot," Jax added before ducking a bit when Ellison made eye contact with them.

"You've been showing up to work unnervingly early and staying late every night," Trina said. "And Katie hasn't stopped by once with lunch in over a week."

"Your point is what, exactly?" Ellison didn't feel like the third degree right now.

"Katie's house is set to close in two days, and you've had me running the paperwork and making all the calls," Jax said, their voice wavering. "I'm certainly up to the task, but it's just that…"

"You're surprised I'm asking you to take on more responsibility?" Ellison bit back.

"It's your job, not Jax's," Trina corrected, always the boldest in the room. "That's your case. Your contract. Your girlfriend."

Ellison gave her a look, holding her gaze. Her voice was flat as she replied, "Not anymore."

A look of understanding settled on Trina's face. "Okay," she said, her tone soft and compassionate. "Do you want to tell us what happened?"

Ellison would have been annoyed by her directness had the buzzing of her phone not distracted her. It was a text from Terry with a baby emoji and a milk bottle and three fireworks symbols. Ellison couldn't believe it. The results were in. She was pregnant.

"Oh God, she's crying," Lauren said. "Why is she crying? Someone broke Ellison. We need to call 9-1-1."

Ellison laughed as the tears poured down her face, and the feeling of relief washed over her like a tidal wave. She sank to the floor in front of her desk, dropping her head into her hands as the shittiest week of her life showed a glimmer of improving. Terry was pregnant. With her baby. She was finally going to be a mom.

Ellison heard furniture being moved around her and felt three sets of hands as her friends—no, her family—encircled her with hugs.

After Ellison's ugly crying slowed, Trina asked, "Are you ready to tell us what's going on now? I don't sit on the floor for just anyone."

"This is true—she's got a thing about germs," Lauren supplied as she rubbed Ellison's back.

Ellison laughed, looking at Jax first. "I'm sorry."

Jax was crying, but Ellison had no idea why. "You're not mad at me, right? Because as dapper as I look on the outside, we all know I'm soft and gooey on the inside. And I don't think I can take that kind of disappointment from you."

Ellison laughed again. "No, I'm mad at myself. And I'm sorry if I took that out on you." She reached out and brushed a tear off Jax's cheek before handing them the tissue Trina offered her. "I am so proud of you. And I'm so grateful you're in my life. Sorry, I've been a bit of a wreck lately."

"So, who's having a baby?" Trina said, holding up Ellison's phone and pointing to the still-lit screen.

"Me," she said with a broad smile. It was time to tell the most important people in her life about the most important decision she'd ever made. She couldn't do this alone—she'd learned that this last week and half. If she didn't let people in, she'd never be any good for this baby or anyone else. "I think we need to talk."

CHAPTER TWENTY-SEVEN

K atie slapped at her cell phone alarm, knocking it to the ground with a thud. She reached for it blindly, trying to get to it before it woke Shaina up in the next room.

She'd been sleeping on Shaina's couch since she'd left Ellison's beach house. Until the house sold, she didn't have much extra money to spare, since she'd increased the supplemental therapy hours at New Beginnings for her mother. Plus, she needed time to find a place, so Shaina's couch was perfect for right now.

Shaina had assured her nightly since she'd shown up at her door in tears that this wasn't an inconvenience. And Katie hoped she was being honest, but she knew she wouldn't stay longer than she had to. It was hard to feel sorry for yourself when someone else was always around. Katie wanted to be able to lock herself in a bedroom and close a door to the world. But that was impossible when you were couch surfing. Though that would change soon enough.

Katie didn't have the stomach to attend the open house, but Shaina went and said it was a mob scene. And she must have been right because Jax had called Katie with six offers before the end of the day on the Sunday of the open house weekend. After going over the details with Jax and weighing her options, Katie chose a cash offer—the second highest on the table. The cash offer afforded her a fast turnaround, and that was what she wanted—to put this whole thing behind her. And start her life over again.

She found the phone, shutting off the horrible alarm sound as she looked at the date. Today was the closing. She was a few signatures away from a big check and handing over the keys of her house for the last time. All she had to do was show up at Gamble and Associates and sign and initial where their attorney told her to. But that's what she was dreading most, going to the office.

Katie hadn't even thought of the home sale when she'd driven to Shaina's from the beach house. She'd barely kept the car on the road through all her tears—she wasn't thinking about anything else but arriving alive. She'd been surprised when she saw *Gamble and Associates* come up on her cell phone screen a few days later. She almost didn't answer it, but at the last minute, she did. And hearing Jax's voice on the line gave her a mix of sadness and relief. She was relieved it wasn't Ellison calling—she wasn't ready to face her yet. Or hear her voice. Or deal with how devastating driving away from her had been.

She'd worked with Jax since then, all via phone and email exchanges. But today was the day she'd have to see everyone face-to-face. She wondered if Ellison would be at the office. She figured she would be. Her Maserati had been in the parking lot every day that Katie had worked at the spa and was there most evenings after her last client of the night. Ellison seemed to be working a lot. Because even when the office lights were dim, Katie could see a light in the window of Ellison's spacious corner office. There had been a dozen times in the past few weeks that she'd started walking toward that office and stopped herself. But that was nothing compared to the hundreds of times she'd picked up her phone to call or text her and stopped. Because that just seemed cruel to both of them.

She slinked into the bathroom and dressed quickly. Shaina had early clients today, and Katie didn't want to be underfoot. She planned to visit her mom in the morning until the meeting and then spend the afternoon under a pile of tissues and a blanket until Shaina came home and she had to be presentable.

When she exited the bathroom, Shaina was at the kitchen table, stirring a cup of something.

"Did I wake you?" Katie asked as she padded over to her duffel bag in search of fresh socks.

"No. Your alarm did," Shaina said playfully.

"Shit. I'm so sorry." Katie ran a hand through her hair. "I'll be out of your space in no time, I promise."

"I'm teasing. And you don't have to be," Shaina said. "I've told you that no less than a million times the last month."

"A month. I've been living on your couch for a whole month. That's ridiculous. You should hate me," Katie replied, shaking her head.

"You're an excellent cook, and you're very tidy," Shaina said. "Truly, your only flaw is that you fall asleep during every movie we watch. Every time."

Katie laughed until déjà vu hit her like a ton of bricks. She'd heard that before.

"You're thinking about her again," Shaina said.

Katie didn't bother trying to hide it. "I am."

"You know, it's been a minute," Shaina said. "Don't you think you should call her?"

"And say what?" Katie asked as she flopped onto the couch. "*I've missed you every day since I broke your heart in your luxurious driveway.* Or would *Leaving you was the stupidest thing I ever did* suffice? Or my favorite usual nighttime ache of *No one will ever love me or kiss me or make me feel like I'm the whole world like you did.* That's a special dagger-to-the-heart kind of realization. I have it almost nightly."

Shaina frowned. "Just call her. Start with one of those. All of them are pathetic enough to get her not to hang up on you."

"Seriously? You're picking on me right now?"

"No," Shaina said as she came over to sit next to her. "I'm talking some sense into you."

"Good luck," Katie said, dropping her head back against the couch.

"Look. I'm going to be honest with you. I love you. But you have been a fucking mess since that night."

Katie sat up bolt upright. "I told you me being here was an inconvenience."

"It's not. That's not what I meant," Shaina said, shaking her head. "What I mean is that you're not happy, Katie Cat. You cry during commercials about toilet paper, you barely eat the amazing meals you cook, and half the time you're sitting next to me, you're staring off into the distance. Thinking about her. You do it so often I've started to recognize the Ellison Look out of my periphery. I don't even bother trying to engage with you until you're back."

Katie sighed. "I know. I guess I don't know what to do about it."

"Call her," Shaina repeated.

"I can't. I left," Katie said, exasperated.

"And why did you do that?" Shaina asked, though they'd talked about this dozens of times.

"Because nothing in my life is stable. I'm living on your couch. I'm a disaster," Katie said, hating how much verbalizing that made her feel small.

"You're wrong. What you had with Ellison *was* stable. You're a mess and living on my couch because you got scared, and you left the best thing that's ever happened to you."

Katie felt tears prick at the edges of her eyes again.

"So I'll ask you again. Why did you leave?" Shaina placed her hand on Katie's knee.

"Because I was scared. I was scared how much she meant to me. I was afraid of selling the house. I was afraid of not having a plan. I was afraid of investing more time into the life she had already built so successfully, just to find out I wasn't meant to be in it." Katie's imposter syndrome reared its ugly head in her honesty. "I was afraid of being trapped like I was when my mother was in the accident. And I was afraid of falling in love with that perfect child the way I fell for her mother. And being stuck all over again."

"You wouldn't be stuck, though," Shaina said. "You'd be in love. And living a life that was yours, not just hers. Right? I mean, if it was just about her and what was ideal for her life, don't you think she would have spent a hell of a lot less time trying to help you fit in to it? Because from what I saw, she opened her life like a book to you and rewrote the chapters with you in it."

Katie didn't know what to say.

"Is she really having a girl?" Shaina asked.

"I have no idea. She's just always been a girl in my head," Katie said. It occurred to her that Ellison would know now if Terry was pregnant. It pained Katie to know she wasn't there for that reveal, whether it be good or bad. She should have been there. "I miss her."

Shaina nodded. "Close this chapter today. Sell that house, spend a few days in a hotel somewhere, and get your head on straight. And call her. Be honest with her. Even if it goes nowhere, at least then you'll have some closure."

"I suppose." Katie wasn't sure she had the nerve to face her. She was already trying to figure out ways to get out of going to her office today. But she knew that was impossible.

"It'll all work out, Katie Cat," Shaina said, pulling her in to a hug.

"I hope you're right."

❖

It was midafternoon when she walked into Gamble and Associates. Her stomach was in knots as she waited for someone to respond to the chime that rang out when she entered the front door. After a beat, Lauren and Jax turned the corner, deep in conversation.

"Oh, hey, Katie," Lauren said, her smile small but genuine. "It's good to see you."

"Hey," she replied, shifting from left to right. Ellison's door was closed. Katie hadn't noticed her car in its usual spot, which she figured meant she was out today. though Katie couldn't imagine why. Ellison always worked on Fridays.

"She's not here," Trina's voice sounded from nearby.

"Oh," Katie said, surprised at the sadness that statement evoked.

Jax cleared their throat. "The buyers are in the conference room with their lawyer. We're ready when you are."

Katie looked between the three friends and recognized their strained expressions. They knew about her and Ellison. At least some of it. "Where is she?"

Trina stepped forward. "Not here."

Lauren gave Trina a look, and Trina sighed. "She's in meetings off-site and then taking the rest of the day off."

"She didn't want to see me," Katie replied with a nod.

"Yes," Trina answered. And though that felt like a gut punch, Katie appreciated her candor. "Look. I won't pretend to know what happened, nor is it any of my"—she motioned toward Lauren and Jax—"or our business, but I promised her I would take care of you today. And I plan to make good on that."

Katie looked at Jax, surprised. "You aren't handling the closing?"

Jax shook their head. "Trina is lead today. There have been some…issues."

"Like what?" Katie felt herself getting more anxious, which didn't seem possible.

"Like the buyers and their lawyer are trying to push and pull a little bit. It happens," Lauren supplied with a shrug. "Trina is better at biting off their heads and pissing down their throats than Jax is."

"I'd argue with that, but I'm secure in my masculinity," Jax replied. "It's a stone-cold fact. Trina's terrifying."

Katie laughed. "I had gleaned that."

"See? We're good then," Trina said with a smile. "Let's go sell a house and get you a fat check."

Katie gave one last look to Ellison's closed office door. Her heart felt so heavy today. And though she had tried to tell herself that was because of the house sale, she knew it was because Ellison wasn't a part of this. Or her life. And that was all her fault.

CHAPTER TWENTY-EIGHT

"Can you explain that to me once more?" Katie felt like a moron, but the math didn't seem right.

Trina gave her a sympathetic nod. "Sure. It's confusing, I know."

The buyers had left over thirty minutes ago, and everything was signed, but Katie still couldn't believe the check that was in front of her. "It's a misprint, right? There are too many zeros here."

"It's not." Trina pulled out the paperwork and started at the last few pages. "This is the credit you got from the insurance filing. This was Zander's fee for renovation—that includes labor, supplies—the whole shebang. And this check is the final amount of the sale, minus Zander's fee. Which you can see was significantly decreased by the insurance filing. So almost burning your house down worked to your benefit," Trina joked.

Katie held up the check from Gamble and Associates like it was made of glass. "Wait, I know. There's no mention of the Realtor fee here. Why?"

"Oh." Trina shifted in place. "You paid the buyer's Realtor fee, here." She pointed to a line on the page before them.

"No, Ellison's fee. Or, I guess, your fee. Jax's fee? Someone should be getting paid for this, right?"

Trina shifted again, and Katie took that to mean she was uncomfortable. "Ellison waived her fee. That money is yours."

"That's not right. That's not fair," Katie argued, but Trina held up her hand.

"Never have I ever seen her waive a fee before. But she did. I can't explain her rationale. She didn't offer any explanation. And something in my gut told me not to ask," Trina said as she closed the folder, sliding it toward her. "You're free, Katie. The house is sold. And you're a multimillionaire. The check is legit. Go forth and live your life." Trina paused. "That's what she would want, I think."

Trina was almost at the door when Katie got up the nerve to ask, "Did the transfer work?"

Trina looked at her, stone-faced. "I can't—"

Katie stood and closed the distance between them before she took Trina's hand in hers. "Don't tell me then. Maybe, just, squeeze my hand if it did. Please. Just that. I'll leave here and never bother her again, but I have to know."

Trina pulled her hand away. "I don't think she'd want that."

Katie dropped her head, devastated.

Trina ducked down, making eye contact with her. "Meaning, I don't think she'd want you to leave and never see her again."

Katie wiped the tear off her cheek as her heartbeat picked up. "Don't screw with me, Trina. I'm newly wealthy and very unstable."

Trina laughed. "She's at the beach house. Construction in the city got extended. But I didn't tell you that. Also, I didn't tell you that she might be missing you as much as you seem to be missing her. I've said nothing of the sort. Got it?"

"Got it," Katie said, feeling hopeful.

"Good luck out there in the world," Trina said as she walked with her to the front door. "It was a pleasure working with you today."

Katie shook her hand, grateful that Trina—and all of Ellison's family—had continued to show her the kindness and welcoming they always had, but her breath caught as Trina gave her one brief extra squeeze before letting go.

"Drive safe," Trina said with a wink.

❖

Katie fumbled with the keys, dropping them twice before successfully fitting them into the lock of the storage unit. She pushed up the garage-type door with a grunt and was immediately overwhelmed by what awaited her.

After the closing, Trina had given her the storage unit key she'd forgotten at Ellison's beach house. Though she'd always had access to the unit—much like the house—she'd never bothered coming by. She'd been driving around with all the boxes she'd sorted and taken from Ellison's that night, because she had nowhere to put them since she'd left the key at Ellison's in true Katie fashion. But now that the house was sold, she was responsible for retaining the unit. Or discarding the contents.

Katie swallowed hard at the sight before her. All of the salvageable furniture, antiques, heirlooms, and the like were carefully wrapped in plastic or moving blankets and labeled with color printouts and descriptions. Katie ran her hand along the antique writer's desk her grandfather had made for her grandmother. It was wrapped in cloth and then double-wrapped in plastic and labeled *Fragile*. The movers Ellison had hired had pulled out all the stops. They had taken such care with Katie's things. Just as Ellison had taken care of Katie.

Ellison. The woman who had infinite patience and kindness and charm. The same woman who gave affection so freely and deeply to Katie the entire time she had known her. She was passionate in everything that she did—it was no surprise that she had been as successful in life as she had been. She was the total package: beautiful, smart, kind, generous, and loving. And until Katie left, she had also been *hers*. All hers. Parts of Katie's fear, from that night and since then, were based in what she knew to be fact—Ellison would ask her to stay once the house sold. She knew that Ellison would continue to share her opulent life and connections with her. She knew she'd share her love with her. Like she had all those weeks. And as those weeks turned to months, Katie knew that the love she felt for Ellison wasn't a fast, quick-burning kind. It was the forever kind. And that had scared her, too.

She sighed as she headed to her trunk, figuring she might as well unload the baggage she'd been carrying around all these weeks. One by one she unloaded the boxes that she and Ellison had sorted when they were together. The boxes full of memories that they'd combed through and laughed over. These were things she wanted to keep, but things that she didn't need on an everyday basis. They were things she'd put back into a new home or space of her own. When that day came.

She dropped the last box unceremoniously, and it slid back, dislodging something from its resting place against the wall. She put her hand up just in time to stop the one-by-eight board from hitting her in the head.

She cursed as she righted the wood, putting it back against the storage unit wall. It was only then, once it was upright again, that she noticed what it was—the inside doorframe of the kitchen pantry. This piece of wood held all her family's heights and age markers for each year and decade that they lived in the house. It was an irreplaceable piece of history that she had overlooked and forgotten about, but one that would have haunted her when she realized she'd left it behind. A sign was attached to the top of the board that read in bold but elegant slanting letters: *Family Heirloom—Handle with Care, Do Not Sell, Do Not Scrap.* That was Ellison's script. She had saved this plank. Like she had saved Katie.

Katie closed her eyes as the sobs racked through her. She was in love, and she wasn't sure what that meant for the future, but it felt amazing and scary at the same time. She let herself feel all the feelings as she sank down onto her mother's garden bench. She cried because her mother was better. She cried because the fire had terrified her but also changed her life for the better. She cried because her heart ached for a woman who was selfless beyond anyone she had ever met. She cried because she felt so deeply about her that she was crying in a storage unit. She cried because she missed her. She cried because Ellison was having a baby, and she wanted to be a part of that. And finally, she cried because she didn't have all the answers—but for the first time since leaving that night, she realized she didn't have to. Because Ellison was at the beach, and every moment Katie was here, she wasn't there.

And as she closed the storage unit and locked the door, she smiled the first genuine smile she'd had in over a month. Because even though she didn't know what to expect when she got there, she knew this—she was heading home.

CHAPTER TWENTY-NINE

Ellison was starving. Which must be a good sign because food hadn't much inspired her lately. She checked her cell phone, wondering where the food was. Had she really called that long ago? Or was she just hangry?

She padded barefoot across the kitchen toward the living room. She sipped her glass of wine as she surfed the channels aimlessly, looking for something, anything, to distract her from how hungry she was. She shivered at a commercial for a popular ski resort that had already begun promoting winter activities. Sure, they were at the last golden days of summer, but skiing? That was just rude.

She reached for the cashmere throw, wrapping it around herself to warm up, when she noticed it—Katie's scent. This blanket smelled like Katie. Ellison sat with that a moment, not wanting to give up the soft, luxurious warmth of what had once been her favorite blanket, but also unsure if she wanted the memories that this scent brought flooding back.

"As if you ever forgot," she said bitterly.

As much as she hated to admit it, she thought about Katie every moment of every day. She thought about her when she made coffee in the morning. Or when she had a salad for lunch. She thought about her when she ordered her favorite pizza on Saturday nights, like the one she was waiting for tonight. Because she had shared so much of her life with Katie, the fact that she was gone made Ellison feel like there was a hole in her whole world. Not just in her heart, which was certainly also true. But her actual existence felt like there was an irreparable tear right through its center. And it ached. It ached like a coldness that never faded. She *ached* for her. And that was the worst part of it all.

In the month that she'd been gone, Ellison missed her as much now as she did the day after she left. That hadn't lessened. Time hadn't taken some of the pain away. And maybe that was because she had still been interconnected with Katie—at least in some way—until yesterday. Now that the house was sold and the paperwork complete, she was no longer linked to her. Which should bring her respite from the sadness, but it didn't. If anything, Ellison felt like she was more down today than she had been yesterday. Because now she had no reason to maybe accidently cross Katie's path. There wasn't one last thing that she needed to do or say to her, because that moment ended when Trina closed the deal.

Ellison was so grateful to Trina. And Jax and Lauren. All of them. Because she finally came clean about everything—the miscarriages, the hostile uterus, Peyton's baby shower, the surrogacy, how things ended with Katie—all of it. And they didn't even blink. Their support never wavered, and gratefully, they stepped up in a big way. She knew she didn't have to worry about anything because between the three of them, she knew Katie would be taken care of, and so would she. They helped heal her heart and get her functioning again. Which was all Ellison could ask for.

The driveway signal sounded, indicating someone was headed to her front door.

"Pizza," she said with a smile. Finally. She was famished.

She didn't bother shrugging off the blanket. Instead she wrapped it a little more tightly around herself. Summer wasn't quite gone yet, but the fall weather was slowly creeping in. And weather on the coast in New England could be unpredictable. So she would retrieve her beloved shrimp scampi pizza in a blanket burrito. That was the sensible thing to do.

"Thank you—" she started but the rest of the words died on her lips at the sight of Katie holding her Reeled In dinner.

"Hi," Katie said, looking tentative. She held up the pizza with an uneasy smile. "I come bearing food."

"Food that I ordered," Ellison replied.

"Mostly," Katie said with a nod. "But—full disclosure—I added an item or two."

Ellison stood there, unsure of what to say. "You commandeered my dinner order and made adjustments?"

"Additions, not adjustments," Katie corrected.

Ellison took in Katie's appearance. She looked great as usual. Her long, dark, curly red hair looked healthy and shiny. And her T-shirt, skinny jeans, and flip-flop ensemble was flirty and cute. Her toes were painted bright red, and she had a little anklet on her right ankle. Ellison took her time bringing her eyes back up to Katie's before asking, "Why are you here?"

Katie seemed to expect this question. "To bring you dinner."

Ellison raised an eyebrow.

"And to ask you to consider talking to me. Not necessarily over dinner. But maybe in the future. Sometime. Ever." Katie ran her hand through her hair, and Ellison knew what that felt like. She missed the weight of those curls in her fingers.

"What did you add to the order?" Ellison asked, curious.

"The calamari. And I convinced Chelsea to let me take two Watermelon Sugars to go," Katie said, looking bashful.

"Why am I not surprised Chelsea had something to do with this?" Ellison asked, leaning against the doorframe.

"She's a sucker for a good love story," Katie said with a shrug. "But just know, she'll probably have questions. You know, if you decline my request to speak at some point. And again, not necessarily tonight. But you know—"

"At some point in the future," Ellison replied.

"Right. That," Katie said with a small smile. "She's sort of invested because I completely involved her. So that's on me. Sorry," Katie said, and Ellison could tell she was being genuine.

"Well, I'm in no rush to piss off my favorite bartender," she said, stepping back and motioning for Katie to come in. "Might as well come in since you're here. Just don't forget the martinis."

Katie gave her a measured smile, but Ellison could see her eyes light up. She'd missed seeing that.

Ellison went right to the bar to get martini glasses. She took the opportunity to observe Katie in her space again. Katie placed the pizza box and extra bag on the counter. She washed her hands at the sink and delicately touched Ellison's giraffe. Her eyes lingered on the sea glass mason jars that Ellison hadn't had the heart to get rid of, even though seeing them pained her a bit.

Ellison filled the shaker with ice as she poured the first cocktail bag into it. She shook the liquid, straining it into both glasses. Chelsea might have told Katie she sent her with two martinis, but clearly, she'd sent her with enough for four. Ellison was sure that wasn't a miscalculation. She made a mental note to tip Chelsea well the next time she saw her.

Katie moved with a comfortable ease through the kitchen. She grabbed plates and utensils with such familiarity that Ellison smiled. She seemed at home here, which brought on feelings that Ellison wasn't quite sure what to do with.

"Couch? Or table?" Katie asked, though she was more than halfway to Ellison's living room.

"Couch," Ellison confirmed, following her with the nearly full martini glasses.

She sat on the couch where she had been and noticed that Katie seemed to hover near the love seat. Prior to Katie leaving, these positions were reversed. Katie was usually snuggled in her favorite blanket and on the couch, and Ellison was often working on the love seat until Katie pulled her over, nudging the work out of her hand.

Katie's eyes lingered on the blanket, and Ellison was sure she was thinking the same thing.

"Please, sit," Ellison said, motioning for her to get comfortable on the love seat. She wasn't ready to give up the blanket or the prime seating. They weren't exactly on friendly terms yet.

Katie gave her a small smile before filling Ellison's plate with food. She gave Ellison a piece of pizza that was heavy on the shrimp and moved a handful of calamari legs to the outer edge, clearly remembering Ellison's preferences from before. "I brought salad bowls, too. I just assumed you'd want to eat these things while they were still warm."

"I do," Ellison replied. As she always did. But Katie knew that. "Here," Ellison said, placing Katie's martini on the table in front of her.

"Thanks," Katie said as she picked it up, though she didn't drink it.

"You're not thirsty?" Ellison asked.

"I'm nervous," Katie admitted. "And I don't want to drink without you."

Ellison eyed her glass on the table. "Are you worried about being rude? By drinking first, I mean?"

Katie shook her head. "I'm worried about my hand shaking and me spilling this bright pink drink on the love seat."

Ellison laughed.

"I'd feel less like I was going to spill it if you were also drinking yours," Katie said with a shrug. "I think. I don't really know."

Ellison picked up her glass and took a hearty sip. She let out a contented sigh. "These are always perfect."

Katie matched her sip, then took another before placing the glass down and pushing it away, farther than was necessary. "Best martini I have ever had, hands down."

"Is that why you pushed it out onto the back deck, then?" Ellison asked as she nibbled the pizza she had been lusting over.

"I just want to make sure I remember to eat enough," Katie replied, her nerves showing again.

"I'm not going to bite you," Ellison said.

"You have every right to," Katie replied, not looking relieved at all by her attempt at humor.

Katie took a few bites of her pizza, seemingly lost in thought. She shivered, and Ellison found herself shrugging off the blanket and handing it to her. Katie reached for it, seeming unsure still.

"Take it. I've warmed up," Ellison said. "Plus, it still smells like you. So I think that means it's part of your DNA now."

"I did tell you we were one," Katie said, wrapping herself up the way she used to before everything changed. She was so cute in that blanket. Ellison tried to ignore that as she took another bite of pizza.

"What did you want to talk about?" she asked, not ready to let her guard down.

"You. And see how you've been. And…" Katie paused. "Honestly, I'd only planned what I was going to say at the door. I wasn't expecting to get inside. Or to be on the couch—"

"Or to be reunited with your cashmere bestie?"

"Exactly," Katie said, smiling. "All of this is going better than I was expecting."

"What were you expecting?" Ellison asked.

Katie put down her plate and clasped her hands on her knee. "Well, I'd envisioned you turning me away at the door. And maybe throwing the pizza box at me like a Frisbee."

"I would never." Ellison put her hand to her heart. "To think you'd believe me to be the type of monster that would waste a shrimp scampi pizza. Unbelievable."

Katie laughed that easy, melodious laugh Ellison loved so much. "I suppose you're right. How dare I."

"Precisely." Ellison gave her a wink. "If I threw anything, it would be the house salad."

"But not the dressing," Katie replied astutely. "You're far too attached to that cilantro lime vinaigrette to waste it."

"Touché."

Katie looked at her martini before reaching for it and finishing it off in another large swig. She took two bites of pizza before putting her plate on the table between them.

"Do you need liquid courage for whatever it is you seem to be struggling to say?" Ellison asked as she took her own sip.

Katie laughed. "No. My mouth feels like cotton. But that's probably anxiety. I'm not afraid of what I want to say to you. I'm not even afraid of what you'll say or not say in response. I'm afraid I'll forget the most important parts. And I expect to only get one shot at it."

"Well, start with those, then," Ellison offered. "Start with the most important parts and see if you even need the rest. That way you won't forget them."

"I love you." Katie started with a bang. "And I miss you. And I want to tell you that I was scared and insecure and in my own head about so many things that I forgot to breathe when I was around you. Because I was afraid I would lose you and that it would be my fault when it happened. And it inevitably was."

Ellison wasn't prepared to hear those words. She wasn't even prepared to sit across from Katie. But to hear I love you? I miss you? That was too much.

She shook her head, but Katie ignored her.

"You cross your ankles when you're on business calls. You spin the ring on your middle finger when you're annoyed at a client. You don't snore, but you breathe softly in this way that is so relaxing that I counted on it to lull me back to sleep if I woke up before you did."

Katie inched forward. "You hum when you wash dishes. You always smell amazing, and you smell even better after you've been in the sun a bit. Your hands are always soft, like you wear moisturizing gloves at night even though I know you don't. And I know that because whenever we shared a bed, you never kept your hands to yourself. You always had one on my hip or resting on my low back, connecting you to me in a subtle, affectionate way."

Katie let out a shaky breath. "The important things—I love you. I miss you. I never should have left the way I did, and I have regretted that night since I pulled out of your obnoxiously long driveway."

Ellison laughed. "It is rather long, isn't it?"

"Ridiculously so," Katie replied. "I see why you always turned your car around. Backing out was hell and a half."

Ellison tried to let Katie's words sink in, but her mind still raced. "Is there more?"

Katie nodded. "I want a relationship with you, if you're open to it. Maybe a wave when we're in the parking lot at the same time. Or a funny meme exchange via text. Maybe a friendship? If that's possible. I want—" She paused, seeming to reconsider her words. "I'd like that more than anything—a chance to have you still in my life. Even casually."

"Just casually?" Ellison asked.

"I mean, how truthfully do you want me to answer?" Katie's green eyes looked so bright and alive right now. Like she was energized with truths.

"The most truthful," Ellison replied, hoping she didn't regret it.

Katie stood, moving slowly to Ellison's couch and sitting beside her. She placed a tentative hand on Ellison's knee. She studied Ellison's face before barely touching her cheek as she said, "I want to go to sleep next to you every night and wake up with you every day. I want to forget to turn on the dishwasher before bed and leave the cap off the toothpaste in your bathroom." She dragged her thumb over Ellison's lower lip, breaking down the last of Ellison's walls as she whispered, "I want to be constantly reminded how much you mean to me by these lips. I want to remember."

"Then remind yourself," Ellison said, holding Katie's hand to her cheek. "Because I never forgot."

"Me neither," Katie said as she leaned in, kissing her softly.

Ellison leaned in to her touch, breathing out slowly against Katie's mouth as she tried to silence the fears in her heart that told her Katie would leave again. Try as she might to ignore them, she couldn't.

Ellison pulled back, shaking her head to clear the lust fog. "I can't do this with you again. I can't have you just freak out and leave. I'm too old for that. I'm too in love with you for that. I have too much at stake now."

"Because she's coming, right?" Katie said, reaching out to caress her cheek again. "You're gonna be a mom, huh?"

Ellison nodded, unable to hold back the tears. "It's not just about me anymore. It can't be."

"I'm not going anywhere," Katie said, reconnecting their lips. "I will wait for the rest of my life for you to give me another chance. And I'll babysit for free, forever. Even if you go out with someone younger and prettier. I'll still babysit."

"Younger and prettier than you?" Ellison laughed. "Unlikely."

"Then don't. And let's find a slightly less qualified sitter than I would have been to have a date night together instead. But let's not stay out late because we'll miss her." Katie brushed the tears off Ellison's cheeks. "And just to be clear, when I say slightly less qualified, I still expect them to be childcare professionals, licensed and certified to practice in multiple states, and with a list of references as long as your ridiculous driveway."

"Oh. Is that all, then?"

"I mean, I'm open to some negotiation about it, but not much," Katie replied.

"You're lucky I love you and find you irresistible—because otherwise, I might consider your standards unrealistic."

"Really? Because I was thinking maybe they were a little lax. Maybe we don't go on a date at all. We bring her with us and do early bird everything. That way we know she's getting all the love, all the time."

"And what if she's not a girl?" Ellison asked.

Katie gave her a look. "She is. But if she isn't, then we'll love her all the same."

"You're really sure about this girl thing, huh?" Ellison said, loving how close Katie was.

"As sure as I am about this." She motioned between them. "I want this. Forever. Long driveway and all. I'm in. Both feet. All the way. I let myself get in my own head before. I convinced myself I wasn't good enough for this life you have. But the reality is that I've never felt more alive and comfortable in my own skin than when I was with you. I don't have to have everything figured out. I needed to take time to see that and really understand that."

"You've always been enough. Just as you are," Ellison replied, as the last of her hesitance slipped away.

"I know that now." Katie watched her intently as she said, "I'm not perfect, but I'm willing to work hard to be perfect *with* you. I want to take on all of life's adventures with you, Ellison. Even the baby ones. Especially those."

Ellison's heart overflowed at Katie's words. She reached for her as she asked, "That's all the important stuff, huh?"

"I think so, but I'm sure I'll remember something else later." Katie climbed into her lap, looping her arms around Ellison's shoulders. "That is, if you'll have me."

"Forever and always." And Ellison meant that with every fiber of her being.

EPILOGUE

Two years later

Katie walked through the door with a triumphant smile. "Vivienne's asleep."

Ellison shook her head, not believing it. "No way. That was too easy."

Katie did a victory dance. "Two 'Ants Go Marching,' some super rocking skills, and the delicate sway and shift lowering into the crib of a boss bitch." Katie pretended to brush off her shoulder. "Super Mom strikes again."

Ellison smiled. "She is obsessed with you."

"It's a ginger thing," Katie said with a shrug. "We've got a special connection."

"I'll say," Ellison said happily. "She wore herself out at the beach today."

Katie nodded. "It's been a busy couple of weeks. Between Trina and Kendall's wedding, and your annual end of summer beach house party, she's maxed out. That's a lot of toddlering for a toddler."

Ellison beckoned for Katie to join her in bed. "Come celebrate the fact that our beautiful little cherub is in her crib, sleeping soundly."

"Yes, ma'am," Katie said as she stripped out of her clothes and scooted under the covers that Ellison held up. "Why am I naked and you aren't?"

Ellison tossed her shirt to the floor as she joined Katie in her nakedness. "Honestly? I thought you'd be in there longer. She's been teething up a storm. I expected to see you in an hour."

Katie ran her fingers along Ellison's naked stomach. "You underestimate me."

"I'm pleasantly surprised and elated you're here now," Ellison said, kissing her.

"There's nowhere I'd rather be," Katie said, and Ellison warmed at the statement that had become commonplace between them. These past two years had been an adventure and a half. After Katie showed up with pizza that night, they'd slowly rebuilt their relationship together. Eventually, Katie moved in with her full-time, and they anxiously awaited the birth of Ellison's little girl.

She looked over at the folder on her desk in the corner.

"I'm so glad that's official now," Katie said, following her gaze. "I want to frame it."

Ellison laughed. "Do people frame adoption papers?"

Katie looked offended. "Do they not? I want to make sure Vivi knows that I did a whole song and dance in front of a judge to make it legit."

Ellison brushed a hair off Katie's forehead. "She knows how much you love her, babe. You've been there since she was handed to me at the hospital."

"I know," Katie said, crinkling her nose. "But the paperwork says she's mine, too. That's important."

Ellison didn't argue with her. She knew that was something that Katie had wanted to have done as soon as possible.

She took Katie's left hand, toying with the engagement ring on her finger. "You know, we should probably set a date or something. Now that the adoption is finalized."

"Oh, you know I love a party," Katie said, pushing Ellison on her back and leaning over her. "You think Reeled In will send appetizer shrimp scampi pizzas over?"

"Over where?" Ellison asked, amused. They hadn't talked about a venue or anything, only that they wanted it to be during the summer months and somewhere local, so Katie's mom could make it.

"Here," Katie said matter-of-factly.

"You want to get married here?" Ellison asked, not hating the idea.

"Of course," Katie replied without hesitation. "The beach is where our love grew. This place is as special to me as you and Vivi are."

"Okay," Ellison said.

"Okay?" Katie asked, looking excited.

"I love that idea. We have so many wonderful memories here. That would be one more to add to the list." Ellison smiled. "We could do it on a weekend your mom is in the guesthouse—that way she could be involved in all the activities."

Katie beamed. "She loves that space. It's nice that she comes to stay a couple weekends a month."

Ellison couldn't agree more. With Katie's help, she'd finished the apartment over the garage and had it fully equipped for Katie's mother to stay with an aide for short periods. They'd even installed a chair lift for days when Mae was too tired to take the stairs up to the unit.

"So, when were you thinking for the big day?" Ellison asked as Katie started to kiss along her collarbone.

"Mmm, maybe late spring? The first week in June?" Katie said between hot, openmouthed kisses to Ellison's chest.

"That close to your graduation?" Ellison asked. Katie would be finishing her doctorate in physical therapy around that time. She'd been working hard over the past two years to finish up the classes she'd started before she and Ellison had met. It was finally paying off. Katie was two semesters away from being Dr. Crawford, and Ellison could not be prouder.

Katie's mouth settled on her nipple, and she sucked gently before saying, "Yeah, I want to get married before July."

Ellison moaned as Katie's hands started to wander. "What's happening in July?"

Katie propped herself up on her elbow, and Ellison missed her mouth immediately. "I was thinking, we should talk about another baby."

Ellison blinked. "A what?"

"A brother or sister for Vivi." Katie smiled as she moved, straddling Ellison's hips and looking down at her. "If I get pregnant in July, then our new little bundle of joy will be big enough to safely enjoy the beach with their big sister the following summer."

"You've given this some thought," Ellison said, loving the idea. "You sure you want another?"

Katie nodded, resting her hands on Ellison's chest as she leaned in to connect their lips. "And I want to carry the last kid-sicle of yours."

Ellison chuckled against her mouth. "Kid-sicle?"

Katie nodded, chasing her lips. "Embryo sounded less sexy in my head, but now that I said it out loud, so does kid-sicle."

Ellison pulled back, cradling Katie's jaw in her hands. "Do you really mean that?"

Katie gave her a broad grin. "I do. Well, I do, after I say *I do* to you. You know, after I graduate and pass the boards."

Ellison kissed her long and slow, loving the feeling of her weight on top of her. "Then I guess we're filling this house up after all, huh?"

"Maybe that beginner's bet you always talked about wasn't such a mistake after all, was it? We're going to need *all* the bedrooms. Seems like your heart knew more than your head did," Katie said, her green eyes sparkling.

"Seems like it." Ellison had never been so happy to be wrong. "Hey, Katie?"

"Yeah?"

"Let's make a baby."

"I thought you'd never ask."

About the Author

Fiona Riley was born and raised in New England, where she is a medical professional and part-time professor when she isn't bonding with her laptop over words. She went to college in Boston and stuck around because the seafood is fresh, and the ocean is only minutes away. When she isn't working or writing, she enjoys spending time with her wife and kids. She can often be found taking too many pictures of her beautiful family and probably eating too much charcuterie.

Fiona has always had a love for writing but lost touch with that connection when it was time to grow up and get a "real job." Luckily for her, a cancer diagnosis paused life long enough to remind her to nurture the one relationship that had always made her feel the most complete: artist, dreamer, writer.

Contact Fiona and check for updates on all her new adventures at:

Twitter: @fionarileyfic
Facebook: "Fiona Riley Fiction"
Website: http://www.fionarileyfiction.com/
Email: fionarileyfiction@gmail.com

Books Available From Bold Strokes Books

All That Remains by Sheri Lewis Wohl. Johnnie and Shantel might have to risk their lives—and their love—to stop a werewolf intent on killing. (978-1-63555-949-1)

Beginner's Bet by Fiona Riley. Phenom luxury Realtor Ellison Gamble has everything, except a family to share it with, so when a mix-up brings youthful Katie Crawford into her life, she bets the house on love. (978-1-63555-733-6)

Dangerous Without You by Lexus Grey. Throughout their senior year in high school, Aspen, Remington, Denna, and Raleigh face challenges in life and romance that they never expect. (978-1-63555-947-7)

Desiring More by Raven Sky. In this collection of steamy stories, a rich variety of lovers find themselves desiring more: more from a lover, more from themselves, and more from life. (978-1-63679-037-4)

Jordan's Kiss by Nanisi Barrett D'Arnuck. After losing everything in a fire, Jordan Phelps joins a small lounge band and meets pianist Morgan Sparks, who lights another blaze—this time in Jordan's heart. (978-1-63555-980-4)

Late City Summer by Jeanette Bears. Forced together for her wedding, Emily Stanton and Kate Alessi navigate their lingering passion for one another against the backdrop of New York City and World War II, and a summer romance they left behind. (978-1-63555-968-2)

Love and Lotus Blossoms by Anne Shade. On her path to self-acceptance and true passion, Janesse will risk everything—and possibly everyone—she loves. (978-1-63555-985-9)

Love in the Limelight by Ashley Moore. Marion Hargreaves, the finest actress of her generation, and Jessica Carmichael, the world's biggest pop star, rediscover each other twenty years after an ill-fated affair. (978-1-63679-051-0)

Suspecting Her by Mary P. Burns. Complications ensue when Erin O'Connor falls for top real estate saleswoman Catherine Williams while investigating racism in the real estate industry; the fallout could end their chance at happiness. (978-1-63555-960-6)

Two Winters by Lauren Emily Whalen. A modern YA retelling of Shakespeare's *The Winter's Tale* about birth, death, Catholic school, improv comedy, and the healing nature of time. (978-1-63679-019-0)

Calumet by Ali Vali. Jaxon Lavigne and Iris Long had a forbidden small-town romance that didn't last, and the consequences of that love will be uncovered fifteen years later at their high school reunion. (978-1-63555-900-2)

Her Countess to Cherish by Jane Walsh. London Society's material girl realizes there is more to life than diamonds when she falls in love with a non-binary bluestocking. (978-1-63555-902-6)

Hot Days, Heated Nights by Renee Roman. When Cole and Lee meet, instant attraction quickly flares into uncontrollable passion, but their connection might be short-lived as Lee's identity is tied to her life in the city. (978-1-63555-888-3)

Never Be the Same by MA Binfield. Casey meets Olivia, and sparks fly in this opposites attract romance that proves love can be found in the unlikeliest places. (978-1-63555-938-5)

Quiet Village by Eden Darry. Something not quite human is stalking Collie and her niece, and she'll be forced to work with undercover reporter Emily Lassiter if they want to get out of Hyam alive. (978-1-63555-898-2)

Shaken or Stirred by Georgia Beers. Bar owner Julia Martini and home health aide Savannah McNally attempt to weather the storms brought on by a mysterious blogger trashing the bar, family feuds they knew nothing about, and way too much advice from way too many relatives. (978-1-63555-928-6)

The Fiend in the Fog by Jess Faraday. Can four people on different trajectories work together to save the vulnerable residents of East London from the terrifying fiend in the fog before it's too late? (978-1-63555-514-1)

The Marriage Masquerade by Toni Logan. A no-strings-attached marriage scheme to inherit a Maui B&B uncovers unexpected attractions and a dark family secret. (978-1-63555-914-9)

Flight SQA016 by Amanda Radley. Fastidious airline passenger Olivia Lewis is used to things being a certain way. When her routine is changed by a new, attractive member of the staff, sparks fly. (978-1-63679-045-9)

Home Is Where The Heart Is by Jenny Frame. Can Archie make the countryside her home and give Ash the fairytale romance she desires? Or will the countryside and small village life all be too much for her? (978-1-63555-922-4)

Moving Forward by PJ Trebelhorn. The last person Shelby Ryan expects to be attracted to is Iris Calhoun, the sister of the man who killed her wife four years and three thousand miles ago. (978-1-63555-953-8)

Poison Pen by Jean Copeland. Debut author Kendra Blake is finally living her best life until a nasty book review and exposed secrets threaten her promising new romance with aspiring journalist Alison Chatterley. (978-1-63555-849-4)

Seasons for Change by KC Richardson. Love, laughter, and trust develop for Shawn and Morgan throughout the changing seasons of Lake Tahoe. (978-1-63555-882-1)

Summer Lovin' by Julie Cannon. Three different women, three exotic locations, one unforgettable summer. What do you think will happen? (978-1-63555-920-0)

Unbridled by D. Jackson Leigh. A visit to a local stable turns into more than riding lessons between a novel writer and an equestrian with a taste for power play. (978-1-63555-847-0)

VIP by Jackie D. In a town where relationships are forged and shattered by perception, sometimes even love can't change who you really are. (978-1-63555-908-8)

Yearning by Gun Brooke. The sleepy town of Dennamore has an irresistible pull on those who've moved away. The mystery Darian Benson and Samantha Pike uncover will change them forever, but the love they find along the way just might be the key to saving themselves. (978-1-63555-757-2)

A Turn of Fate by Ronica Black. Will Nev and Kinsley finally face their painful past and relent to their powerful, forbidden attraction? Or will facing their past be too much to fight through? (978-1-63555-930-9)

Desires After Dark by MJ Williamz. When her human lover falls deathly ill, Alex, a vampire, must decide which is worse, letting her go or condemning her to everlasting life. (978-1-63555-940-8)

Her Consigliere by Carsen Taite. FBI agent Royal Scott swore an oath to uphold the law, and criminal defense attorney Siobhan Collins pledged her loyalty to the only family she's ever known, but will their love be stronger than the bonds they've vowed to others, or will their competing allegiances tear them apart? (978-1-63555-924-8)

In Our Words: Queer Stories from Black, Indigenous, and People of Color Writers. Stories Selected by Anne Shade and Edited by Victoria Villaseñor. Comprising both the renowned and emerging voices of Black, Indigenous, and People of Color authors, this thoughtfully curated collection of short stories explores the intersection of racial and queer identity. (978-1-63555-936-1)

Measure of Devotion by CF Frizzell. Disguised as her late twin brother, Catherine Samson enters the Civil War to defend the Constitution as a Union soldier, never expecting her life to be altered by a Gettysburg farmer's daughter. (978-1-63555-951-4)

Not Guilty by Brit Ryder. Claire Weaver and Emery Pearson's day jobs clash, even as their desire for each other burns, and a discreet sex-only arrangement is the only option. (978-1-63555-896-8)

Opposites Attract: Butch/Femme Romances by Meghan O'Brien, Aurora Rey & Angie Williams. Sometimes opposites really do attract. Fall in love with these butch/femme romance novellas. (978-1-63555-784-8)

Under Her Influence by Amanda Radley. On their path to #truelove, will Beth and Jemma discover that reality is even better than illusion? (978-1-63555-963-7)